PUFFIN BOOKS

Loamhedge

A TALE *of* REDWALL

BRIAN JACQUES

Loamhedge

A TALE *of* REDWALL

Illustrated by David Elliot

PUFFIN

PUFFIN BOOKS

Published by the Penguin Group
Penguin Books Ltd, 80 Strand, London WC2R ORL, England
Penguin Group (USA), Inc., 375 Hudson Street, New York, New York 10014, USA
Penguin Books Australia Ltd, 250 Camberwell Road, Camberwell, Victoria 3124, Australia
Penguin Books Canada Ltd, 10 Alcorn Avenue, Toronto, Ontario, Canada M4V 3B2
Penguin Books India (P) Ltd, 11 Community Centre, Panchsheel Park, New Delhi – 110 017, India
Penguin Group (NZ), cnr Airborne and Rosedale Roads, Albany, Auckland 1310, New Zealand
Penguin Books (South Africa) (Pty) Ltd, 24 Sturdee Avenue, Rosebank 2196, South Africa

Penguin Books Ltd, Registered Offices: 80 Strand, London WC2R ORL, England

www.penguin.com

First published in the USA by Philomel Books, a division of Penguin Group (USA), Inc., 2003
First published in Great Britain in Puffin Books 2004
Published in this edition in Puffin Books 2004
2

Set in MT Palatino

Made and printed in England by Clays Ltd, St Ives plc

British Library Cataloguing in Publication Data
A CIP catalogue record for this book is available from the British Library

ISBN 0–141–31282–3

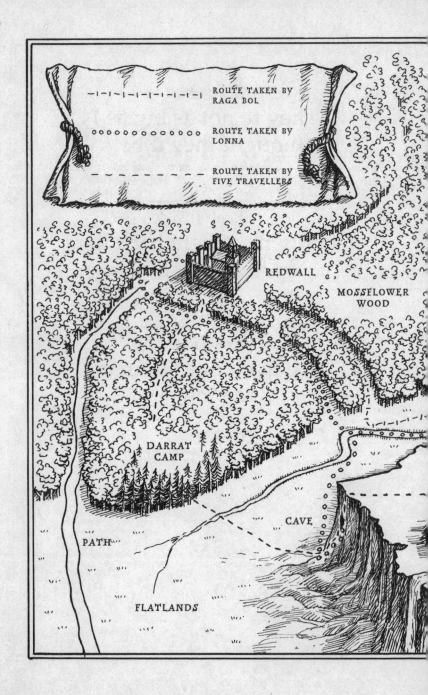

ROUTE TAKEN BY
RAGA BOL

ROUTE TAKEN BY
LONNA

ROUTE TAKEN BY
FIVE TRAVELLERS

REDWALL

MOSSFLOWER
WOOD

DARRAT
CAMP

CAVE

PATH

FLATLANDS

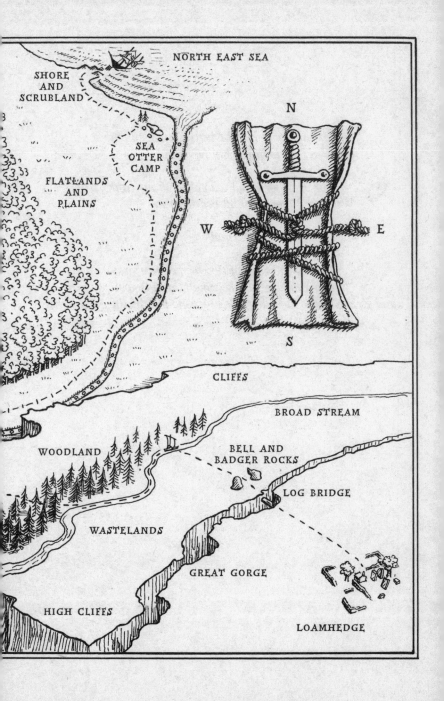

*For my good friend Martha Buckley who
inspired my Martha.*

*For Heather Boyd who cheered me from
her hospital bed to mine*

and

*to the memory of two brave warriors:
Nolan Wallace who became Lonna Bowstripe
and Eric Masato Takashige Boehm who fought the good fight.*

Prologue

Have you been travelling, my young friend? Come in out of the darkness and rain. Sit by the fire, eat, drink and rest yourself. Life is one long journey from beginning to end, you know. We all walk different roads, both with our bodies and our minds. Some of us lose heart and fall by the wayside, whilst others go on to realize their dreams and desires.

Let me tell you a story of travellers, and the paths they followed. Of young ones, like yourself, sometimes uncertain of their direction, and often reluctant to listen to the voices of sense and wisdom. Of a mighty warrior, set on a course of destiny and vengeance, unstoppable in his resolve. Of an evil one and his crew, cruel and ruthless, bound on a march of destruction and conquest. Of a simple maid and her friends, homebodies whose only aims were peace and well-being for all. Of wicked, foolish wanderers, chasing fantasies and fables, consumed by their own greed. Of small babes who dreamed small dreams, not knowing what the future held in store for them. And, finally, of two friends, faithful and true, who had roamed many highways and together chose their own way.

The lives I will tell you of are intertwined by fate – good and evil bringing their just rewards to each, as they merited them. Listen whilst I relate this story. For am I not the Teller of Tales, the Weaver of Dreams!

BOOK ONE

'They're not as big as I thought they'd be'

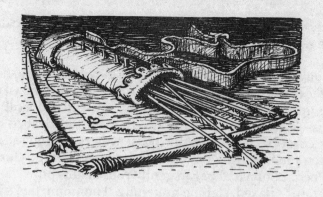

1

Lashing rain, driven by harsh biting winds from the sea, scoured the land from the bleak salt marshes to the stunted scrub forest. Abruc the sea otter bent against the strain of a loaded rush basket. It was tied to his shoulders and belted across his brow to stop it from spilling backwards.

Holding on to his father's paw, young Stugg trotted alongside, plying his parent with interminable questions, which Abruc did his best to answer.

'H'are you veddy veddy strong?'

Scrunching his eyes against the wind, Abruc could not help smiling at his inquisitive little son. 'I have t'be strong. I've got to feed you, your mamma an' the whole family. That's my job, I'm a father.'

Stugg sucked his free paw, digesting this information whilst he thought up another question. 'Den why can't Stugg sit atop of your basket no more?'

Abruc adjusted the belt to ease the strain on his neck. 'Because you've growed since last season. Yore gettin' to be a big feller now, a fine lump of an otter. Soon you'll be carryin' yore ole dad an' the basket. Let's put a move on, Stugg, so we can make it into the woods by dark. It'll be good to take a rest out o' this weather.'

With the sound of the grey northeast sea pounding in

5

their ears, both the sea otters squelched through the desolate salt marshes towards the weather-bent scrub forest.

Daylight ebbed into early evening as they entered the shelter of the trees. With a grunt of relief, Abruc swung his basket to the ground. It was brimfull of edible seaweed, scallops, mussels and shrimp – a full two days' work, gleaned from the coast of the barren northeast waters. Abruc sat on a fallen pine. Sensing his father's weariness, Stugg climbed up behind him and began gently rubbing his brow.

Abruc relaxed, sighing gratefully. 'Hmmmm, that's nice. I was beginnin' to think that strap'd cut the top off me skull. Huh, where'd I be then?'

Stugg giggled. 'Wiv a half offa head, silly ole farder!'

The sea otter cautioned his son. 'Hush now, not so loud. There might be Coast Raiders about. Huh, they'd cut the tops off'n our skulls, just to watch us die.'

Wide-eyed, Stugg crouched down against his father, speaking in a hushed whisper. 'Mamma says Coaster Raiders be's naughty vermints!'

His father pushed dry pine needles into a small heap, shaking his head grimly. 'Naughty ain't the word for that scum. They're evil, cold-blooded murderers. Cruelty is just fun to the likes o' them. Right, young 'un, I suppose yore hungry now?'

Nodding eagerly, Stugg whispered, 'I'm starfished!'

Abruc chuckled. *Starfished* was a word all the young ones used, a cross twixt *starving* and *famished.*

He patted Stugg's head fondly. 'Nothin' worse'n a starfished otter. You stay here, keep yore eyes'n'ears open, an' lay low. I'll go an' find us a snug berth for the night.'

He pulled a sack from under his cloak, tossing it to his son. 'Sort through the rest of those rations an' see wot you want for supper. I'll be back soon.'

Abruc knew the woods well; he recalled a spot not too far off. It was a good dry place, sheltered by a rock ledge. Silent

6

as a night breeze, he weaved his way through the dark, twisted trees, straight to the exact location. He had camped there before. Halting slightly short of his destination, he paused. Something did not feel quite right about the area. Abruc sniffed the air and listened carefully, his animal instinct aroused. He caught the faint sound of ragged breathing. Drawing his long dagger, he crept forwards, peering keenly into the shadows, his neck hairs bristling.

For supper Stugg had selected two flat loaves, some of his mamma's apple and blackberry preserve and their last flask of plum cordial. If his father lit a fire, they could make toasted preserve sandwiches and warm cordial. The young otter was a pretty fair cook, often having helped his mamma to prepare meals. There was not much else to do but wait in silence for his father's return. Stugg set out the food and sat next to the basket of supplies.

Abruc came speeding out of the darkness to his son's side. Crouching beside Stugg, he gripped his paws tightly. The sea otter's voice was urgent and breathless from running.

'Listen carefully, little mate. Could you find yore way back home to our holt on yore own?'

Stugg was taken aback by the unusual request. 'Er, I fink so, what's a matter, farder?'

Abruc gripped his son's paws tighter. His voice sounded harsh. 'Answer me – yes or no! Could you find yore way back home?'

Stugg had never seen his father like this. He nodded, his own voice sounding small and scared. 'Yes, Stugg know d'way!'

Abruc released the young otter's paws. 'Good, now here's wot y'must do, son. Find Shoredog. Tell him to bring the crew to the spot by the rock ledge, he'll know where I mean. Say that they best bring rope, canvas an' poles. Enough t'make a stretcher to carry a wounded, giant stripedog. That's if'n he's still alive when they reach here.'

Words poured from Stugg's mouth like running water. 'A giant, a stripedog, a wounded one? I never see'd a giant stripedog afore! What happened? Will he get deaded . . .'

Abruc grabbed Stugg and shook him, something he had never done before. He hissed at him through clenched teeth. 'Shut yore mouth, son! Don't stand here askin' questions! Go now, run, don't stop for anythin'. The life of another creature depends on you. Go!'

Young Stugg took off like a madbeast, pine needles scattering from under his paws as he tore homewards through the nighttime forest. Abruc watched until his son was out of sight, then gathered up their belongings and dashed back to the camp beneath the ledge.

Swiftly he heaped dry pine needles and cones with a few twigs. Using the steel of his knife blade against a chunk of flint, he soon had a small fire burning. It was sheltered by the overhanging rock and could not be seen from a reasonable distance. Abruc viewed the scene around him. Two badgers, one very old, the other about two seasons into his adult growth, lay stretched out, side by side. Small and grizzled, the oldest of the pair was obviously dead, slain by various weapon thrusts. As he turned to the younger badger, a brief glance at the churned-up ground and the blood-flecked rock confirmed the sea otter's suspicions. His jaw clenched angrily. 'Dirty murderin' Raiders!'

The younger badger was still alive. Abruc had seen one or two badgers in his lifetime, but not as big as this fellow. He was truly a giant – tall, deep of chest and broadbacked with massive paws and powerfully muscled limbs.

The sea otter winced as he inspected the fearsome wound to the badger's head. A long jagged slash, from eartip to neck, had ripped across the badger's face. Narrowly missing the eye, it had ploughed across the brow, through the wide-striped muzzle, across the jaw line to the side of the creature's throat.

Abruc, with only a limited knowledge of healing, staunched the blood with his cloak. Lifting the badger's

8

head, he cradled it in his lap, dabbing away at the dreadful rift and murmuring to the unconscious beast.

'Seasons o' salt, matey, 'tis a miracle yore still alive! Y'must have a skull made o' rock. I know you can't hear me, but don't worry, big feller, our crew will do the best we can for ye. There's one or two good healers at our holt.'

Abruc sat rambling away to the senseless badger, knowing he could do little else until help arrived.

It was close to midnight. Rainladen wind hissed through the scrub forest, carrying with it salt spray from the thundering seas. Beside the guttering embers of his little fire, Abruc had dozed off, still holding the badger's head.

At the front of the otter crew, Shoredog pointed with his lantern, hurrying forwards. 'There they are, mates!'

Little Stugg reached his father first. 'I bringed them, farder!'

Abruc patted the youngster's paw. 'Yore a good ole scout. Unnh, somebeast get me out from under this giant's head. Me limbs have gone asleep on me from holdin' his weight.'

Willing paws assisted him upright. Shoredog shook his head as he viewed the injured badger. 'Great seasons, lookit the mess the pore creature's in. I fears there ain't much hope for 'im. I never set eyes on a wound bad as that 'un!'

Stugg caught sight of his mother and tugged at her paw. 'Issa giant stripedog goin' to die, mamma?'

Abruc's wife Marinu nodded at Shoredog's grandma, Sork. 'Not if'n we can help it, Stugg. Come on, crew, get some warm blankets around that badger an' strap him to a stretcher. Easy now, don't jolt the pore beast too much.'

Everybeast knew that Marinu and Sork were the best healers in all the southeast.

Stugg grinned broadly. Now that he had succeeded in his mission, he proceeded to take charge of the situation, striding about and issuing orders. 'You all hear my mamma, pick dat stripedog up careful!'

Marinu was about to pull her son to one side when Abruc murmured to her, 'Let the young 'un be, he did well tonight.'

As the otter crew manoeuvred the huge badger on to the huge stretcher, Shoredog gave a surprised bark. 'Blood'-n'thunder, lookit that!'

Beneath the injured creature a mighty bow and a quiver of long arrows lay half covered in the loose sand and pine needles. The badger had fallen backwards upon the bow, his hefty bulk breaking the weapon in two pieces. One jagged half was stuck into his hip. Marinu halted the bearers until she and Sork had extracted the splintered yew wood. The big fellow grunted faintly as they padded and dressed the wound.

Stugg jumped up and down triumphantly. 'He be's alive, d'stripedog maked noise!'

Old Sork looped the birchbark quiver over Stugg's head. It scraped the ground; the arrows were taller than he. Sork shooed the young one aside. 'Aye, mayhap he is. Now you carry those an' stay out the way.'

A score of otters bore the badger off on a litter of pine poles, sailcloth and rope, padded with dead grass and soft moss. Stugg stayed behind with his father and Shoredog to bury the dead badger. It was only a shallow grave, but they found slabs of rock to top it off with. Abruc wedged the two pieces of broken bow, with the string still joining them, into the foot of the grave. They would serve as a marker. All three sea otters gazed down at the sad resting place.

Abruc shook his head. 'Pore old beast, we don't even know wot name he went by. He looked weak, an' small. A badger that age should've spent out his seasons restin' in the sun. I wonder wot kin he was t'the big 'un. Mebbe his father?'

Stugg pressed his face against Abruc and wept. He could not imagine anybeast losing a father. He sobbed brokenly. 'Who would kill someone's farder like that?'

Shoredog looked up from smoothing the earth around

the stones. 'Only beast I knows who kills like that is Raga Bol.'

The name struck fear into Abruc. 'Raga Bol! Has he been here?'

Shoredog stood upright, dusting off his paws. 'While you an' Stugg were gone, Rurff the grey seal visited our holt. He saw the sea rats' ship wrecked on the rocks, further north up the coast. Raga Bol an' about fifty vermin crew came ashore. They headed down this way, but pickin's are scarce on this northeast coast, so they've probably marched inland. They ain't got a ship anymore. I was just rousin' our crew to search for you an' Stugg, when the young 'un comes runnin' to tell me you need help.'

Shoredog took one of the straps on Abruc's basket. 'Let me help ye with this, mate, 'tis a good haul.'

They set off back to their holt, with Stugg stumbling over the quiver of long arrows.

Abruc shrugged philosophically. 'It's a bad spring, cold an' stormy. Let's hope summer's a bit better when it comes. At least we won't have Raga Bol an' his villains to worry about. I suppose we should count ourselves lucky, really.'

Young Stugg hitched the arrows higher on his back. They still dragged along the ground as he muttered aloud. 'More luckier than d'poor stripedogs, I appose.'

A brief smile crossed Shoredog's weathered face. 'That young 'un of yores is growin' up quick, mate!'

Dawn glimmered chill and blustery over the heathlands some two leagues west of the northeast sea. Wet, hungry and dispirited, Raga Bol's crew of sea rats huddled round a smoking fire down a ravine. They stared miserably at a deep, rain-swollen stream running nearby. From further up the bank the vermin could hear their captain's shrieks and curses rending the air.

Rinj, a sly-faced female, gnawed at a filthy clawnail, glancing from one to the other. 'Ye t'ink Bol's lost the paw? I t'ought Wirga cudda sewed it back on, she's a good 'ealer.'

A lanky, gaunt rat named Ferron picked something from his teeth and spat it into the stream. 'Sewed it back on! Have ye gone soft in the skull? Last I saw, Cap'n Bol's paw was 'angin' on by a string o' skin. We should've stayed well clear o' those two stripedogs!'

Rinj wiped firesmoke from her blearing eyes. 'The little ole one wuz no trouble, he didn't know wot 'it 'im, gone afore ye could wink.'

Ferron winced as Raga Bol's screeches and curses redoubled. 'Aye, but wot about the big 'un, eh? I thought Cap'n Bol killed him wid the first blow of his big sword!'

Glimbo, the captain's first mate, pushed Rinj away from the fire and installed his fat, greasy bulk close to the flames. One of his eyes was a milky sightless orb; the other roved around the crew as he warmed his paws.

'Never in me days seen Bol 'ave to strike a beast twice wid that blade. But that big stripedog came back after the first whack an' got his teeth in good. Just as well that Bol struck again, or he would've lost more'n one paw. Mark my words, stripedogs are powerful dangerous beasts!'

The heathland was a barren region, made drearier by the day's unabated rain. Down in the ravine a huge bonfire blazed to dispel the harsh weather. Every sea rat of the crew sat watching their captain. Tall and sinewy, with a restless energy that could be glimpsed in his fiery green eyes, Raga Bol was an impressive rat by any measure. He sat wrapped in a fur cloak, his left pawstump hidden from view. The sea rat's right paw rested on the carved bone hilt of a heavy, wide-bladed scimitar, protruding from his waistband. The crewbeasts could feel Raga Bol's eyes on them. Rain sizzling on the fire and wind fanning the flames were the only sounds to be heard as they waited on their captain's word.

Finally, Raga Bol rose and snarled bad-temperedly at them, firelight reflecting from his hooped brass earrings and gold-plated fangs. 'We march west at dawn. Anybeast who don' want to go, let 'im speak now, an' I'll bury 'im right 'ere!'

Not one of the sea rat crew said a word. Raga Bol nodded. 'West it is then. Blowfly, get me two runners.'

An enormously fat rat, with a whip curled about his shoulders, motioned two lean crew members forwards.

Raga Bol sat looking at them in silence, until they squirmed under his unwinking gaze. His jaw clenched as he moved the stump where his left paw had been. 'You two, go back to where I slew the stripedog. Find the carcass, an' bring me back his head.'

Each of the runners touched a paw to his ears. 'Aye aye, Cap'n!'

Raga Bol stood watching them climbing the sides of the ravine, then turned his attention to an old female sea rat crouching nearby. 'Wirga, is that hook ready yet?'

'It'll be ready by dawn, Cap'n.' The old one gave him a toothless grin. 'So thee wants the big stripedog's head, eh?'

Raga Bol drew his cloak tight and sat, staring into the fire. 'Nobeast ever took a paw o'mine an' stayed in one piece, dead or alive. Now get that hook ready if'n ye want to keep yore head, ye withered old torturer!'

2

Far over to the west, a brighter spring day had dawned. Ascending meadowlarks heralded the sun beneath a soft, pastel blue sky. Drawn by the sudden warmth, mist rose from the greenswards, transforming dewdrops to small opalescent pearls amid the dainty blossoms of saxifrage, buttercup, capsella and anemones. Mossflower woodland trees were blessed with a crown of fresh green leaves. Life was renewed to the sounds of little birds, calling to their parents with ceaseless demands for food.

Toran Widegirth loosed his apron strings, satisfied that he had completed his duties as Redwall Abbey's Head Cook. Leaving his kitchens, the fat otter sought the beautiful spring morn outdoors. Heaving a sigh of relief, Toran sat down on an upturned wheelbarrow at the orchard entrance. He was joined by his friend Carrul, the Father Abbot of Redwall. The mouse sat down beside the otter, both relaxing in silence, blinking in the sunlight and savouring the first good weather that spring.

Carrul glanced sideways at his companion. 'Not going with Skipper and the otter crew this season?'

Toran watched an ant negotiating its way over his foot-paw. 'Much too early, it ain't summer yet. But you know

Skipper an' the crew, first sign o' sun an' a skylark an' they're off like march hares to the west seashores for the season.'

Abbot Carrul chuckled. 'Fully provisioned I trust?'

Toran nodded wearily. 'Aye, I saw them off myself at dawn. Pushin' a cartload o' victuals I'd made special for 'em. Singin' their rudders off, dancin' like madbeasts!'

Carrul's smile widened. 'I know, they woke me up, I saw them from my window. Good luck and fair weather to them. So why didn't you go? I gave you permission to take as long as you wanted to go on leave.'

Toran shrugged. 'Oh, I'm gettin' too old for that sort o' thing. Leave it to the younger ones.'

Carrul snorted. 'Too old? Too big in the tummy, you mean! If you're too old, then what about me, eh? I was your teacher when you were only a tiny Dibbun at Abbey School!'

The ottercook tweaked his friend's bony paw. 'Aye, an' ye haven't gained a hair's weight since then. How d'ye do it, you skinny, ancient mouse?'

The Abbot looked over his small square spectacles good-humouredly. 'I don't spend my whole life down in those kitchens like you do, my friend. Oh, Toran, isn't it just a glorious day? I hope the summer is a really golden one.'

Toran snuggled more comfortably into the wheelbarrow. 'Makes ye feel good t'be alive, don't it, Carrul?'

They both lapsed into silence again, gazing around and taking in the beauties of their Abbey.

Behind them, Redwall reared – a legend in pink, dusty sandstone with its high walls and turrets, stained-glass windows and buttressed arches, belltower, attics and steeple, all complemented by a background of verdant woodland and cloudless blue sky. Toran took in the stout battlements and picturesque gatehouse of the outer wall, whilst the Abbot contented himself by viewing the lawns and orchards, peacefully shimmering in the sunlight.

Carrul's gaze took in the Abbey pond, down near the south ramparts. 'What creature could not count himself lucky to be dwelling in such a paradise? Ah, look Toran, there's our young friend Martha, taking a little nap in her chair, just by the rhododendron bushes on the far side of the pond.'

Toran saw the young haremaid, her head nodding down to a heavy volume, which lay open on her lap.

The ottercook eased himself from the barrow. 'I'll just take a stroll over there and check she's alright.'

The Abbot stretched luxuriously into the position Toran had vacated. 'Dearie me, you're like an old mother hen with that young 'un. Why don't you tell her that lunch will be served late, out in the orchard? In fact, tell everybeast, 'twill cheer them up after being kept indoors by the rain for so long. We'll all lend a paw to help.'

Toran smiled happily. 'What a good idea!'

The ottercook approached Martha carefully, not wanting to disturb her. She was very special to him. Toran could recall the winter's day, twelve seasons ago, when Martha Braebuck had arrived at Redwall. She had been nought but a tiny babe, strapped to the back of her ancient grandmother. Her brother Hortwill, two seasons older, had stumbled along, clutching the old hare's cloak. Toran's heart had immediately gone out to the pitiful trio. They had walked from the far Northlands, the only survivors of a vermin attack which had wiped out an entire colony of mountain hares. No sooner were they through the Abbey gates than the poor grandmother had collapsed and died from exhaustion. A sad occurrence, made sadder by the fact that Martha had never learned to walk from that day forth. Her brother grew up as sprightly as any young hare, but despite the most tender care, the babe Martha was immobile from her knee joints to her footpaws. There were no signs of any apparent wound or injury, no scarring or broken bones. No reason, in fact, why the little one should not learn to walk. Some of the wiser heads, like old Phredd the Gatekeeper, Great Father Abbot Carrul and Sister Setiva, the healer shrew who took care of the Abbey infirmary, said it was due to shock. That perhaps Martha's long trek from the Northlands, strapped to her grandmother's back, coupled with witnessing the murder of her family and kin, had caused the problem. Still, the Redwallers were completely puzzled.

Toran did everything possible to help her. He believed firmly that one day she would stand and walk. Meanwhile, the kind ottercook provided Martha with the means to get about. Taking a light comfortable chair, he fixed it to the base of a kitchen trolley, adding two large wheels to the back. The young haremaid learned to propel herself about quite easily. Toran also fashioned a crutch for her, but Martha used it only to get at things which were beyond her reach.

Martha Braebuck grew up an extremely bright young creature with a thirst for knowledge. She was a formidable reader and scholar, the equal even of the venerated mouse, Sister Portula, Redwall Abbey's Recorder. Martha could solve riddles and equations, write poems, ballads and even sing. According to popular opinion, she had the sweetest singing voice ever heard within the Abbey walls. She never complained about being chairbound, and was invariably cheerful and willing to help others. The maid was a welcome and useful member of the Redwall Abbey community.

Toran watched silently as her head drooped lower. The volume slid from her lap rug on to the grass. Toran grunted as he bent to retrieve it.

Martha came awake, stifling a yawn and rubbing her eyes. 'Dearie me, I must have nodded off!'

Returning the hefty volume to Martha's lap, the otter-cook winked at her. 'Who'd blame ye, with all this sun about. I could lie down right here an' take a nap myself!'

Martha saw a group of Dibbuns approaching from

around the orchard hedge. 'You wouldn't sleep for long, my friend. Look, here comes trouble!'

The Abbeybabes descended upon the haremaid's chair. Muggum, a tiny mole who was their ringleader, climbed up on to Martha's lap, rumbling away in his quaint molespeech. 'Yur, Miz Marth', do ee singen us'n's ee song?'

The haremaid eyed him good-naturedly. 'Which one would you like me to sing?'

Toran interrupted with his suggestion. 'A pretty day deserves a pretty song, miss. Sing a spring song!'

The squirrelbabe Shilly added her request. 'Da one where uz clappa paws!'

Buffle the shrewbabe, who was the smallest of all, nodded solemnly. 'Gurbbadurrguddun!'

Shilly translated. 'Him says that be a good 'un.'

Martha sat up straight, exchanging a smile with Toran. 'Well, Buffle's word is good enough for me. Here goes.'

The Dibbuns raised their paws, ready to clap, as Martha's melodious voice soared out.

'The rain has gone away . . . Clap Clap!
and larks do sing on high.
Sweet flowers open wide . . . Clap Clap!
their petals to the sky!
'Tis spring . . . Clap clap! 'Tis spring,
let us rejoice and sing,
the moon is queen, the sun is king,
so clap your paws and sing . . . Clap Clap!

There's not a cloud in sight . . . Clap Clap!
the leaves are bright and new.
This day was made for all . . . Clap Clap!
for me, my friend and you!
So sing . . . Clap Clap! . . . So sing,
let summer follow spring,
from golden morn to evening,

we clap our paws and sing . . . Clap Clap!
. . . Clap Clap!'

Although the clapping missed its beat once or twice, it was with joyous vigour. The little ones danced around, whooping and squeaking wildly, 'Sing us'n's a more!'

Martha was coaxed into singing the lively air again. She finished quite out of breath, amid yells for a third performance.

Toran took charge, slapping his rudder loudly on the bankside. 'Hold up there, ye rogues, pore Miz Martha's tuckered out. Now lissen t'me. If ye promise t'be good, we'll have lunch out in the orchard today, seein' as 'tis sunny!'

His suggestion was greeted with roars of approval. 'Lunch inna h'orchard, 'ooppee!'

Martha smiled happily. 'Oh, what a splendid idea!'

Little Shilly sped off towards the Abbey, calling to the other Dibbuns. 'Come on, we 'elp Granmum Gurvel wiv lunch!'

Toran watched them go. 'I don't think old Gurvel will thank me for lettin' that lot invade the kitchens.'

Martha settled the big volume more comfortably on her lap. 'Bless their little hearts, they mean well.'

Toran cast a glance at the haremaid's book. 'That's a heavy ole thing t'be readin', miss. Wot's it all about?'

Martha opened the book at a page marked by a silken ribbon. 'I borrowed it from Sister Portula's library. It's a rare and ancient account of Loamhedge mice.'

The ottercook looked thoughtful. 'Loamhedge mice, eh? I've heard of them. Weren't they the ones who helped t'build our Abbey? Aye, they were led by old Abbess, er, wotsername?'

'Germaine,' the haremaid corrected him. 'It was she and Martin the Warrior who helped to build and design Redwall. Germaine and her followers once lived at the place they called Loamhedge. It was a peaceful and prosperous community, almost as large as our Abbey, some say. But they were forced to abandon it and flee for their lives. Loamhedge was left deserted to the four winds.'

Toran's interest was roused. Although he was no great reader himself, he liked to hear his friend tell of what she had read. 'Why did they have to leave? Does the book explain?'

Martha riffled back to a previously read page. 'It says here that a great sickness fell upon Loamhedge. A plague, brought by vermin, possibly sea rats. First there was sickness, then a few deaths. Abbess Germaine was wise enough to realize that it would grow into an epidemic, which would wipe them all out. So she took her mice and fled. They went wandering for many seasons, far from home. One day their journey took them into this part of Mossflower territory. It was here they met Martin the Warrior and his friends. Germaine joined forces with the Woodlanders, helping to rid the lands of powerful enemies. When peace was achieved, Martin and Germaine were free to realize their dream. They built a mighty stone fortress, an Abbey, where goodbeasts could live in safety and happiness together. That's how, countless ages ago, Redwall came into being . . .'

Martha was interrupted by her brother Hortwill. He came bounding and splashing through the shallows and threw himself upon her.

'Wot ho, wot ho, wot ho, me pretty young skin'n'blister!'

She ducked her head, laughing as he showered her face with kisses. 'Stop that this instant, Horty! I'm not your skin'n'blister, I'm your sister. Oh, look now, you've splashed water all over Sister Portula's precious book!'

Hortwill Braebuck, or Horty, as everybeast knew him, was Martha's brother, older than her by two seasons. An overpowering character – ebullient, quaint of speech, always in trouble, he was roguishly gallant, sentimental to a fault, and possessed a gluttonous appetite. In short, a typical hare.

Throwing up both paws and ears in mock horror, Horty declaimed, 'Well, flog me twice round the jolly old orchard an' chop off me ears with a rusty blinkin' axe, wot! Splashed a bally spot o' water on Sis Peculiar's blessed book? Lack a day, fifty seasons in the cellar for me. What say you, Toran old scout? Either that or instant death. Wot wot?'

Toran played along with Horty's dramatic mood. Squinting an eye, he growled fiercely, 'Instant death's the only thing!'

The young hare threw him a smart military salute. 'As y'say, sah, sentence t'be carried out on the blinkin' spot!'

Without further ado, Horty flung himself into the pond and vanished underwater, still saluting.

Martha sat bolt upright in her chair. 'Oh the fool, save him Toran, quickly!'

Lumbering into the pond, the ottercook fished Horty out with one huge paw.

Grinning like a madbeast, and still saluting, Horty spouted a mouthful of water into the air. 'Beloved blinkin' friend, you've saved me life. I'll never forget you, an' I'll always dine at your excellent kitchen!'

Keeping a straight face, Toran looked at Martha. 'I'd better chuck him back in, miss; think of the food we'd save!'

Martha nearly fell out of her chair with laughter. 'Hahahaha! Oh no, please sir, hahaha! I beg you, spare his gluttonous young life. Hahahahaha!'

Shooting a last jet of pondwater skywards, Horty said fondly, 'A chap's confounded lucky to have such a merciful sister, wot!'

Toran growled as he frogmarched Horty ashore. 'Ye certainly are, matey. But if'n I hears ye callin' Sister Portula, Sis Peculiar again, back in the pond ye'll go. Aye, an' those two ripscuttle pals o' yores, Springald an' Fenna. A lesson in manners wouldn't harm them, either!'

Martha dabbed the book pages dry with her lap rug. She could never be angry with her boisterous brother. Horty had always been close by, ready to cheer her up when she was sad or depressed. Her inability to run free like other young ones sometimes put Martha in low spirits.

She held up the volume for Toran to see. 'No harm done really, it's perfectly dry now. Come on you two, let's go back to the Abbey!'

On the way up, they met Muggum and several other Dibbuns who had been banished from the kitchens by Granmum Gurvel, the old assistant molecook.

Muggum tugged his snout respectfully to the haremaid. 'Yur, mizzy, oi'll push ee to ee h'orchard furr lunch.'

Reaching down, Martha lifted the molebabe on to her lap. 'That's very thoughtful of you, Muggum, but I'm sure Horty and Toran can manage the job quite well.'

Patting the young haremaid's paw, the molebabe nodded sagely. 'Oi thankee, Miz Marth'. Coom on, zurrs, you'm pushen us faster'n'that, us'n's bee gurtly 'ungered furr lunch!'

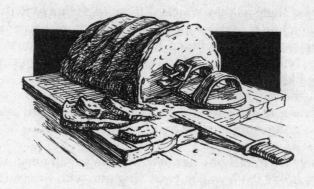

3

Redwall orchard was a riot of blossoming fruit trees and bushes. Pink and white flowers clustered thick on every branch, their petals carpeting the grass. Apple, pear, cherry, beech, hazelnut and almond trees flourished in rows, fronted by raspberry, strawberry, redcurrant and whortleberry. Summer promised an abundant yield.

Toran cast an eye over three trolleys laden with buffet lunch – spring vegetable soup, brown bread and cheese, dandelion and burdock cordial, followed by a dessert of damson preserve pie. 'Who did all this?'

Abbot Carrul bowed apologetically, knowing how touchy the ottercook could be about trespassers in his kitchen domain. 'I offered to help Granmum Gurvel. You looked so hot and weary when I met you in the orchard for a breath of fresh air. Gurvel and I decided to help you out. Is it to your liking, my friend?'

Toran bowed thankfully to them both. 'My thanks to ye. I couldn't have done it better!'

Redwallers sat in the tree shade, laughing and chatting amiably as lunch was served. Sister Portula spread a rug, and Toran lifted Martha on to it. All four sat beneath a wide chestnut tree at the orchard's far end. Sunlight and shadow dappled them as they watched the inhabitants of Redwall enjoying lunch. Martha appreciated such moments because the elders always included her in their discussions. The young haremaid felt she had become an honorary member of the Elders Council.

Martha laughed at the antics of the Dibbuns, who were beginning to get a bit rowdy. 'They do get excited after a rainy spring indoors. Look at baby Yooch, he's eating flower petals!'

Sister Portula shook her head. 'There's Shilly and some others doing it. I'll wager 'twas Muggum who started it all. Muggum, Shilly and Yooch are more trouble than any ten Dibbuns. I call them the Terrible Trio!'

Toran's stomach shook as he chuckled. 'Yore right, marm. Hi there, Springald, go an' tell those little 'uns to stop eatin' the petals, or Sister Setiva will have to dose 'em with physicks.'

The mousemaid Springald shrugged carelessly. 'Flowers won't do 'em any harm. I used to eat petals myself.'

Abbot Carrul glanced sternly over his glasses at her. 'Do as you are bidden, miss, and don't argue!'

Springald curtsied slightly, then flounced off to do as she was told.

Sister Portula pursed her lips and tutted. 'Yonder goes more trouble. She's one of the other three. Horty, Springald and Fenna, the young rebels. They aren't babes anymore; they should know better.'

Martha put aside her cordial beaker. 'Oh, they'll grow out of it, Sister, they're all good creatures at heart, I'm sure.'

Portula helped herself to bread and cheese. 'Huh, let's hope they do, before there's really trouble. I'm sure we were never like that at their age, were we, Father?'

Abbot Carrul raised his eyebrows. 'Weren't we, Sister? I can recall two young ones sailing a dining room table on the pond. Aye, with an embroidered linen tablecloth for a sail. Hmm, let me see now, what were their names?'

Sister Portula fidgeted uncomfortably with her sleeve

hem. 'But that was only a bit of fun. You and I were well behaved as a rule.'

Martha could scarcely believe her ears. 'You two? Well, you rascals! Did you get caught, Father?'

Behind his small glasses, the Abbot's eyes twinkled. 'Oh, we were caught sure enough, and both set to work in the kitchens as punishment. Remember that, Sister?'

Portula nodded ruefully. 'How could I ever forget five days of scrubbing greasy pots and scouring pans? My little paws stayed wrinkled for half a season!'

Martha winked cheekily at the Recorder. 'Horty and his two friends seem innocent compared to you and Abbot Carrul. What a pair of rogues you were!'

A light smile hovered on Portula's kind face. 'Listen, missy, if you think we were naughty, you should have seen two Dibbuns who were younger than us at the time. Bragoon and Saro, an otter and a squirrel. Now those two really were a twin pestilence!'

Martha turned to Toran. 'I've heard you telling the young ones tales about Bragoon and Saro, but I always thought they were make-believe creatures. Were they actually real?'

The ottercook nodded vigorously. 'Oho, missy, that they were! Bragoon was my big brother, five seasons older'n me. Sarobando, or Saro, as everybeast knew her, was a Dibbun squirrel, his best little pal. Sister Portula's right, ye never saw two villains like 'em! Hah, 'twas just as well they ran off whilst they was still young 'uns. If'n Bragoon an' Saro had stayed, we mightn't have a roof over our heads. They would've demolished the Abbey between 'em!'

Whilst Toran had been talking, some of the Dibbuns and a few of the young 'uns had gathered around.

Muggum scrambled up on to Toran's lap. 'Yurr zurr, you'm tell us'n's ee story 'bowt Zuro an' Burgoon!'

Toran chuckled. 'I can't bring one to mind right now, but I can recite a poem I wrote about 'em for the Harvest Feast many seasons back.'

Taking a swig of cordial, he tried to recall the words.

Shilly waggled her tail impatiently. 'Well, 'urry up an' gerron wiv it, Cooky!'

The ottercook twitched his nose at her. 'Silence, ye liddle rip!'

Draining his beaker, Toran launched into the recitation.

'I'll tell ye a tale of two Dibbuns,
who lived here long ago,
an otter who was named Bragoon,
an' a squirrel known as Saro.
Aye, little Bragoon an' Saro,
what a pair o' scamps they were,
their names rang through the land oh,
there was nought they didn't dare!

Good Granmum Gurvel molecook,
made puddens, cakes an' pies,
they vanished off the kitchen shelf,
before her dear ole eyes.
"Bragoon an' Saro, I'll be bound,"
the poor ole beast would say,
"they'll eat me out of house an' home,
they'll turn my fur to grey!"
Bragoon an' Saro, gracious me,
I dread to hear those names,
come hearken whilst I tell ye,
of those two scoundrels' games.

Who filled the Abbot's bed with ants,
who nailed up all the doors,
who was it glued the bellrope,
and stuck the ringer's paws,
who filled the pond with beetroots,
and turned the waters red,
who baked poor Foremole's sandals,
inside a loaf of bread?

The dreaded Bragoon an' Saro,
I'm here to tell ye all,
there's never been two like 'em,
at the Abbey of Redwall!'

The Dibbuns jumped up and down in delight, roaring with laughter at the escapades of the infamous pair. Horty and his friends, Springald and Fenna, laughed too.

Toran put on a stern face, wagging a cautionary paw at his listeners. 'I tell ye, 'twasn't so funny for the poor creatures who were the butt o' those tricks!'

Horty scoffed. 'Oh I say, sah, you don't actually believe all that dreadful twaddle about Bragoon an' Saro, wot?'

Abbot Carrul answered him. 'Toran's right, 'tis all true. I was a young 'un here myself at the time. I saw it!'

Fenna fluttered her long eyelashes prettily. 'Oh really, Father Abbot, you don't expect us to believe all that about Bragoon and Saro. We're not Dibbuns anymore. Toran makes up the stories to amuse the little ones – they'll believe anything, but we know better.'

Martha spoke out sharply. 'If the Abbot and Toran say it is true, then I'm certain it is. What reason would we have to doubt them?'

Her words, however, went unheeded by the three young 'uns, as they strolled off together, still unwilling to credit the existence of the fabled duo.

Horty scoffed again. 'Bragoon an' Saro, wot? Load of jolly old codswallop, if y'ask me. Tchah!'

Springald giggled. 'If I swallowed that lot, I'd be looking out for fishes nesting in trees and flying!'

Martha was so angry that she almost rose from the rug, but then she fell back again.

Abbot Carrul helped her to sit up. 'Don't upset yourself, Martha. One day our young friends will wake up and find themselves somewhat older and a little wiser, just wait and see. I was a bit like them at that age, but one lives and learns.'

The young haremaid sighed. 'I hope it happens to my brother soon. I don't like to say this, Father, but Horty seems to behave more outrageously each day.'

Toran helped Martha into her chair. 'Don't ye worry. Horty's a hare; they're always a bit wild when they're young.'

Martha retrieved her volume and straightened her rug. 'Perhaps you haven't noticed, Toran, but I'm a hare, too!'

Sister Portula dusted a stray flower petal from Martha's head. 'Ah, but you're a very rare and special kind of hare, my dear. Anybeast can see that!'

Hostile weather still reigned on the plains and heathlands of the far east. Raga Bol and his sea rats had not made much headway in three days of trekking westwards – the sea rat captain's pawstump pained him abominably. They camped on high ground, in the lee of a rocky projection. Apart from a few chosen cronies, the crew avoided the captain, making their own fire sufficiently far away to evade his sudden wrath.

Raga Bol sat by his own fire, with Glimbo and Blowfly in attendance. The two runners had been sent out to retrieve the badger's head but had returned empty-pawed. They crouched at the far side of the blaze, panting from their long journey. Raga Bol watched reflecting flames glinting from the polished silver hook where his paw had once been. His luminous eyes shifted to the runners.

'Are ye certain 'twas the spot where I slew the giant stripedog?'

Both heads nodded. 'Certain shore, Cap'n!'

'I'd swear me oath on it, Cap'n Bol. The stripedog was gone; there was no sign of 'im anywhere's about!'

The sea rat captain's terrifying stare never left either of the two quivering vermin. 'But the old one, 'e was buried there?'

'Aye, Cap'n, right on the spot where ye slew the big 'un.'

'He's right, Cap'n, the very spot. All the tracks were wiped out, too. Wasn't nothin' we could do but come back 'ere, fast as we could, to tell ye!'

Raga Bol dropped his gaze to the steaming ground at the fire's edge. 'Speak to none about this, or yore both deadrats. Now get out o' my sight!'

Glimbo and Blowfly scuttled off, relieved to be still among the living, after having brought their murderous captain such bad news. Hunching against the bleak cold at his back, Raga Bol sat silent. His eyes roved between the silver hook and the roaring, wind-driven fire.

Blowfly whispered to Glimbo, 'I reckon dat giant stripedog must still be alive, mate!'

The fat sea rat's hushed whisper was barely audible, but Raga Bol heard it. He stood slowly and faced them both. With lightning swiftness his hook shot out, latching on to Blowfly's broad belt. The sea rat was dragged forwards to find himself facing Bol's upraised blade and threatening snarl.

'Did ye ever see a beast alive after I'd struck 'im wid me blade? Well, did ye?'

Blowfly watched the heavy scimitar poised, one stroke away from his quivering double chins. The rat's voice went squeaky with panic. 'N . . . no, Cap'n!'

Raga Bol bared his gold-plated teeth in a wolfish grin. 'Shall I prove it to ye, Blowfly?'

The rat sobbed brokenly. 'Aw, don't do it, Cap'n Bol, please. Nobeast ever lived after yew 'it 'em wid yore sword!'

The captain's pale eyes lighted on Glimbo. 'You should know, mate, tell 'im!'

Glimbo loved life too much to remain silent. Words poured from his mouth like running water. 'Dat stripedog's kinbeasts must've carried 'im off, fer a fancy buryin'. I bet they buried the old 'un where he fell, 'cos they couldn't haul two carcasses. Mark me words, Blowfly, it don't matter 'ow big the stripedog was, he's deader'n any doornail now. Once Cap'n Bol's sword swipes 'em, they're well slayed. I'd take me affydavy on it!'

Blowfly fell to the ground as the hook pulled loose from his belt. Bol ground the scimitar and leaned on it.

'There's yore answer, mate; the stripedog's dead. I don't want to 'ear no more talk of such beasts from my crew. Now set four guards around me, so I can sleep.'

The sentries crouched miserably in the darkness, waiting for the dawn. Wrapped in his cloak, Raga Bol lay alongside a roaring fire. But sleep did not come easily, and, when it did, his dreams were troubled by visions of the giant stripedog coming slowly but surely after him with the light of vengeance burning in his eyes.

Abruc the sea otter, his wife Marinu and their son Stugg sat on the streamside, beneath an overhanging bank canopy. They enjoyed their evening meal outside, away from the bustling noise of the holt. Stugg sucked noisily at the contents of his bowl.

Abruc patted his stomach and winked at the young creature. 'Now that's wot I calls a sea otter chowder. Nobeast can make it like yore mamma does, ain't that right, me 'eart?'

Marinu refilled her husband's bowl. 'I wager you used to say that about yore own mamma's chowder. All it takes is clams, mussels an' shrimps, with some beans, chestnut flour, seaweed, carrots an' a few pawfuls of sea salt an' hotroot pepper. 'Tis simple to cook up.'

Young Stugg held out his bowl for a refill. 'But you make it da best, 'cos yore our mamma!'

Marinu dipped her ladle into the pot they had brought out. 'You'll soon be as big a flatterer as yore dad! Wipe that chin, you've got chowder all over it.'

Abruc looked over the rim of his bowl at Marinu. 'So, how are you an' old Sork gettin' along with our big badger? D'ye reckon he'll live?'

Marinu wiped Stugg's chin with her apron hem as she spoke. 'It looks like he will, though whether or not he'll waken fully we don't know. He might just fade away, after one of those death sleeps that last a few seasons. I never thought anybeast could be so deeply wounded an' live. Sork used fish glue to mend his skull bone. When that was all clean and set, I used long hairs from his own back as thread to stitch the skin back over. We set lots of spider web over it all. Give it a few days, then we'll wash it gently with valerian and sanicle to deaden any pain. Shoredog says he'll have to be moved to the old cave where it'll be quieter. We'll make him a big bed of silver sand and moss.'

Abruc nodded. 'That should help. I'll keep a warm fire of pine an' sweet herbs burnin' there, night an' day.'

Marinu rose. 'I'm going back inside. Sork wants to borrow some of the broth off'n my chowder to feed him. A hard task with such a big beast who's still senseless.'

When she had gone inside, Abruc and Stugg finished off the remaining food. The young otter sat watching his father attach a slim line from the end of his rudder to a thick root growing from the bankside. Abruc took a chunk of beeswax and began rubbing it into several more loose lines of tough flaxen fibre.

The sea otter eyed his young son. 'Shouldn't you be off to yore bed? 'Tis getting' late.'

Stugg rubbed some of the beeswax on his paw curiously. 'Wot are you doin' wiv dat stuff, farder?'

Abruc explained as he worked. 'I'm makin' a bowstring, a good stout one that won't rot or break under strain.'

Young Stugg pursued his enquiries. 'Wotta you be wantin' a bowstring for, farder?'

Abruc answered patiently. 'T'aint for me, it's for our big badger. I've got a feelin' he'll be well again some day. When the time comes, he'll be leavin' us to go westwards.'

Stugg persisted. 'Is a bowstring good to go westwards wiv?'

His father began deftly plying the waxed fibres together.

'Aye, son, that big feller's an archer. He'll have t'find 'imself the right wood t'make a new bow, but the least I can do is to plait him a proper bowstring. Then he'll be well armed to settle up with the vermin who tried to slay him an' murdered his ole friend.'

Stugg nodded. 'I bet they be sorry then!'

Abruc stopped working momentarily. 'Sorry ain't the word, young 'un. When a badger goes after his enemies, there ain't noplace they can run or hide from him. I'll wager our big beast will come down on 'em with the Bloodwrath!'

Unfamiliar with this strange word, Stugg posed a new question. 'Wot's a Bloodraff, farder?'

Abruc shook his head decisively. 'Bloodwrath is terrible, somethin' you don't ever want t'see or know about. Go on now, off to bed with ye, me son!'

4

Old Father Phredd was the Redwall Abbey Gatekeeper. He had once been Abbot, but his seasons caught up with him. Passing the position over to Carrul, he retired to the gatehouse. Phredd was ancient, probably the oldest hedgehog in all Mossflower, and enjoyed being very old, and rather eccentric as well. Although the Old Gatekeeper sought the privacy of his beloved gatehouse and slept a lot, when he was up and about, he could be rather sprightly. His skinny form, with drooping silver spikes, often caused a smile around the Abbey and its grounds. Phredd spoke to stones, trees, plants and flowers, carrying on long conversations and debating with the most everyday objects.

He had arrived late for lunch, shunning the main crowd that was now gathered in the orchard. Preparing his own plate in the deserted kitchens, Phredd first chose a scone. He prattled on to it as he made his way around the tables.

'Hee hee, you're a fine fresh fellow. Now what'll I have to go with you, eh, eh? Speak up!'

Placing an ear close to the scone, he cackled. 'Teeheehee! Of course, some honey, a piece o' cheese and a beaker of soup – not too hot, just right for swigging, eh?'

Granmum Gurvel, the old molecook, came in from the orchard to draw off more cordial. She spied Phredd and watched him chatting away to the food until he caught sight of her.

Phredd waved his scone at her. 'Oh, er, young Gurvel, g'day!'

She chuckled. 'Hurr hurr, goo day to ee, zurr. Wot bee's ee soup sayin' to ee; sumthin' noice oi 'opes?'

Phredd sipped at the beaker and smacked his lips. 'Oh yes, indeed, miss. 'Tis saying that you cooked it very nicely. Oh, it also asked if there was any pie about, eh?'

Gurvel went to her larder and took out a large pie. It was preserved plum and apple, the golden crust liberally dusted with maple frosting.

She cut a generous slice and gave it to him. 'Thurr naow, old 'edgepig, doant ee let nobeast see that. Oi baked it speshul furr supper.'

Phredd nodded his thanks and skittered off out of the kitchens, conversing with the pie slice. 'My my, you're a handsome fellow! What a splendid dessert you'll make. Come on, let's find a nice quiet corner, eh?'

Granmum Gurvel shook her head at Phredd's antics. She picked up the remainder of the pie. 'Coom on, pie, back in ee larder again!'

The realization of what she was doing caused the old molecook to smile. 'Gurr, lack ee day, that Phredd got oi a talkin' to moi own pies naow, gurt seasons!'

Martha had finished her lunch. She, too, sought peace and quiet to continue her reading. Leaving her friends, she wheeled the chair indoors. Crossing Great Hall, she went straight to her favourite place. Harlequin hues of sunlight shafted down through the high, stained-glass windows on to the worn stone floor. Between two towering sandstone columns, a lantern glowed beneath a wondrous woven tapestry with a sword suspended to one side of it. The haremaid halted her chair in full view of the scene, golden motes of sundust floating slowly on the serene air.

Martha paused before opening Sister Portula's heavy book. She gazed up at the central figure in the tapestry, Martin the Warrior. A heroic, armour-clad mouse, the hero and champion of Redwall Abbey. Martha loved looking at his face – so strong and protective yet kindly, with a secret smile forever hiding in his eyes. The sword he was leaning on was the very same one that hung on the wall – a legendary warrior's weapon, its only adornment, one red pommel stone set on the hilt. Martin's swordblade had been forged at Salamandastron, the badgers' mountain fortress on the west seashore. It had been made from a star fragment that had fallen from the skies.

No matter what position Martha took up when she visited the tapestry, Martin's eyes always seemed to be watching her. The haremaid could feel his presence so strongly that she often spoke to him. Keeping her voice low in the echoing hall, she nodded towards the warrior mouse.

'The rains stopped today. You can see by the sunlight in here that it's a beautiful spring day outside. I've come to do a bit of reading in peace. You should hear those Dibbuns singing in the orchard – they're so happy! Did you ever do much reading, Martin?'

'Hee hee, I don't suppose he did, a warrior like him, eh?' Phredd emerged from the shadows, where he had installed himself behind a column to enjoy his lunch.

Martha was slightly surprised at the old hedgehog's appearance. 'Oh I'm sorry, sir, I didn't know you were here.'

Phredd picked pie crumbs from his cheek spikes. 'No need to be sorry, pretty miss, you carry on talking to your friend. I've had many a long chat with him, eh!'

The haremaid continued looking at the tapestry. 'He looks so understanding, like a friend anybeast could talk to. Do you think he can hear us?'

Phredd patted her shoulder lightly. 'Of course he can. I'm sorry for intruding. You carry on, miss. I'll just pop off to my gatehouse for an afternoon nap. Good day to you.'

He shuffled off, though Martha heard him reprimanding a corner bench. 'You mind your own business an' don't be eavesdropping now, eh, eh!'

Martha opened the book but was only able to concentrate on it for a short while before her eyelids began to flicker and then droop. The peacefulness of her surroundings, combined with the warm sunlight pouring down from the windows, had woven its own spell. There, in the silence of Great Hall, the small figure in the chair slept in a pool of tranquillity. Floating through the corridors of her mind came two mice – one, a maid of her own age clad in a gown of green; the other, Martin the Warrior.

His voice was as reassuring as soft breezes through a meadow. 'I never did read much, Martha. It is good to read, all learning is knowledge. Read on, young one. Learn of Sister Amyl and the mice of Loamhedge.'

The haremaid could hear her own voice replying, 'Learn what? Who is Sister Amyl?'

The young mousemaid standing beside the warrior pointed to Martha and spoke, every word burning itself into Martha's mind.

'Where once I dwelt in Loamhedge,
my secret lies hid from view,
a tale of how I learned to walk,
when once I was as you.
Though you cannot go there,
look out for two who may,
travellers from out of the past,
returning home someday.'

Both Martin and Sister Amyl raised a paw in farewell. The dream faded like wisping smoke as Martha slept on.

Around midnoon Martha was awakened rudely, her chair jolted as three pairs of paws latched on to it. Horty,

Springald and Fenna ran her speedily across Great Hall, whirling perilously around the huge stone columns.

Martha gripped the chair tightly. 'Whoo! Slow down, please. Where are we going?'

Horty jumped up beside her, shouting, 'Out to enjoy the jolly old fresh air, my beautiful skin'n'blister; you'll go mouldy sittin' indoors, wot! I say, you chaps, can't you make this thing go faster? Yaaaah!'

The chair struck a table edge and upturned. Springald and Fenna leapt aside, but Martha and Horty were shot out. Luckily, Martha landed on top of her brother, clutching Sister Portula's volume to her. The chair skidded on a short distance, then lay still, one of its wheels still turning slowly.

Horty looked up into his sister's face. 'Dreadfully sorry about that, old gel, just a bit of fun, wot. I say, are you hurt?'

Martha glared down from where she was sitting on him. 'Lucky for you I'm not. Is my chair damaged?'

Springald and Fenna set the chair upright and examined it. 'No, not a mark on it, Martha!'

'Haha, old Toran knew what he was doing when he built this thing. Stay there, we'll lift you back in!'

In frosty silence, Martha allowed them to lift her back into the chair. The trio fussed about, folding the rug neatly about her lap and laying the volume on it.

Fenna smiled sweetly. 'There, no real harm done, Martha. We were only trying to cheer you up, didn't mean to throw you like that.'

Hastily Springald backed her up. 'Yes, we were going to take you for a quick spin around the walltop. Lovely view from there on a day like this.'

Horty waggled his ears in agreement. 'Right you are, m'dear. There's still time for a toddle round the battlements, though we'll go slower this time. Word of honour, wot!'

Martha shook her head firmly. 'Oh no, you three wild-beasts aren't taking me anywhere. Now go away! Please, leave me alone, I'm quite happy here!'

Horty scuffed his footpaw guiltily along the floorstones.

'I say, y'won't tell anybeast about what happened, will you?'

Martha tapped her chair arm pensively. 'Anybeast like who?'

Horty fidgeted with his belt tab. 'Er, like Toran, or Abbot Carrul or blinkin' old Sis Peculiar.'

Martha reminded him of the Infirmary Keeper. 'Or Sister Setiva?'

Fenna's eyes went wide. 'Oh please, don't tell her!'

The other two miscreants joined in with their pleas.

'She'll make us scrub the infirmary out and stitch sheets!'

'Aye, an' physick the blinkin' life out of us. Oh come on, charmin', beautiful Sis, say y'won't snitch to that monster!'

They looked so sorry for themselves that Martha relented. 'Alright, I won't say anything – provided you go away immediately and leave me in peace.'

Without a word the trio began to scramble away and were almost at the door when Martha suddenly recalled her dream.

'Wait, come back here, there's something I need you to do!'

Horty dashed back so hastily that he almost tripped and fell on to his sister's lap. 'Anything, dear old skin'n'blister, we're yours to flippin' well command!'

Martha issued her modest requests, but she spoke firmly. 'Fenna, I want you to go and seek out Abbot Carrul. Horty, you go and find Sister Portula, and mind how you address her. The message for both of them is this: ask politely that if neither is too busy, would they please come to the gatehouse. There is an important matter I would like to discuss with them. Springald, push my chair to the gatehouse – at a reasonable pace, please.'

Brother Phredd poked his head around the gatehouse doorway, blinking and yawning. 'Ah yes, young wotsername, come in please, and your friend, too. Always nice to have afternoon visitors, eh!'

As Springald pushed Martha over the threshold, the haremaid heard the mousemaid muttering, 'Huh, I'm not stopping in some dusty old gatehouse on an afternoon like this!'

Martha fixed her with an icy smile. 'Oh, you don't have to stay, you run off to the kitchens now. Have a word with Gurvel or Toran – tell them I'd like afternoon tea for four.'

Springald looked puzzled. 'Afternoon tea for four?'

Martha wheeled round to face her. 'Yes, afternoon tea, you know, scones and slices of cake, and a large pot of mint tea with honey. Hop along now, bring them straight back here, and don't spill the tea. Off you go, miss!'

To ensure Martha's silence, Springald had no option but to obey. With a sweep of her skirt she flounced off.

Old Phredd addressed the chair he was about to sit on. 'Afternoon tea, how does that sound to you, quite nice, eh?'

In due course, Abbot Carrul and Sister Portula arrived. Both knew that Martha was a sensible creature and would not summon them on some foolish errand. Brother Phredd had just seated them both, when another knock came on the door. He scratched his drooping spikes and muttered. 'More visitors, quite an eventful afternoon, eh?'

Springald pushed the laden trolley in. She curtsied impudently at the Abbot. 'Afternoon tea for four, Father!'

Martha forestalled any further smartness by nodding graciously at the mousemaid. 'Thank you, miss, you may go now!'

Sister Portula watched the back of Springald's head shaking with rage as she exited the gatehouse and slammed the door. 'Gracious me, you certainly put that young mouse in her place!'

Martha smiled demurely. 'Yes, Sister, but she does need it now and again, doesn't she?'

Abbot Carrul took the haremaid's paw. 'What was it you wanted to see us about, Martha?'

Over afternoon tea, Martha explained to her friends how she had fallen asleep. She told them of Martin's visitation, and of the young mouse who had accompanied him, ending with the short poem, which she recalled precisely.

'Where once I dwelt in Loamhedge,
my secret lies hid from view,
the tale of how I learned to walk,
when once I was as you.
Though you cannot go there,
look out for two who may,
travellers from out of the past,
returning home someday.'

Abbot Carrul sat forwards in his armchair. 'Strange. What do you think, Sister?'

Portula put aside her tea. 'Not many Redwallers are honoured by a visit from Martin the Warrior. We must heed all he says. His spirit is not just the essence of valour and honour, he is also the voice of knowledge and wisdom. Now, what is your own opinion of this incident, Martha?'

The haremaid tapped the cover of the book. 'This is the history of Loamhedge that you loaned me, Sister. I think the answer lies inside it. That's why I called you here. I am still young, but you three have the knowledge of seasons on your side. I was hoping that you could help me. I never dreamed that there might be an answer to why I can't walk. Do you think there is?'

Old Phredd picked up the big tome and laid it on the table. He spoke to it, as if it were a living thing. 'Well now, you dusty old relic, are you going to assist us with this little one's problem, eh, eh?'

He turned and gave Martha a toothless grin. 'Heeheehee, I think he will. Though one can never really tell what a book says until one reads it, eh?'

Abbot Carrul opened the book. 'This may take some time, but we're on your side, Martha. If there is a way to make you walk, rest assured, we'll find it.'

Martha could feel tears beginning to brim in her eyes. She blinked them away swiftly. 'Thank you all, my good friends. But there is something that I don't think the book can tell us. Who are the ones we must look out for? The two travellers from out of the past, returning home someday?'

Sister Portula gazed out the window into the sunlit noon. 'You're right, Martha. I wonder who they could be.'

5

North of Redwall, spring eventide filtered soft light through the leafy canopy of Mossflower Wood. Amid aisles of oak, beech, elm, sycamore and other forest giants, slender rowan, birch and willow stood like young attendants, waiting on their stately lords. Blue smoke drifted lazily upwards through the foliage which fringed a shallow stream. Somewhere nearby, a pair of nightingales warbled harmoniously.

The tremulous beauty was lost upon a small vermin band who had trekked down from the far Northlands. They had camped on the bank to fish. A fat, brutish weasel called Burrad was their leader. Beneath his ragged cloak he carried a cutlass, its bone handle notched with the lives he had taken. Burrad's sly eyes watched his band closely. They were spitting four shiny scaled roach on green willow withes to grill over the fire.

Drawing the cutlass, Burrad pointed it at the biggest fish. 'Dat'n der is mine; yew cook it good fer me, Flinky!'

The stoat called Flinky let out a pitifully indignant whine. 'Arr 'ey, Chief, I caught dis wun meself, 'tis me own fish!'

Despite his bulk, Burrad was quick. Bulling the stoat over, he whipped Flinky mercilessly with the flat of his blade.

Covering his head, the victim screeched for mercy. 'Yaaaaaargh, stop 'im mates, afore he kills me pore ould body! Yeeegh, spare me, yer mightiness, spare me. Aaaaagh!'

Cruel by nature, Burrad thrashed Flinky even harder. Throwing himself upon the hapless stoat, he pressed the blade against Flinky's scrawny neck, snarling viciously.

'Wot d'yer want, the fish or yore 'ead? 'Urry up an' speak.'

The cutlass blade pressed savagely down. Flinky wailed. 'Yeeeeh, take de fish, I've only got one 'ead. Take de fish!'

Burrad rose, grinning wolfishly as he kicked Flinky's bottom. 'Cook dat fish good, or yore a dead 'un!'

He turned on the other eleven vermin gang members. 'Wot are youse lot gawpin' at, eh? Gimme some grog!'

A female stoat called Crinktail, whose tail was shaped almost like a letter Z, passed Burrad the jug of nettle grog. Snatching it roughly, the bully sat down, taking long gulps of the fiery liquid.

He watched Flinky like a hawk. 'Crispy outside an' soft inside, dat's de way I likes fish.'

The others averted their eyes; there was no doubt about who the leader of their gang was.

Crouched low in the reeds on the far bank, two creatures viewed the scene. One was an otter, the other a squirrel, both in their late middle seasons.

The otter squinched his eyes, letting them rove over the gang. 'Hmm, about twelve o' them over there, I'd say.'

The squirrel nibbled on a young reed. 'There's thirteen.'

Her companion shrugged. 'I won't argue with ye, 'cos my eyes ain't as good as they used t'be. I tell ye though, mate, that's one sorry gang o' vermin. Looks as if they got rocks in their skulls instead o' brains.'

The squirrel chuckled. 'Aye, campin' there without a single sentry posted, an' a fire smokin' away like a beacon. 'Tis a wonder their mothers let 'em out alone.'

The otter nodded. 'See ole lardbelly yonder, the big weasel? Leave him t'me, I enjoy takin' bullies down a peg.'

The squirrel commented drily, 'Watch he don't fall on ye, he'd flatten ye like a pancake. Are those fish ready yet?'

Her companion sniffed the air. 'I'd say so. Right then, are we ready t'go an' pay 'em a visit?'

The squirrel sighed. 'Aye, layin' here won't get us any supper. You go in the front, an' I'll make me way around back.'

The lean, ageing otter grumbled, 'It's always me wot has t'go in the front. Why can't I go in the back?'

The squirrel cut left along the streambank, replying, ''Cos I'm the best tree climber. Give me time t'get ready, mate, don't walk in too early. Good luck!'

Tucking his rudder into the back of his belt, the otter draped his ragged cloak to conceal it. He bound a faded red bandanna low on his brow, disguising both ears and scrunching down over his eyes to make them look short-sighted.

Picking up a polished hardwood staff, he splashed into the stream shallows, muttering to himself, 'Huh, I'm gettin' too old for this game!'

Little Redd was the youngest of the vermin gang. Small and runty, he was often the butt of their coarse jokes.

Seeking about for firewood, Redd glanced sideways. He saw the bedraggled creature wading across the stream, and called to Burrad. 'Aye aye, Chief, looks like we got company!'

Burrad took his mouth from the grog jug. He cast a contemptuous glance at the hunched figure struggling towards the bankside. 'Wot'n de name o'bludd is dat?'

The otter sloshed ashore, calling in a quavery voice. 'A good evenin' to one an' all. Seems I'm just in time for supper. Mmm . . . roasted roach, me favourite vittles!'

Burrad's cutlass was drawn and wavering a whisker's breadth from the unwanted visitor's nose. 'Who are ye? Huhuhuh, or should I say, wot are ye?'

The stranger avoided the blade neatly. Ducking under it, he stood at the vermin leader's side, wrinkling his nose comically. 'Wot am I, young feller? I'm a ferroat, o' course!'

Flinky looked up from the cooking fire. 'A ferroat? Ah sure, an' wot sort o' beast is dat now?'

The intruder replied airily, 'Oh, just a cross twixt a ferret an' a stoat. I was a small sickly babe, or so me ole mum'n'dad told me. That's why I look like this.'

Ignoring his fish-cooking task, Flinky continued. 'An' who, pray, was yore muther an' father?'

The stranger replied, straight-faced, 'A rat an' a fox, I s'pose, but they was terrible liars.'

Flinky scratched his head. 'Liars? Huh, I'll say they was!'

Burrad interrupted by thwacking Flinky between both ears with the flat of his blade. 'Who asked yew, puddle'ead? Gerron wid cookin' dose fishes!'

He turned to the odd-looking creature. 'Wot's yore name, ferroat, an' wot d'ye want 'ere?'

The newcomer pointed to himself. 'Just told ye, haven't I? Me name's Ferroat, an' I'll sing an' dance fer me supper. That's if ye'll allow me, kind sir.'

The vermin gang winked and sniggered among themselves. Burrad, a kind sir? This old fool was begging to die.

Testing his cutlass blade by licking the edge, Burrad leaned close to his intended victim and grinned. 'Allow ye, eh? If'n yore dancin' an' singin' ain't to me likin', I'll allow this blade to chop ye into ten pieces. Then I'll allow me gang to roast ye over that fire. If ye don't taste nice, we kin always use ye fer fishbait!'

Smiling affably, the odd beast bowed creakily. ''Tis a fair offer, sir, I thankee kindly.'

Shuffling about in a curious jig, the creature twirled his staff and began singing.

'I'll always recall wot Ma said to me,
ere I went a rovin' a minstrel to be,

45

"Beware of the vermin, they ain't got no class,
an' they ain't got the brains Mother Nature gave grass!"
Rowledy dowlety toodle um day.

I soon found out me dear mother was right,
I met up with some vermin the followin' night,
they were strangers to bathin', an' that made me think,
why didn't Ma tell me that all vermin stink?
Rowledy pong and a toodledy pooh!'

The comic-looking old ragbag of a beast jigged and shuffled around. Raucous laughter greeted his performance followed by tears of merriment that coursed down the vermin's cheeks. It was only at the start of the third verse, when vermins' faces were compared to toads' bottoms, that Burrad realized the singer was insulting him and his gang.

Roaring with rage, the fat weasel rushed at the disguised otter. Whirling his cutlass, Burrad aimed a mighty swipe that should have left the singer headless. However, far from being slain, the odd creature ducked under the blow, came up under Burrad and tweaked his snout.

Purple with spleen, the gang leader grappled with his opponent, yelling to his second in command, 'Skrodd, gut this old fleabag wid yer spear, I've got 'im!'

The tall, evil-looking fox dashed forwards, plunging with his spear. But the otter was fast and more clever than both vermin. He butted Burrad under the chin, wriggled from his grasp and scuttled to one side in the blink of an eye.

Burrad stood gaping at the spear protruding from his stomach. He raised his clouding eyes to the open-mouthed fox, faltering, 'Ye've killed me, yer blather-brained foo ...!'

Burrad crashed over backwards, slain by his own gang member. Amid the drama, nobeast noticed the four fish vanish up into the willow foliage, hauled on a thin twine by the green withes they were spitted upon.

Skrodd's surprise was only momentary. His brain was already reacting to the fact that he was now the vermin gang's new leader. Leaving the spear stuck in his former chief, the tall fox grabbed the cutlass from Burrad's limp grasp. He came at the otter with a blurring barrage of swift slashes.

Whizzzzzthonk! A slingstone from the trees suddenly rendered him senseless. Skrodd's fellow vermin looked on in horror as his body collapsed in a heap. Before the gang could move, the squirrel dropped from her perch. Danger glinted in her eyes as she twirled a loaded sling expertly.

'There's twoscore more of us layin' in the bushes, just waitin' on the word!'

Shedding his disguise, the otter knocked daggers and other weapons from the vermins' paws, with sharp raps of his polished staff. He looked nothing like the ragged, dancing fool he had been a moment ago. His voice was stern and commanding.

'Everybeast stand still, right where ye are! Believe Saro, we've got a full crew ready to pounce on ye!'

Halfchop, a rat who was minus a paw, gulped. 'If'n that 'un's called Saro, yew must be Bragoon?'

Flinky looked at the pair in astonishment. 'I've heard of ye, Bragoon an' Saro. Two mighty warriors!'

Bragoon leaned on his staff and nodded. 'That's us, an' there's forty more trained fighters like us, just waitin' to get a crack at you lot. So have the brains to stay alive an' listen to wot we say.'

Flinky bowed politely. 'Anythin', yer honour, sure we're in no position to be arguin' wid ye.'

Saro pointed at a wobbly-nosed ferret called Plumnose. 'You, where have ye come from? Speak!'

Gesturing back over his shoulder, Plumnose replied, 'Durr, we cummed from der Nort'lands.'

Saro nodded. 'The Northlands, eh? Then listen carefully to my friend Bragoon.'

The otter let his fierce eyes wander round the hapless vermin as he ground out an ultimatum. 'Get yoreselves back to the Northlands, 'cos if yore anywhere south of here by nightfall, yore all deadbeasts! We're goin' now, but our mates'll stay hidden, watchin' ye. Sit still here until 'tis properly dark, then break camp an' get back to where ye came from – sharpish! We'll be passin' this way again tomorrow. Make sure yore not still here. Is that clear?'

Flinky's head bobbed up and down like a yo-yo. 'Ah, sure, 'tis certain clear, yer mightiness. We've all got the message, an' a fine important one it is, sir!'

Bragoon and Saro backed out of the camp. A moment later they were lost in the surrounding trees. The vermin sat wordlessly staring at one another until Plumnose broke the silence.

'Wodd duh we do now?'

Flinky's mate, Crinktail, was in no doubt. 'Like they said, we wait 'til it's dark, then we gets out of here. I don't know about youse, but I'm goin'.'

Flinky agreed. 'Aye, ye don't disobey two like Bragoon an' Saro. Best do the sensible thing, mates.'

Recovering from the slingstone blow, Skrodd sat up groaning. 'Unnnh, wot hit me?'

Slipback, a weasel with most of his back fur missing, toyed with the cutlass that had belonged to Burrad.

'Ye were knocked cold by a slingstone, mate.'

Skrodd felt the lump on his skull and winced. 'Who did it?'

Flinky chuckled. ''Twas none other than a famous squirrel called Saro. Yore lucky she did, 'cos the one you was goin' after wid yore blade was 'er partner, Bragoon.'

Skrodd stood slowly and walked across to Slipback. Suddenly he dealt the weasel a swift kick to the chin. As Slipback fell, the tall fox grabbed Burrad's cutlass.

'Keep yer paws off dat blade, 'tis mine now. I slew Burrad, an' I'm the new chief round 'ere!'

Slipback avoided a second kick. 'Only by accident – dat don't make yew chief!'

Skrodd turned to face the rest of the gang, wielding his new weapon. 'Accident or not, Burrad's dead. Does anybeast want to challenge me? Come on!'

None came forwards. They knew the tall fox's reputation as a fighter; even Burrad had never kicked him about.

Skrodd smiled grimly. 'Right, up on yore hunkers, we're goin' to track those two down!'

Little Redd exclaimed, 'Didn't ye hear Flinky? Those two are dangerous warriors, Bragoon an' Saro.'

Skrodd turned on the little fox. 'Ye mean that ole ragbag who was jiggin' about an' tryin' to sing for his supper? Wot did the other one look like, Flinky?'

The stoat shrugged. 'Small an' oldish, why d'ye ask?'

Skrodd curled his lip scornfully. 'A pair o' little ole tattered ragamuffins, an' ye lot believed they was Bragoon an' Saro. Real famous warriors are big an' tough. Any two beasts could say they was Bragoon an' Saro. Those two were nothin' but a pair of ole impostors. Now come on, let's get after 'em. Nobeast knocks me down wid a slingstone an' lives t'brag about it. I'll gut the two of 'em!'

A hefty-looking rat called Dargle remained seated. 'They said we was to sit 'ere 'til it was dark, then head back t'the Northlands. The otter said there was twoscore fighters layin' nearby, an' that we'd be dead meat if'n we didn't do like we was told.'

Skrodd shook his head in disbelief. 'An' ye believed 'im? That's the oldest trick in the book. Watch, I'll show ye twoscore o' fighters!'

Furiously grabbing anything that came to paw – firewood, pebbles and soil – the tall fox flung them at the surrounding trees, yelling out defiantly, 'Now then, ye mighty fighters, come out an' show yerselves. I'll fight ye all at once, or one by one if'n ye ain't frightened o' me! Get out 'ere, ye mangy frogbait!'

Silence greeted the challenge. Skrodd spat contemptuously into the fire, glaring at the vermin gang. 'Wot a bunch of addlebrains! Up on yore paws an' get movin' ye bunch o' ditherin' oafs. After I've slain those two ole relics, we'll get the rest o' this job done. Move!'

As they moved southwards into the woodlands, Little Redd discussed the situation with Flinky. 'Skrodd ain't takin' us to that Abbey place that Burrad was always goin' on about, is he?'

Flinky nodded. 'Ah sure, it looks like he wants t'be the big bold beast who gets the magic sword. Huh, magic sword! I wonder where ould Burrad heard that tale?'

Juppa, the weasel who was Slipback's mate, joined the conversation. 'Burrad said his father told 'im about it, just afore he died. Said there was an Abbey, a big place called Redwall. Accordin' to 'im, there's only a few peaceful woodlanders lives there. They keep a magic sword at Redwall. 'Tis said that the warrior who holds that sword is the greatest in the land!'

Slipback confirmed his mate's story. 'Aye, none can stand against the sword owner, I've heard the tale meself.'

Skrodd, who was leading the gang through the darkened woodlands, overheard Slipback's remark. He stopped and questioned the weasel. 'Wot have ye heard? Tell me.'

The garrulous Flinky spoke up. 'Ah sure, 'twas me that told him. I sat wid Burrad's ole dad many a night, yarnin' away. He was a fine ould feller, not like his son. Anyhow, he told me all about the magic sword, so he did.'

Skrodd was fired with the idea of possessing such an enchanted blade. He stared hard at the gabby stoat. 'Right, then, you tell me everythin' the ole beast said.'

Flinky liked to talk, but he was also aware that the tall fox was not one to be taken lightly. 'Ah, well let me see now. There's this place, see, a grand ould Abbey called Redwall that stands on a path somewhere in the centre of the land. Sure, an' a fine buildin' it is!'

Little Redd interrupted. 'I've 'eard o' Redwall.'

Skrodd froze him with a glare, gesturing Flinky to continue.

'Aye, Redwall was built by a mighty warrior long ago. He carried a great sword made from bits o' the moon 'n' stars. A marvellous blade, magic enough t'make a champion fighter out o' anybeast. That warrior's long dead now, but the sword still hangs in the Abbey.'

This time it was Skrodd's turn to interrupt. 'Then why doesn't one of the creatures at Redwall Abbey wear it?'

Flinky shook his head. 'Ah no, they're all only simple woodland beasts. They're farmers an' such, not fighters. Hah, what need d'they have o' swords? 'Tis said that Redwall is a place of peace an' plenty.'

Little Redd's eyes shone with longing. 'I wish I had a magic sword!'

Skrodd shoved him roughly. 'A runt like yew, huh, you'll have to fight me fer it. That sword is goin' t'be mine!'

The hefty rat Dargle muttered under his breath. 'If ye think ye can take it, fox!'

Skrodd looked around at the vermin behind him. 'Did somebeast say somethin'?'

Flinky rubbed his stomach. 'Ah no, Chief, 'twas just me ould guts rumblin' away. I knew that fish wasn't fer me somehow.'

Bragoon and Saro had made camp in a grove of conifers, some miles south of where they had encountered the vermin.

Burying the fishbones beneath the deep layer of pine needles, the otter wiped his mouth. 'Bit o' fish like that makes a nice change, eh mate? Did ye manage to lay paws on any o' that stuff they was drinkin'?'

The ageing squirrel wrinkled her nose disgustedly. 'That poison? Vermin-brewed nettle grog. Small wonder they're stupid – it must've rotted what little brains they had. Best stick with clean streamwater until we get back to Redwall an' get some decent drink.'

She lay back, viewing the star-dusted skies through the treetops. 'Aah, t'be back home in the good ole Abbey.

D'ye think they've forgiven us for the old Dibbun days?'

Her companion chuckled. 'I certainly hope they have, we were a fearsome pair, mate. Hmmm, wonder if ole Granmum Gurvel's still the Abbeycook. Hoho, the pies'n'scones we swiped off'n her kitchen windowsill. No wonder she turned grey!'

Saro shrugged. 'There's a lot o' seasons run under the bridge since we were Abbeybabes. I don't suppose pore old Gurvel will still be livin'. She was a great cook though.'

Bragoon nodded. 'Aye, she was that. I'll bet that little brother o' mine Toran is Abbeycook now. Gurvel taught him a lot, y'know. He was always a goodbeast around kitchens an' ovens.'

Saro hopped up and spread herself along a bough, directly above Bragoon's resting spot. She reminisced hungrily. 'Scones, or fresh bread, with meadowcream an' damson preserve. That's what I could eat right now!'

Stretched on the ground, Bragoon yawned and sighed. 'Don't even mention it, mate. Let's get a good night's shuteye. We could make Redwall by afternoon tea tomorrow. You can fill yore face then. G'night, Saro.'

The squirrel ignored her friend and continued yearning. 'October Ale! What could be nicer than a foamin' beaker o' good October Ale. Mmmm, with some brown farlbread an' some yellow cheese with roasted hazelnuts in it. Simple but satisfyin', eh Brag?'

The otter opened one eye. 'Very acceptable. Now go t'sleep!'

Saro carried on as if she had not heard. 'What would y'say to an apple'n'blackberry crumble, spread thick with meadowcream?'

Bragoon growled. 'I'd say button yore lip an' sleep. So goodnight!'

But Saro could not forget the subject of food. 'Howsabout ice cold mint tea an' a thick slice of heavy fruitcake with honey crystals in it. Ooooh!'

Bragoon sat up slowly. 'I'd say ye was makin' my pore stomach gurgle with all this vittle talk. Good . . . night!'

Saro licked her lips. 'Or some of yore favourite, a big carrot'n'mushroom pasty, with onion gravy drippin' an' oozin' out the sides, an' . . . Yaahooooow!'

She was catapulted into the air as Bragoon hauled down hard on the bough, letting it go suddenly. Rising from the ground, Saro dusted herself off indignantly.

'Gettin' touchy in yore old age, aren't ye? Goodnight to ye, ole grumpy rudder!'

Bragoon snorted. 'I swear ye were born chatterin'. Now goodnight, old gabby whiskers!'

Silence fell over the glade. Both lifelong friends drifted into the realm of slumber. They dreamt golden-tinged memories of their Dibbun seasons at the place they called home – Redwall Abbey.

6

The big badger's eyes flickered, then opened slowly. He lay quite still, taking in his strange surroundings – a cave, peaceful and warm, with sweet aromatic wisps drifting languidly from a rockbound hearth. A fireglow cast flickering shadows across the rough-hewn walls. He felt secure and safe there with moss and soft, silver sand beneath him.

A movement near his head caught the badger's attention. A young sea otter emerged.

'De old stripedog who was slayed, was he yore farder, sir?'

Though it pained him, he strained his neck to get a closer look at the young one. The badger's voice, echoing in the cavern, sounded strange to his ears. 'Nay, he was my friend, though a father could not have been kinder to me. He was called Grawn. I trust you put him to rest decently.'

The youngster nodded several times. 'Shoredog an' my farder made a bury hole. They putted rocks on him an' yore bow, 'cos it was broked in halves.'

The badger's big dark eyes glistened wetly. 'I must thank your father and Shoredog. What do they call you?'

The young beast held out his paw politely. 'I bee's Stugg, son of Abruc an' Marinu, sir.'

A massive paw took Stugg's smaller one, enveloping it.

''Tis a pleasure to meet ye, Stugg. I am called Lonna Bow-stripe. Is your father hereabout? I would speak with him.'

Lonna listened to young Stugg scamper from the cave calling shrilly, 'Farder, farder, come quick! De big stripedog bee's awake, his name be Lonna!'

In a short while, two male sea otters entered the cave, fol-lowed by two females, one very old, and Stugg following up the rear.

Lonna leaned forwards slightly. 'Thank you, my friends, for saving my life, caring for me and putting old Grawn to rest. Stugg told me you buried him well.'

Abruc pressed Lonna back down gently. 'We did what was right for your companion. Only vermin leave the dead unburied. As for ye bein' cared for, 'twas my wife Marinu an' ole Sork who saw to yore well-bein'. You lie still an' rest now, Lonna. By an' by ye'll get stronger. We'll see to that.'

The big badger's paw touched the long scar ridge that crossed his face diagonally from eartip to jaw. 'I must grow strong again to repay the vermin who did this and murdered poor Grawn. Did you see them?'

Sork placed Lonna's paw by his side. 'Be still, bigbeast, an' thank the seasons ye are still alive. That face still needs a lot of healing, aye, an' yore back, too. We'll bring ye food an' drink.' Sork and Marinu departed.

Shoredog stood over Lonna, looking down into his in-jured face. 'We never saw the vermin, but we know 'em. Raga Bol the sea rat an' his crew were the ones. His ship was wrecked beyond repair. They have gone westwards, inland to where the weather's fair an' the pickin's easier. Do ye know Raga Bol?'

Lonna's scar twitched faintly. 'I do not know the scum, but I know of him. They say he kills for fun.'

Young Stugg scowled. 'My farder says Raga Bol be's wicked!'

Abruc tugged his son's rudder. 'Go an' help yore mamma now.'

55

Lonna watched the young otter shuffle off. 'He'll grow up to be a fine big creature someday.'

Abruc smiled. 'Aye, Stugg's a good liddle son.'

Abruc sought Lonna's paw and pressed something into it. 'Yore weapon was too badly broken to fix. I wove ye a new bowstring. Mayhap ye'll need it when y'leave here.'

Lonna held the cord where he could see it better. 'Thankee, friend. 'Tis a fine, tough one, well woven and waxed. This is a good and thoughtful gift.'

Abruc flushed with pleasure. 'Ye have only to ask if ye need ought else. We'll do our best to find it.'

The giant badger closed his eyes, speaking softly. 'I'd be obliged if you could get some ash shafts for arrows, and a few long stout yew saplings, so I can choose one to make a new bow from.'

Shoredog replied. 'We saved yore quiver an' the arrows, too. Me an' Abruc know some stream otters not too far from here. They coppice a yew grove. We can have ye a selection of good saplings by tomorrow night. Now sleep, Lonna, ye must rest if yore goin' to get better. Relax an' sleep.'

A short time thereafter, Lonna allowed Marinu to feed him. Then he drifted off into slumber whilst Sork tended to his hurts. In his sleep he visioned Raga Bol, swinging down at his face with the broad-bladed scimitar. The big badger concentrated all his energy and thoughts on the sea rat's savage features.

Mentally he began chanting, over and over, 'Look and you will see me! Know that I am Lonna Bowstripe! The earth is not big enough for us both! I will come on your trail! I will find you, Raga Bol! I will seek you out no matter where! The day of your death is already written on the stones of Hellgates!'

Whilst the big badger was sleeping, young Stugg crept in to see him. The expression of hatred on Lonna's ruined features was so frightening that the young sea otter ran from the cave.

Raga Bol was still out on the heathlands, trekking west with his sea rats. They were camped on the streambank in what had once been a vole settlement. Amid the smoke and carnage of burning dwellings and slain voles, the barbarous crew fought among themselves over the pitiful possessions and plundered food.

Wirga, the wizened old sea rat who had healed Raga Bol's severed stump, stood watching her master chewing on a strip of dried fish.

With the silver hook tugging at the fish as he pulled to tear it apart, Bol grinned wickedly at Wirga. 'See, I told ye, the further west we go, the better the pickin's get. This stump o' mine ain't painin' so much now. Aye, an' the weather's gettin' better, too.'

Wirga gestured round at the slain vole bodies lying on the bank. 'Fling 'em in the stream an' this'd make a good camp for the night, Cap'n.'

Bol picked his teeth with the hooktip. 'Aye, 'tis nice'-n'restful 'ereabouts now. Hahaha!'

Dutifully, Wirga laughed with him. Her cackling trailed off as she saw her captain go off into a vacant silence, his eyes opening wide as the fish fell unheeded from his mouth.

Wirga stared at him anxiously. 'What is it, Cap'n, a bone stuck in thy gullet? Let me take a look!'

As she bent towards him, Raga Bol recovered and kicked her roughly away. 'Break camp, we're movin' out!'

The healer was bewildered at this sudden change. 'But Cap'n, thee said . . .'

Wirga narrowly dodged an angry slash from the silver hook.

Bol booted the fire left and right, scattering it. 'I said we're movin' out, we ain't stayin' in this place. Now shift yoreself an' get the crew together!'

He strode off, to the top of a small rise, peering back at the route they had come along. Wirga passed the word on to Glimbo.

The one-eyed sea rat rolled his milky orb in puzzlement. 'Why does 'e wanna move? 'Tis nearly dark!'

Wirga picked up her stolen belongings. 'Hah! Yew go an' ask 'im, if'n thee feels tired o' livin'.'

The crew gathered in sullen silence, watching their leader. He was still gazing eastwards from the top of the rise. None of them dared make a move until he did.

Raga Bol stared at the hostile heathland, muttering to himself, 'Yore dead, stripedog, or ye should be. In the name o' blood an' thunder, where are ye?'

He drew his cloak about him and shivered. Somewhere in Raga Bol's evil mind he had felt Lonna Bowstripe's threat.

In the gatehouse at Redwall Abbey, Martha and her friends were studying the history of Loamhedge. It made harrowing reading.

Abbot Carrul shook his head sadly. 'This is not the story of one creature, it is the history of many, all related to one writer, who set it down as a chronicle. I think that this poem, "The Loamhedge Lament," by Sister Linfa, sums up most of the tragedy. I'll read it out to you.'

Martha's eyes misted over as the Abbot recited the poem.

'Where are the carefree sunlit days,
when once amid tranquil bowers,
Loamhedge mice would take their ease,
to dream away happy hours?
Where did the laughter go?
Who stole the joy away?
Heavy the heart that goes
far from its home to stray.
A sickness stole in to blight our lives
like a spectre of unwanted doom.
Midst grief and anguish it lingered,
creeping through hall and room.
Like wheat before the sickle,
it laid our loved ones low,

leaving us only one answer,
to flee our home and go!
Stalked by desolation now,
left open to wind and rain,
only in old memories dim
would Loamhedge live again.'

The day's last gleaming shone through the open door. Toran stood framed there, wiping his eyes on his cook's apron. He had entered unnoticed and heard the whole thing.

'Leave this now, and come back to the Abbey for supper, friends. Tomorrow morning ye can sit out on the wallsteps in the sunlight and study some more. Martha, come on, 'tis far too sad, sittin' here at night readin' of sickness an' death.'

The haremaid cast an imploring glance at Abbot Carrul. 'But we must find out about Sister Amyl's secret, and we must find out a way to discover where Loamhedge lies!'

The Abbot shepherded her to the gatehouse door. 'Toran's right, miss, the night hours can be long and oppressive for such heavy stuff. Let's go to supper in Cavern Hole and shed our sad mood for tonight. We'll be much brighter, and more alert, in the morning.'

Old Phredd the Gatekeeper waved them off. 'Hmm hmm, you run along now. I'll stay here awhile.'

He watched them go, then wandered back into the little building, talking to a cushion he had picked up. 'Hmm, the way to Loamhedge, now where've we seen that before? Chronicle of some bygone traveller I expect, eh, eh?'

Climbing upon a chair, he peered at a row of books on a high shelf. Selecting one, Phredd blew the dust from its covers and smiled benignly at it. 'Ah, there you are, y'old rascal. Hiding up there, heehee. Didn't think I could see ye? Now what've you got to say for yourself, eh, eh?'

Settling down in an armchair, he brought a lantern close and opened the book's yellowed pages. 'Heeheehee, we've met before, haven't we? The recordings of Tim Churchmouse, now I recall ye! The journey to seek out Mattimeo, son of the warrior Matthias. Aye, that covered the Loamhedge Abbey territory, I'm certain it did!'

Toran had been keeping his eye on Martha throughout supper. The ottercook did not like to see his young chum so downcast. He chivvied her, hoping to lighten Martha's mood.

'Cheer up, beauty. If'n ye keep lookin' like that, it'll teem down rain tomorrow. Wot's the matter, my mushroom 'n'barley soup too cold? Has the bread gone stale, the cheese too hard, not enough plums in the pudden? Speak up, droopy ears, does that strawberry fizz cordial taste musty?'

The haremaid managed a wan smile. 'No, Toran, it's not that, the supper is delicious. It's just that . . . oh, I don't know.'

Toran collared Horty, just as he was reaching for another helping of plum pudding. 'Hear that, young starvation face? Yore sister doesn't know wot's wrong with her. Sing her a song an' liven her up, or y'don't get any more plum pud!'

Horty had done this once or twice before, when Martha was a bit down. That, and Toran's threat to cut off his plum pudding supply, galvanized the greedy young hare into action. He let rip with a special ditty he saved for such occasions.

'What a gloomy little mug, wot wot,
come on, let's see you smile.
With a scowl like that you'd frighten
every beast within a mile.
So chortle hahaheeheehoho!
and brighten up for me,
or I'll send you to that Sister
from the Infirmary.

She'll say "Wot have we here, wot wot?
A face like a flattened frog?
This calls for a bucket o' physick, aye,
now that should do the job!
Will somebeast grab her nose,
so she can't hold her breath,
then I'll be able to grab a ladle,
an' physick the child to death!
I'll not have it said of me, I couldn't do my job,
an' send a young 'un to her grave,
with a grin upon her gob!"

So chortle hohohahahee,
an' smile an' giggle a lot,
you can't sit there all evenin'
with a face like a rusty pot. Wot wot!'

Martha was chuckling when she spied Sister Setiva, the Infirmary Keeper, making a beeline for her brother.

Setiva had a stern manner, and a marked northern accent, coupled with a dislike for impudence. 'Ach, ye flop-eared wretch, ah'll physick ye tae death if'n ah lay paws on ye!'

Horty hid behind Toran. 'I say, sah, 'twas only a blinkin' joke, y'know. Don't let that old poisoner get me!'

Martha wiped tears of merriment from her eyes as the Abbot leaned across to her and asked, 'Better now, miss?'

She nodded. 'Yes, thank you, Father. Oh, that Horty!'

Sister Portula gave the Abbot a sidelong glance. 'It's all very well making plans to continue our studies out on the steps tomorrow, but look at the ruckus today. They were crowded around the gatehouse to see what we were doing inside. I think we'd best get ready to have lots of company tomorrow, Father – unless you can think of another way to keep our creatures distracted.'

Abbot Carrul touched a paw to the side of his nose. 'I've

already thought of that, Sister. Do you not know what day it is tomorrow?'

Portula shrugged. 'A day like any other. Sunny, I hope.'

Abbot Carrul stood up and murmured to her as he banged a ladle upon the tabletop to gain order. 'Tomorrow is the first day of summer.'

He raised his voice. 'Your attention please, my friends!'

A respectful silence fell upon the boisterous Redwallers. Everybeast was eager to hear what their Abbot had to say.

'It is my wish that, as tomorrow is the first day of Summer Season, a sports day and a feast shall be held within the grounds of our Abbey. My good friend Foremole Dwurl will be in charge of the proceedings. I trust you will cooperate with him. Foremole Dwurl!'

Redwall's mole leader, a kindly old fellow, bowed low to the Abbot. Amid the raucous cheering and shouting, he climbed upon the table and stamped his footpaws to gain order.

'Thankee, zurr h'Abbot. Naow, you'm all coom to ee h'orchard arter brekkist, an' oi'll give ee yurr tarsks. Hurr hurr, an' all you'm Dibbuns make shore you'm be proper scrubbed!'

Abbot Carrul looked over the top of his tiny glasses at Sister Portula. 'Does that solve your problem, marm?'

The good Sister looked slightly nonplussed. 'But Father, Summer Season doesn't start for two days yet.'

Foremole Dwurl wrinkled his snout confidentially. 'If'n you'm doant tell 'um, marm, us'n's woant. Hurrhurr!'

Silence reigned in Cavern Hole. Every Redwaller was tucked up in bed, anticipating the coming day's delights. Summer Season feast and sports was always a joyous event on the Abbey calendar.

Abbot Carrul pushed Martha's chair across Great Hall to her bedroom, which was next to his on ground level. His voice echoed whisperingly about the huge columns as they went.

'Did you notice that Old Phredd didn't come in for supper this evening?'

Martha voiced her concern. 'Oh dear, I do hope he's not ill!'

The Father Abbot reassured her. 'Not at all, that old fogy's fit as a flea. He was rather anxious for us to get out of the gatehouse, though. I'll wager a button to a barrel of mushrooms that rascal has information about Loamhedge hidden in his dusty archives, sly old hog!'

Martha sat up eagerly. 'Do you really think so, Father?'

Carrul nodded. 'I'm certain of it, miss. D'you know, I think our search is going to turn up some interesting and exciting stuff tomorrow.'

The young haremaid wriggled with anticipation, since any prediction the Abbot made invariably came to pass. 'Oh, I do hope so, Father. Maybe we'll discover Sister Amyl's secret. Wouldn't that be wonderful!'

Martha looked up as they passed the great tapestry. Was it just a trick of the flickering lanterns, or did she really see Martin the Warrior's eyes twinkle at her?

7

Some leagues north of Redwall Abbey, the ragtag vermin gang blundered their way through the nighttime thickness of Mossflower woodlands. Skrodd swiped at the undergrowth with his former leader's cutlass as he led the party.

The big rat, Dargle, kept muttering under his breath, continuously criticizing Skrodd. 'Fancy trackin' two beasts when yore lost, huh!'

Tired and sleepy, the other vermin managed a weary murmur of agreement. Skrodd did not want to challenge Dargle directly – it was the wrong time and place for such a move. So he asserted his authority by bullying all and sundry. He turned on them, brandishing the cutlass.

'Shut yer gobs an' keep movin'. Lost? Hah! Youse'd be the lost ones if'n I wasn't leadin' ye!'

Flinky enjoyed causing trouble. Disguising his voice, he called out behind the big fox's back, 'That's no way t'be talkin' to pore pawsore beasts!'

Little Redd agreed with him. 'Aye, we should be sleepin' now instead o' wanderin' round an' round all night long!'

Although Flinky was the instigator, Redd was the unlucky one whose voice Skrodd identified. With a savage kick, Skrodd sent the small fox sprawling.

Laying the cutlass blade against his neck, he snarled, 'Ye

liddle runt, say the word an' ye can sleep 'ere fer good. I've took enough of yore moanin'!'

Realizing that he had gone too far, Flinky tried to remedy the situation by pulling Redd upright as he appealed to Skrodd. 'Ah, come on now, sure he's only a tired young whelp. No sense in slayin' one of yore own mates. Let's step out a bit, an' I'll sing a song to help us along, eh?'

Skrodd relented, pointing his blade at the stoat. 'Right, you sing. The rest o' ye march, an' shuttup!'

Flinky's ditty put a little fresh life into the gang's paws.

'Ferrets are fine ould foragers,
though frequently furtive an' fey,
stoats can sing sweetly fer seasons,
so me sister used to say,
but foxes are fine an' ferocious,
when faced with a fight or a fray,
an' rats remain rambunctious but only for a day!
But wot about weasels, those wily ould weasels,
they're woefully wayward an' wild,
the ones they've whipped an' walloped,
will wail that weasels are vile,
they've bullied an' beaten an' battered,
they've tormented tortured an' tripped,
I'm sure any day their pore victims would say,
steer clear o' the weasel don't get in his way,
for of all the vermin ye'd care to recall,
the weasel's the wickedest wretch of all.
An' virtuous vermin will all agree,
any weasel is worse than me!'

There were four weasels in the gang: Slipback; his mate, Juppa; and two taciturn brothers, Rogg and Floggo. All of them protested volubly at Flinky's song.

'That ain't right, foxes are worse'n weasels!'

'Ye sing dat again, an' I'll wallop ye alright!'

Skrodd's bad-tempered shout quickly silenced them.

'Shut yore faces back there, or I'll show ye 'ow ferocious foxes can be. Sing somethin' else, Flinky, an' don't insult nobeast!'

Dargle called out, 'Aye, an' be nice to foxes, they're easy hurt!'

Skrodd fixed the big rat with an icy glare. 'Aye, an' they can hurt rats easily, too!'

Dargle stared fearlessly back at him. 'Ye don't scare me, fox. Burrad was slayed by mistake. Us rats don't make mistakes when we fight!'

Skrodd never answered. Turning away, he continued to march, but the challenge was out in the open now. The rest of the gang exchanged nods and winks – a fight to the death was not far off. Skrodd pulled Little Redd up to the front with him and allowed him to walk by his side. The small fox felt honoured; normally he would be left trailing at the back of the gang.

Keeping his voice low, the bigger fox took on a friendly tone with the young one. 'You stay by me, mate. Us foxes've got to stick together.'

Little Redd had to glance around to make sure Skrodd was not talking to some other beast. He was more used to kicks and insults than to kind words.

The big fox winked at him. 'I been keepin' an eye on ye, mate. Yore a smart little feller, not like this other lot!'

Redd hated being called 'little', but he was quite pleased to know that Skrodd thought of him as smart. He returned the wink, speaking out of the side of his mouth.

'I ain't no fool, an' I ain't so little, either. I'm growin' fast. One day they'll call me Big Redd.'

Skrodd got to the point. 'Lissen, mate, I want ye t'do me a favour. Do ye think yore smart enough t'be useful to me?'

Little Redd walked on tippaw, swelling his chest out. 'Just tell me wot ye want doin', mate!'

Skrodd leaned close. 'Keep an eye on the gang, especially Dargle. That rat's gettin' too big fer his boots. I want ye to watch my back, sort o' be my second in command.'

Redd hid his delight, replying gruffly, 'I'll do that, just watch me. Soon they'll be callin' me Big Redd. I won't let ye down, mate!'

Skrodd patted the small fox's back. 'Good! When I gets this gang sorted out, we'll give ye a proper vermin name. Big Redd don't mean nothin'. How does Badredd sound to ye, eh?'

The young fox was squirming inside with joy. However, he kept his voice tough, in keeping with his new position. 'Sounds great t'me, mate. Badredd – I like that! 'Tis a real killer's name. Badredd!'

After a fruitless night rambling through woodland thickets, the gang watched a rose-tinged dawn break over the tree-tops. They were soaked through by heavy dew, which was dripping everywhere from boughs and leaves.

Dargle's temper was on a short fuse. Emerging into a clearing on the bank of a stream, he struck out at Little Redd with his spear haft.

'Keep outta my way, runt! Every time ye come near me, I get soaked wid the water ye knock off the bushes.'

Redd looked appealingly at Skrodd. The big fox cast a glance of mock pity at Dargle and snarled scornfully. 'Scared of a few drips o' dew, are ye? Look at us, we're all wet through, an' we ain't moanin'.'

Dargle faced up to Skrodd right away. 'Hah! Wet through an' weary, an' wot for, eh? We never found the otter an' the squirrel. No, we just tramped around all night followin' you, an' now we're good an' lost. Some leader you are, Skrodd!'

The big fox bristled. 'Don't talk silly, we ain't lost!'

It was Dargle's turn to sound scornful. 'Oh, ain't we now? See that rowan tree, I marked it wid me spearblade not long after we started marchin'. Look!'

Flinky inspected the fresh scar on the rowan bark. 'Aye, 'tis a new spearmark sure enuff. Dargle's right!'

Leaning on his spearbutt, the hefty rat grinned teasingly.

'We've been goin' round in circles, mates, an' now our great leader's got us lost. Well, Skrodd?'

The fox held his blade at the ready and challenged Dargle. 'If'n yore so clever, then you find the way. 'Tis easy to stand there talkin' smart all day, Dargle. Go on, show us how clever ye are, an' find the right way!'

The rat squatted down on his haunches, chuckling. 'Sort out yore own mess, I'm stoppin' here an' restin'.'

Halfchop ventured a suggestion. 'Burrad would've sent Plumnose to find the way, 'cos he's a good tracker.'

Relief flooded through Skrodd as he realized that Halfchop had provided the solution to a sticky problem. Taking advantage, he quickly re-established his position as leader of the gang.

'Right, Plumnose, get on yore way! Ferget the two beasts we were trackin', they'll keep for another day. Find us the way to this Redwall Abbey place an' report back here.'

Always one to seize an opportunity, Flinky nodded his head admiringly. 'Ah, that's a grand ould move, Chief. I see ye noticed the fine campsite we're at. We can lay up here fer a day or two an' rest, once we're sure of the way. Lookit, we got a stream wid fish an' freshwater an' lots o' trees full of fat birds sittin' on nests packed wid eggs. The place is filled wid roots an' fruit an' firewood!'

Skrodd looked sage. 'That's wot I was thinkin', a day or two here'll freshen us up for the rest o' the journey. We'll make camp an' rest awhile, mates.'

Only Plumnose was not happy with the new plans. His huge nose wobbled from side to side as he complained. 'Duh, id's nod right. I'b tired, too, j'know!'

Rogg and Floggo, the weasel brothers, notched arrows to their bows and fired a pair of shafts near Plumnose's paws.

'Yore the tracker, Plum, now git goin'!'

'Aye, ye could track a butterfly underwater wid a hooter like that. Hohoho!'

Throwing twigs and grass clumps at the unfortunate creature, the gang drove Plumnose from the camp. Glad they had not been selected to go tracking, they shouted after him.

'Don't trip over yer nose, Plum!'

'Aye, an' don't sniff any big boulders up. Heeheehee!'

The tension was broken for the moment. Gathering wood and foraging for victuals, the gang busied themselves.

Flinky dug a firepit on the streambank, singing a cheery ditty.

'Ah 'tis luvverly bein' a vermin,
'cos ye lead a simple life,
leave the snufflin' babes behind,
run off from the naggin' wife.
There's nought to do but ramble,
an' plunder on the way,
just look bold, rob all ye can hold,
an' bid 'em all good day.
A vermin, a vermin, that's wot I'll always be,
I'm base an' vile, 'cos that's me style,
an' I'll bet ye envy me!'

By late morn they had a good fire burning. Flinky and his mate, Crinktail, were in their element. They boiled wood-pigeon eggs, grilled fish, and made a passable vegetable stew from various roots and wild produce which grew plentifully roundabout. Neither Dargle nor Skrodd made any move to help. Sitting close to the fire, they helped themselves, glaring at each other across the flames.

Skrodd collared Little Redd and gave him whispered orders. 'Scout round an' find me somewheres safe to rest. Make sure 'tis soft an' comfortable. Pick a place far away from that rat, an' someplace close for yourself, so ye can guard me. Go on!'

Puffed up with his own importance, Redd went to seek a suitable resting spot. He chose the base of a spreading oak, not too close to the stream. It was a basin-shaped depression between two thick roots.

When the gang finished eating, they settled down for a much-needed sleep. Most of them stayed by the fire, but Dargle chose a fernbed on the opposite side of the camp from Skrodd. From there the rat could see his enemy and lay plans.

Little Redd proudly showed Skrodd the spot at the base of the oak trunk. 'That's it, mate, nice an' snug, see!'

The small fox lay down, gesturing. 'There's plenty o' room for both of us. I can guard ye good from here, mate.'

Skrodd shook his head disapprovingly. 'Nah, ye go an' lay by the fire with the others. That'll put ye halfway twixt me'n Dargle. But don't go sleepin'; keep yore eyes peeled on those ferns where he's layin' low. Soon as Dargle makes a move, come runnin' an' let me know.'

Little Redd rose reluctantly. 'I kin watch him just as well if'n I stop 'ere with you, mate.'

Skrodd hauled him roughly upwards, thrusting him towards the fire. 'Ye'd do better to heed my orders. Now get goin'. I'm chief round 'ere, see!'

Stinging from the rebuke, Redd slouched over to the fire. Sullenly, he slunk down amid the snoring vermin.

With not a breeze to rustle the trees, warm noon sunlight shone down on the camp. Bees hummed gently, and butterflies fluttered silently around blossoming bushes. Near the ashy embers of the cooking fire, Little Redd drifted into a slumber. Only one of the gang was still awake – Dargle. Now was the time to put his plan into action. Draping his cloak over the ferns so it would look like he was still there, the rat inched his way backwards out of the foliage. Flat on his stomach, he took a careful route, circling the campsite. When the rear of the spreading oak came in sight, Dargle rose into a half crouch. Gripping his spear firmly, he crept up on his sleeping enemy.

Skrodd woke momentarily, but only to die. A muffled grunt of agony escaped him as Dargle's spear thrust into his body.

Dargle leaned down on the spearhilt, grinning triumphantly. '*Now* who's the chief, eh?'

It was the rat's only mistake – it turned out to be his last. Skrodd had lain down to sleep with the cutlass held tight in his paw. Now, with one spasmodic jerk, he whipped the broad blade across his assassin's neck, almost severing Dargle's head. The ambitious rat fell slain on top of his victim's dead body.

Little Redd was wakened by Flinky kicking him in the back. The small fox sat up rubbing his eyes and muttering at the still-sleeping stoat, 'Keep yore paws to yoreself, ye great lump!'

Flinky rolled over and emitted a huge snore. To avoid a second kick, Redd rose stiffly and looked around. Dargle's cloak was still draped over the ferns. He let out a sigh of relief and wandered over to check on Skrodd. Redd was dumbfounded by the sight that greeted him – Skrodd and Dargle, both dead!

Little Redd circled them slowly, poking both beasts with a stick and uttering their names softly. There was no doubt about it, they were still as stones. His first thought was to run and tell the others. He had already opened his mouth to shout when a thought struck him. Who would be the next to claim leadership of the gang? Little Redd sat down and did some serious thinking. It did not take him long to reach a decision. He would be the new chief. Getting the cutlass loose from Skrodd's paw was a difficult task, but he managed it somehow. Dargle was almost decapitated by Skrodd's death blow. Two good chops of the hefty blade finished the job.

Flinky was roused by a painful feeling he knew well, the slap of a flat cutlass blade. He sprang upright, rubbing his rump, expecting to see Skrodd standing over him. Instead, there stood the small fox, whacking away at the other gang vermin and yelling aloud.

'Up on yore hunkers, all of ye!'

The weasel Juppa grabbed a chunk of firewood and advanced on the small fox, snarling, 'Ye snotty liddle runt, who do ye think y'are, smackin' me wid the chief's blade?'

Redd jarred the wood from Juppa's paws with a blow from the cutlass. His voice was shrill but commanding. 'I'm the new chief round here, that's who I am. Come an' see this, all of ye!'

The gang stood around the two carcasses in awed silence as the small fox explained. 'I saw Dargle run Skrodd through with his spear. So I rushed in, grabbed the cutlass an' slew the dirty murderin' sneak with one swipe!'

Crinktail looked at him disbelievingly. 'You, Little Redd, took off Dargle's block in one go?'

Redd was getting the feel of the heavy sword now. He took a pace back, then leaped forwards, swinging the cutlass in both paws, shouting fiercely, 'Aye, one swipe! D'ye want me to show ye how? I'm the chief now, this sword's mine, I killed to get it!'

He was gratified to see fear shining from Crinktail's eyes as she backed away from him swiftly. 'No, no,' she pleaded, 'if you say ye did it, I'm not one to argue with ye!'

Ever the one to seize an opportunity, however, Flinky confronted Redd and held out his paws placatingly. 'Ah now, don't go upsettin' yoreself, Little Redd. We all think ye'll make a grand chief. Anyway, better'n the last two. Isn't that right, mates?'

He turned to the gang, winking broadly at them but making sure the small fox could not see his gesture.

'C'mon now, raise yer paws an' salute the great new chief!'

A newfound confidence flooded through Redd as he watched the remaining nine vermin acknowledging his leadership with raised paws. He suppressed a shudder of joy. For as long as he could recall he had been ignored, bullied or pushed about. Now, in the course of one day, he was in command of the gang.

Deciding to assert his authority, Little Redd glared haughtily at the ratbag vermin. 'My name ain't Little Redd no more. From now on ye'll all call me Badredd. Is that clear?'

Flinky threw him an elaborate salute. 'Badredd it is, yer honour, sure an' a fine ould name it is! Well now, Badredd sir, wot's yore pleasure – do we stop 'ere awhile in this grand camp? There's water an' vittles aplenty roundabout, an' 'tis a pleasant spot.'

Badredd nodded imperiously. 'Aye, we'll stop 'ere awhile!'

As they prepared the evening meal, Flinky's mate, Crinktail, whispered to him, 'Badredd, huh! Wot'n the name o' blood made ye support that liddle fool?'

Flinky winked at her as he turned a roasting woodpigeon on a willow spit over the fire. 'Trust me, mate, better a liddle fool than a big bully. I can 'andle this 'un. Badredd'll do like I suggest, ye'll see. We've 'ad enough o' weasels, big foxes an' bullyrats in this gang. This Mossflower territory's a good soft place to stay, plenty of everythin'. Better'n those ould Northlands. Leave the thinkin' t'me, we'll live the good life from now on. Badredd'll do like I tell 'im.'

The newly elected Badredd sat on the streambank, picking at a roasted woodpigeon leg and watching the westering sun die in a crimson haze. He listened to Flinky singing as he dished out supper to the gang, who lay about looking contented enough.

'Oh this is the place to be,
where the fruit falls from the tree,
where eggs an' birds jump out of the nest,
right in me pan they come to rest.
Oh this is the place for me,

73

far from that Northland sea.
Here the good ould fish leap out of the stream,
an' shout, "Please, sir, cook me,"
where the sun shines all the day,
an' the cold wind stops away,
an' the water's clean 'n' fresh 'n' clear,
I'll make ye a promise now, me dear,
I'll take a bath so don't ye fear,
in ten summers' time if I'm still here,
'cos this is the place for me!'

Badredd, however, had totally different plans. Not for him all this lying about on sunny streambanks. Ambition had entered his being. To be the owner of the magic sword and ruler of that place Skrodd had spoken of – Redwall Abbey.

8

Lonna Bowstripe sat outside the cave, savouring the approach of summer in the harsh northeast coastlands. Pale sunlight glimmered out of a watery, cloud-flecked sky. It was breezy, but the chill had died out of the wind. Green buds were shooting out of the scrublands, seabirds mewed across the marshes.

The huge badger shifted his position near the fire, wincing momentarily and arching his back. Young Stugg sat beside him like some constant shadow, always close to the big creature. Lonna fascinated the young sea otter.

'You back still be hurted, Lonn'?'

Lonna smiled down at his companion. 'A bit, but it's getting better every day, mate. Pass me the bow, please.'

Stugg ambled across and carried the yew sapling to him. Out of six lengths, this was the one Lonna had chosen to use for fashioning his bow. Stugg inspected it closely. The wood had seasoned out until it was strong as sprung metal. Lonna had shaved away the bark, leaving a broad band at its centre that he had bound and whipped with green cord to make a pawhold. At both ends, the wood was circled and notched deep to accommodate bowstrings. Stugg watched as the badger tested the yew's strength by bending it against his footpaws.

'Wot you think, Lonn', bee's it ready?'

The badger applied heavy pressure, bending the bow until it formed a deep arc. He straightened it slowly and then responded, 'As ready as it will ever be, young 'un. This is a good bow!'

Stugg jumped up and down impatiently. 'Putta string on it, Lonn'. Fire a h'arrow for Stugg!'

Abruc wandered out of the main holt cave towards them. 'Ahoy there, young pestilence! Are ye still botherin' Lonna? Yore more trouble than a sack o' frogs!'

The giant badger tugged Stugg's little rudder fondly. 'Oh, he's no trouble, Abruc. Stugg's my good old workmate.'

Abruc sat down beside them. He could not keep the curiosity out of his voice. 'Well, bigbeast, is yore bow finally ready?'

Lonna used the bowstaff to pull himself upright. 'Let's string it and see, shall we?'

A short time thereafter, all the sea otters had gathered to watch the testing of the bow. Lonna limped slightly as he went back into the cave to fetch his quiver of arrows.

Stugg stood outside, holding the bow and declaiming proudly to everybeast, 'All stan' back now, please. I help Lonn' to make dis bow. 'Tis a very dangerful weapon, so watch out!'

The big badger emerged with the birchbark quiver. It was packed heavily with two score of long ashwood shafts, which Abruc and Shoredog had helped to fashion. Each one was fletched with grey gull feathers, gleaned from the shoreline. The arrows were tipped with flint shards, sharpened and ground to lethal points.

Lonna took the bowstring which Abruc had woven and looped it over the notch in the yew staff.

After knotting it with a skilful hitch, he remarked, 'If this bow fails, it won't be for want of a good string. This is the finest one I've ever seen, thanks to you, friend.'

Abruc flushed with pleasure. 'Thankee. 'Tis a special string, worthy of a mighty bow.'

Lonna braced the yew sapling against his footpaw, with the string at the bottom end. Tying a loop into the free end, he leaned down heavily on the centre of the wood.

A gasp arose from the otters as the yew bent in a great arc. With the graceful ease of an expert bowbeast, Lonna slipped the loop deftly over the notched top end. It was a bow now, a mighty and formidable longbow that only a beast the size and strength of Lonna Bowstripe could draw. Taking three arrows, he set them point down in the earth and selected one, explaining as he did, 'Height, distance and accuracy are what an archer needs.'

Whipping the bow up, he laid the first arrow on it, heaved back powerfully and let fly, all in a split second. Swift as lightning the shaft sped upwards and was immediately lost to sight.

Shoredog let out a growl of surprise. 'Whoo! Where did it go?'

Stugg gestured airily. 'Stuck inna moon I appose, eh Lonn'?'

A rare smile creased the badger's scarred face. 'Aye, I suppose so, mate. Let's try for distance next.'

The second arrow he laid flat against his jaw, squinting one eye and holding the bow straight.

Zzzzip! Out across the stream over marsh and scrubland it flew, until it was lost on the seaward horizon.

Abruc clapped his paws in delight. 'Speared a big fish I bet, eh Stugg?'

The young otter smirked. 'Prolably two, anna big crab!'

Lonna scanned the countryside. 'I need a target now.' He bowed to Abruc's wife, Marinu. 'Lady, would you like to choose one? Anything will do.'

She looked around, then pointed. 'There's a piece of driftwood just beyond the marsh, see? To the right of that rivulet which runs out on to the shore. I don't know if you can reach that far, Lonna. Shall I pick something a little closer? I'm afraid I don't know much about firing arr . . . !'

Her words were cut short as the chunk of driftwood went end over end, pierced through by the badger's arrow. A rousing cheer went up from the spectators.

Lonna unstrung his bow, passing it to Stugg. 'Well, mate, it looks like we made a proper bow. Thank you for all your help.'

The young otter nodded. 'Sea rats better watch out now!'

Lonna took supper in the sea otters' main cave that night – a large seafood pie, followed by a preserved plum crumble, washed down with beakers of last summer's best cider. He sat by the fire with Abruc and Shoredog, with Stugg dozing on his lap.

Old Sork made Lonna hold still whilst she inspected his facial scar. 'A luckybeast is what ye are. 'Tis healin' better'n I hoped. So what are ye lookin' so miserable about, eh?'

The big badger shrugged. 'Every day that I sit here, Raga Bol and his crew get further away. Soon there'll be no trace of them to follow.'

Abruc refilled his beaker with cider. 'Never fear, Lonna. A sea rat like Raga Bol always leaves a trail, a path of murder an' destruction that anybeast with half an eye could follow. I've been watchin' ye since you've been up an' about. I know yore impatient to begone from here. Well, summer's almost in, the time'll soon be ripe.'

Lonna stared into the flames as he replied. 'Raga Bol and his crew won't live to see the leaves turn gold this autumn. I leave tomorrow!'

Shoredog helped himself to more cider, peering curiously at the big badger. 'Then we'll go with ye, Lonna, us an' a dozen of our best fighters. Even a warrior as big as yoreself will need help with Bol an' his crew!'

The badger shook his huge scarred head. 'I'm grateful, friend, but this is a thing I must do alone. You stay here and care for your families. There will be a hard time ahead for me. Raga Bol knows I am coming.'

Abruc replenished the fire with driftwood and sea coal. 'He probably thinks yore dead, mate. How could he know yore comin' after him?'

Lonna never took his eyes from the flames as he explained. 'I never knew my mother and father. Grawn, the wise old badger you buried, was the one who reared me. Not only did he teach me all the skills of a bowbeast but also many other things. When I was very small, Grawn told me that I was gifted with something few other badgers possess. He said that I was born with the power of a Seer. Old Grawn used to question me a lot. One day he said to me, 'You have the keenest eyes of any bowbeast I have known, but you also have another eye, inside your mind. You can see things the rest of us cannot, strange things that will shape your destiny.' It has always been so with me. Even when I was lying wounded in the cave, I could see Raga Bol. I can stare into this fire and see his face. Believe me, he knows I am coming. I want him to know, to fear me. He is evil and must die!'

Shoredog felt the fur on the nape of his neck begin to prickle. 'But if yore a Seer, ye must have known Grawn was goin' t'die, didn't ye?'

Lonna's eyes left the flames momentarily. 'Aye, I knew the old beast had not long to go, but I didn't know the manner of his death. Grawn was old and very ill. He wished to end his days at the badger mountain of Salamandastron. I was taking him there, and I knew my own fate was also linked to the mountain.'

Abruc leaned forwards. 'Do ye know where this mountain is?'

Lonna turned back to contemplating the fire. 'I have never been there, but I feel I am guided to it by my mind's eye. It is far to the west, on the shores of the great sea. When my business with the sea rats is done, that is where I'll go. I will not return to this place again. That is why I must travel alone.'

*

79

As they sat silently by the fire, Marinu came and lifted the sleeping Stugg from Lonna's lap. All the other otters had retired for the night. Only the three of them – Lonna, Abruc, and Shoredog – remained.

Shoredog broke the silence. 'Garfo Trok, he's the answer!'

Abruc nodded vigorously. 'Right, mate, good ole Garfo!'

Lonna stared from one to the other. 'What are you talking about – who's Garfo Trok?'

Shoredog rose and picked up his warm cape. 'Skipper o' the Nor'east Riverdogs, that's who Garfo is. He runs a riverboat. Garfo will take ye westwards along the waterways. That should save time an' strain on that back o' yores, Lonna. Ye'll pick up Raga Bol's trail in half the time ye'd take limpin' along step by step.'

Shoredog hurried from the holt, calling back to Abruc. 'I'll be back with Garfo by midday. Tell the cooks to pack plenty o' vittles, especially nutbread!'

Abruc nudged Lonna cheerfully. 'Ye'll like ole Garfo; that otter knows waterways like the back of 'is rudder.'

Happy but puzzled, Lonna smiled at the sea otter. 'I'm sure I will, but what's all this about vittles and nutbread? I eat only lightly when I'm travelling.'

Abruc stood up and stretched. 'Ye may do, Lonna, but Garfo Trok ain't a beast that's ever stinted 'isself when it comes to vittles, particularly nutbread. Why, that ole dog'd go to Hellgates for a loaf! Now get yoreself off an' rest, ye've a big day tomorrow!'

After Abruc had gone, Lonna stretched out by the fire, intending to sleep there for the remainder of the night. Before he closed his eyes, he spent several minutes intensely concentrating on the red embers, repeating mentally, 'Rest not too deeply, Raga Bol! Know that I am coming for you! As surely as night follows day, I am coming!'

Raga Bol and his crew were sleeping. They had made it out of the hills and moorlands into the first fringes of heavy forest. A spark from the campfire touched Ferron's nose, startling him awake. The gaunt rat sat bolt upright, rubbing at the stinging spot. He saw Raga Bol sit up as well, waving his silver hook and mumbling as he tried to come fully awake.

'Go 'way, yore dead! Get away from me, d'ye hear?' The sea rat captain caught Ferron looking strangely at him across the fire. 'Who are ye gawpin' at, long face, eh?'

Ferron knew better than to answer back. Instead, he lay back down and closed his eyes. All the crew had been saying the same thing. Lately Cap'n Bol was acting very strange.

9

Dawn was only moments old, but Redwall Abbey was awake and buzzing. Today was the special day Abbot Carrul had promised. Breakfast was already being served from a large buffet table, set up in the passage outside the kitchens. With laden platters, the Redwallers sat down to eat at anyplace which took their fancy. Horty and his friends looked out from the dormitory window at the scene below. Dibbuns thronged together on the broad front step of the Abbey, spooning down bowls of oatmeal mixed with honey and fruit. Anybeast wanting to dine outside had to step carefully over them to reach the lawns or the orchard. It was a jumble of happy confusion.

Muggum waved his beaker at the passing elders, who tippawed around him. 'Yurr, moind ee paws, you'm nearly trodded in this choild's brekkist. Whurr's ee manners? Hurr!'

Warm sunlight was rapidly dispersing the mist into a golden haze. Fenna the squirrelmaid leaned out over the dormitory sill and dropped a fragment of scone down into the hood of Sister Setiva's habit, giggling as she drew back inside.

'Did she notice it?'

Horty reassured her. 'Not at all. She's toddled off down to

the pond with Brother Gelf. Hahaha! I expect old Setiva'll be set upon by the first blinkin' bird that spots it. Should liven her up, wot!'

Springald watched the Infirmary Sister balancing her tray gingerly as she crossed the lawn. 'Huh, pity help the bird who tries to set upon her. She'll bath it in the pond and physick it silly. Look out, here comes Father Abbot!'

The mischievous trio ducked below the windowsill as Abbot Carrul, Toran, Sister Portula and Martha emerged from the Abbey. Toran lifted Martha's chair over the step and assisted Portula with a trolley full of food. They set out for the gatehouse together, with Abbot Carrul stretching his paws and breathing deeply.

'My my, it's a good-to-be-alive day. Let's hope we get a few hours of peace to tackle our studies.'

Toran had to rap loudly on the gatehouse door to gain attention. Old Phredd could be heard inside, arguing with an armchair.

'Come out my way and let me see who 'tis. It's your fault, being so comfy and allowin' me to sleep like that!'

A moment later, his frowzy, prickled head poked around the door. 'Oh, er hmm. Good morning, I suppose it's morning, isn't it? Of course, if 'twas noon, the sun would be much higher, eh, eh?' Dabbing his face in a bowl of water, the ancient hedgehog absentmindedly wiped his eyes on Martha's lap rug. 'There, that's better. Oh good, I see you brought breakfast with you. Splendid, I'm starving!'

Martha ate very little, trying to hold back her impatience as Phredd slowly munched his way around the food. Toran, however, got to the point right away.

'Well then, sir, how did yore studyin' go? Did ye find out anythin' useful about Loamhedge?'

Phredd nodded towards a dusty book lying on his bed. 'Oh, that. Take a look in the old volume there. I read it until I could keep my eyes open no longer. Hmm, quite interesting really, an exciting little story, eh?'

Martha opened the book, its pages yellow with age and

so brittle that they were cracking and beginning to flake. She read aloud from the neatly scribed lines of purple, faded ink. 'Written by Tim Churchmouse. Recorder of Redwall Abbey in Mossflower country . . .'*

Phredd interrupted her as he dealt with a hazelnut roll. 'It was written in the seasons of Abbot Mordalphus. The account of Mattimeo, son of Matthias the Abbey Champion. All about abduction and slavery, a search, a chase and so on. If you're looking for a route to the old Abbey of Loamhedge, the descriptions are very long and complicated, but there's a map included that should be a help. Actually I only got a third of the way through the account before I dropped off . . .'

Abbot Carrul shook his head in wonder. 'In the seasons of Mordalphus . . . Dearie me! That book must be nearly as old as time itself!'

Sister Portula put aside her beaker of mint tea. 'The land will have changed a lot since then, what with rains and floods altering water courses and storms blowing down trees. There'll be new areas of woodland grown over the ages, and I don't know what. Do you think it will be much help, Toran?'

As she had been speaking, the noise of stamping paws and singing voices had been swelling outside.

Toran went to the door. 'Who knows, Sister? Great Seasons, what's all that rackety din about?'

Old Phredd chuckled. 'They're singing the Summer Feast song. What a happy sound! Let's go out and watch, eh, eh?'

Martha was less than enthusiastic, since she wanted to continue studying the book. But the Abbot patted her paw encouragingly. 'You know, we can study the problem at our leisure, but next summer's first day is a long time away. They sound so joyful and excited! Come on, young 'un, let's go and see.'

*See *Mattimeo*

Smilingly, the haremaid relented.

Up and down the wallsteps and all over the lawns, Redwallers, led by Horty, were joining paws and skipping about, singing lustily to the jolly tune.

'The sun could not shine brighter
upon this summer's day,
my heart could not be lighter.
I've heard our Abbot say
there'll be a feast this evening,
so listen one and all:
This afternoon we'll run a race
around the Abbey wall!

Come form up in a line, pals,
and listen for your names,
it's ready steady set and go,
for Redwall Abbey games!

There's vittles in the kitchen,
good ale and cordials, too,
fine singers and musicians,
to play the evening through.
But first I'll gird my robe up,
so I don't trip or fall.
I'm going to be the first around
that high old Abbey wall!

Come form up in a line, pals,
and listen for your names,
it's ready steady set and go,
for Redwall Abbey games!'

Martha could not resist the merry cavalcade. Clapping her paws in time to the lively song, she laughed happily. Sister Portula, whooping like a wildbeast, grabbed Martha's chair and dashed off into the throng.

Abbot Carrul winked at Phredd. 'My mistake for starting all this, but who could sit indoors studying on such a wonderful day?'

Toran, in complete agreement, shepherded both of his friends out of the way of the dancers. 'You two stay here. I'll go an' bring two armchairs an' the rest o' the food out of the gatehouse. Ye can sit back an' watch the whole thing in comfort. We can always look through dusty ole books tomorrow.'

Old Phredd spoke to a buttercup growing by the wall. 'Heehee, now there's a sensible young creature. Beasts like that make a body enjoy his old age, eh, eh?'

Bragoon and Saro stood outside the main gate. Memories flooded back as they touched the stout oak timbers.

The ageing squirrel looked misty-eyed. 'Dear ole Redwall Abbey! Sounds like they're havin' a good time in there, mate. Well, do we knock for the Gatekeeper?'

Bragoon scuffed the gravel path with his rudder as he pondered the question. 'Hmm, we've been a long time gone. Suppose nobeast knows us anymore. Or worse, supposin' they do recognize us an' recall wot a pair of scoundrels we were! They might not want us back. Wot d'ye think?'

Saro gnawed at her lip. 'Aye, I think yore right, Brag. Tell ye what, let's just slip in unnoticed an' sort of mingle with the crowd. That way we can judge the lay o' the land.'

The otter grinned furtively at his companion. 'The way we used to come an' go, through the ole east wallgate. I'll bet ye can still open it.'

Saro clapped his back with her bushy tail. 'Great idea! Come on, let's give it a try. We'll disguise ourselves up a bit so as not to cause too much of a stir!'

Brother Weld, an old bankvole who was Abbey Beekeeper, perched on the arm of Abbot Carrul's chair to watch the fun. Some of the other games were in progress, and competition among the Dibbuns was fierce.

The Abbot watched them fondly as he reminisced. 'I was pretty good at the nut and spoon race in my younger seasons.'

Weld kept his eyes on the games as he observed drily, 'Aye, Father, you beat me three seasons on the run. Then they caught you sticking your nut to the spoon with honey.'

Abbot Carrul cautioned him. 'Not so loud, Weld, keep your voice down. We can't have the young 'uns discovering that a Dibbun who cheated at nut and spoon is now their Abbot!'

Three of the Dibbuns – Muggum, Shilly and Yooch – were trying madly to win the greasy pole event. A big bag of candied chestnuts hung from the top of the pole. It resisted all their efforts. Each time, they ended up skimming dismally down to earth, caked with a mixture of soap and vegetable oil. After some earnest plotting, they hatched up a joint plan. Muggum stood tippaw, grasping the base of the pole. Yooch scrambled up the molebabe's back and stood on his head. Both clung tightly to the pole, then Shilly climbed up over them on to Yooch's head. Holding the pole with one paw, the squirrelbabe strove with her free paw to reach the bag. Unfortunately, the combined height of all three Dibbuns was still short of the prize. Muggum could not look up, his tiny face squinched by the weight of his two pals. But that did not stop him yelling out words of encouragement.

'Gurr, goo on Shilly, grab ee chesknutters naow!'

Shilly roared back at him, 'I carn't not gerrem, me paw bee's too likkle'n'short!'

Yooch the molebabe grunted his contribution. 'Moi pore bee's flattinged, 'urry up!'

Amid the spectators' shouts of support and hoots of laughter at the spectacle, Fenna came bounding out. The squirrelmaid hopped up the backs of all three Dibbuns.

Launching herself from the top of Shilly's head, she made a graceful leap. Fenna effortlessly unhooked the bag of candied chestnuts. Performing a spectacular somersault, she landed neatly on the ground, without a speck of grease anywhere on her.

She smiled smugly. 'No trouble at all, the prize is mine!'

Martha's voice cut across her jubilant cries. 'Not fair! it's the greasy pole you're supposed to climb, not the greasy Dibbuns. You should forfeit the nuts, Fenna!'

Fenna stuck her lip out and pouted. 'But I won them!'

The Abbot left his armchair and took possession of the bag. 'The object is to get the nuts. There's no hard-and-fast rule about climbing greasy poles. But be fair, Fenna. The little ones tried so hard, and they gave us all such fun. I suggest we split the nuts four ways betwixt you and them.'

Whilst everybeast was applauding the decision, Toran caught Shilly and Yooch as they fell backwardss from the pole. Horty was left with the task of unsticking Muggum, who was practically plastered to the pole with grease. He tugged his snout politely to the young hare.

'Thankee, zurr, oi thort oi wuz stucked thurr fer loife!'

Horty gazed down at his clean tunic, now coated with the mess. 'Oh, think nothin' of it, old lad. My pleasure, wot!' He slipped and fell flat as he stumbled away from the pole.

By the pondside an old female squirrel, her face hooded against the sun by a cowl, was bathing her footpaws in the reeded shallows. An otter of medium size, his face also hooded, sat next to her. Sister Portula sought a seat in the reedshade alongside them, fanning her face with a dockleaf.

'Whew, this is certainly going to be a memorable summer!'

The otter glanced sideways at her. 'Has afternoon tea been served yet, Sister?'

Portula swiped at a flying midge which was tormenting

her. 'We never serve afternoon tea when there's going to be an evening feast. You knew that, didn't you, Brother?'

The female squirrel sighed. 'Oh no, I was lookin' forward to some nice scones with strawberry preserve an' meadow-cream.'

Portula had to raise her voice to be heard over the sounds of sporting revellers. 'The walltop race will be starting soon. I think first prize for that might be a cream tea with scones.'

The squirrel jumped upright, surprisingly spry for one of her long seasons. 'Right, I'll enter an' win first prize!'

The Sister shook her head doubtfully. 'You'll have lots of competition from younger and fitter creatures, I'm afraid.'

The otter smiled knowingly. 'Oh, don't ye worry about that, Sister. If'n there's a prize of afternoon tea goin', my mate'll win it. Right, Saro?'

The squirrel threw off her cowl. 'I'll give it a good try, Brag, an' maybe I'll share it with ye.'

The good Sister stared open-mouthed at the ageing squirrel. 'Saro, is it really you?'

Saro took the old Recorder's paw and shook it warmly. 'Aye, Portula, my ole friend, an' guess who this creakin' ruddered lump is?'

Portula was all aflutter. 'Wait, don't tell me now . . . Oh, seasons o' mercy, it's Bragoon!'

She raced off, waving her paws wildly and shouting, 'They're back! It's Bragoon and Sarobando! They're back!'

The squirrel watched her go. 'Hear that, I got me full title!'

The games were abandoned for the moment. Redwallers crowded to the pond to see the legendary duo. Both beasts were overwhelmed by pawshakes, kisses, backslaps and the embraces of old friends. Banter and welcomes went back and forth as they were reunited with the comrades of long-gone seasons.

'Saro, you bushy-tailed rogue, 'tis me, Phredd the Gate-keeper!'

'Old Phredd? I don't believe it. Are you still here?'

'Och, 'tis that dreadful Dibbun Bragoon! Where've ye been, ye bold wee scamp?'

'Sister Setiva, a pleasure t'see yore face, marm. Been? Oh me'n Saro've been as far as there an' back a few times!'

'Yurr, oi'd know ee thievin' likkle face anywhurrs, Miz Saro!'

'Granmum Gurvel, my ole beauty, give me a hug, quick!'

'Haharr, who's that – not young Carrul the nut'n'spoon cheat?'

'Bragoon, friend of my Dibbun days, oh 'tis so good to see you! Ahem, the name's changed now; I'm Father Abbot Carrul. But what a pleasure to see you, and Saro, too!'

'Look out, who's this big, rough-lookin' villain, eh?'

'Oi bee's Muggum, marm, bee's you'm really Sabburandum?'

Suddenly Bragoon found himself swept off his paws and hugged in a vicelike grip. Tears flowed freely down Toran's face.

'Brother Brag, you've come home to Redwall!'

Planting a kiss between Toran's ears, Bragoon wheezed, 'Brother Toran, I won't see sunset if'n ye crush me t'death. I missed ye, Toran, y'great lump of an otter!'

Greeting upon greeting followed, everybeast seemed at once to be embracing the pair. The air resounded to cries of, 'Well I never, my oh my, just look at ye, welcome home!'

Springald, Horty and Fenna stood to one side. Like most teen-season creatures, they were embarrassed by all the hugging and kissing among elders.

Springald muttered in resignation, 'I suppose that means the end of the Games Day. Huh, I'd have won the wall race easily if they hadn't turned up.'

Fenna passed each of them a piece of candied chestnut, musing aloud, 'So, that's the famous Bragoon and Saro. Huh, they're not as big as I thought they'd be. They look pretty old, too – creaky, I'd say. What do you think, Horty?'

The young hare shrugged. 'After all the tall stories we've

heard about 'em, wot? Actually, old bean, you could be right. Those two ain't exactly the huge giants we've been told about. A bit blinkin' old, an' jolly ordinary, too, though everybeast seems tip over tail to see 'em back, wot? Let's toddle over there now that the huggin'n'kissin' is all done with. Come on, chaps, I want to get a closer dekko at the bold blinkin' Bragoon an' the startlin' Sarobando.'

Martha was being introduced to the pair by Sister Setiva.

Bragoon shook the haremaid's paw gently. 'Martha, eh? A pretty name for a pretty maid. Well, Martha, you don't look anything like us two when we were young. I wager you've heard a lot o' stories about the villainy we got up to in the old days.'

Martha thought Bragoon had a kind face; she liked him immediately. She tried changing the conversation from his past misdeeds. 'How did you and Sarobando get into the Abbey, sir, with the gate locked and barred?'

Old Phredd scratched his scrubby beard. 'Aye, how did you get in, eh, eh?'

Saro shrugged modestly. 'Oh, 'twas nothin' really, just a little trick we used to do with the east wallgate. Don't worry, Phredd, we locked it behind us.'

Fenna interrupted. 'Mister Bragoon, I heard that you were once a Skipper of Otters. Is that true?'

The ageing otter nodded. ' 'Tis true enough, miss, but ole Saro didn't fancy bein' an otter. So I gave it up to go rovin' with her.'

Springald enquired, rather pertly, 'Are you as good a cook as your brother Toran?'

Bragoon chuckled at the idea. 'Wot, me? No, pretty one, I'll wager that Toran's the best cook anywhere. Huh, I'd prob'ly end up burnin' a salad!'

Ignoring the Abbot's stern gaze, the mousemaid continued. 'Miz Saro, are you as quick as they say you are? I bet I'm faster than you. I won the Abbey wall race last summer.'

Saro grinned from ear to ear and shook Springald's paw.

'My congratulations, missy! So then, I'll have a bit o' competition in this wall race. I'm plannin' on runnin' in it for a prize of an afternoon cream tea. Mmm! 'Tis many a long season since I tasted one.'

Springald blurted out, 'You're too old, I'll beat you easy!'

Abbot Carrul was shocked by her behaviour. 'Springald, show some respect for your elders!'

However, it was Saro who interceded on her behalf. 'Not at all, Father, I like to see a young 'un with a bit o' spirit. She's like me at her age. Don't ye fret now, 'twill be a fine race, I'm sure. Let's go to the wall an' get it started. No time like the present, eh, mate?'

Supremely confident, Springald winked at Horty and whispered to Fenna, 'That old relic's in for a surprise.'

Turning to Saro, she bowed mockingly. 'After you, marm!'

10

The crowd gathered under the threshold of the gatehouse. None of the wall racers was interested in entering. Everybeast was talking about it, eager to see the race between Springald and Saro.

The Abbot held up his paws. 'So be it, the wall race will start from the threshold above this gate. One circuit of the entire rampart's area, ending back on the same spot. Pushing or shoving means instant disqualification. Runners may use all of the walkway, including the battlements. Any questions?'

Shilly the squirrelbabe piped up. 'Farver h'Abbot, worrabout uz likkle 'uns an' the very very h'old 'uns?'

She was referring to the ground race, which was run over the same distance but from the ground level. This was for Dibbuns and Elders, mainly to avoid the dangers of falling from the walltops, where only fit and experienced runners competed.

The Abbot watched as Foremole Dwurl scored a deep line along the ground with his formidable digging claws. 'Of course, we mustn't forget the ground race. All competitors come up to the line, please. No crowding or jostling!' He checked the walltop, where Springald and Saro were standing level.

Brother Weld, acting as walltop official, waved down to the Abbot. 'All ready up here!'

Bragoon and Toran sat on the lawn where they could see both races at the same time. Toran patted his ample stomach.

'Me racin' days are long gone. What about ye, Brother? Yore the same age as Saro, why ain't you runnin'?'

Bragoon folded his paws and settled back. 'I'm far too old. Saro was born on the same day as me, but she's an hour younger.'

Toran scoffed. 'An hour, that's nothin' in a lifetime!'

His brother Bragoon maintained a straight face. 'Oh it isn't, eh? Ye try holdin' yore breath for an hour, matey!'

Every Dibbun in Redwall was hopping and leaping on the line, waiting for the start.

Abbot Carrul held up a big spotted red 'kerchief, taking one last look around as he called, 'Is that all now, last chance for any late entrants!'

Horty came bowling up, pushing Martha in her chair as she protested, 'No, please Horty, I've never raced before!'

The garrulous hare pushed his sister on to the line. 'Oh piffle'n'twodge, miss. We'll show these blighters what us Braebucks are jolly well made of, wot! Two stout runnin' paws an' a splendid set o' wheels. Hahah, we'll leave 'em all bally well standin', wot wot!'

Toran and Bragoon applauded from the sideline. 'That's the stuff, give it a go, miss!'

Springald stood in a ready stance. Saro glanced sideways at her as she pawed the line.

'Good luck to ye, young 'un!'

The mousemaid kept her eyes set on the course ahead. 'Aye, good luck to you, too, old 'un. You're going to need it!'

Several of the Dibbuns made overenthusiastic false starts, causing a slight delay as Toran and Bragoon got them back into line.

Abbot Carrul stood out on the lawn and shouted as the 'kerchief fluttered in the breeze.

'On your marks . . . Ready . . . Steady . . . Go!'

Away everybeast went, young and old, on walltop or ground, running at top speed.

Carrul sat on the grass with the two otters. 'Dearie me, some of those Dibbuns have raced off in the opposite direction.'

Toran laughed. 'Oh, let 'em go. They'll still run the same distance at the finish. Flyin' fur 'n' feathers! Lookit young Springald go; ye'd think she had wings on 'er footpaws. Looks like Saro is laggin' behind a bit. D'ye think she's in trouble already, Brag?'

The otter shook his head. 'She's just pacin' herself, keepin' the mousemaid lookin' back over her shoulder, ye'll see.'

Both walltop runners were almost at the north wall corner, with Springald a good two paces in front.

Below on the grass, chaos ensued. A molebabe and a tiny shrewlet had decided to stop and share some candied chestnuts between them. Another molebabe tripped over them. He forgot the race and joined the pair.

'Hurr, worrum ee got thurr, candee chesknutters, oi'm gurtly fond o' they'm, boi 'okey oi arr!'

The shrewlet passed him a few. 'Den h'eat dese up, nuts make y'go faster, we still winna race, mate!'

Martha clung tight to the chair as the little cart bounced and bumped furiously forwards, with Horty yelling out a warning to them, 'I say there, you bounders, make way or we'll run ye down. Watch out for the corner, me old skin'n'blister. Steer quicker, or we'll knock a hole in that wall, wot!'

Abbot Carrul shook his head in admiration as he viewed the walltop runners. 'My word, the speed of those two, they're nearly at the east corner already. Look at them go!'

As Toran saw them negotiate the corner and tear off along the parapet southwards, he groaned softly, 'Aaaah, pore ole Saro's flaggin' now. See, Springald's stretched her lead, I think she's bound to win.'

A slight smile played about Bragoon's lips. 'The race ain't over 'til the winner crosses the line. You watch, Saro'll soon take the spring out o' Miss Springald.'

But by now the mousemaid had turned the south wall-corner, leading by three paces.

The Abbot commented, 'I think that young 'un's got the field to herself now.'

Bragoon did not answer; instead, he put both paws to his mouth and emitted a single sharp whistle.

Springald was panting heavily, but still she took time to glance back at Saro as she gasped, 'Give up, old 'un, you're beat!'

Saro was breathing like a bellows, still hard on her opponent's heels. At the sound of Bragoon's whistle, Saro summoned up all her energy and put on a massive burst of speed. As the finishing line loomed up, Springald set her eyes dead ahead, racing wildly for it. Saro made a mighty leap. She sailed up and over, passing above the startled mousemaid's head, to land beyond the line, half a pace ahead, right beside Brother Weld, who roared out, 'Saro wins!'

Completely shocked, Springald collapsed in a heap on the walkway. Fighting for breath, she gasped, 'Wh . . . wh . . . what h . . . happened?'

Weld the Beekeeper was holding Saro's paw high, shouting, 'The winner by a half pace – Miz Sarobando!'

On the ground, three-quarters of the way around, more contestants were put out of the race as they met the reverse runners. They collided and fell in a jumble, roaring and arguing.

'Yurr, wot ways bee's you'm foogles a runnen?'

'Uz norra foogles, you knock uz over 'cos we winnin'!'

Martha steered the cart around them, yelling in panic, 'Slow down, Horty, watch out for those Dibbuns!'

Her brother narrowly missed the melee, speeding up as he shouted, 'Forwards the buffs! Onward t'death or flippin' glory! Blood'n'vinegar, me jolly lads! Redwaaall!'

Howling and hooting, he rushed over the finishing line, grinding to a halt and losing a back wheel in the process. 'Hoorah, me beautiful ole skin'n'blister, we won. Wot Wot Wot!'

'Nay, you'm diddent, zurr. Uz wunned – Shilly an' oi!'

Horty's mouth fell open. 'But . . . but . . . how . . . wot . . . but?'

Martha almost fell from her chair laughing. 'Hahahahaha! Muggum and Shilly were first over. Heeheeheehee, they won. Stop your but butting, Horty, we were second. A great effort on your part, sir. Thank you kindly!'

She did not tell him that, when they almost collided with the fallen Dibbuns, she had rescued Muggum from the heap as they whizzed by. Muggum had hold of Shilly's tail, so she, too, was swept aboard the chair. Both of the little ones hopped off the cart, over the line, just ahead of it. Luckily they landed either side of the vehicle.

The Abbot, who had his suspicions as to who the real winners were, eyed the Dibbuns sternly. 'Who won? I want the truth!'

Muggum was the picture of infant innocence. 'Troofully, we'm wunned, zurr. Us'n's farster'n woild bunglybees, moi paws nurrly tukk foire!'

The Father Abbot shook his head in disbelief until Martha reassured him. Toran and Bragoon backed her up stoutly.

'Aye, 'twas the Dibbuns who won, fair'n'square!'

'Right, mate, would we lie to a great Father Abbot?'

Folding both paws into his wide sleeves, the Abbot wandered off, muttering, 'Why shouldn't I believe three good and honest creatures? Frogs can fly, fish make nests in trees. Who am I but a poor Abbot who knows nothing?'

It was still some time until nightfall and the commencement of the Summer Feast. Under the Abbot's instructions, the kitchen crew had already made a substantial afternoon tea.

Saro threw a friendly paw around Springald's shoulders.

'That was the closest race I've ever run. Come on, young 'un, you'n yore friends must take tea with me. Let the winnin' Dibbuns an' Martha sit with us, too.'

The banks of the Abbey pond made a perfect setting as the Redwallers sat in the lengthening afternoon shadows, watching sungleams on the cool, dark water. Junty Cellarhog, the big hedgehog who took care of Redwall's famous cellars, personally served them with ice-cold rosehip and mint tea. Everybeast gossiped animatedly whilst enjoying the excellent food. Most Redwallers wanted to know more about the famous pair and their adventures. Bragoon had to do most of the answering, as Saro was lost in the ecstasy of scones, meadowcream and strawberry jam. Even Horty was amazed at the amount of food that Saro could put away.

He remarked in awed tones, 'Good grief, marm, you can certainly deal pretty roughly with scones when you've a blinkin' mind to, wot!'

Bragoon shoved more meadowcream over to his companion. 'Don't disturb Saro while she's eatin', she gets fierce.'

Horty nodded politely. 'Know wotcha mean, sah. I expect it was jolly tough, wot. All those seasons o' fightin' rascally vermin. Must've given the lady a confounded keen appetite!'

Bragoon nodded. 'Many's the time I've had to count me paws after sittin' too close to Saro at vittlin' time!'

Toran beckoned to his friend Junty. 'Now then, ole cellarspikes, wot about a bit o' music? Brought yore fiddle?'

Junty Cellarhog took a small, beautifully crafted fiddle out of the hood of his cloak. He tuned it deftly. 'Rightyo, any pertickler tune ye'd like?'

Horty volunteered, 'Play the Dawnsong. I'm sure Martha will sing for us. The jolly old skin'n'blister has a rather charmin' voice, y'know.'

Everybeast began calling for Martha to sing. Junty played

a chord or two. The haremaid bowed in deference to the two guests.

'Only if Bragoon and Sarobando would like to hear it.'

The otter chortled. 'Like to hear it? I'd *love* to hear ye sing, Martha. All I ever hear is my mate Saro, an' she's got a voice like a frog bein' strangled!'

The squirrel looked up indignantly from a half-eaten scone. 'Hah, lissen who's talkin'. Let me tell ye, missy, to hear ole Bragoon singin', 'tis like listenin' to a nail trapped under a door!'

Fenna giggled. 'Then you'd best be singing, Martha. Those two'll curdle the meadowcream if they start warbling.'

Martha paused until Junty's fiddle had played the opening bars, then she began to sing.

'I have a friend as old as time,
yet new as every day.
She banishes the night's dark fears,
and sends bad dreams away.
She's always there to visit me,
so faithfully each morn,
so peaceful and so beautiful,
my friend whose name is Dawn.

She fills the air with small birds' song,
and opens all the flowers.
She bids the beaming sun to shine,
to warm the daylight hours.
She comes and goes so silently,
to leave the earth reborn,
serene and true, all clad in dew,
my friend whose name is Dawn.'

There was silence as the last poignant notes hovered on the still air, then wild applause.

Bragoon's tough face softened as he sniffed, 'I never heard anythin' so pretty in all me days!'

Horty puffed out his chest. 'I told you she could sing!'

Saro, having forgotten her afternoon tea, sat transfixed. 'Sing, did ye say? Listen, even the birds've gone quiet at the sound of the maid's voice. I'm retirin' from singin' as of now. Wot d'ye say, mate?'

Bragoon had borrowed Junty's fiddle. He plucked the strings as he gazed in admiration at the haremaid. 'Our lips are sealed, Miss Martha, ye put us t'shame. Mind ye, I can still knock a tune out on the ole fiddle, an' Saro ain't a bad dancer. Shall I play a jig for ye?'

Muggum had a swift word in Martha's ear, causing her to smile. 'Do you know a Dibbun reel called Dungle Drips?'

The Abbeybabes leaped up and down, shouting eagerly, 'Play ee Dungle Drips, zurr!'

Bragoon raised the fiddle bow, winking at Saro. 'Haha, Dungle Drips. We danced to that 'un a few times when we was Dibbuns, eh mate?'

The ageing squirrel leaped up. 'Aye, I'll say we did! Right, c'mon, me liddle darlin's, I'll show ye a step or two. I once was Redwall's Champion Dibbun Dancer!'

Even before the first notes rang out, the Dibbuns clasped paws and whooped. Saro was whirled off amid a crowd of molebabes, tiny mice, infant squirrels and small hoglets. All the Dibbuns roared the molespeech lyrics with gusto, hurtling themselves into the wild reel. Martha was convulsed with laughter at their antics and amazed at Saro's skill. The squirrel was a born dancer, twirling and somersaulting recklessly as she sang out in mole dialect along with the Dibbuns.

'Whooooaaah! Let's do ee jig o' Dungle Drips,
woe to ee furst likkle paw wot slips,
chop off ee tail, throw um in bed,
wiv a bandage rownd ee hedd!
Feed ee choild on strawbee pudd,

gurt fat h'infants uz darnce gudd,
Dungle Drips naow clap ee paws,
tug moi snout an' oi'll tug yores.
Bow to ee h'Abbot, gudd day zurr,
twurl ee rounden everywhurr,
Dungle Drips bee's gurt gudd fun,
oop t'bed naow likkle 'un. Whoooooaaah!'

The dance grew more frantic, the singing faster as Bragoon speeded up his fiddling. Muggum and his crew performed some very fancy pawwork – shuffling and high kicking, raising raucous cheers and calling for the fiddler to play even faster. The scene of wild abandon suddenly stretched out into a double line with Saro bringing up the rear as the Abbeybabes cavorted furiously across the lawns and vanished into the Abbey.

Bragoon stopped playing and blew upon his heated paws. 'Whew! Wot happened there, Carrul?'

Bewildered, the Abbot shook his head. 'I've no idea. Sister Setiva, do you know what those babes are up to?'

The shrewnurse shrugged. 'Och, the wee beasties must have danced off tae their beds. 'Tis no great surprise, ah'm thinkin', after all that racin', eatin' and jiggin'. Ye ken, they must be rare wearied.'

The Redwallers sat sipping tea for quite some time. There was no sound from within the Abbey. Then Saro emerged. Chuckling to herself, she sat down wearily, accepting a beaker of tea gratefully.

'Whew, I ain't as young as I used t'be! That was some dance, I tell ye. Those Dibbuns jigged through the Abbey, up the stairs they went, straight into their dormitory. Before you could say boo, they were flat out on their beds an' snorin'! I felt like joinin' 'em myself. Huh, looks like the liddle 'uns have called it a day.'

Toran looked perplexed. 'But wot about the Summer Feast?'

Abbot Carrul saw the look of disappointment on his friend's face. 'Cheer up, Toran, we'll have it at midday tomorrow. 'Twill keep until then.'

Horty's ears drooped mournfully. 'I say, you chaps, all I've had to eat is a few measly scones an' a drop o' tea.'

Martha slapped his paw playfully. 'Shame on you, I wouldn't call three plates of scones measly. Don't pull such faces, you'll last until tomorrow.'

The gluttonous young hare went into a sulk. 'Jolly easy for you t'say, wot. Skin'n'blisters never scoff much anyway, not like us chaps. So be it then! If none of you lot see me round an' about tomorrow, you'd best take a blinkin' good search. You won't be smilin' then. Not when you find the skeleton of a gallant young hare in some lonely corner. Oh yes, indeed, that'll be me, perished t'death from flippin' hunger, wot! Woe is us, you'll cry, an' weep absolute buckets o' tears, thinkin' we should've let the poor brave lad have a small extra scoff last night.'

Bragoon played along with Horty, shaking his head sadly. 'An' wot'll yore skeleton reply to us, ole mate?'

Horty sniffed. 'It'll say, too blinkin' late, but I told you so, an' yah boo sucks to you, cruel rotten lot! I leave you to your guilty consciences, you heartless bounders. My famished lips are sealed. Wot!' He stalked frostily into a corner whilst stealing the last scone from under Sister Portula's nose.

11

It was still warm as darkness fell. When the Redwallers stopped by the water, enjoying a faint breeze, talk turned to the life of Redwall Abbey and gradually to Martha's story. Bragoon and Saro, who had become very fond of the pretty young haremaid, listened intently. Abbot Carrul, Sister Setiva, Toran and Sister Portula all contributed to the narrative, with Martha filling in the details.

When the tale ended, Bragoon sat staring at the haremaid's unmoving footpaws, peeping from under her lap rug. The ageing otter's voice was extremely sympathetic. 'What a terrible thing t'happen to a young 'un! An' you've never been able to walk since ye can first remember?'

Martha shook her head. 'No, sir, though 'tis not for the want of trying. I collapse every time I do, as if my footpaws were held there by two pieces of wet string.'

Saro was impressed by the young one's frankness. 'That's a hard thing for anybeast t'bear. If'n ye don't mind me askin', Martha, wot d'ye do with yourself all day?'

Martha shrugged. 'Oh, I get around. There's always my kind friends to push me, though I can wheel myself around if I need to. I do a lot of reading and studying, too. Oh, that reminds me, Sister Portula, I left your book in the gatehouse. Old Phredd's still up, I can see the light at his window from here. Let's pay him a visit.'

They all strolled across to the gatehouse with Bragoon and Saro pushing Martha's chair. Unusually for Phredd, he was wide awake and answered the door promptly.

'Young Martha, I was hoping you'd come. I see you brought all your friends, eh? Well come in, everybeast. You'll have to find somewhere to sit, there's not much room, y'know!'

Phredd spoke to the latch as he closed the door behind them. 'Heehee, got something to show this haremaid, haven't we?'

Martha sat up eagerly. 'Have you found anything, sir?'

The old hedgehog sat on the side of his bed, opening Sister Portula's book at a page he had marked. 'Found something? Hah, the moment that race was over and I could rescue my armchairs back in here, I did some serious reading. There's more important things in life than running oneself silly around walltops, y'know. After all, Martin the Warrior sent you a message that mustn't be ignored, missy.'

Bragoon suddenly became interested. 'Martin the Warrior sent ye a message, Martha? What did he say?'

The haremaid explained. 'I fell asleep near the tapestry. Martin and another young mouse named Sister Amyl appeared to me. Martin told me to read, because reading is knowledge, then Sister Amyl spoke this rhyme to me.

'Where once I dwelt in Loamhedge,
my secret lies hid from view,
the tale of how I learned to walk,
when once I was as you.
Though you cannot go there,
look out for two who may,
travellers from out of the past,
returning home someday.'

Saro looked very serious. 'I remember Martin the Warrior spoke to me an' Brag when we were young.'

Abbot Carrul peered over his spectacles in astonishment. 'Martin spoke to you two? Did he really?'

Saro kept her face straight. 'Oh aye, I'll tell ye wot he said.

"Seek adventure, liddle mates,
go ye forth from Redwall's gates.
Both of ye, wild and unchecked,
begone afore my Abbey's wrecked!"'

Bragoon chuckled. 'She's only jokin', of course.'

Old Phredd glared at them both. 'This is no joking matter. As soon as I saw you down by the pond today, I knew you were the two travellers from out of the past. Eh, eh, the two that Sister Amyl's poem spoke of, right?'

Horty's eyes went wide as saucers. 'Right indeed, wot!'

Phredd tapped the open book he held. 'Stop jabbering and listen, please, this is most important. I have found the story of Sister Amyl. It was written by another, Recorder Scrittum. He was the Loamhedge brother who put most of this story together – and very well he did it, too. Listen to this!'

They sat entranced as Phredd's wavery tones brought the past back to life for them.

'"The plague has come to Loamhedge, a great sickness is upon us. This morning we buried four, three sisters and one brother. Our infirmary is packed with the ill and suffering. I fear this Abbey has become a pest hole. Abbess Germaine and her Council have reached a bitter decision: if we are to survive, we must leave Loamhedge. It is almost unthinkable, is it not? Having to forsake our beautiful old home to wander in the wilderness. Germaine speaks of travelling to Mossflower country, where she has friends who will give us shelter. We are to take very little with us and live off the land as we go. These are hard and sad times, indeed.

' "However, there is no other way for it. Poor Sister Amyl is a young mouse who has never walked. She makes her way about in a wheeled chair. Amyl has decided not to go with us. I pleaded with her, saying that I would care for her and push the chair to wherever we were bound, but she would not hear of it. Amyl said that the journey would be far too arduous and feared that she would hold us back. In a way she is right, since a wheeled chair cannot be hauled over hill and dale. There would be bad weather to contend with – rivers, swollen streams, rocks and swampland. Also, it will soon be wintertide. The Abbess does not know of Amyl's decision yet. It is my sad duty to tell her of the situation. Young Sister Amyl is such a good creature. It will break my heart to leave her at Loamhedge, amid the dying." '

Toran interrupted the narration by sniffing loudly and grubbing a paw across his moist eyes. 'Pore liddle thing, left t'die in a deserted Abbey. I'd never leave ye to a fate like that, Martha, no matter wot it took!'

Bragoon grasped the haremaid's paw. 'Me either, miss!'

Martha forestalled Saro and the rest by holding up a paw. 'I know you wouldn't, none of you . . .'

She caught sight of Old Phredd, glaring about impatiently. 'Oops, sorry sir, we'll be quiet, I promise!'

The Gatekeeper huffed, then leafed on to another marked page. 'Thank you! Now let me read further into this narrative. Here is a section by Recorder Scrittum, concerning setting up camp on the first evening of the journey.

' "Let me tell you of a miracle! Can I believe my eyes? You must take what I tell you as true; I have always been a faithful recorder, and never given to lying. Here was I, trudging along carrying my writing equipment and a sack of provisions. We were heading for a streambank with high sides, where there would be shelter for the brothers and sisters. I was travelling somewhere in the centre of the column, not having seen the Abbess, as she was leading up at the front. I came away from Loamhedge, filled with shame and remorse, being too overcome with grief to bid Sister Amyl farewell. I slunk off like a thief. Then, from the rear of the marchers, a mighty cheer rose up. I trekked back to see what was causing such jubilation. There across the heathland, limping slowly but walking without any shadow of a doubt, came young Sister Amyl!"'

Again, Phredd's recital was interrupted when a hearty cheer came from his listeners. The old hedgehog made as if to slam the book shut.

'Do you want to hear the rest of this, or shall I lay back on my bed and go to sleep, eh, eh?'

Somewhat embarrassed, Abbot Carrul replied, 'Forgive us, friend, we'll stay silent. It was just that we felt so happy for Sister Amyl, we had to cheer.'

Phredd went back to his book, muttering, 'Aye, so did I when I first read it. Ahem, allow me to continue. "Was it a miracle, or some sort of magic? I had told the Abbess of Amyl's plight. She was sorrowful, of course, but informed me she would have a word with Amyl. What came of their conversation, I did not know. But here was my young friend, as large as life and up on her footpaws. Later that evening we sat by the fire, exhausted after the day's long march. Sister Amyl lay wrapped in her cloak sleeping deeply. I sought out Abbess Germaine and spoke to her about the amazing happening. Here is what our great and wise Mother Abbess told me. She said that she had recalled a formula, given to her by an old healer, many seasons ago. Searching through her belongings, she had found the parchment. This she gave to Amyl, telling her that she must decide on her own whether to stay or whether to read the formula, learn from it and undertake the journey. Obviously, Sister Amyl must have read what was written on the parchment. Was it a magic spell, or some remedy of herbal medicine? The Abbess would not tell me."'

Martha stifled a cry of disappointment, nevertheless listening dutifully as Phredd continued reading.

'"Next morning I dropped to the rear of the column and

walked with Sister Amyl, whose pace was getting stronger and more sure as the day went on. I told her what I had gleaned from the Abbess and faced her with the question: What was written on the parchment?

'"Amyl gave me one of her rare, secretive smiles and refused to speak of it. All that day I persisted, harassing her to divulge the information. It was only after a full day's march through sleeting rain and harsh country that she relented. We were camped beside a rocky tor, huddled in our cloaks around the fire, when she finally spoke. Her words are etched into my memory, and here they are, for what it's worth. 'The message on the parchment would be of no use to you. It would only have a meaning for somebeast who is greatly troubled in mind or body. Once I had learned what the old healer's rhyme was, I left the parchment behind at Loamhedge. I carry its power within me now, but any creature in need of those words must seek it out for themselves:

Beneath the flower that never grows,
Sylvaticus lies in repose.
My secret is entombed with her,
look and think what you see there.
A prison with four legs which moved,
yet it could walk nowhere,
whose arms lacked paws, but yet they held,
a wretched captive there.'"'

Phredd closed the book decisively, addressing its cover. 'My bed calls me. I bid you a weary goodnight.'

Bragoon protested, 'Is that all there is?'

Abbot Carrul reassured the otter, 'If there was more, my old friend would have told you. Right, Phredd?'

The ancient Abbey Gatekeeper reached for his nightshirt. 'Right indeed, young Carrul. I have given you all the information that is of interest to you, namely, Sister Amyl's story. We already have a map of the route to Loamhedge that was used by Matthias in his search for his son Mattimeo.'

Saro yawned and stood up stretching. 'We'll look at that tomorrow. After all that racin' an' jiggin', I'm ready for bed, too. That poem of Sister Amyl's, 'tis a real tail twister an' no mistake. Flowers that never grow, prisons with four legs an' no paws. An' who in the name o' fur'n'bush is Sylvaticus lyin' in repose?'

Old Phredd poked his head through the neck of the nightshirt. 'Sylvaticus was the first Abbess of Loamhedge. Don't know where I learned that, must have been at Dibbun School. Hmmm, that was more seasons ago than I care to remember. Funny how old little facts stick in one's mind. Don't slam my door when you leave, it doesn't like being slammed. Goodnight!'

They strolled back to the Abbey through the balmy night air, discussing the whole thing.

Martha turned to Bragoon and Saro, who were pushing her chair. 'Phredd said that you were the two travellers from the past. Do you believe him?'

Bragoon nodded. 'Of course we do, beauty. Don't ye fret now, me'n my mate'll bring that parchment back from Loamhedge for ye. Ain't that right, Saro?'

The ageing squirrel's reply left Martha in no doubt. 'Aye, I'll wager a split acorn to a cream tea on it, missy. We'll have ye up'n'dancin' in no time!'

The haremaid's face was a picture of joy to behold. 'I will dance someday just for you, my good friends. Tomorrow I'll make a copy of Sister Amyl's poem so you can take it with you in case you forget the words.'

Horty did a small hopskip of eagerness. 'Splendid idea, my wise an' pretty sis. I'll take charge of it, like a sort of jolly old mapfinder. Wot!'

Bragoon and Saro exchanged glances, and the otter murmured, 'We'll have to see about that.'

Further discussion was cut short. Sister Setiva met them at the Abbey doorway. She stood in a pool of golden light, holding up a lantern. The stern old Infirmary Keeper cast a jaundiced eye over the new arrivals.

'Ah'm tae shew ye to yore beds. There's two spare ones in the room next tae mine.'

Bragoon bowed appreciatively to her. 'It'll be a treat to sleep in a real bed again, Sister.'

Saro agreed. 'Aye, after some o' the places we've laid our heads down. But we'll be up at the crack o' dawn, ready to lend a paw with yore problem, Martha.'

Bragoon thumped his rudder down firmly. 'Ye can bet yore brekkist on that, missy. We won't let ye down!'

Martha clasped their paws fondly. 'Pleasant dreams to both of you.'

The pair found themselves being prodded, none too gently, with Setiva's blackthorn stick.

She commanded them in a no-nonsense voice, 'Follow me tae mah sickbay, an' 'twill be woe betide either of ye if ah hear just one wee snore disturbin' mah rest, d'ye ken?'

Bragoon saluted her smartly. 'Oh, we're kennin' away like a pair o' good 'uns, Sister. Lead on!' They grinned at each other, listening to the shrewnurse while she chunnered away to herself as she shuffled upstairs.

'Ach, I'll have tae dig oot fresh sheets an' coverlets! Ah'm thinkin' they're big enough tae make their ain beds, great roarin' villains! Ah'll nae sleep a whit taenight, knowin' they two are in the next room tae mine!'

Opening the infirmary door, she glared at her guests. 'Wipe the mud off ye're paws an' the silly grins offn'n ye're faces. Ah'll be inspectin' yon sickbay on the morrow, an' ah'll skelpit the pair o' ye if'n there's one wee thing oot o' place, d'ye ken? Ah bid ye a silent guidnight!' She slammed the door and retreated into her own chamber.

Bragoon burst out sniggering as Saro called out in imitation of Setiva's far northern accent, 'Aye, we ken, Sister, an' a guidnight to ye, too, the noo!'

The Sister's strict tone rang out from the adjoining room. 'Ah'll be in there wi' mah stick if there's anither sound, so get tae sleep an' no talkin'!'

Saro whispered in Bragoon's ear, 'Goodnight, mate.'

12

Early morn found the northeast skies showing more promise of decent weather. Outside the holt of Shoredog, pleasant sunlight was turning the mist into a warm yellow haze over the stream.

Lonna Bowstripe limped out with the rest of the sea otters to witness the arrival of the otter known as Garfo Trok. He had come in a peculiar-looking craft, a long, battered old boat with rounded stern and for'ard ends. It had a rickety cabin erected amidships and sported a square, heavily-patched sail, which was furled around a much repaired crosspiece.

Garfo was a stream otter, a jovial, fat beast. He wore an old iron helmet that resembled a cooking pot, and a permanent smile on his broad, friendly face. Shipping his paddling pole, Garfo waddled ashore and began singing in a dreadfully toneless voice.

''Tis a long ways down the stream, me lads,
when a beast ain't got no grub oh,
wid a belly like a wind-blowed sail,
aboard this leaky tub oh.
If I fell overboard like this,
all thin'n'pale'n'slack oh,

111

a pike'd take one look at me,
an' quickly chuck me back oh!

Me ribs are showin' through me fur,
I'm frightened o' the weather,
in case a sudden gust o' wind,
whips me off like a feather.
Me cheeks are sunken hollow,
an' me nose is wintry blue, lads,
me rudder's covered in green mould,
I'm sufferin' from the Doodads!

Take pity on this riverdog,
an' feed me good ole vittles,
some skilly'n'duff to stop me bones,
a-clackin' round like skittles.
A pot or two o' barley stew,
an' nutbread by the plateful,
an' a bathtub full o' custard, lads,
would find me ever grateful!'

The sea otters laughed and applauded Garfo heartily, then gathered round as he shook paws, patted backs and kissed babes, all the while hooting in booming tones, 'Whoohoohoo, slap me rudder an' curl me whiskers! Lookit ye lot. Wot 'ave youse been feedin' yoreselves on? Y'all look so chub'n'sparky! Ma Sork, me ole tatercake, are ye still bakin' the primest nutbread in the northeast?'

Old Sork whacked him playfully with her ladle as he picked her up and hugged her. 'Put me down, ye great fat-barrel. I've been up all night bakin' nutloaves to feed yore hungry gob!'

Garfo put her down and cast a jolly eye over Lonna. 'Whoohoo, shrivel me snout an' gravel me guts! So this is the giant stripedog I'm carryin' as cargo. Hah, I thought I was a big 'un, but ye could eat dinner of'n me head, mate!'

Lonna shook Garfo Trok's paw. 'Pleased to meet you,

mate, but I'm not just cargo. My name is Lonna Bowstripe, and I can wield a paddle as good as most.'

Garfo was big and well built for an otter, but Lonna's giant frame towered over him. He released the badger's huge paw.

'Wield a paddle, big feller? Whoohoo, ye look strong enough t'carry me an' my old boat *Beetlebutt* up a waterfall on yore back! Belay, Lonna, let's get some brekkist afore we sail.'

Lonna had already eaten, so he sat nibbling a crust of ryebread and sipping some plum cordial whilst Garfo dealt with breakfast. The otter was a mighty eater and extremely odd in his choice of food. He spread nutbread with honey and dunked it into hotroot soup. Breaking up an apple pie, he crumbled it into a bowl of mushroom stew, daubing plum preserve on an onion-and-leek pastie.

Clearing the lot in a remarkably short time, Garfo stood up, patting his big stomach. 'Ahoy, Lonna, pack that bow'n' arrers an' let's go sailin'. Can't waste a fine mornin' sittin' here vittlin', like some I've seen. Never could abide greediness in a beast!'

The otters had packed *Beetlebutt* with an amazing array of provisions. Lonna looked around at the faces of all these otters that he had come to like so much. It was going to be a sad experience saying goodbye to them. Garfo stood, waiting to push off, as the badger went in turn to each of his otter friends – Shoredog, Sork, Marinu and many others, saving his last farewell for Abruc and young Stugg. Lonna embraced Abruc warmly and clasped his paw. A tear coursed down the big badger's scarred face.

'Farewell to you and your family, my good friend. I will never forget you and your son. You saved my life, cared for me, fed and nursed me. All I can give you in return are my thanks and undying friendship!'

Abruc scuffed the ground with his rudder, then looked up at the big badger. 'Friendship is the greatest gift one can give to another. You are a goodbeast, Lonna. I know ye would've done the same for me an' mine if'n ye found us lyin' hurt. Go on, mate, you go now, an' know our thoughts are always with ye!'

Stugg tugged at Lonna's paw until the badger lifted the young otter and held him level with his eyes. His face solemn, Stugg wiped a tear from Lonna's striped muzzle.

'Lonn', der is somet'ink you can do for me an' my farder. Get Rag' Bol an' dose sea rats, so they don't hurt no more pore beasts!'

The badger put Stugg back down and stepped aboard the boat. Raising his bow, he called out as Garfo pushed off into the midstream.

'Stugg, my little mate. I swear by the fine string your father made for this bow. I will wipe Raga Bol and his sea rats from the land forever. This is my oath, and my promise to you. Goodbye!'

Putting aside the bow, he joined Garfo Trok at the paddling poles.

Fighting away the tears, Lonna did not look back as they sped downstream. Behind him the tribe of Shoredog stood on the banks, singing an old sea otter song of farewell.

'When the sun sets like fire,
I will think of you,
when the moon casts its light,
I'll remember, too,
if a soft rain falls gently,
I'll stand in this place,
recalling the last time,
I saw your kind face.
Good fortune go with you,
to your journey's end,
let the waters run calmly,
for you, my dear friend.'

Garfo Trok had spent his life amid the northeast streams and rivers. There was no waterway for leagues that the burly otter was not familiar with. Lonna obeyed his every order, backing and tacking down the broad stream. They made good progress. Midday found the *Beetlebutt* running smoothly with a fair breeze running astern.

Garfo shipped his long paddle, gazing up at the blue, cloud-flecked sky. 'Let the ole lady drift for awhile, mate. Belay that paddle an' we'll haul sail an' take a bite o' lunch.'

They released the sail and made its ends fast to the cleats. Lonna had been wondering when the otter's appetite was going to reappear. Together they sat on the roof of the little midships cabin, drinking cider and eating nutbread.

Garfo chuckled as he watched the big badger consume his lunch. 'Whoohoo, ain't nothin' wrong with a beast who kin eat hearty, mate! That limp o' yourn will soon clear up with a good cruise. Ye won't be walkin' so much.'

Lonna liked the feel of a boat beneath his paws; he felt rested and well. Gesturing ahead, he enquired, 'How long can we go by water, Garfo?'

The otter refilled his beaker. 'Almost into Mossflower. This ole stream takes a turn there an' runs back east. I kin see yore wonderin' 'ow far ahead those vermin are.'

Lonna eyed him keenly. 'Aye, can ye tell me, mate?'

Garfo scratched his rudder thoughtfully. 'Raga Bol has t'go by land since they ain't got no boat an' there's too many of 'em for small rivercraft. Those sea rats should be well into Mossflower Wood by now. I'd say ye was about ten days behind 'em, Lonna. But I kin cut that down to eight, wid some canny sailin'. Don't fret, mate.'

The badger's eyes narrowed; the look on his ruined face caused the otter to shudder. Lonna laughed mirthlessly. 'Oh, I'm not fretting at all. I'll catch up to them for sure!'

The country they were sailing through was open, with no tree cover. Gradually it ran into hills and gorges, the stream-banks growing higher on either side.

Garfo pointed to a steep bend up ahead. 'When we round the point of yon bend, we'll be meetin' up with Buteo. Now

I know yore not a-feared of anybeast, but don't start anythin' wid him. I've knowed Buteo a long time.'

Lonna was intrigued. 'Just as you say, mate, but who is Buteo?'

Garfo crumbled some nutbread on the cabin roof. 'Oh, ye'll find out soon enuff, matey, soon enuff!'

Beetlebutt took the bend smoothly, keeping to midstream. Halfway around it, Lonna was startled to feel a slight cuff on the back of his head. Buteo landed like a bolt of lightning, silent and menacing. He was a honey buzzard – a large, savage-looking bird of prey. From fawn-barred tail to mottled chest, and huge wingspan to lethal-hooked beak and a fierce eye, Buteo looked every inch a killer. Folding his wings, the buzzard stared disdainfully at the crumbled nutbread that Garfo had put out for him, then pointed a lethally sharp talon at them.

'Heek! This be Buteo territory, I rule here. Heeeeeekah!'

Garfo replied cheerily, 'So ye do, me ole burdy, but we ain't trespassin', just passin' through.'

Buteo cocked his head to one side, glaring at them. 'Yaheeek! I riddle you riddle, you spin me a spin. Only pass here if you win. Good?'

Garfo cautioned Lonna to silence with a warning glance. The badger watched as the otter appeared to consider this proposition.

'Good it is, Buteo. You go first.'

The honey buzzard stared up at the sky, a thing that honey buzzards do when trying to appear mysterious. 'Heeeeekoh! What be brown'n'yellow, fat'n'mad, an' if you slow, sting you bad?'

Garfo scratched his rudder, shaking his head, as if really perplexed. 'Frazzle me whiskers, Buteo, that's a real poser!'

Buteo pecked up the crumbled nutbread, sniggering. 'Keeheeheehee! Stupid riverdog not crossing through my country. Buteo much clever. Keehar!'

Garfo tipped a sly wink to Lonna, then jumped up shouting, 'I got it, 'tis a bumbly bee!'

Both Garfo and Lonna had to avoid the buzzard's wings as he beat the air in frustration. 'Yeekeeha! How you know?'

The otter twitched his nose modestly. 'Oh, I just took a guess. But it was a great an' clever riddle.'

Buteo stalked up and down, digging his talons angrily into the cabin roof. Then he turned and wheeled on Garfo. 'Yeeee! You still not go 'til you spin me. This time I win!'

The crafty otter produced a flat pebble from his helmet, spat on one side of it and held it up for the bird to see. 'Right, I'll spin ye – dry side I win, wet side you lose. Good?'

The honey buzzard nodded eagerly. 'Keehee! I take wet!'

Garfo spun the pebble into the air, chanting, 'Up she comes, down she goes, how she lands, nobeast knows!'

Buteo's keen eyes watched every spin of the stone until it clacked down flat on the deck.

Garfo grinned from ear to ear. 'Wet side, you lose!'

The buzzard hovered over the otter, glaring murderously at him. Garfo sat munching a chuck of nutbread, looking the fierce bird straight in the eye. 'Ye've got to let us pass now, mate, or you ain't a bird whose word can be trusted.'

Fearing that the buzzard was going to attack Garfo, Lonna braced himself to spring upon it.

The bird's black and gold eyes dilated wildly as it screeched, 'Allbeast know Buteo be a bird of honour, my word always good. I slay anybeast who say different. Yeeeeeekaaaah!'

Snatching the nutbread from the otter's paw, he soared off into the air – up and up, until he was a mere dot in the sky.

Lonna relaxed gratefully. 'That was a close call, my friend. Buteo looked like a bird who would fight to the death. How did you manage to hoodwink him like that?'

Garfo Trok winked knowingly. 'I been doin' it a long time, mate, whenever my journeys take me by this way. Pore ole Buteo's memory's scrambled from too many battles. Besides, he ain't the brightest o' birds. Funny how he loses every time. I'll let him win on the return trip, 'cos I'll be bound back nor'east anyway. That's fair enough.'

Lonna could not help laughing at the sly otter. 'You great fat fraud! Shame on you, Garfo Trok!'

Nibbling on a piece of cheese he had found, Garfo waved his rudder nonchalantly. 'Better'n havin' to fight t'the death wid a mad buzzard. You said so yoreself, mate. Anythin' for an easy life, that's my motto.'

13

The sea rat Blowfly sat on a rotten log, cooling his footpaws by rubbing them in the rich, damp loam. Gazing up at the trunks of mighty woodland trees, with their canopy of sun-pierced green, he murmured to the sea rat sitting alongside him, 'I likes this 'ere Mossflower place, better weather 'ere than on that nor'east coast. Plenny o' shelter an' prime vittles, too!'

His companion, a sad-faced sea rat called Rojin, rubbed his blistered footpaws tenderly as he complained, 'Huh, if only we wasn't marchin' so much. I ain' cut out fer all this trekkin'. I'm a sea rat, norra landlubber!'

Hangclaw, another rat, limped over to join them. Rooting with his daggerpoint at a splinter in his footpaw, he spat in disgust.

'Right y'are, shipmate, just look at me pore trampers. Why are we walkin' all the time? Where's ole Bol got us bound to? We're traipsin' around all day an' 'arf the night!'

Glimbo, the one-eyed rat who had been first mate aboard ship, had been loitering nearby, eavesdropping on the three crewrats. Sneaking up behind them, he gave the rotten log a hard shove with his spearpoint, sending the trio sprawling into the loam.

'Gerrup on yer paws an' quit whinin', ye slab-sided sons o' worms. If the cap'n catches ye, he'll leave youse here to rest as food fer the ants. Now march!'

Raga Bol had been marching up in front of the others but had looked back over his shoulder so often that the crew could not fail to notice. The sea rat captain dropped back until he was level with Glimbo. Catching his mate's sleeve with the deadly silver hook, Bol swiftly dragged him behind a broad sycamore trunk.

Glimbo's sightless eye rolled in its socket as he saluted. 'They're all on the march, Cap'n!'

Raga Bol poked his head out from behind the tree and snarled at the backstragglers, 'Keep movin', I'm watchin' ye!' Then he turned his attention to the trembling Glimbo. 'They're talkin' about me, wot're they sayin'? The truth!'

The mate was trembling so hard that the back of his head made a noise on the tree trunk like a woodpecker. 'N . . . nothin', Cap'n, they ain't sayin' nothin'.'

He heard the slither of cold steel as Bol drew his scimitar. As Raga Bol pulled him close, Glimbo could see the glint of his captain's gold teeth. He knew how dangerous the captain's moods were becoming.

With his scimitar upraised, Bol hissed, 'They must be sayin' somethin', ye mud-brained idiot!'

Words poured out of Glimbo at breakneck pace. 'On me oath, Cap'n, the whole crew's sayin' 'ow thankful they are to ye for bringin' 'em 'ere, where 'tis sunny an' there's easy pickin's. It's just that they ain't used to all this marchin' . . . some of 'em gotten sore paws.'

Thunk! The scimitar blade cut deep into the sycamore, taking off a tuft of Glimbo's whiskers. 'Sore paws, is it? You tell anybeast moanin' about sore paws that I'll chop 'em off an' make 'em march on the stumps! Aye, an' ye can tell all the crew to quit starin' at me all the time. An' ye can tell 'em another thing, too. Any rat I 'ears mentionin' that giant stripedog, I'll make 'im eat his own tongue. There ain't no big stripedog follerin' me, d'ye hear?'

Glimbo gulped hard, knowing how close to death he had come. Raga Bol wandered off without warning, leaving him to pull the scimitar loose and return it. The mate was surprised to see his captain sit down in the loam and speak in a voice that almost had a sob in it. 'I ain't been sleepin' at nights. Post extra guards around me when it gets dark.'

Glimbo dislodged the blade and returned it to his captain. Raga Bol grabbed the scimitar, staring suspiciously at him.

'Stop starin' at me like that, thick'ead. Gerrabout yer business an' make 'em march faster!'

Glimbo saluted and walked off bemused. This was not the Raga Bol he knew from the seafaring days. The captain was definitely acting strange. He glanced back at Bol, but the captain did not notice him looking, because he, too, was peering back over his shoulder.

Badredd felt the early sun on his muzzle as he lay on a soft patch of moss, with both eyes closed, feigning sleep. He listened to the voices of the gang, identifying each one as they spoke.

'Sure 'tis a luvly morn, an' a grand ould spot t'be enjoyin' it in!' Flinky had an unmistakable accent.

His mate, Crinktail, was next to speak. 'Which way d'ye want these woodpigeon eggs boilin'?'

Flinky replied, 'Keep 'em nice'n'soft, me ould darlin'. I've never been fussy on hardboiled eggs.'

Crinktail sounded cheerful. 'I'll cook night an' day for ye, if'n yew can fool that little fox into lettin' us stay by this water for a few more days.'

Badredd heard Juppa's voice chime in. 'Aye, this is a prime spot. See if'n ye can fool the liddle idjit to stop 'ere fer a score o' days!'

Flinky oozed confidence. 'Leave it t'me, mates. I'm a silver-tongued ould charmer when I wants t'be!'

Badredd yawned convincingly, then, opening his eyes, sat up lazily and stretched. 'Boiled woodpigeon eggs, eh? Bring 'em over here, Flinky, I 'ope they're done nice'n'soft.'

The stoat gritted his teeth but obeyed the new chief's orders. 'Top o' the mornin' to ye, sir, an' another grand day 'tis, t'be sure. Now ye enjoy those eggs, there's plenny more around. We was just sayin' wot a fine spot ye chose fer us. Yore a wise leader, so y'are!'

Badredd put the eggs to one side and stood up, sword in paw. Scowling darkly, he asserted his authority. 'Don't get to like it too much, you lot, 'cos we're movin' on as soon as we've eaten. So pack up yore gear an' stand by, ready t'march as soon as Plumnose gets back!'

Halfchop's face was the picture of dismay. 'But didn't ye say we wuz stayin' 'ere for a coupla days?'

The little fox gripped his cutlass tighter. 'Well, I just changed me mind. A chief can do that!'

Slipback stood paws on hips, facing up to Badredd. 'Changed yore mind, eh, jus' like that! An' where d'ye think yore takin' us, eh?'

Raising the cutlass, Badredd took a pace forwards and snarled nastily at the weasel, 'We're goin' to this Abbey place, if 'tis any business of yores. So git yore tackle t'gether!'

Slipback turned to the others, scoffing insolently, 'Hah, looks t'me like the liddle fox needs a magic sword t'make 'im look bigger!'

Badredd's temper snapped. He swung at the weasel's unprotected back, chopping off his tail with a single blow.

Slipback screeched in pain. 'Yeeeaaaargh, me tail!'

His mate, Juppa, hastily slapped a pawful of bank mud on the severed stump. Slipback lay moaning, half fainting with the agony.

Juppa glared accusingly at Badredd. 'Ye had no call t'do that to 'im!'

As the fox once again flourished his cutlass, the gang fell back. He saw the fear in their eyes and exulted in it. 'Next time anybeast talks t'me like that, I'll slay 'im! Oh, I know wot ye've been sayin' be'ind me back. Think ye can fool me, do ye? Well, dig the dirt out yore lugs an' lissen. I'm rulin' this roost, an' wot I say goes! I'm goin' to own that magic sword, aye, an' take the Abbey, too. Anybeast who sez diff'rent, let 'em speak now!'

Flinky raised his paws placatingly. 'Ah, sure now, who'd be wantin' t'get themselves slayed by battlin' wid a fine great warrior like yoreself? 'Tis just that we thought ye was goin' to stop 'ere a few days.'

It was then that Badredd knew he was really the leader of the gang. A feeling of power surged through him. Now he could be as cruel and commanding as Burrad or Skrodd. Had he not just drawn blood? Curling his lip contemptuously, he growled, 'I do the thinkin' from now on. We're goin' to the Abbey. Come on, Slipback, up on yer hunkers, ye ain't dead yet.'

With a poultice of mud and dockleaf tied to his severed tail, the weasel rose slowly, fixing Badredd with a stare of hatred. 'There's eight of us an' only one of you, fox. Don't get too big'n'fancy wid yore ideas, 'cos ye've still got to sleep at nights. I wouldn't turn me back on us too often if'n I was you – ye can't kill us all!'

Badredd realized the truth in Slipback's statement, but now that he had all this newfound power he was not backing down. With his cutlass blade, Badredd upset the small cauldron of water over the campfire. It went out with a hiss and a cloud of steam.

At that moment, Plumnose came lumbering back through the woodlands. The ferret's oversized nose wobbled from side to side as he took in the scene. 'Huh, wod's bin goin' on, mates?'

Flinky began explaining. 'Ah well, Plum, me ould messmate, wait'll I tell ye wot . . .'

Badredd shoved the stoat roughly aside. 'I'm the chief now – make yore report t'me. Well, wot did ye find?'

Plumnose pointed in the direction he had been scouting. 'Er, over der, I'b found a path dat runs south't'north. I t'ink dat's der way to the h'Abbey. Id's aboud h'a day's march, Chief, to d'path I mean.'

Badredd pointed with his blade. 'Get movin', you lot. Plumnose, you go up front an' show 'em the way. Slipback, Juppa, Crinktail, Flinky an' Halfchop, up front wid 'im. I ain't walkin' wid youse behind me. Rogg an' Floggo, you bring up the rear wid me.'

He shook the cutlass at Flinky. 'An' remember this, old silver tongue, no gossipin' an' plottin', 'cos I'll be watchin' ye. There'll be no more coaxin' me inter things wot I don't wanna do. Now move yoreselves!'

It was pleasant walking through the woodlands. Patches of light and shade mottled the grass, and many forest blossoms were coming into bloom. The weasel brothers, Rogg and Floggo, were a taciturn pair. Since both of them carried bows and arrows, Badredd had kept them back with him. He explained their duties as he watched the backs of the gang, marching ahead. Badredd confided to the weasel brothers as though they were lifelong friends.

'Stay by my side, mates, I'll make ye both my seconds in command. Keep yore eyes on the rest of that gang an' watch me back. Aye, ye two look true'n'blue t'me. When we conquer that Abbey place, I'll reward ye well. Mark my words, ye'll live the lives o' kings!'

Rogg and Floggo were not at all impressed by the little fox's brags and promises. They had seen gang leaders come and go, each one as ruthlessly cruel as the next. Keeping a stolid silence, the brothers marched dutifully on. Badredd kept a half pace behind them, carrying the cutlass over one shoulder like a spear. He had tried wearing it thrust into his belt, but the blade was too long. It dragged along the ground and got caught twixt his footpaws, causing undignified stumbles. Leaders could not afford to look foolish to those serving them.

Morning wore on to midday. The gang's initial feelings of a brisk march through pleasant country began to pall as the going got more difficult. Those who were marching in front began complaining when they had to pass through a wide area of stinging nettles. Badredd roared at them to carry on in silence, which they did but only briefly. They had come upon marshy ground – not too deep but very uncomfortable – and soon were grumbling loudly. Swarms of midges attacked as the vermin struggled through the smelly, oozing mud. This time they ignored Badredd's shouts and threats, even hurling insults back at him. After what seemed like hours, the front marchers emerged on to firm ground. Badredd and his bodyguards Rogg and Floggo hurried to catch up with them.

The gang had found a dry, sunny clearing where they lay, looking sullen and rebellious. One glance at their mud-splashed, insect-bitten faces warned their leader of trouble to come should he start roaring out orders to continue marching. Badredd forestalled this by sitting down wearily and commenting, 'Ye did well there, mates, let's rest 'ere awhile. Ahoy, Plum, are ye sure this is the right way? Are ye sure that hooter o' yores didn't wobble in the wrong direction, eh?'

Not even a snigger greeted his little joke. Picking dried mud from his nosetip, the ferret replied dully, 'Dis is duh way h'I went awright.'

The vermin gang had no supplies with them and were too tired to forage. Crinktail and Halfchop stretched out and began taking a nap in the warm sunlight. Plumnose, Juppa, Slipback and Flinky sat in a group, conversing in muted tones. Rogg and Floggo slouched nearby, their eyes half closed.

Badredd began feeling dozy in the midday heat, but he forced himself to sit up and look alert. He saw Slipback glance his way, then whisper something to Juppa. The little fox pointed the cutlass at them.

'Cut out the whisperin', I'm warnin' ye!'

Flinky grinned impudently and threw a lazy salute. 'Ah sure, they wasn't sayin' ought bad about ye, sir. Wid yore permission, would it be alright if we was to sing?'

Badredd relaxed, shrugging indifferently. 'Sing 'til yore

tongues drop off, if'n ye've a mind to. But none o' that gossipin' an' whisperin' to each other!'

The four exchanged sly winks. Flinky began singing a lullaby in a soft soothing voice.

'All the walkin' today that I've done, done, done,
trampin' through mud in the sun, sun, sun,
it reminds me of the days when me dear ould mother
  said,
come on now liddle feller, time for bed . . . bed . . . bed.
So hush a-bye, looh ah-lie, baby close yore eyes,
an' dream about the moon up in the starry skies.'

He repeated the verse again, even softer, with the other three vermin humming gently in the background.

Badredd's head drooped forwards slightly, the cutlass lying limp in his open paw. His thoughts drifted back to his own young seasons. Through a golden haze of memory, he was barely aware of Flinky's singing. It was the same tune but with different words.

'It looks like the fox has gone to sleep, sleep, sleep,
Slippy now be quiet as ye creep, creep, creep,
an' stick a good sharp spear straight through his head,
then the moment that he wakes up he'll be dead, dead,
  dead!
So hush a-bye, don't ye cry, foxy close yore eyes,
an' ye'll soon make lovely vittles for the ants an' flies!'

The murderous scheme might have worked out successfully had it not been for Plumnose. He thought that the altered words were so funny that he clapped his paws and broke out into hearty guffaws.

'Duh, haw haw haaaw! Dat's a gudd 'un, I like dat, Flink! Haw haw haw, wake up dead, berry gudd!'

Badredd snapped immediately back to reality. He caught

Slipback, brandishing a spear not three paces from him. Grabbing up his cutlass, the fox raised it threateningly.

'Wot are yew up to, weasel?'

Slipback veered and went past him. He started jabbing at the shrubbery at the edge of the glade.

'Thought I saw those bushes movin', Chief. It might've been that otter an' the squirrel, er, Sagroon an' Bando!'

Flinky interposed, 'I know who ye mean, Bragoon an' Saro. I saw the bushes move, too, Chief. Slipback could be right!'

Thinking swiftly, Badredd turned the situation to his advantage. 'No sense in takin' chances then. We'd best git movin' fast. Come on, up on yore paws!'

Badredd drove them hard for the remainder of the day by adopting a simple but effective scheme. He ordered Rogg and Floggo to fire off arrows from time to time. The deadly shafts fell just short of the marchers' rear, causing them to hasten forwards. Oaths and curses accompanied the arrival of each arrow, but they kept going, knowing they were only getting tit for tat. The plot to rid themselves of the little fox had failed, but they realized that, had it been Burrad or Skrodd in Badredd's place, Flinky and Slipback would have been slain as retribution. They were getting off lightly.

Progress was good. By evening, Badredd was heartened to hear Plumnose calling out, 'Dere's duh path at de end ob the trees!'

Sure enough, they had reached the border of the woodlands. In front of them lay the path, which ran down from the north to the south.

Flinky leaned on an elm trunk, smiling cheerfully as the fox came up to see. 'Ah well, there ye are now, Chief. All we gotta do is follow that road t'the left an' keep goin' 'til we hit Redwall Abbey!'

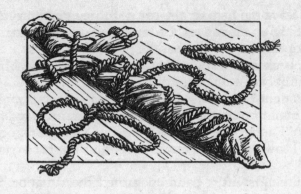

14

Larks soared joyfully on the flatlands outside of Redwall, singing their hymns to the newborn day. Chiming a melodious bass line, the Abbey's twin bells boomed out warmly. Indoors, all the young ones were already up and about, anticipating the arrival of Summer Feast.

Sister Setiva invariably rose to the tolling bells. Up and dressed, tidy and neat, she rapped on the sickbay door with her blackthorn stick, berating the sleepers within.

'Oot o' those beds, ye great dozy lumpkins. If your no' out here in a brace o' shakes, ah'll be in there an' haul ye both oot by your tails!'

Bragoon poked a sleepy head from beneath his coverlet. 'Hear that, mate? I think we'd best get up. Huh, I'd sooner face a regiment o' vermin than that ole shrewnurse!'

Reaching out a paw, Saro grasped a bedside stool and rattled it noisily on the floor, calling out, 'We're both up, Sister, just makin' the beds an' tidyin' round. We'll be out there in a tick!'

Setiva's shrill warning came back loud and clear. 'Och, you're a braw fibber. Ah'll be doonstairs, keeping an eye out for ye. Laggardly sluggards!'

The pair sat up at the sound of her retreating stick taps. Saro yawned and thumped her head back on the pillows.

'Just leave me here for the rest o' the season, Brag. I'd forgotten how comfy a real bed feels. Mmmmmmmmm!'

Leaping out of bed, the otter swished water from a ewer on his face and towelled it vigorously. 'Fair enough, me ole bushtail, you stop there. I haven't forgotten how good a Redwall brekkist tastes.'

Without bothering to wash, Saro pursued him downstairs. 'I'm right with ye, ole ten bellies. You ain't scoffin' all the vittles afore I gets a crack at 'em!'

Martha had just finished making up a tray for herself and Old Phredd when she saw the pair rush in and begin loading up two trays from the long buffet tables set up in the kitchen passage. She giggled at the sight of them, helping themselves to some of everything, chuckling with delight at the food.

'Almond wafers with raspberry sauce, my favourite!'

'Oatmeal with apple'n'honey, just the stuff! Granmum Gurvel, me ole beauty, pass me some o' that pastie. Wot's in it?'

'Burr, ee mushenrooms an' carrot, zurr, wi' h'onion sauce.'

'Onion sauce! Gimme two portions, one for Starvation Saro!'

'Hah, lissen to ole bucket mouth! You get us two mint teas, Brag, an' I'll fill two beakers o' Junty Cellarhog's best damson cordial. Oh great, hot scones! Gimme, gimme!'

Leaving the buffet, they beamed at the haremaid over the tops of their laden trays. 'Mornin', Miss Martha, we're just makin' up for the lost brekkists, ain't that right, Bragg?'

The otter winked roguishly. 'Haharr, sleepin' in a real bed gives a beast a powerful appetite.'

Martha looked up at their heaped trays. 'I'm sure it does. Perhaps you'd like to take breakfast in the gatehouse with Phredd and me, away from all this bustle.'

Balancing the tray skilfully on his head, Bragoon began wheeling Martha's chair. 'An honour an' a pleasure, miss. Besides, 'twill get us out of Sister Setiva's way. Come on, afore she finds we ain't made our beds or tidied the sick-bay.'

Halfway across the lawn, Abbot Carrul caught up with them. 'Oh dear, Martha, I've brought breakfast for Phredd, too.'

The haremaid indicated her two companions. 'Don't worry, Father, it won't go to waste!'

The old hedgehog Gatekeeper welcomed them in. He reached for his nightshirt, then shook his head absent-mindedly. 'Hmm, must've gone to bed in my daytime habit. Look at me, putting my nightshirt on to start the day. What's it all coming to, eh, eh?'

Phredd gestured at the volume lying on the table. 'The account by Tim Churchmouse about the route to Loam-hedge, when Matthias was searching for his son. If you two read it, you'll learn of how to get there.'

Saro leafed briefly through the ancient pages. 'Me'n Brag ain't champion readers like you, sir. We'd rather see the map – that'll tell us more.'

No sooner had Martha showed them the copy she had made of the map, than the squirrel and the otter glanced at one another and nodded.

Bragoon tapped his paw upon the map. 'We've travelled this country afore. I can recall most of it – those high cliffs, the pine forest, river, desert an' the great gorge. Dangerous country, eh Saro?'

The ageing squirrel held the map this way and that as she studied it. 'Aye, bad territory, though we came to it a different way. I remember those rocks, the ones shaped like a bell an' a badger's head, but I can't bring that tall tree to mind.'

Bragoon tapped his rudder thoughtfully against the floor. 'It prob'ly collapsed with age. This map was made seasons afore we were born. But 'tis the same area alright, riddled with vermin an' all manner o' perils. I was glad to get away from it!'

Martha looked disappointed. 'Does that mean it's too dangerous to make the journey?'

The otter laughed. 'Haharr, wot ever gave ye that idea, me beauty? Danger's wot me an' Saro live on. We'd both end up dead afore our seasons was out livin' at Redwall.'

The squirrel nodded mournfully. 'All the good vittles an' soft beds, that'd finish us off. Huh, if Sister Setiva didn't.'

Abbot Carrul poured mint tea for Old Phredd. 'Then when will you be going?'

Saro selected a hot scone and bit into it. 'Straight after the Summer Feast, if'n we can still walk. Late noon prob'ly. We'll travel southeast.'

After breakfasting they set off for the orchard to help with the festive preparations. Horty, with his two friends, Springald and Fenna, came out of the Abbey, carrying a trestle board. The young hare hailed Bragoon and Saro.

'Hello there, you chaps. Well, have you sorted out a jolly old way to Loamhedge for us, wot?'

Bragoon answered him rather abruptly. 'Aye!'

Springald bounced up and down eagerly. 'Oh good, when are we leaving?'

Fenna's eyes shone happily. 'A journey to Loamhedge. Great seasons, I've been looking forward to this!'

Horty looked from Bragoon to Saro excitedly. 'Come on then, you bounders, who's got my copy of the bally map? Remember, I'm the flippin' pathfinder, y'know.'

Bragoon turned to face the trio, his voice stern. 'This ain't no daisy dance! Me'n my mate Saro'll be makin' the journey to Loamhedge . . . alone!'

Horty's ears drooped. 'But you said . . .'

Saro interrupted him. 'We never said nothin', young 'un. Yore the one whose been doin' all the sayin'. Bragoon an' me knows the country we got to go through. We can make it alone, but it'd be far too dangerous with three young 'uns in tow.'

Fenna was outraged. 'You mean you aren't taking us?'

Bragoon nodded. 'That's right, missy. 'Tis too much

responsibility. We couldn't show our faces back in this Abbey if'n ye were slain by vermin or killed in an accident. We're goin' alone, an' that's that!'

Springald tried to make an appeal to the Abbot. 'What's he talking about? We've as much right to go as they have! Martha's our friend, too. Father, you're the Abbot of Redwall. You make all the decisions here, tell them!'

Abbot Carrul beckoned the three young ones to him. Putting his paws about their shoulders, he spoke kindly. 'Now, now, what Bragoon and Saro say makes sense. None of you has ever been further than the main gate. You're far too inexperienced to make such a trip, trust me. Our two friends are thinking of your own good.'

Horty pulled away from the Abbot, his ears standing stiffly with indignation. 'Tosh'n'piffle, sah! We're young and strong. We can put up with anythin' those two old fogies can! Bragoon and Saro are old chums of yours. That's why you're blinkin' well siding with 'em. And anyhow, what flippin' right have you to stop us goin', wot?'

Springald and Fenna supported him volubly. 'Horty's right, it's not fair. You let us think we were going all along, then changed your mind at the last moment!'

'Aye, it's just because we're young, and those two old wrecks want to grab all the glory for themselves. What do you think, Martha? Come on, tell them we're right.'

Martha shook her head. 'If the message from Sister Amyl, when she appeared in my dream with Martin the Warrior, had mentioned that you should go, I'd be the first to say yes. But only the two travellers, Bragoon and Saro, were included in the rhyme. So I'm afraid I must say no – not that my decision matters. Our Father Abbot has forbidden you to journey to Loamhedge, so you must abide by his word. Also, I trust Bragoon and Saro. They know of the dangers and are far more experienced at things like this than the three of you.'

Horty exploded. 'It's nothin' but a confounded plot against us. Shame on all of you, shame I say!'

Abbot Carrul put his footpaw down sternly. 'Enough of this talk! Arguing and casting insults is not the way in which any decent Redwaller should behave. Any more of this from you, Horty, or your two friends, and there'll be three empty seats at the Summer Feast this afternoon!'

Horty glared back at the Abbot, his temper completely out of control. 'Keep your rotten feast, blinkin' bounders!'

The Abbot's paw shot out. 'Go to your rooms and stay there until you are ready to apologize, all three of you!'

The trio ran off, shouting, 'Don't worry, we wouldn't be seen dead at your feast!'

'Come on, leave those old greywhiskers to themselves!'

'You'll be jolly well sorry, we'll stay in the blinkin' dormitory until we die of flippin' starvation. So there!'

Abbot Carrul comforted Martha, who had become so upset that she had begun weeping. 'There, there, Martha, don't you waste tears on those three. Could you imagine Horty starving himself to death? 'Tis as unlikely as me trying to leap over the belltower. Give them a day and they'll have changed their minds, trust me.' Carrul bowed slightly to Bragoon and Saro. 'Please forgive the bad manners of those three young ones.'

Saro smiled wryly. 'No need to apologize to us, friend. I can recall two, younger'n'Horty an' his pals, two more bad-mannered liddle scuts ye never did see!'

Martha blinked through her tears. 'Were you really that bad?'

Bragoon shuffled his rudder awkwardly. 'Oh, much worse, missy. Take me word fer it!'

Abbot Carrul chuckled heartily. 'Aye, now that you've come to mention it, 'tis a wonder you turned out so well!'

Bragoon clapped him on the back. 'An' ye, too, Carrul. Ye wasn't exactly a model Dibbun as I remember!'

Whipping out a clean 'kerchief, the Abbot busily wiped away at Martha's eyes. 'Yes, well, that was a long time ago. Now then, missy, are you going to keep weeping and bring on the rain, or are you going to smile for our Summer Feast?'

133

She smiled happily. 'Are you still going to carry on with the feast, Father, I mean after what just took place?'

Abbot Carrul reassured her, 'Of course I am, no need to halt it because of three surly young 'uns. If they want to join in, all they have to do is apologize for their bad manners. Come on, friends, I wouldn't miss my Summer Feast for anything!'

Set in the orchard against a background of ripening fruit and summer flowers, complete with sumptuously decked tables, the feast turned out to be a huge success. Freshly washed and dressed, the Redwallers took their places, waiting on the Abbot to start the proceedings. Martha sat - between Bragoon and Saro. The three of them stared in awe at the magnificent spread. Salads, pasties and savouries were still being brought on trolleys by the servers. These were placed among the pies, tarts and flans. Jugs of various cordials and fizzes stood between trifles, crumbles, puddings and candied fruits. Loaves of many shapes and types, still fresh from the ovens, were set amid cheeses of different hues – from pale cream to golden yellow.

Everybeast, even the Dibbuns, ceased their chatter as Abbot Carrul stood up and recited a verse, specially written for the event.

'We celebrate this happy day,
with fair and right good reason,
in friendship, let us share the fruits,
of this fine summer season.

We seed and plant the fertile earth,
to use what she may give,
and thank the kindly summer sun,
which gives us joy to live.'

Granmum Gurvel, resplendent in a new floral-embroidered apron, called out, 'You'm never spoked truer wurds, zurr!'

With that, the Summer Feast began in earnest. Junty Cellarhog tapped a barrel of strawberry fizz, which he had made the previous summer. Dibbuns squealed with delight as the bubbles tickled their mouths. Carving a wedge from a soft hazelnut cheese, Bragoon added it to his salad. Toran noticed him brushing away a teardrop.

'Wot's the matter with ye, brother?'

The otter looked mournfully at the festive board. 'Nothin' really, I was just thinkin' of all the Redwall feasts I've missed since me'n Saro left the Abbey.'

Toran scoffed, 'Don't fret, it looks like yore makin' up for it with a will!'

Saro adopted a wheedling tone towards the ottercook. 'Anybeast who can cook vittles like these should be famous. Toran, ole pal, why don't ye come adventurin' with me'n yore brother? You could cook for us an' everybeast we meet.'

Toran lowered his eyes modestly. 'No thankee, marm. I'm a mite too round in the waist for travellin'.'

Sister Portula put aside her plate in mock indignation. 'Take our ottercook, indeed! Mayhaps you'd like to take Junty Cellarhog, too, in case you feel the need of a drink?'

Bragoon chortled, 'Haharr, a capital idea, Sister!'

Abbot Carrul's eyes twinkled as he joined the conversation. 'I'm with you, Bragoon, a marvellous scheme! Take Toran and Junty, they'd make life much easier for you and Saro. However, I must insist that you take Sister Setiva along. If ever you are wounded, or fall ill, you'll surely need a dedicated creature to care for you both. Agreed?'

Bragoon suddenly became interested in a bowl of plum pudding and meadowcream. He mumbled hastily, 'Me'n' Saro will make the journey alone, thankee Carrul.'

Good-humoured banter and cheerful gossiping carried on into the warm summer noontide, a perfect accompaniment to the delicious feast. Having eaten their fill, the Dibbuns ran off to play within the Abbey grounds.

After a while, Saro glanced at the sun's position and announced, 'We'll have t'get goin' soon. Best be on the road afore we lose the daylight.'

Her otter friend patted his stomach. 'Aye, though I reckon we won't need much feedin' for a day or two. That was the nicest food an' the best company I can ever recall. Thankee, friends, for everythin'.'

The Abbot smiled. 'It was our pleasure. I knew you'd be going today, so I've had two packs of provisions made up by Granmum Gurvel. They should last you quite a time. Inside them you'll find all you need – the map, the poem telling of the location of Sister Amyl's secret and extra garments to wear. Now, is there anything else you two would like to take – anything?'

Bragoon replied without hesitation, 'I'd like to take with me the memory of a sweet song. Martha, would ye sing us a song to send us on our way?'

Saro added, 'Aye, go on, missy, put the birds t'shame!'

The haremaid's clear voice rang out into the still noon air. She sang for her two friends as she had never sung before. They sat entranced by Martha's beautiful voice.

'I planted her gently last summer,
all in quiet evening shade,
within an orchard bower,
her little bed I made.
Alone I sat by my window,
as autumn leaves did fall,
they formed a russet cover for
My Rose of Old Redwall.

Through winter's dreary days she slept
beneath the cold dark ground,
when all the earth was silent,
white snows lay deep around.
Bright stars came out above her,
as to the moon I'd call,

take pity on my dearest one,
My Rose of Old Redwall.

How the grass grew green and misty,
soft fell the rain that spring,
her dainty budded head arose,
and made my poor heart sing.
Then summer brought her just one bloom,
so white, so sweet and tall,
with ne'er a thorn to sully her,
My Rose of Old Redwall.'

Both the hardy old adventurers were sobbing like babes. Saro scrubbed roughly at her eyes. 'Come on, mate, time to go. We'll push ye as far as the gate, missy, so ye can wave us goodbye.'

They were met at the gatehouse by Foremole Dwurl and Granmum Gurvel, each carrying a pack of provisions. Old Phredd emerged from the gatehouse with a long, slender bundle, which he presented to Bragoon.

The otter stared at the strange object. 'Thankee kindly, Phredd. What is it?'

Abbot Carrul answered. 'It is the sword of Martin the Warrior. I want you to take it on your quest for Loamhedge. Should you need a weapon to defend yourselves, you could not have a finer one. I trust you both with the sword, and I know when the journey is done, you will bring it back safe to Redwall. May the spirit of Martin go with you, my friends, and the good wishes of all in this Abbey!'

Bragoon bound the still-wrapped sword across his shoulders. 'Ye do us great honour. How could we fail with Martin's sword to keep us company? Go back to yore Summer Feast now, an' don't fret. Me an' Saro'll bring back Sister Amyl's secret – that is, providin' it makes ye walk, Martha.'

The young haremaid's eyes shone with resolution. 'Walk? I'll do better than that! One day I'll dance for both of you. I'll dance on top of that wall, right over the threshold, for my heroes Bragoon and Sarobando. I swear it upon my solemn oath in front of you both!'

Bragoon laughed. 'Haharr, that's the stuff, me darlin'!'

Saro swung her pack up on one shoulder. 'So ye will, beauty, so ye will. Goodbye!'

They had only taken a dozen paces down the path to the south when Toran came running up and threw himself upon Bragoon. 'Take care of yoreself, brother, an' look out for Saro, too!'

Bragoon gasped for breath as he tried to pull free of Toran's embrace. 'We've taken care o' each other since we was Dibbuns. If'n ye don't let go of me, I'll get me ribs crushed afore the journey's started!'

Toran released his brother and stood weeping on the path. Bragoon looked away as Saro kissed the ottercook fondly.

'Go on now, ye great lump, back to yore feast. We'll be just fine. But keep this in mind, Toran Widegirth, when we come back to Redwall ye've got to make us a feast, as good as the one we had today. Promise?'

Toran ran back to the Abbey, shouting, 'That 'un today'll look like afternoon tea to the feast I'll make ye when ye return, I promise!'

They watched him go inside, then walked to the south wall gable and struck off southeast into Mossflower.

15

Horty stood at the dormitory window, watching as Toran returned and assisted Old Phredd in closing the main gate. Both beasts then headed for the orchard and what remained of the Summer Feast. The young hare turned to his two companions, who were sprawling about on their beds.

'Well, chaps, Toran's back an' the gate's closed, wot! That means those two ageing relics have finally gone off on the quest. Is everything ready, you blighters?'

Springald leaned over and pulled three bulging sacks from under her bed. 'These are going to take some carrying!'

Horty scoffed. 'Pish an' tush, m'gel, one can't have enough tuck. It's vital, mark m'words, bally vital!'

Fenna gathered their walking staffs and three travelling cloaks from the wall closet. 'But how do we get out of the Abbey without being spotted? It won't be dark for hours yet. Huh, you'd think Bragoon and Saro would've waited until dawn tomorrow.'

Horty sat down on his bed, ruminating. 'Hmm, you've got a jolly good point there. I'll have to think up a cunning plan. Spring, pass me one of those sacks. A chap can't think on a blinkin' empty tummy, wot!'

Springald kept a tight grip on the foodsacks. 'Forget your

confounded stomach, Horty! Get thinking, and be quick about it. We can't sit around here until it's dark and we've lost their trail.'

Horty rose and strode back to the window, muttering, 'Forget one's tum, wot? Easy for you t'say, Miss Mouse. I'm a flippin' hare, y'know. Forgetfulness of the old stomach is bally impossible to types like me . . . Ahah, Dibbuns, the very chaps!'

Flinging the window open, Horty called down to Muggum and a crew of Abbeybabes who were cavorting on the lawn below, 'What ho there, my pestilential friends!'

Shilly the squirrelbabe looked up and pointed an accusing paw. 'Naughty 'orty, you been sended up t'stay inna dormitee.'

Horty stared down his nose at the little squirrel. 'Let me inform you, my broom-tailed friend, I am here merely out of choice. I can come down when I flippin' well please. Now listen closely, you little bounders. Would you like to hear a secret, wot?'

Muggum wrinkled his button nose. 'Ee seekurt? Us'n's gurtly fond o' seekurts. Ho urr aye!'

Fenna called out in a hoarse whisper, 'Horty, what are you up to? Who are you talking to?'

Waggling his ears at her, the young hare looked secretive. 'I've just thought up a super wheeze, a plan t'get us out unnoticed, wot. Create a diversion, that's the idea. Leave this to Hortwill Braebuck, marm!'

A hogbabe named Twiglut, having grown impatient, squeaked up at the window, 'Are ya goin' a tell uz dis seekrut? Well 'urry h'up, or we go an' play wiv sticks!'

Horty waved his paws earnestly to gain the Dibbuns' attention. 'No no, don't go an' play with sticks, my tiny pincushion. I'll tell you the secret. This mornin' we went down to the pond, an' guess what? We saw lots of big fishes . . .'

Muggum butted in, 'Wurr they'm gurt hooj fishies, zurr?'

Horty stretched his paws wide, indicating their size.

140

'Huge? They were blinkin' colossal! Anyhow, they gave us rides on their backs all round the jolly old pond. Oh, it was loads o' fun, I can tell you, absoballylutely top hole an' all that, wot!'

The Dibbuns began dancing with excitement.

'Will ee fishies still be thurr?'

'Uz wanna ride on der fishies!'

Horty scratched his ears. 'Hmm, they said they'd be there late afternoon, just before evenin'. I say, you chaps, it's round about that time now, isn't it?'

Roaring delightedly, the Dibbuns thundered off in the direction of the Abbey pond.

Horty called after them, 'Have fun, you little savages. Tell the fishies Horty sent you!'

The realization of what was taking place suddenly hit Springald. Leaping up, she hurled Horty away from the window. Cupping both paws to her mouth she yelled, 'No, don't go! Come back this instant, all of you, come back!'

But the Dibbuns could not hear because of the din they were setting up. Like a small stampede, they ran out of sight around the Abbey corner.

Springald turned on Horty. 'You blathering fool, what have you done? Idiot!'

Horty flapped his ears airily. 'Creatin' a small diversion. No need to get your fur in an uproar, old thing, wot?'

Fenna's tail went stiff as Horty's foolish act dawned on her. 'You puddenbrain! Can't you see that those babes will be drowned if there isn't anybeast responsible to watch over them?'

The young hare slapped a paw to his brow. 'Oh corks, you're right! I never gave that a flippin' thought.' Leaning wide out of the window, he bellowed, 'I say, little chaps, come back this very instant. D'ye hear?'

'Dearie me, what's all the shouting about?'

Horty found himself staring down into the questioning face of Brother Gelf, who was returning some bowls to the kitchen when he heard the commotion.

Fenna pushed past Horty, her voice shrill with anxiety. 'Hurry, Brother, the Dibbuns are down at the pond alone. There's nobeast with them. Oh hurry, please!'

The mouse sped off as fast as his paws would carry him.

In a trice, the bells of Redwall were tolling out an alarm. Creatures could be seen hurrying towards the pond. Toran was out in front, shedding his apron as he ran and plunging straight into the water. Luckily, none of the Dibbuns was harmed. Most of them were garnered from the shallows by willing paws, though Toran had to swim for Muggum. The molebabe was well out of his depth, floating about like a ball of downy fur. Foremole Dwurl's resounding bass tone could be heard, calling to the Abbot, as he panted up, pushing Martha's chair.

'They'm awright, zurr h'Abbot, oanly ee bit wetted!'

Horty was shaking all over as he turned to his friends and laughed with relief. 'No harm done, chaps. At least my diversion worked, wot?'

Springald and Fenna leaped upon him, boxing his ears and kicking his bottom. They were furious.

'No thanks to you and your bright ideas!'

'You great waffling flannel-brained nincompoop!'

Horty broke loose and seized the travelling gear. 'What's done is done. Sorry, chaps, an' all that. We'd better make ourselves scarce. Let's go while the goin's good!'

Sister Setiva was towelling the babes dry with Toran's apron and her shawl; others were helping, using anything that came to paw. The shrewnurse railed on at the Dibbuns, alternately drying and hugging each one.

'Och, why wid ye want tae do sich a silly thing, mah babbies? Have ye no been told aboot playin' alone by the water, eh?'

Under the stern eyes of Abbot Carrul, Martha and a dripping wet Toran, the whole story emerged. Martha could scarcely believe her ears when she heard that it was her brother who had encouraged the little Dibbuns. Seething with righteous wrath, she turned to Toran.

'Mr Widegirth, would you kindly push me up to the Abbey? I wish to have some severe words with that brother of mine!'

The ottercook bowed politely. 'Certainly, Miz Braebuck. I'm shore there's one or two wants words with Master Horty, one of 'em bein' me!'

A procession of Redwallers followed Martha into the Abbey. The Dibbuns were enjoying the affair hugely, seeing some other beast getting blamed for their escapade. They tagged along, muttering darkly of tail chopping and bottom-skelping punishments. Some were even speculating that Horty would be boiled in a soup pan.

Their delight, however, was short-lived. Sister Setiva and some molewives whisked them off, down to Cavern Hole.

'Intae the bath, ye filthy wee beasts. Och, there's nae tellin' whit muck'n'mire ye picked up in yon pond!'

The Abbeybabes wailed piteously but to no avail.

Boom! Boom! Toran's hefty paw reverberated on the dormitory door. After a moment's silence, his voice rang out harshly.

'Master Horty, yore sister an' Father Abbot want a word with ye downstairs. Miz Fenna an Miz Springald, ye'd best show yoreselves, too!'

Martha sat down in Great Hall and waited. Soon she heard the dormitory door slam, followed by the sound of Toran's footpaws pounding down the stairs. Abbot Carrul looked over his glasses as the grim-faced ottercook entered the hall.

'Don't tell me they're gone?'

Toran sat down on a table edge. 'No trace of 'em, Father. I searched that dormitory from top't'bottom, but I'll wager they're hidin' someplace. You leave it t'me, I'll find those villains.'

The Abbot began pushing Martha's chair towards the

kitchens. 'I don't think you will somehow. Follow me, please.'

Granmum Gurvel met them as they entered the kitchen. Clearly in a proper tizzy, the poor old molecook began chattering angrily. 'Foive gurt h'apple puddens, ee gurt meadowcreamy troifle, strawbee scones, celery an h'onion flans, pasties full o' carrut'n'gravy. They'm all be gonned! Burrrrrooooh! Wait'll oi get'n moi paws on ee Dibbun rarscalls. H'all moi luvverly arternoon bakin' furr tomorrers lunchen an' supper. Varnished!'

Martha kept her eyes downcast as she informed Gurvel, 'It wasn't Dibbuns, Granmum. It was my brother Horty and his friends, Fenna and Springald. They're the thieves who raided your kitchen. Now they've run off to join Bragoon and Saro on the quest.'

Toran's rudder rapped loudly on the floor. 'Of course, that's it, Martha! But why'd they have to cause so much upset to everybeast – us, an' the Dibbuns, an' Gurvel? Why?'

Abbot Carrul raised his eyes and sighed. 'Sadly, that's the way most young 'uns behave at that age. Forbidding them to do something is like encouraging them. Unfortunately, they do things without thinking.'

Old Phredd shuffled in, bowing creakily to the Abbot. 'I just found my main gate open, but me and young Toran barred it shut this afternoon. How did that happen, eh, eh?'

Carrul patted the Gatekeeper's bony paw. 'No doubt you've closed it again, Phredd. It was Horty, Fenna and Springald – they've gone off adventuring.'

Phredd chuckled drily. 'Just like Bragoon and Saro when they were younger, eh, eh?'

Junty Cellarhog, who had just come into the room and heard Phredd, thrust his big paws into his apron belt. 'No, ole feller, not like Saro an' Bragoon at all. Them two was born tough, rovin' was in their blood. But young Horty doesn't remember anytime afore comin' to Redwall, an' both maids was borned 'ere. They don't know wot 'tis like

144

out there in the big world. I think they'll 'ave to learn t'grow up fast.'

Martha felt a pang of alarm at Junty's words. 'What does he mean, Toran?'

The ottercook explained. 'Well, miss, look at their vittles. Apple puddens, strawberry scones an' a meadowcream trifle? No proper travelbeast'd take such stuff along. Huh, it'd be smashed t'bits afore they got a day's march in, eh Gurvel?'

The old molecook nodded wisely. 'Aye, et surpinkly wudd, zurr. Oi maked speshul marchin' vikkles furr ee uther two. Lots o' cheese, ee h'oatbreads, summ candied fruits an' canteens o' moi gudd dannelion'n'burdock corjul furr drinken.'

Martha grasped Toran's paw. 'You don't think they'll come to any harm, do you?'

The ottercook's eyes softened. 'Don't ye fret yoreself, Martha. If'n they picks up my brother an' Saro's trail, they'll be safe enough. Mind, though, they won't get no special treatment. Horty an' his pals will learn the hard way. Now, if'n they lose the trail, Redwall's stickin' up in plain view for a good distance. Once yore brother gets hungry, he'll dash back to this Abbey like a scalded toad. The others are sure to follow. If'n ye pardon me sayin', Martha, Horty's a natural glutton. He won't stray too far without vittles – starvation's a hard taskmaster!'

The haremaid fiddled with the fringe of her lap rug. 'I'd feel happier if somebeast could overtake them and bring them back, so they don't get lost or hurt.'

The Abbot looked at Toran and Junty Cellarhog, both big, stout beasts and very competent. 'Perhaps our Martha is right. Do you think you two could catch up with them before it gets too dark?'

Junty took off his canvas apron and nodded to the otter-cook. 'We'll give it a try, Father. Are ye ready, mate? Come on!'

They left the Abbey by the main gate. No sooner had

Carrul and Old Phredd closed and barred it than Junty and Toran were pounding on the timbers to get back in.

Toran's voice was loud and urgent.

'Open up quick! There's vermin comin' down the path from the north! They're headin' this way. Hurry and let us in!'

BOOK TWO

'If only they were back here at Redwall'

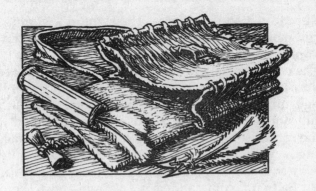

16

Late that same afternoon, the vermin gang had been keeping to the woodlands. On Badredd's orders they followed the path. Stopping for a breather, the little fox sighted Redwall Abbey in the distance, showing above the trees. He scurried out on to the path, pointing and yelling, 'Aharr, there 'tis, mates, the Abbey place! I told ye I'd find it, 'twas me who saw it first!'

As he ran forwards, the cutlass, which he had pushed into his belt, tangled in his footpaws, causing him to trip. He lay sprawled on the path, still shouting, 'Wait'll I gets me paws on that magic sword!'

Halfchop sneered, 'Look at 'im, willyer, the flamin' fool. I swear, Flinky, dat stoopid oaf'll get us all killed!'

The crafty stoat chuckled. 'Ah, sure enough, he's a grand, brave beast. I'd sooner serve under Badredd than Burrad or Skrodd. Those two would have made us march in front, an' led from the rear. Let the fearless chief run an' meet the foe. Us pore ould pawsloggers will just keep our heads down an' follow from a safe distance.'

Crinktail was in agreement with her mate. 'Aye, whoever's inside o' that place will prob'ly see us comin' from their walltops. Wot was it that Burrad said, that those Abbey creatures was all peaceable Woodlanders? So we may as well put on a show o' force. The sight of a vermin gang might make 'em open up those gates to us – providin' they knows wot's good for 'em!'

The crew strolled out on to the path, deliberately setting a slow pace, keeping Badredd well ahead of them. Flinky sang a quiet ditty as a warning to his mates. The little fox could not quite hear the words, but he assumed it was some sort of song for marching into battle. He swaggered along, a good half-spearthrow in front, waving the unwieldy cutlass with regained dignity, feeling every inch the great Badredd, commander of a vermin crew. The others followed at a safe distance, sniggering at the words of Flinky's song.

'When the clouds of arrows fly,
keep yore heads down.
Let the brave ones charge on by,
keep yore heads down.
When the heroes' blood runs red,
an' yore scared to raise yore head,
just be glad that you ain't dead,
keep yore heads down!

Ye won't win no medals here,
keep yore heads down.
Don't be fools who know no fear,
keep yore heads down.
We can all lay low an' sing,
duckin' spears an' stones from sling.
Let 'em chuck most anything,
but keep yore heads down!'

Amid smothered giggles and hoots, Slipback and Juppa made disparaging remarks behind their leader's back.

'Haw haw, lookit the way 'is bottom waggles when 'e puts on a swagger. Looks like two sour apples in a sack!'

'Aye, an' if'n 'e don't stop wavin' that blade around, 'e'll chop 'is own tail off. Wot d'ye reckon, mate, does that liddle smidge look like a vermin warrior who'd terrify those Abbeybeasts?'

'Maybe they'll laugh theirselves to death at the sight of 'im. Heeheeheee!'

Flinky gazed up in awe as the impressive red sandstone Abbey loomed closer. He muttered to Rogg and Floggo, 'Huh, if Badredd gives the order to charge that place, well, I'll be chargin', shore enough. I'll be runnin' the other way, like a duck wid its tail on fire!'

The weasel brothers were not much given to merriment, but Flinky's remark tickled them so much that they guffawed loudly.

Badredd came running back brandishing his cutlass. 'Wot's so funny, eh, can I share the joke?'

Flinky shrugged disarmingly. 'Ah now, we wasn't laughin' at ye at all. 'Twas just that we're 'appy for ye. Yore a good chief, an' soon the magic sword'll be yores. Ye deserve it fer bein' a grand ould leader, so ye do. Ain't that right, mates? Badredd's the best boss we've ever 'ad!'

Half believing Flinky's flattery, Badredd eyed the gang and nodded approvingly. 'Lissen, mates, we could be a good crew if'n we tried. Now wipe the grins offa yore gobs an' form up in twos. We'll march straight up to that Abbey an' put the fear o' Hellgates into those peaceable bumpkins. Try t'look more like a gang o' killers. Wave yore weapons about an' snarl loud, as if yore ready t'do murder!'

Flinky glanced up at the high battlements. Already he saw heads poking up over them in the gathering gloom. Thinking quickly, the stoat slid down into the ditch on the path's opposite side. He beckoned Badredd. 'A nighttime charge might go wrong, Chief. D'ye not think we oughta figger out some kind of ould plan, afore we go rushin' at a buildin' that size?'

The little fox turned his attention to the walltops. Lots of heads were beginning to appear there. He climbed down into the ditch, alongside Flinky, knowing that what the stoat said made sense. 'Aye, let's, er, make up a scheme . . . Every-beast down 'ere!'

The remaining gang members obeyed promptly. Flinky patted Badredd's back. 'Sure, that's wot I likes about ye, Chief, yore a true fox, a born slayer, but a grand an' crafty ould planner. Hoho, those creatures in there'll get the shock o' their lives when we turns up outside their doorstep tomorrer!'

Badredd was puzzled. 'Tomorrer?'

Crinktail caught on, knowing her mate was trying to put off invading Redwall for as long as possible. She backed Flinky up. 'Haharr, clever move, Chief. Tomorrer's the best time t'do it!'

Beyond a straight charge, Badredd had no real plan. He decided to hear Flinky out, knowing the stoat was no fool.

Flinky explained eagerly. ' 'Tis dark now, y'see, an' we're in strange territory. The gang can get a good night's rest down 'ere. When you've thought up yore scheme, we'll be ready fer a fresh start, an' catch 'em nappin' at dawn! Now that's wot I calls a smart move, thought up by a smart fox!'

Unaccustomed to compliments, Badredd enjoyed the feeling of having everybeast waiting on their leader's word. Flicking his tail round slowly, he stroked it as foxes do when they are pleased. 'Right, we rest 'ere, gang, that's my orders!'

He missed the nudge exchanged between Crinktail and Flinky as they lay down and closed their eyes. Flinky murmured but loud enough to be heard by all, 'Ain't we the lucky ones, havin' a gangleader like Badredd.'

Starlit darkness had fallen as Abbot Carrul made his way up the north wallsteps on to the ramparts. A frown creased his brow when he saw the throng of Redwallers crowding the parapet.

'Friends, listen to me, please. There's no need for all of you up here. With vermin about, it's not safe to stand look-ing over the battlements. Anybeast who is not required up here, please go down now. Sister Setiva, Sister Portula, will you see those Dibbuns down the stairs, it's time they were in their beds anyhow.'

Toran and Junty, who had already joined Foremole Dwurl and Brother Weld, were at the northwest wall corner. Carrul hastened to join them. 'Is there really a vermin band out there? Where are they now?'

Toran answered reassuringly, 'There's no great army o' them, Father, I only counted about eight. Might be more to come, but I ain't spotted 'em yet.'

Junty made way for the Abbot to look between the battlements as Toran pointed. 'Look, they've lit a small fire, in the ditch, just further up the path there. Wonder wot they're up to?' A red-gold glow showed from the ditch, where Toran was pointing.

Foremole blinked. 'Oi aspeck they'm cooken ee supper.'

The Abbot looked to Toran. 'What do you think?'

Thumping his rudder thoughtfully against the wallside, the ottercook speculated, 'Well, there's no way a crew that size could attack Redwall. I think we'd best do nothin' for the present, Father. But let's watch every move they make. We'll post sentries on the walls, just a few who can watch 'em, while keepin' low. Who can tell – maybe they're only passin' by this way. Per'aps they're bound someplace else. I wish Bragoon an' Saro would've stayed a day or two longer – we could really do with 'em right now!'

Foremole smote the wall with a heavy digging claw. 'Boi 'okey we'm cudd, they'm udd know wot to do abowt ee varmints. But thurr bee's h'only us'n's, yurr!'

Toran could sense that the Abbot was waiting for him to take charge. He waved down to Martha, waiting in her chair on the lawn, then spoke. 'Father, maybe ye an' Martha could get a few helpers an' search around for anythin' that would be useful as a weapon. I've got a feelin' they won't make a move 'til tomorrow. We should be ready for 'em by then, though it prob'ly won't come to that. I'll stay up here with Junty, Weld an' Foremole on watch.'

The Abbot went down to the lawn and pushed Martha back to the Abbey, explaining what was happening and what he had seen. The young haremaid could tell by Abbot Carrul's face that he was very worried.

Wirga was long past her best seasons, a wrinkled, toothless old sea rat, yet Raga Bol kept her with his crew. She was useless as a fighter or a forager, but she possessed other skills. There was little that Wirga did not know about wounds and the treatment of injuries. Her powers as a healer and her knowledge of herbs, nostrums and remedies made the old vermin invaluable to the ignorant crewrats. But there was yet another art Wirga practised – that of a Seer. Raga Bol, as captain, was the only one she allowed to consult her, and then only in times of crisis.

Wirga crouched by the fire, watching Bol. They were camped among some wooded hills where the red sandstone rocks of Mossflower jutted out in shelflike formation. It was twilight. The sea rat crew had slain a small colony of wood-mice, and were leisurely plundering their shattered dwellings. Raga Bol and Wirga sat on a hilltop, isolated from the noisy rabble below.

The old sea rat knew that her captain wished to consult her. He had given her half a roasted dove and a goblet of his personal grog – this was always a sign that she was needed. Wirga took out her pouch of charms and selected half a large musselshell. It was edged with yellow on the inside, glistening grey at the centre, with three partially grown purple mussel's pearls protruding from its broad end.

Filling the shell with water, she gazed into it. 'Thy appetite is not good of late?'

Raga Bol licked the sharp tip of his silver pawhook in silence as Wirga continued.

'Sleep eludes thee, thou are weary. None can rest easy in thy presence. Even I fear to speak of certain things – aye, things that trouble thee.'

With a curt nod, the sea rat captain dismissed the four guards who attended him from twilight to dawn. When they had gone off to join the others, he took a furtive glance over his shoulder.

Drawing close to the Seer, Raga Bol dropped his voice to a hoarse whisper. 'Fear not, speak openly to me, ye won't be harmed.'

Keeping her eyes on the water-filled shell, the old Seer proceeded, her voice now a sibilant hiss. 'If thine enemy lives, he must die. Only then can Raga Bol find peace of mind. Thy foe's death will release thee.'

The sea rat captain's eyes shone feverishly. 'Does the stripedog still live? Tell me!'

Wirga turned away from the shell, confronting him. 'When did thou last see this stripedog?'

Bol's red-rimmed eyes stared back at her. 'This very noon, aye, in full sunlight. 'Twas when we stopped to rest. I was so tired that I dozed off awhile. The sun beat through my closed lids, makin' everythin' go red. That's when I saw the stripedog. Gettin' off a strange craft he was, where that broadstream from the nor'east bends away from the trees an' woodlands. Ye recall the spot, 'twas where we slayed those two shrews. The stripedog pointed to the bodies an' looked straight at me. "They will be avenged, I am coming for ye, Raga Bol!" Those were his very words.'

Wirga went back to contemplating the water in the shell, then continued, 'Thee told him to go away and join the deadbeasts at Hellgates, because he was already slain by thee. But the giant stripedog kept coming. He was frightening to look upon, with his face cleaved wide, but scarred an' stitched together by somebeast. Do I not speak truly?'

Raga Bol gasped, in awe of the Seer and her powers. 'Aye, true, but how did ye know? Did ye see the beast, too?'

She smiled. 'Wirga sees many things unknown to others.'

What she did not say was that she had been observing her captain for days – listening, watching, taking all in. Every nightmare, every time Raga Bol called out, in the brief times he did sleep, were memorized by Wirga. She had a complete picture of it all – from the moment Raga Bol had struck the badger to every event since.

The sea rat captain brought his face even closer to the Seer. His breath was hot on her jaw, his voice half threat and half plea. 'I can't fight a dream, so I'm waitin' on yore word. Tell me wot t'do, I must be rid of the stripedog!'

Wirga replied, 'Knowest thou my three sons?'

Bol knew the ones she spoke of, though not too well. They were a furtive trio, a bit undersized for sea rats, always last to fight but first to grab the plunder. He was not impressed with them, and saw the three as background vermin who never put themselves forwards or appeared bold, like proper sea rats often do.

The captain shrugged. 'Aye, I know 'em, they ain't no great shakes as fighters. That big stripedog could eat the three of 'em!'

Wirga rocked back and forth on her haunches, chuckling. 'Heehee, well said. But give 'em a skilled tracker, one who could lead 'em to the place of thy dream, an' my sons will make an end of thy stripedog, believe me!'

Raga Bol drew his scimitar, allowing the firelight to gleam across its lethal blade. 'If'n' I never finished the bigbeast with a blow o' this, how could three runts like that do the job?'

Wirga drew from her pouch a section of bamboo, cut off near the joint and sealed at one end with beeswax. Carefully, she broke away the wax and upended the cylinder. Six long thorns spilled out, each one tipped with crimson dye and plumed with the short feathers of some exotic bird. She stayed Raga Bol's paw as he reached to pick one up.

'Keep away from such things. They can kill ten times more swiftly than the most venomous snake!'

The sea rat captain pulled back his paw. 'Poison?'

Using her long pawnails, the Seer divided the thorns into three groups of two. 'Once one of these little beauties pricks the skin, even the greatest warrior cannot stand. Poison, from far isles across the southern seas. My three sons know how to use these darts. Warriors they may not be, but assassins they surely are. Give 'em a tracker to lead 'em to the streambend. They will seek out thy stripedog an' slay 'im.'

Raga Bol stood abruptly, peering over the hilltop rocks at his crew below until he saw the one he required. 'Ahoy, Jibsnout!'

A big, competent-looking sea rat saluted. 'Cap'n?'

Raga Bol called back to him, 'Bring Wirga's three sons up 'ere. I've got a task for the four of ye.'

Night had fallen as the sons of Wirga left the hilltop, following Jibsnout. The tracker had a blanket with some food rolled into it thrown over his shoulder, and a well-honed dagger dangling from a cord around his neck.

Once they were off the hill and bound back along the trail, Jibsnout halted and glared contemptuously at the three smaller rats. It was obvious he did not enjoy their company. He pointed the dagger at each of them in turn.

'Lissen t'me, slimesnouts. I don't like yew three one liddle bit. But I gotta do the job wot Cap'n Bol gave me – to take ye back to where the broadstream bends at the edge o' this forest. Wot ye do then is carry out the cap'n's orders. 'Tis up to ye how y'do that, an' nought t'do wid me. But get this straight: ye do yore job an' I'll do mine. So stay outta my way an' mind yore manners around me. Step on my paws or look the wrong way at me an' I'll gut all three o' ye wid this blade o' mine! Unnerstood?'

The sons of Wirga never answered; they merely looked at one another and exchanged sly leers. This did not improve Jibsnout's opinion of them. Turning on his paw, he set off at a rapid pace into the dark woodlands, growling back to the odd trio, 'Move yoreselves! We'll be marchin' night'n'day, an' only stoppin' for a bite or a nap when I says so. If'n ye don't keep up, I'll leave ye behind. Hah, try explainin' yoreselves to Raga Bol when ye get back then, I dare ye!'

17

Three days earlier, Lonna had bid farewell to Garfo Trok at the broadstream bend. The last he saw of the otter was Garfo singing loud ballads about food, or the lack of it, paddling back upstream to the northeast country. Lonna had enjoyed his time with the garrulous otter aboard his boat *Beetlebutt*. The big badger felt lonely as he trudged off into Mossflower, but soon his loneliness was replaced by rage, as he remembered the pitiful bodies of the two dead shrews. Before they parted, he and Garfo had buried them on the bankside.

All that day the scar across Lonna's face felt sore and tight. His head ached whenever he thought of Raga Bol and his murderous crew, and his back wound began bothering him, causing him to limp as he pressed doggedly onwards. The woodlands were quiet and peaceful, with sundappled green light cascading through the overhead foliage. Distant birdsong sounded muted, bees droned lazily in the midday calm. Lonna ignored the beauties of nature, his eyes constantly darting from side to side, paws ever ready to seek bow and shafts.

At midnoon the big stripedog halted by a rippling brook in a mossy sward. Resting awhile, he ate sparingly from the sea otter's food pack – a crust of nutbread, some fine ripe cheese and a few scallions he found growing nearby – and drank deeply from the brook. Still sitting with his footpaws in the water, Lonna washed his head and face, then, leaning forwards, immersed his face and head for several long intervals. The cold, clear brookwater refreshed him greatly. He stood up to leave, rubbing the small of his back and swaying from side to side, testing the limp in his footpaw, to judge how it was feeling.

A sense that he was being watched came over Lonna. Continuing his exercises, he spoke out in a voice loud enough for any eavesdropper to hear.

' 'Tis not good manners to spy on a beast. Come out and show yourself. Don't be afraid, you can see I'm no sea rat!'

An elderly female squirrel, clad in a russet and yellow tunic, dropped out of the trees, landing right in front of him. She was a perky, cheerful-looking creature, but he could see by the way she toted a small javelin she was ready for anything.

Looking him up and down, she chattered boldly away, 'Chahah! Me could tell ya wasn't sea ratta. Warramarrer bigbeast, ya back be hurted?'

Completely disarmed, Lonna smiled ruefully. 'Just a bit, marm, but 'tis getting better by the day, thank ye. My name is Lonna Bowstripe.'

The squirrel bobbed him a neat curtsy. 'Me's Figalok Twigbenda, pleasin' t'meetcha. I fix ya back, Lonna, folla me!'

Lonna took an immediate liking to Figalok, following her without question. She was so very swift that he had to hurry to keep up. Figalok halted alongside a big, ancient hornbeam tree and began giving rapid orders.

'See da branch stickin' out up above? Me wancha t'jump up an' grab it tight. Chakahoo! Berra take offa dat bigbow an' arrers. Cheeh! Howcha make dat – cut a yewtree down an' purra string on it? Dat a big bow, sure 'nuff!'

Lonna smiled at her observation. When he took off his bow, it stood near three times the height of Figalok. Placing his quiver of arrows to one side, he leaped up, grabbed the hornbeam limb and hung there, dangling. The branch was quite stout enough to hold his weight.

'Is this alright, marm? What do I do now?'

Figalok walked around him. 'Ya jus' hang there like a h'apple. Are ya plenny strong, Lonna?'

He stared down at her. 'Aye, strong enough.'

Figalok jumped up and sat on Lonna's footpaws, facing him. She grabbed his legs to steady herself. 'Keep ya paws still now, bigbeast, don't ya kick me off!'

Figalok began jerking Lonna back and forth, using him like a swing. 'Chahah, dis do ya good, keep tight hold!'

For what seemed like an eternity she continued the swinging motion, back and forth, forwards and back. Lonna's own bodyweight, with the added burden of the squirrel, began to tell after awhile. She stared up at his clenched jaws.

'Ya wanna leggo now? Dat was a good ride.'

Lonna gasped, 'Aye, I'd best come down before I drop!'

Figalok leaped to the ground, skipping to one side. 'Rightee, ya can leggo, Lonna!'

He dropped gingerly, expecting the fall to jolt his back. Surprisingly, it did not.

The squirrel gave his back a thump. 'Wassamarra witcha? Walk round, jump 'bout! Chahah, ya back be good as new now. Me fixed lotsa backs!'

Lonna's back felt easy and relaxed, and he was not getting a single twinge from the footpaw, which had been bothering him. He walked, then trotted, jumping up and down forcefully, putting all his weight on back and footpaw. Revelling in the newfound freedom of movement, Lonna dashed at Figalok, meaning to embrace her.

'I'm better, there's no more pain! Figalok, you marvellous creature, how can I thank you?'

She shot up the trunk of the hornbeam, protesting, 'Keep ya big paws offa me, or I be crushed flat! Betcha hungry, eh? Bigbeasts must get plenty hungry. Folla me!'

Figalok scuttled through the woodlands, with Lonna hard on her tail. She halted at the base of a three-topped oak, which grew in close proximity to a beech, an elm and a sycamore. The upper limbs of all three trees intertwined with the oak, forming a wide platform.

The squirrel twitched her tail at Lonna. 'Ya wait der, me send ya rope down!' She shot lightly up the oak trunk, vanishing into the foliage.

A moment later Figalok reappeared, surrounded by a crowd of tiny squirrelbabes. They squeaked and squealed at the size of Lonna, pointing and giggling.

'Cheehow, nanny, wherecha find dat 'un?'

'Weehoo, must be da biggest beast in alla lands!'

'Choowhee, never see'd not'ink like 'im in me life!'

Shoving them out of her way, Figalok pushed a thick rope down. It was knotted at close intervals to make climbing easy. Shouldering his bow and quiver, Lonna began scaling the rope. Figalok was hard put to keep back the press of little squirrels.

'Chahah, gerra ya back an' make way for me friend. Take no notice a dese likka pesters, Lonna, up ya come!'

Lonna found the climb quite easy. The squirrelbabes shrieked and scurried off as he joined Figalok on the bough. She nodded approvingly.

'Not'ink wrong wirra dat back now. Me make a squirrel outta ya, bigbeast. Berra get vikkles quick, afore they alla gone!'

The squirrels' dray was an amazing sight. Branches were cunningly woven twixt the network of bows and limbs between the four trees. Lonna found it safe to walk upon, though he trod carefully. At the oak's centre was a wide platform with a charcoal oven set on slabs of slate. Upwards of a dozen older squirrels were preparing a meal there.

Literally scores of babes and young ones festooned the place, hanging by their tails or balancing nimbly on the slenderest of twigs.

Figalok proudly introduced her newfound friend to the assemblage. 'Ya see this 'un, he be Lonna bigbeast. Figalok finded 'im. Lonna be hungry, berra give 'im lotsa vikkles!'

Four older squirrels hurried to serve the big badger, plying him with huge portions of a thick, sweet porridge. It was a mixture of wild oats, fruit and nuts boiled in honey and rhubarb juice. Lonna was given a full flagon of elderflower and pennycress cordial. Both the food and drink tasted delicious. Figalok sat beside him, watching in awe as he satisfied his considerable appetite.

'Cheehoo! Betcha mamma was glad when ya leaved home!'

Lonna chuckled. 'Who knows, maybe she might have been, but I don't ever remember having a mother.'

Gradually the squirrelbabes had been inching closer to the big badger. When he mentioned that he had never known a mother, their sympathy was instantly aroused. They surrounded Lonna, sitting on his lap and shoulders, climbing on his back and paws. He was totally engulfed by the babes, one of them even perched upon his head.

Their tiny paws patted him as they squeaked sorrowfully, 'Aaaaah, never haved no mamma, pore bigbeast!'

'Must bee'd tebbirle, not 'avin' no mamma!'

'Didya cried an' weeped alla time for ya mamma?'

Figalok waved her paws at them. 'Chachafah! Shooshoo! Gerroffa 'im, leave Lonna alone!'

But the badger defended them. 'Let them be, marm. I like the little 'uns, they're so small and friendly. Besides, they're not at all afraid of my face, the scars and stitching.'

Figalok shrugged. 'Chaaaah, why be they 'fraid? Likkle 'uns never see'd a bigbeast afore. They know ya be a goodbeast, me see dat, too. Not matter what ya lookin' like.'

Before he could express his gratitude for the kind words,

a tubby squirrel mother, with a fine bush of tail, took the empty bowl from Lonna and called to the little ones. 'Hachowa! Sing for a bigbeast, sing 'im Twing Twing.'

The elders stood by, smiling fondly as the squirrelbabes sang their simple song for Lonna. What they lacked in melody, they made up in raucous enthusiasm, some of them performing dancing leaps and hops in time to the tune.

'Twing twing up inna trees,
twirlin' me tail around,
lighter'n fevvers onna breeze,
never not fall to a ground!'

These were the only words they seemed to know, but they carried on singing the verse again and again, with the renewed gusto of babes enjoying themselves. Lonna held both paws wide, his face wreathed in a happy grin. The little ones swung on him, squeaking away lustily.

They were well into the seventh repetition of their song when one of the elders gave forth a piercing whistle. Like lightning, both infants and elders vanished into the foliage. A massive black shadow flew low overhead.

Lonna looked around, but not a squirrel could be seen anywhere. He called out into the densely leafed treetops. 'Figalok, where are you, what's going on?'

The elderly squirrel popped her head out from behind a branch, her eyes wide with fright as she chattered, 'Bad, bad! Rakkaw Ravin badbird! Look ya uppina sky!'

Glancing upwards, Lonna beheld a raven of startling wingspread, circling high in the bright afternoon sky. Reaching for his bow, he picked an arrow from the quiver and laid it on the string, keeping his eyes on the raven.

'Don't worry, marm, that bird won't harm you while I'm here.'

Figalok stayed under cover, shaking her head sadly. 'Rakkaw Ravin after babes, ya watch 'im, he soon be down.

Steal likkle 'un, take what he want. Badbird, bigga strong an' fast. Nobeast stoppa Ravin!'

As Figalok spoke, a tiny squirrel panicked. Squealing shrilly, she hopped out on a long branch. There she stood, covering her face, rigid with terror, and in clear sight of the foe. Sensing a quick kill, the raven folded its wings and dropped down like a thunderbolt.

Instinctively, Lonna stretched the bowstring tight against his clenched jaw. Closing one eye, he aimed at the bird and loosed his shaft. With a sound like an angry wasp, the arrow zipped upwards, taking the raven through its glossy, plumed body. Instantly slain, its huge wings spread wide open, the raven cartwheeled through the air like a dark, tattered cloak, landing with a thud on the woodland floor beneath the oak, transfixed by the badger's well-aimed arrow.

Chattering madly, the squirrels started pounding the body. The older ones used small slings, from which they hurled small pebbles. Emerging from cover, the babes tossed down pawfuls of leaves and pieces of twig, all the while screeching insults at their slain enemy.

'Yaa yaa, not eat us no more, Rakkaw!'

'Yeeheeee, eata dis twig if ya be hungry, bigbird!'

'Hahaaay, Rakkaw, we burn ya, burn ya, burn ya!'

Some of the older squirrels threw down glowing charcoal from their oven. The smell of charring feathers reached Lonna's nostrils. Shocked by the frenzy of hatred the squirrels were working themselves into, he called out in a stern voice, 'Here now, stop that, you'll cause a woodland fire!'

Sensing the danger, Figalok joined Lonna. 'Chahah, ye heara bigbeast, stoppa throwin' fires!'

They obeyed reluctantly. Figalok sent some older squirrels down to fetch water and quench the smoking embers. She touched the big badger's taut bowstring.

'Dat a good bigbow, me thank ya, Lonna. Rakkaw Ravin gone'd forever now, thank ya!'

Hanging up his bow and quiver on a nearby branch, Lonna sighed, 'I wish that had been a sea rat!'

Figalok pointed west and slightly south. 'Sea ratters over data way.'

The badger became immediately alert. 'Where, over that way, have you seen them?'

Smiling slyly, the elderly squirrel nodded. 'Ho, me see 'em, awright! Lotsa sea ratters marchin' through. Chahah, they no see us, though. Squirrel know how ta hide.' She tapped her paw four times against the oak tree. 'Me see dat many sea ratters a-comin' back thisaway though.'

Lonna grabbed up his bow and quiver. 'Where, when?'

Figalok explained. 'Yistaday. Me was far from this place, lookin' for h'almind nuts. See dem, one bigbeast.'

She tapped her paw on the oak three times. 'Dis a many smalla sea ratters comin' disaway. No worry, Lonna, dey not see ya, we hide up here plenny good, eh? Asides, dey still more'n a day 'way, not travel fast like squirrel.'

Lonna seized the thick, knotted rope and began clambering down to the woodland floor. 'Sea rats at last! I've got a score to settle with those murdering scum. Figalok, will you show me where they are?'

The squirrel made it down to the ground before him. 'A course me will – least I can do for ya, bigbeast. We go now, catch 'em around at dawn, travel alla night, eh?'

Lonna shook her small paw gratefully. 'Thank you, my friend!'

The squirrels appeared much upset at Lonna leaving, particularly the little ones. 'Don't go bigbeast, ya stay here wid us for longa time!'

One bold little maid thought she knew the reason for the badger's departure. She shook her head at the others. 'Gorra let Lonna go, he gotta find 'is mamma.'

Lonna ruffled her downy little brush. 'That's right, miss. Now take care of your mammas, and watch out for ravens.'

Figalok kicked the dead bird's carcass scornfully. 'No

more Rakkaw Ravin come here. We hangin' dis one up inna tree, dat scare 'em off. Chahaah, you betcha!'

Following the agile Figalok, Lonna trotted off south and west into the thickness of Mossflower. As they went, he envisioned the evil face of Raga Bol – concentrating hard on it, as only a creature of fate and destiny like a badger can.

'I'm coming, Raga Bol! I am Lonna Bowstripe, and I'm coming!'

18

After marching all night on what he had fondly imagined was a southeast course, Horty was totally fatigued. In dawn's pale light, he slumped down in a fern grove, grumbling.

'It's no blinkin' use, you chaps, I've got to take a jolly old snooze. Ahah! But first we must deal with the inner hare. Brekkers beckons the poor lad's slim stomach, wot?'

Furious, Springald grabbed the provision sack from his paw, ranting on at him, 'Food, food, food, don't you ever think of anything else? Here we are, in the middle of nowhere, and you're yowling about brekkers after eating all night as we marched! We're lost, you lop-eared oaf, lost!'

Horty tried unsuccessfully to tug the sack back from her. 'Lost? Don't talk piffle'n'woffle, m'dear gel, we're merely restin'. Now don't be so flippin' moody, an' pass the scoff!'

Springald dealt him a wallop with the soggy ration sack. 'You've no idea where we're going. You've completely lost Bragoon's and Saro's tracks, and we could have been walking in circles for all you know! You're an idiot, d'you hear me?'

Horty twiddled his ears and smiled at Fenna. 'Rather pretty when she's angry, ain't she? Spring, me old beauty, why don't y'give your face a rest. We'll find the right track sooner or later. Or would you prefer to toodle back to the Abbey an' face the blinkin' music, wot wot?'

Fenna sat down wearily beside Horty, then closed her eyes. 'Good grief, I'm bone worn-out. He's right y'know, Spring, arguing isn't going to get us anywhere. Let's have a bite to eat and a rest. Give him the bag.'

Springald threw herself moodily down amid the ferns. 'Here, take your confounded food. I wish I'd never left Redwall in the first place.'

The gluttonous young hare seized the sack eagerly. 'I wish you hadn't, either – there'd be more scoff for me an' Fenn, wot. Hawhawhaw!'

Fenna looked into the sack to select her breakfast. She drew back with a look of disgust. 'Yukk, I'm not eating any of that mess. Look at it, pie and trifle squashed up with onion gravy pastie. Just the sight of it makes me sick. Nobeast could stomach that!'

Horty dipped his paw in and came up with an unappetizing lump of sludge. 'Well tut tut, little miss fussy apron. What's wrong with the flippin' scoff, it's good food ain't it? Please yourself, marm, but I'm jolly well starved.'

He began eating with evident relish. 'Mmmmm, you bods don't know what you're missin'. Nothin' like a spot o' tucker to settle the old tum for a good sound snooze, wot!'

This time it was Fenna who lost her temper. She tugged Horty's ears sharply. 'Listen to me, you great ten-bellied buffoon, you were supposed to be supplies officer, remember? You appointed yourself in charge of provisions. There'll be no naps or snoozes for you while us two are still hungry, so shift yourself and get us some breakfast, right away!'

Horty made a languid gesture. 'There's two other sacks there, or ain't you blinkin' well noticed? You can open 'em yourself!'

Where Fenna upended one of the sacks, a great splodge

of squashed pastie and meadowcream trifle splattered among the ferns.

Springald inspected the contents of the other sack. 'Ahah, scones and cheesebread. But guess what, pals? Our genius packed 'em along with a flask of mint tea and one of strawberry cordial. Of course he never made sure the stoppers of the flasks were on tight, so we've got another sackful of sludge. Oh, Horty, how could you?'

The gluttonous hare was munching pawfuls of the mixture from the second sack. He smacked his lips loudly. 'Sorry about the blinkin' flask stoppers, chaps, but I didn't want to make too much noise, y'see. Mmmm, rather good this stuff. Hawhaw, I've just invented apple'n'rhubarb'n'-gooseberry surprise. Hmm, there's some soft white celery cheese in here, too . . . excellent mixture. I must give old Gurvel the recipe when we return t'the jolly old Abbey, wot!'

Springald peered into the third sack, wrinkling her nose in distaste. 'How could anybeast even think about eating that?'

Horty took the sack and sampled a pawful. 'An' what, pray, is the matter with it? 'Tis perfectly top-hole scoff! Trouble with you two is y'don't know how to blinkin' rough it. You've become spoiled by Abbey life, too picky by far!'

Springald took hold of a sack. 'Go and get a bath, Horty.'

The young hare grinned at her. 'Not right now, thanks, I don't need a bath.'

She upended the sack over his head. 'You do now!'

Horty rose slowly, making two eyeholes in the mess of flan and pudding, then sucked his paws. 'Gettin' a bit touchy, aren't we?' He saw Fenna take hold of another sack and fled. 'Hello out there, any frogs or tadpoles know a good stream where a chap can get a wash an' brush up, wot?'

Fenna sat down and rested her head between both paws. 'We should've known better than letting him go for supplies. 'Tis our own fault, I suppose. The fool never even thought of bringing a flint along to make fire.'

Springald produced a chunk of crystal from her belt pouch. 'That's no trouble. I got this off Old Phredd. He told me how to use it . . . watch this.'

She held the crystal close to some unlit twigs and moss, focusing until it caught the sunrays and concentrated them in a small bright point. Instantly, the moss began smouldering. After a short while, a single puff of the mousemaid's breath caused a slim column of flame to rise.

Fenna was both delighted and astonished. 'That's marvellous! At least we can boil some water and pick mint leaves to make tea. There's plenty of wild mint growing round here. What's the matter, Springald?'

The mousemaid kicked the sack she had upended. 'Guess what? Horty forgot to bring anything along to boil it in.'

Fenna sat down beside her friend. 'Right, that's the last time I listen to the mad plans and stupid ideas of a hare. We'd best go back to Redwall!'

Springald did not relish the suggestion. 'Redwall? Imagine having to face the Father Abbot, and Sister Setiva, and Granmum Gurvel and all the rest! I'd sooner sit out here for a season or two and starve, until they've forgotten about us drowning those Dibbuns, plundering the kitchens and disobeying the Abbot. Lack a day, we'd be scrubbing floors and washing pots until we were old and grey!'

Springald's despairing thoughts were interrupted by Horty's voice. 'Yowch ouch, I say, leggo me blinkin' ears, you bounders!'

Horty appeared, dripping wet, with six big, mottled rats dragging him along. Their garb was a curious mixture of leaves, shrubbery and purple tattoos. All of them were armed with cudgels and long knives.

Springald let out a cry of alarm, Fenna seized an old kitchen knife and leaped up. Soon they were surrounded, as more rats stepped out from the trees.

Their leader – a tall, brownish-white mottled vermin

carrying a long spear – growled warningly, 'T'row down der knife, or you're deadbeasts!'

Something about his bleak stare told Fenna it would be wise to obey the order. She let the knife fall.

Horty indignantly took up his case with the tall rat. 'I say, d'you mind tellin' these chaps to stop swingin' on me blinkin' ears? They'll pull 'em out by the flippin' roots, tuggin' at 'em like that, wot!'

A sudden jab of the tall rat's spearbutt jolted into the young hare's stomach, leaving him doubled up and gasping for breath. The rat turned the point swiftly, covering Fenna and Springald as they leaped forwards to intervene.

'Be still or die! I am Birug, High Kappin of de Darrat. You be prisoners for invadin' our lands!'

Springald protested, 'We're not invading anybeasts' land, only passing through. We are innocent travellers!'

Birug sneered, 'Shut you mouth, shemouse, you not talk to High Kappin like dat. Bring dem along!'

Fenna was shocked to see that they were surrounded by at least a hundred rats. Horty regained his breath, but before he could speak he and his two friends were gagged with thick pieces of rope. Darrat rats swarmed over the trio, binding their forepaws tightly and linking their footpaws together on a long rope. They were helpless. The squirrel-maid barely had time to cast a frightened glance at her companions before sacks were pulled roughly over their heads. Cudgels prodded them, none too gently.

Birug's voice rang out. 'March now!'

Stumbling and bumping into one another, they were hauled swiftly along, dragged upright and cuffed soundly whenever they fell by the wayside. The unhappy trio bumbled along in the midst of their captors, terrified witless and ruing the day they had set paw outside of Redwall Abbey.

Sarobando and Bragoon lay in the treeshade, out of the shimmering midday heat. They sipped dandelion and

172

burdock cordial and nibbled at oatcakes, supplemented by some watercress they had found near a stream. Saro tootled a small reed flute and played a melody. Bragoon sang the tune quietly.

'I know not young 'uns or a wife,
no scolding tongue I fear,
I live a carefree traveller's life,
from yon to hither and here.
O'er mountain, hill and lea,
I'm bound to wend my way,
cross river, lake or sea,
with never a beast to say,
Sit down! Stand up! Stay here!
O ring a lairy lay.
Stand back! Be still! Just wait!
Farewell my dear, good day!'

Saro began piping the tune to a second verse, when Bragoon ceased singing and held up a paw. 'Ssshhh! Did ye hear somethin', mate?'

Ears cocked, the squirrel looked around. Silently she nodded, pointing over to the dense growth of trees on her left. Putting aside the flute, Saro pointed to her friend, indicating that he should stay put. In a flash she was gone, nimbly scaling a beech trunk and vaulting away through the foliaged upper terraces of Mossflower.

Bragoon sat perfectly still, his eyes roving from side to side as he searched the woodlands. Several minutes elapsed before Saro somersaulted back to earth from the high treetops. She picked up a twig, then snapped it and flung it away, muttering darkly to herself.

Bragoon raised his eyebrows. 'Wot's upset ye, matey?'

The squirrel began gathering up her possessions. 'Upset? I ain't upset, buckoe, I'm steamin' fit t'burst! Those three young fools from Redwall, Horty an' the two maids –

they've got themselves captured by a hundred or so big spotty rats!'

Bragoon sighed heavily. Buckling the sword across his back, he dusted himself off and made ready. 'You shore 'twas them?'

Saro checked her sling and pouch of stones. 'Aye, I'm sure enough. They was bound t'gether an' had sacks over their heads, but it's got t'be them. Wot other young hare, squirrel'n'mouse would be wanderin' willy-nilly through these woodlands, eh? They've sneaked out o' Redwall an' come searchin' for us, to share the adventure. Huh!'

Bragoon shook his rudder in disapproval. 'Fivescore o' big spotty rats, ye say? Well, they'll get their share of the fun – that's if'n the three idiots live long enough. Ye recall those spotty rats we battled with last time we was up this way?'

The squirrel nodded grimly. 'Aye, they were flesh eaters!'

19

Evening was crimsoning the sky over the western reaches as Birug led his Darrat vermin into camp. The Darrat tribe gathered around to see what he had captured. A huge old rat – almost white, with a few brown flecks – pulled himself out of a hammock which was slung under a rocky ledge. Bulling his way through the crowd, he indiscriminately kicked babes, young ones, females and males out of his way. Studying the bound and hooded creatures lying exhausted on the ground, he addressed Birug in a shrill voice totally unsuited to his bulk.

'Lemme see dem!'

Horty felt the sack being pulled from his head and a knife slitting the rope gag in his mouth. He spat out the gag and found himself looking at the huge, fat one. Immediately the young hare began complaining.

'Y'don't mind me sayin', sah, but this is all a bit bally much! Is this the way y'treat jolly peaceable wayfarers, wot?'

A slap from the huge rat silenced him. 'Shutcha face, rabbert, d'great Hemper Figlugg don' like talky rabberts!'

He glared at Springald and Fenna, who had been unhooded and had their gags removed. 'Don' like talky mouses or squirrels either!'

A shrunken and incredibly ugly female pushed her way through to Hemper Figlugg's side. Ignoring him, she began pinching the three captives, nodding approvingly as she did so. Hemper Figlugg whispered something in her ear.

She nodded, replying aloud. 'Burcha Glugg!' The Darrat tribe nodded in agreement and laughed.

Always ready to take advantage of a situation, Horty winked at his two companions. 'At least they seem happy, must be a good joke, wot! Burcha Glugg, wasn't it? Watch this.'

He grinned at the assembly and repeated the words, 'Burcha Glugg!'

The Darrat tribe howled with laughter at Horty's remark. A tiny ratbabe wrinkled his nose at the young hare and squeaked, 'Burcha Glugg!'

Horty favoured him with a kindly smile. 'Aye old lad, Burcha Glugg, indeed, wot! Yowhoooo, y'little savage. Gerroff!' The ratbabe, who had bitten Horty's footpaw, clung on grimly. High Kappin Birug pulled the ratbabe off and cuffed it.

Hemper Figlugg nodded at his prisoners. ' Glugg cayjizz!'

They were picked up bodily and borne to two large cages, formed of thick branches lashed together, one of which was open. Into this the three companions were thrown. The Darrat tribe dispersed and went about their business. Seeing they were being ignored, Springald began loosing herself from the ropes binding her forepaws and the running rope about her right footpaw. The other two did likewise.

Fenna watched the fat Hemper Figlugg settling himself back into the hammock. 'What now, I wonder?'

Springald answered hopefully, 'Well, we're still alive, aren't we? Where there's life there's hope, they say.'

Horty rubbed his stomach – as usual, his mind was on food. 'I won't be alive much longer if somebody doesn't feed us. Chap gets hungry, bein' captured an' all that, wot?'

He called out to a passing rat, 'Hi there, I say, me old vermin, how about somethin' to jolly well eat?'

He pantomimed eating and pointed inside his mouth. 'Eat! Y'know, just like starvin' chaps do. Grub, food or whatever you savages call it.'

The rat grinned and pointed to his own mouth. 'Glugg!'

Horty clapped his paws together. 'Hoho, that's the stuff. Glugg!'

Something suddenly dawned on Fenna. 'Glugg, that must be their word for food. Oh, great seasons!'

Horty winked. 'Leave it to me eh, wot! I can translate any bally thing when it comes to food!'

Springald understood all too well. She clapped a paw to her brow. 'Glugg, that's what we are. Food!'

Horty patted her reassuringly. 'No no, old gel, you've got it all wrong. They said Burcha Glugg – that prob'ly means feed them, or give these bally prisoners some food, they look hungry.'

Just then, four Darrat males bore a big cauldron to the cage. They placed it outside the bars, within the captives' reach. It was filled with a form of porridge, full of berries and sliced fruit.

One of the rats indicated they should eat. 'Burcha Glugg, you eat all up.'

Horty smiled. 'Told you so!'

Fenna asked the rat, 'What does Burcha Glugg mean?'

The rat shrugged. 'Old Darrat way of saying good food.'

Springald's worst fears were confirmed. She whispered in a shaky voice, 'They're fattening us up before they eat us!'

Horty dipped a paw into the cauldron and scooped some up. 'Oh, don't be silly! Nobeast'd dare to eat us, shockin' idea. I say, this tastes rather good, wot! Come on, you two!'

They shrank to the back of the cage, shaking their heads. 'I couldn't bear to touch it!'

'Oh Horty, how could you eat at a time like this?'

One of the rats unwound a whip from about his waist, gave it a sharp crack and shouted at the pair, 'Eat or whip!' They were forced to dip their paws in and eat. However, with the prospect of what they were being fed for, the food, as good as Horty said it was, turned to ashes in their mouths.

Fenna and Springald could only manage a small mouthful apiece, but Horty bolted the porridge down until his snout and whiskers were crusted with it.

'Mmmch, no sense in a chap bein' eaten, grmmfff munch, on an empty stomach. Capital stuff, wot!'

Night fell, bringing a cloudless vault of carnelian blue, dusted with stars. Bragoon lay alongside Sarobando, among some rocky hillocks that skirted the Darrat camp. The otter watched as campfires glimmered low.

'Let the vermin settle down, they prob'ly outnumber us by a couple o' hundred to two.'

Saro chewed on a dandelion stalk. 'What then?'

Bragoon raised his head, risking a glimpse of the camp area. 'They're in a cage, over by that long rocky ledge. We'll have to work out a plan to break 'em out an' escape without bein' seen.'

The squirrel lay back and closed her eyes. 'Yore good at schemin', mate. What's the plan?'

The otter lay down and closed his eyes also. 'First a short sleep, wait'll the camp's quiet.'

Saro opened one eye. 'An' then?'

Bragoon stuck Martin's sword into the ground, close to paw. 'I don't know just yet, but ye'll be the firstbeast I tell when a good idea comes along. I'm goin' to sleep; wake me in an hour. Otters get good ideas when they take naps.'

Saro rolled over on to her side. 'No, you wake me, 'tis your turn.'

Her companion watched the starlight playing along the swordblade. 'How can I wake ye when I'm makin' the plan? You wake me!'

The squirrel grumbled. 'Huh, 'tis always me. Alright, you take a nap an' do all the plannin', I'll wake ye in an hour.' The only answer she received was a pretend snore from the otter.

The midnight hour had just passed. Silence reigned over the Darrat camp, broken only by protracted snores mingled with nighttime woodland sounds.

In the cage, Horty sat clasping his stomach and grimacing. Fenna came over to sit by him. 'Tummyache, eh?'

The young hare answered dolefully, 'Absolute agony, doncha know. No use upsettin' you an' Springald, so a chap's got to be brave an' silent, even though he's dyin'. It must've been somethin' I ate.'

Springald overheard him and snorted, 'Something? You great glutton, 'tis not something, but how much of that something you ate. That big cauldron's almost empty!'

Horty winced. 'Ah me! Maids can be beautiful but cruel. I only scoffed that porridge because you two wouldn't touch it after the first mouthful. Ha, 'twas me that saved you a jolly good whippin'. Sacrificed meself for your rotten sakes, that's all the gratitude a chap gets, wot?'

One of the three guards in front of the cage snuffled and grunted at the sound of Horty's raised voice. The captives sat in frozen silence until he settled back down with the other two rats. The three guards snored in soft unison.

Springald whispered, 'Look at them – not a care in the world. We'd be that way, too, snoring in the dormitory. Huh, that's if we'd had the sense to listen to the Abbot and your sister Martha. Wish we were back at Redwall now.'

Fenna murmured, 'Wishing isn't much use. What we should be doing now is escaping while the guards are asleep.'

Horty forgot his pains for a moment. 'By jingo, you're right, old gel. Escape, that's the bally idea! Right, chaps, anybeast got a scheme or a plan of some type, wot?'

They sat racking their brains for a while, until Fenna

admitted limply, 'We've got no chance, locked in a cage and surrounded by armed guards. They'd cut us down before we managed to get two paces!'

Numbly they stared at one another. A tear trickled down Springald's cheek; Fenna's lower lip started quivering. Horty blinked and sniffed.

'We've really gone an' done it now, haven't we, chaps, wot!'

Then a rope fell from above, close to the cage. Attached to it was a sharp knife and a piece of bark that had charcoal writing scrawled on it: 'Hush, take knife, escape. Tie rope to pot. Wait.'

Horty peered up through the bars at the overhead rock ledge. Bragoon's tough-lined face was staring back at him. The otter held a paw to his mouth, signalling silence. Working feverishly, Springald took the knife and tied the rope to the cauldron handle. At a wave from Fenna, the cauldron rose upwards, halting just above the cage.

Gripping the rope firmly, Bragoon began swinging the iron cauldron from side to side until it moved back and forth in mighty sweeps like a giant pendulum. Horty watched it as it swung, lower and lower, whizzing close to the cage front, until it reached the level of the three snoring Ratguards. Then the cauldron jerked outwards. *Kurblungggggg!* It struck two of the rats, laying them out senseless. The remaining one sat up, rubbing his eyes.

'Wot was th . . .' *Podongggg!* The cauldron caught the third rat on the return swing, knocking him head over paws.

Springald was sitting on Fenna's shoulders, slashing at the ropes which kept the wooden roof bars in place. The sharp knife made short work of them.

Hemper Figlugg awoke. He heard the cauldron toll like a muted bell as it hit the last rat. Waddling out of his hammock, he went to investigate the noise. Seeing Fenna's head poking out of the cagetop, he hastened forwards, shouting wheezily, 'Burcha Glugg 'scapin'! Wakey wakey, Darrats!'

Borlonggggggggg! The swinging cauldron biffed him on the back of his great fat head. Hemper Figlugg performed a somersault, raising a big puff of dust as his back hit the ground. His shout, however, had roused the Darrat horde, who came staggering from under the ledges and thick bushes, grabbing for weapons.

Bragoon roared down to the escapers, 'Cut that pot loose an' grab on to the rope!'

Springald slashed the cauldron free, and they took hold of the rope.

Saro's head appeared above the high ledgetop. 'One at a time, we can't pull ye all up t'gether!'

Horty grabbed the spear from a fallen Ratguard. Taking charge, he rapped out orders like a veteran sergeant. 'Steady the buffs, chaps! Spring, you go first, Fenna next! I'll hold these bounders off, wot!'

The Darrat had just realized what was taking place. Around half a dozen of the boldest came at the young hare.

Spear at the ready, Horty challenged them bravely. 'Step up there, laddie bucks, meet a flippin' Redwall warrior, wot! Two or ten at a time, doesn't blinkin' matter to Bone-breaker Braebuck. Have at ye, scurvy nosewipes! Come on, don't be shy, ye wiltin' wallflowers. Wot!'

A big broad mottled rat charged at him, waving a hatchet. A slingstone flew from above, and the rat stood still, tottered, then collapsed in a heap.

Horty threw himself at the other five rats, who had been advancing on him slowly. He was in his element.

'I'm the son o' the roarin' buck! D'ye want to visit your ugly ancestors, eh? Well, I'm the one who'll send ye to Hellgates. Yaaaaaaah!'

At the top of the ledge, Fenna and Springald stood with their rescuers. Bragoon shook his head. 'Is he mad? Look at 'im!'

Horty was like a whirling demon, lashing out with his long hind legs as he thwacked wildly about with the spear. Rats went down like ninepins before his onslaught.

Sarobando nodded in admiration. 'That young 'un's got the makin's of a powerful warrior, but he's still a hotheaded learner. Soon as he tires they'll overpower 'im an' bring 'im down.'

Springald yelled down to her friend, 'Horty, get to the rope, hurry!'

The young hare looked at the pack of rats charging towards him. 'Right away, marm, cover me jolly old back, chaps!'

Saro used her sling, whilst the others pelted the rats with rocks from the ledge as Horty ran for it. He reached the rope and looped it about his waist.

'Haul away!'

Kappin Birug flung a wooden club that caught Horty square between both ears, before bouncing off his head.

Horty grinned. 'Yah missed me!' Then he fell unconscious.

Ducking slingstones and a few arrows, the rescuers – along with Fenna and Springald – hauled Horty's limp figure up on to the ledgetop.

Bragoon peered anxiously down as more archers began appearing. 'Better get goin' an' move out o' range. They mean business!'

They struck off into some thick pinewoods, carrying the senseless figure of the hare between them.

20

It was a long and wearying night, but the Redwallers kept going. Pines grew thick about them, obscuring even the stars in the sky. Stumbling on through the dense carpet of rotting pine needles, Springald bumped into a tree trunk.

'Oof! There won't be a part of me that's undamaged if we go on at this rate. A torch would help us to see where we're going.'

Bragoon urged her on. 'Just keep goin', missy, there'll be no torches. One spark can start a fire among pine trees, an' the whole woodland'd be ablaze bafore ye could blink. Besides, a torch would be like a beacon for those vermin to follow.'

Springald felt foolish. 'I'm sorry, I didn't realize.'

The otter said nothing, but he was exhausted and bad-tempered after having to run all night, burdened with Horty. He snapped at the mousemaid, ''Tis not much good bein' sorry now, Miss Mouse. If'n you three would've stayed put at the Abbey, we wouldn't be in this fix!'

Fenna came to her friend's defence. 'We only came after you because we thought we could help. Besides, now that we're free, we can get on searching for Loamhedge.'

But Bragoon was not to be appeased. 'Free, eh, don't make me laugh! You think those rats won't come after us?

Lissen, I know rats, they won't rest 'til they've got us all in the cookin' pot. Ask Saro, we've fought flesh eaters like them afore. The only way to make 'em give up is to kill 'em, an' there's too many of the scum for that!'

A quavery voice echoed out of nowhere. 'Oh, far too many! They've eaten most of us, you know.'

Bragoon stood stock still, his eyes scouring the night woods. 'Who said that?'

From a small hillock of pine needles built up round the base of a trunk, the voice answered, 'If you remove your great heavy rudder from my neck, I'll tell you!'

The otter leaped to one side as an old rabbit shoved his head through the mound.

'Sorry to startle you like that, I'm sure. If the Darrat are hunting you, I'd be pleased to hide you. Only for awhile, though – they eat anybeast who harbours fugitives.' The ancient rabbit shrugged. 'But Darrat will eat a creature for no reason at all. So, d'you want me to hide you?'

Saro indicated the unconscious Horty. 'Just until this 'un's fit for travel agin, thankee.'

The rabbit's name was Cosbro. He took them to the hollow log in which he lived. It was a cunningly contrived dwelling, a great elm trunk overgrown with all manner of moss and nettles. One end of it backed against a standing rock, the other was artfully concealed by thistles and wild lupins. Cosbro carefully parted these, creating a little gap which allowed them to squeeze through one at a time. Once they were all inside, the old rabbit rearranged the outer thistles and lupins, rendering the entrance invisible to the casual observer.

Springald looked about: it was a very neat little home. Lit by four lanterns containing fireflies, its illumination dim but adequate. They sat down on a carpet of dried grass and springy moss.

Fenna made Horty comfortable, remarking, 'I've never heard of a rabbit living inside of a tree before.'

Cosbro preened his meagre whiskers. 'Neither have the Darrat, young 'un. That's what makes it such a perfect place. I've often sat in here, listening to them digging holes as they searched for rabbits – they dig out anything that looks like a burrow. Clods, they have no imagination at all.'

Bragoon smiled at the old one. 'But where do the other rabbits around here live?'

Cosbro shook his head sadly. 'There are no other rabbits left. Only me, sitting inside this log, poor fool that I am.'

Saro patted his paw gently. 'You ain't no fool, me friend. It takes a clever beast to survive in this country. How many rabbits were there, an' how'd ye come to be livin' here?'

Cosbro shrugged. 'We were too many to count one time, long ago. Our families had no written history. All I have to remember my ancestors by are ancient poems and ballads passed down by word of mouth. Woe is me, sometimes I think I must be the last rabbit left in all the land.'

Saro felt sorry for the pitiful old creature. She passed him a flask of dandelion and burdock cordial.

'Wet yore whistle with this, ole mate. Maybe ye'd like to tell us one of yore poems from the ole days, eh?'

Cosbro sipped the cordial, closing his eyes blissfully. 'Ahhh, dandelion and burdock, tastes like nectar to me. Aye, 'tis many long seasons since I tasted ought as good as this. Have you ever heard of a poem called "The Shadowslayers"?'

He looked from one to the other, but they shook their heads. Helping himself to a longer sip, Cosbro licked his lips. 'When I was younger, I could skip through such verses. But, alas, the weight of seasons has descended upon me. My mind forgets a lot of things these days. So, my friends, here is the poem, as best as I can recall it.

'Lo the golden days are gone,
the happy laughter long fled,
now silence falls o'er Loamhedge walls,

185

lone winds lament the dead.
The Shadowslayers sent us forth,
some south and east, some west and north.

The wise ones said 'twas vermin foul,
their blood, their teeth, their fur,
which brought the plague that laid us low,
with more than we could bear.
When families die before our eyes,
we learned, 'tis folly to be wise.

Leave everything ye own now, flee,
run if ye can, go far and wide,
linger not here, to grieve and weep,
those tears have all been cried.
The mouse Germaine said, "Woe, 'tis true,
The Shadowslayers will come for you."

The mice went first, escaped their fate,
they traversed north and west;
what was left of us remained,
to lay our dead to rest.
We travelled then, us piteous few,
who'd seen what Shadowslayers could do.

My father's father spake these words,
as had his kin, from time untold,
wand'ring exiled o'er the land,
growing up, and growing old.
Recalling to their dying breath,
how once the Shadowslayers brought death.'

Cosbro took another drink and sighed wearily. 'I myself wrote that final verse, though there were many more. They told of our family names and histories. But I've forgotten the words, shame on me!'

Fenna thought it was the saddest thing she had ever heard.

Springald spoke comfortingly to the ancient hare. 'I hope

that if ever I live to your age, I would remember the half of it, sir.'

Horty chose that moment to waken from his stupor. 'Remember what, wot? I say, did we escape those blighters? Jolly good show, chaps, where are we now? Someplace far a-blinkin' way, I hope. Owch, my flippin' head's given me jip!'

He tried to stagger upright and banged his head on the log. 'Yowhooyooch! Who left that up there, confounded oaf!'

Saro threw herself across his face, stifling further cries. She whispered fiercely, 'Shuttup, addlebrain, I can hear somethin' goin' on outside!'

Kappin Birug and a crowd of Darrat rats halted alongside the log. Those inside held their breath in frozen silence. Sounds of the vermin poking about with spearbutts and slashing at shrubbery could be heard by those in the log. Outside, Birug climbed up and sat upon the log. Dawning sunlight slanted through the trees as he glanced down at the Darrat rats resting upon the grass.

'Any of you be High Kappins, eh?' They stared owlishly at one another, then shook their heads. Birug jumped up, performing a dance of rage upon the log. Pointing his spear at them, he screeched, 'Den why you not searchin', mudbrains? Search! Search! Find dem, y'want me to do everythink, eh? Search!'

They dispersed hastily, trying to look busy and diligent as they probed amid the woodland trees. Birug laid about with his spearshaft, spittle going everywhere as he took out his bad temper on anybeast standing close.

'Hemper Figlugg got bad sore skull, big lump onna 'ead! Dose beasts die slow when I catch 'em. Only make Burcha Glugg out of wot be left of dem!'

Birug hurried over to a rat who had returned to investigate the fallen log. Dealing the unfortunate several hard kicks to the rump, the Kappin screeched hoarsely at him, 'Wotcha be doin', dumbum – y'think they be beetles, hidin' inna falled treelog? You never be High Kappin, that be sure!'

As Birug chased the rat back to search with the others, Cosbro crept to the log opening and called out in excellent imitation of the gruff Darrat dialect, 'Der dey goes! Ober dat way, quick!'

There followed a stampede of pounding Darrat paws, with Birug bellowing as he hastened in pursuit, 'Not kill 'em, catch 'em priz'ner, that a h'order!'

As the sounds retreated, the fugitives breathed easier. Springald was visibly shaken. 'Good grief, that was a bit close for comfort!'

Saro removed herself from Horty's face. He was the picture of sputtering indignity.

'Pshaw, phoo! I'll be spittin' wodges of your bally tailfur for days t'come, marm. No blinkin' thanks to you, I was near smothercated, wot! But who am I to complain, chaps? Me flippin' head's poundin', achin' to blue blazes. There's a lump like a duck egg on me young skull. The poor old stomach is painin' an' swollen from savin' the ungrateful comrades. An' to top it all jolly well off, a great lump of a squirrel has been layin' on my tender young mouth for absolute ages. Phwaaaw, phutt! Never feed your young on squirrelhair, tastes vile!'

Bragoon's paw shot out, pinching Horty's nose in a vice-like grip. 'Are ye finished moanin', after ye nearly got us all captured, young sir?'

Horty tried to nod. 'Yith, juth leggo ob be dose pleathe!'

The otter released his grip, growling threateningly, 'One more whimper an' I'll pull it right off, so keep quiet!' He turned to question Cosbro. 'Ye mentioned Loamhedge in yore poem, mate, an' Abbess Germaine, too. She ruled there, from wot I've 'eard. Loamhedge is where we're bound for. Any idea which way it lies?'

The ancient rabbit pointed in a general southeast direction. 'I can't be sure, but I've always imagined it being somewhere over that way. I've heard 'tis savage country – deserts, chasms, wide rivers, and numerous foebeasts.'

Saro nodded. 'Aye, me'n Bragoon have seen a bit of it, though that was quite a few seasons back. Over that way, eh?'

Cosbro began moving the vegetation from his log entrance. 'When you see a great line of very high cliffs, you'll know you're on the right track. Er, by the way, have you any of that excellent cordial to spare? I'm too old to travel now.'

Bragoon passed him a fresh flask. 'Take this, friend, an' thankee kindly for yore help!'

They emerged into calm morning sunlight and fresh, green woodlands.

Saro waved to Cosbro. 'Good fortune be with ye, matey. We'll travel now, while the coast's clear. You take it easy!'

Cosbro brought something out of his dwelling and gave it to Bragoon. It was a large coil of rope – thin but incredibly strong, with big knots every three pawlengths.

The otter inspected it closely. 'Haharr, 'tis a climbin' rope, an' a fine one, too. If'n I ain't mistaken, this'll come in useful at the high cliffs. Where'd ye get it?'

Cosbro explained. 'I made it myself, when I was a lot younger. Never got round to using it, though. I've forgotten my dreams of high cliffs long since. You take it.'

Bragoon drew Martin's sword and held it up in a warrior's salute. 'A gift from a friend is somethin' to be valued. Thankee, sir, an' may the seasons be kind to ye!'

To avoid bumping into the Darrat, they set off at a southerly tangent through the woodlands. Cosbro stood watching until they were out of sight. Wiping a paw across his rheumy eyes, the ancient rabbit murmured wistfully to himself, 'And may the seasons be kind to you, friends. May the breeze be at your backs, and the sun never in your eyes. Ah me, I wish that I were young enough to go with you.'

The lonely rabbit shuffled back to his home, thinking of the high mysterious cliffs and the lost opportunities of his earlier seasons, now that old age leaned heavily upon him. Cosbro took one last look at the far horizon as he bent to enter the log dwelling.

'Ah well, at least my rope won't be wasted – if they live long enough to use it.'

21

Martha did not sleep a wink on the night that the vermin were sighted. It was as if some unreasoning panic was welling up in her. Vermin, at the very gates of her beloved Abbey! Restlessly she roamed Great Hall, propelling the little cart which held her chair, by pulling it along with the crutch that Toran had made for her.

Moonlight sent pale shafts of light in varied hues as it shone through the stained-glass windows on to the worn stone floor. Travelling through the patches of dark and light, the young haremaid arrived at the tapestry of Martin the Warrior. She gazed up at the figure of the heroic mouse. It was illuminated by a small lantern on either side.

Martha voiced her fears and worries to her friend. 'Oh Martin, what shall we do? Sarobando and Bragoon have left the Abbey, and all on my silly little behalf. Abbot Carrul gave Bragoon your great sword to take with him. I'd stay in my chair forever, if only they were back here at Redwall. The safety of this Abbey and all my friends here is far more important than foolish dreams of being able to walk. With my brother and the other young ones gone, who will help us against the vermin? The very thought of those cruel, murderous vermin getting inside our gates is horrible!'

'Here now, young Martha, what's all this?'

She gave a start as the Abbot loomed up out of the shadows. 'Father Abbot, I thought you'd gone to your bed.'

Carrul sat down on the edge of the cart and looked over the top of his glasses at her. 'And I thought you had, too, miss.'

The sound of the main abbey door opening caused them both to pause. The Abbot's loud whisper echoed around the hall columns.

'Who's there?'

Toran's voice replied. ' 'Tis only me an' Foremole Dwurl, Father. We just been relieved o' wallguard by Junty Cellarhog an' Weld.' The pair joined Martha and Abbot Carrul.

Dwurl tugged his snout politely. 'Wot bee's you'm a-doin' settin' daown yurr? Shudd be snorin' abed, 'tis orful late.'

The Abbot put on his wise face. 'Oh, we were just discussing a few things, weren't we, Martha?'

The haremaid managed an important little cough. 'Ahem, yes, just small bits of business. What's it like out there, Toran? Any more news of the, er, vermin?'

The ottercook sat back on his rudder. 'No, miss, they ain't up to much. Their fires are burnt low, I think they're sleepin'. We've been watchin' the ditch outside the front gate, t'other side o' the path, makin' sure they don't try t'sneak along it.'

Martha asked the question she had been anxious to have answered. 'Aren't you afraid?'

Toran rubbed his wide midriff thoughtfully. 'Bless yore 'eart, pretty one, o' course we are. Only a fool'd say he wasn't. We're afraid as any sensible beast should be, but we ain't scared. Wot I mean is, we're only afraid for the safety of others – Dibbuns, an' young 'uns like yoreself. But if'n we got to do somethin' about it, we ain't scared o' vermin.'

Foremole licked his lips. 'Oi'm afeared.'

Toran raised his eyebrows at this remark. 'You, afeared?'

A huge grin creased the mole leader's homely face. 'Aye,

zurr, afeared oi'll fall asleep an' miss ee brekkist. Oi'm a-thinken oi'll go to ee kitchens an' get a h'early wun!'

Martha laughed at the mole's comical logic. 'What a great idea, sir, I think we'll join you!'

The kitchen was crowded with Redwallers of a like mind, even Dibbuns. Nobeast could sleep with the excitement of the night. Granmum Gurvel and three young moles were busy filling baked apples with honey and chopped hazelnuts.

Gurvel curtsied to the Abbot as she bustled by. 'Coom in an' sit ee daown, zurr, an' you'm h'others, too. Et bee's a gudd job moi ole bones can't be a sleepen, so oi'm a keepen moiself bizzied.'

They found seats around the kitchen table and began pouring a sauce of meadowcream and rosehip over their baked apples. Everybeast was watching the Abbot as he paused before eating to address them.

'What we need are some good contingency plans, my friends. Seeing as most of us are here, I'll take any suggestions.'

Muggum was sitting up on a shelf, among the spice jars, with his cohort of Dibbuns. The molebabe raised his spoon. 'Oi says chop ee vermints tails offen wi' a gurt rusty knoife, an' barth 'em in 'ot soapy watter. Hurr, they'm soon bee's glad to run away arter that. Ho urr aye!'

This met with hearty applause and much sneezing from the Dibbuns, two of whom had opened a hotroot pepper jar. Amused by this, Abbot Carrul tried to keep a straight face as he spoke to Sister Portula, who was recording the meeting. 'Not a bad idea! Write it down, Sister, and don't forget the bit about hot soapy water. We'll keep it in mind.'

Sister Setiva, after wiping several noses and glaring the Dibbuns into silence, held up a paw. 'As soon as ah've finished eating, ah hope some o' ye will join me tae search around for more things tae use as weapons.'

Martha was among those who volunteered. But Toran

had other plans for her. 'You'd never be able to search the attics upstairs, me beauty. I think ye should be in charge of the Dibbuns' safety. Seasons forbid that anythin' should happen to the liddle 'uns with vermin camped next to our gates. Will ye do it, Martha?'

Immediately the haremaid agreed. 'I'd be glad to. Right, come on you villains, off that shelf and up to bed. Last one up washes all the pots and dishes, eh, Granmum Gurvel?'

Gurvel picked up her big ladle. 'You'm said the vurry thing oi wuz abowt t'say, Miz Marth!'

An almighty scramble followed as Dibbuns climbed down from the shelves and fled upstairs squealing.

Abbot Carrul waited until the noise subsided. 'Next suggestion please!'

Badredd lay awake down in the ditch, trying to ignore the stentorian snores of those around him. He longed for the dawn, when he could take possession of his magic sword. What did it look like? He imagined it as a solid gold blade with a crosshilt and grip crusted with rubies, pearls and emeralds. Of course, he would not mind too much if it were made from silver with jetstones and sapphires for adornment.

Mentally he went through a speech he had prepared for the woodland bumpkins who lived behind the wall. Badredd silently practised it, making sweeping paw movements to emphasize its drama. 'Throw wide your gates! Tremble at my name, for I am Badredd, commander of a vermin horde.'

He paused here, wondering if his scruffy little band could constitute a horde. No matter, those woodland oafs had probably never seen a horde, much less taken a head count of one. He continued his oratory. 'You are looking at death, all of ye! Unless you deliver unto Badredd the magic sword that is rightfully his.'

He questioned the last phrase – it needed something, a word or two to prove that the sword's ownership was never in doubt. Hah, that was it! He embellished his flowery recitation thus: 'For did not my father, Reddblade, Warlord of the Northern Mountains, proclaim it so? "Give unto my son Badredd his sword. It lies within Wallred, I mean, Redwall. To the mighty warrior goes the magic sword!" ' He flung out his paw and caught Halfchop a smack on the chin.

The rat awoke, holding his chin in his good paw. 'Mmmph, wot did ye do that for, Chief?'

But Badredd was too fired up to waste time with arguments. 'Get further along that ditch an' see if'n ye can make it so that yore level with the big gate!'

Halfchop peered at him in the predawn darkness. 'Wot for?'

Badredd shoved him forwards. 'If'n ye make it safely, give me a signal. I'll follow up with the rest o' the crew. That way we'll be in place when it gets light. They'll get the shock o' their lives when they see me climb out o' the ditch an' demand the magic sword. Go on, don't hang about!'

Blundering forwards, Halfchop stepped on a thistle and banged into the ditch's sidewall. ' 'Tis no good, I can't see a thing. Why don't ye wait 'til dawn?'

Badredd drew his cutlass. 'Because I want it done now. There'll be one less in the crew if'n ye stand there rubbin' yore chin an' makin' excuses. Now get goin'!'

Halfchop picked up a red-ended branch from the embers of a fire. He went off, blowing it back to burning light and muttering, 'Alright, then, but I ain't goin' without a light!'

Up on the northwest rampart corner, Brother Weld nudged Junty Cellarhog. 'Is that somebeast coming along the ditch carrying a light?'

The burly hedgehog watched as a small burning beacon grew closer. 'Aye, so 'tis, Brother. I wager that's a vermin, up to no good, I'll be bound. Better stop the rascal afore he sets fire to our front gate.'

There was always a variety of things in Junty's big apron pocket. He dug a paw in and rummaged about. A slow smile lit up his heavy features as he produced a big barrel bung made from a knot he had gouged out of an oak log. 'This should do!'

Though ponderous and not given to quick flings, Junty was accurate and very powerful.

Halfchop was never very sure of what fractured his muzzle and wrecked his nose. But he never forgot the sound as it hit him. *Kachunk!*

Badredd saw the rat's light snuffed out with a gentle hiss as it fell into some stagnant water. He went and shook the weasel brothers, Floggo and Rogg, awake. 'Rouse yore bones there. Go an' fetch ole Halfchop back 'ere. He went wanderin' off up the ditch. It looks like the idiot's fallen over. Go on, move! It'll soon be dawn.'

When they returned, hauling the senseless rat, Badredd blew on the embers and stirred the fire. He winced as he saw the damage to Halfchop's face. Awakened by the commotion, Flinky dug some dried herbs out of his pouch and lit them so that they smouldered. The weasels held the rat's head steady as Flinky pushed the smoking herbs under his nose. Halfchop's eyes opened immediately when the pungent fumes got to him.

Badredd squatted beside him. 'What happened?' Halfchop looked at the fox quizzically as he repeated the question. 'Who did that to ye, what happened?'

Halfchop spoke . . . just one word – 'Kachunk!'

Flinky put aside the smouldering herbs. 'Wot did ye say, mate?'

Halfchop looked at Flinky as if seeing him for the first time. He looked at Badredd the same way and spoke the word again. 'Kachunk!'

Losing his patience, Badredd pawed the cutlass edge menacingly. 'Talk sense! I asked ye wot happened. Keep sayin' that stupid word an' I'll kachunk ye, good an' proper!'

Halfchop leaned close and whispered in the fox's ear. 'Kachunk!'

As Flinky saw the cutlass beginning to rise, he stepped in and stayed his crew leader's paw. 'Ah now, leave him alone, Chief. The pore ould rat's not in his right mind at all. How d'ye feel, matey, better now?'

Halfchop smiled foolishly over his swollen muzzle. 'Kachunk!'

Dawn crept in from the east, pale pink and lilac in a creamy haze. Dewdrops bedecked the flatlands beyond the ditch. Redwall Abbey's twin bells tolled out the opening of a new summer day. Martha watched Toran, Abbot Carrul and several others mounting the gatehouse steps. Frustration tinged the haremaid's plea to them.

'Let me come up on the ramparts, I want to see what's happening. Oh please, I feel so helpless down here!'

Toran shook his head. 'It might get a bit dangerous up here, me pretty. Best ye stop down there an' look after the Dibbuns.'

Little Shilly the squirrelbabe made a scramble for the steps. 'Cummon, we all go up onna wall. Then Miz Marth' gotta be up dere wiv us'n's!'

Sister Setiva ran down and blocked the Dibbuns' way. 'Och no ye don't, mah wee babes. Ah'll come o'er tae the orchard wi' ye an' Martha. We'll see if any blackberries are ripe enough tae be picked yet. A guid idea, eh?'

Squeaking with delight, the Abbeybabes pushed Martha's chair across the lawns so fast that the haremaid was forced to hold on tight to the arms.

Sister Setiva chased after them, shouting in her thin, reedy voice, 'Slow down, ye naughty creatures, go easy wi' Miss Martha!'

Junty and Brother Weld kept an eye on the ditch as they made their way along to the threshold over the main gate.

Throwing a brief salute, the Cellarhog made his report to the Abbot. 'Looks like they're makin' a move, Father. Comin' this way!'

The wall party was armed with a variety of window poles, kitchen utensils and tools. Apart from one or two slings and bags of pebbles, there were no real weapons to be found within the bounds of the peaceable Abbey. Toran gave Junty a sling and some stones. He tossed a long ash stave to Brother Weld.

'These ain't much, but they're better 'n nothin', friends.'

Now the vermin crew had reached the spot directly below where the Redwallers stood. They halted, only the tops of their heads visible. Silence fell as they waited, standing in a muddy pool of ditchwater.

Toran whispered to Abbot Carrul, 'Let them state their business first.'

The silence from below became rather protracted, then a voice spoke out. 'Kachunk!'

This was followed by Badredd hissing, 'Somebeast, shut that fool up!'

Curiosity overcame Old Phredd the Gatekeeper, who called out, 'What do ye want? Speak up!'

Badredd had envisioned himself leaping boldly from the ditch to state his demands. However, he was far too short for such a thing, so several of the crew had to lift him up and boost him on to the path. It was a totally undignified procedure. The little fox landed, sprawling on the dust and gravel. He sprang up quickly, took a swaggering step forwards and tripped over his cutlass.

Having heard a few stifled giggles from the walltop, Badredd glared up frostily at the assembled Redwallers, putting on his toughest snarl. 'Ye'll laugh the other side of yore faces afore this day's done!' Puffing himself up to his full height, he continued. 'I'm Badredd, Warlord of the Vermin Horde. Nobeast can stand against me. I come from the Northlands where we drink our enemies' blood!'

The Abbot bowed his head politely. 'I bid you a good morning, Sir Badredd. I am Father Abbot Carrul of Redwall. Is there any way I can be of service to you? Mayhaps you might need food or supplies to continue your journey?'

At the mention of food, the rest of the vermin crew climbed out of the ditch eagerly, but the little fox forestalled them by answering the Abbot scornfully, 'We don't want yore food, mouse. Our journey's end is here, at this Wallred place. You've got a magic sword here. I want it – bring it t'me now!'

The Abbot stared coolly down at him. 'There is no such thing as a magic sword at Redwall Abbey.'

Badredd drew his cutlass with a swish, pointing it at Carrul. 'You lie! Bring that sword out to me, old fool, or it will go badly with ye!'

Toran stepped up to the Abbot's side, roaring down at the fox, 'Don't ye dare call the Abbot of Redwall a fool or a liar! If he says there's no magic sword here, then you'd best get the mud out o' yore ears an' listen. Now shift yoreself, vermin. Get up the road with that raggedy-bottomed bunch. Quick, or I'll come down there and kick yore tail back t'the Northlands!'

Shaking with rage, Badredd turned and nodded to his two archers, the weasel brothers. 'Fire!'

Two arrows zipped from their bows. Toran flung himself upon the Abbot, knocking him down below the battlements. One arrow flew harmlessly overhead, the other grazed the ottercook's shoulder.

Toran winced as he yelled, 'Down, everybeast!'

The Redwallers immediately dropped below the parapet. Junty Cellarhog fitted a stone into his sling and whirled it. He popped up and let fly. Though it was a speedy shot, and not too accurate, it did hit Badredd on the footpaw. He screeched out in pain as Crinktail and the rest of the crew jumped back into the ditch, taking him with them.

There was an uneasy silence. Then Flinky called out in a

wheedling voice, 'Ah, look now, friends, why don't ye just throw the ould magic sword to us an' we'll be on our way, I promise!'

This was followed by a tirade from Badredd. 'Sword or no sword, I vow I'll slay ye all an' take yore Abbey from ye. This is war, d'ye hear me?'

Two broken halves of the arrow which had struck Toran were flung into the ditch. The ottercook sat watching Sister Portula bind his wound with her apron. He laughed and shouted back contemptuously to the fox, 'War, eh? Go on then, let's see ye take Redwall from us. A dirty liddle band o' vermin scum, ye'd have no chance!'

Down in the ditch, Flinky gazed levelly at Badredd and nodded. 'Sure an' I believe the big riverdog's right. How could a crew as small as ours take that fine big place? 'Tis all made o' stone an' locked up tight.'

Badredd nursed his footpaw, shooting a hateful glance at the stoat. 'Whose side are ye on, theirs or ours?'

Flinky spread his paws expressively. 'Ah now, Chief, I'm with you. But ye got to admit, things ain't exac'ly goin' our way, are they now?'

Badredd narrowed his eyes, well aware that Flinky could be a sly one at times. 'So, what d'ye suggest?'

The stoat winked secretively. 'Make 'em think we've gone away. I'll wager we could catch 'em off guard after a day or two.'

Granmum Gurvel came panting up the wallsteps, carrying a big wooden pail of kitchen rubbish with the arrow that had missed the Abbot sticking out of it. The old mole blinked indignantly. 'Yurr, see wot appinged? Oi wurr just crossin' ee lawn to put ee rubbish on moi compost 'eap. That thurr h'arrer comed roight out'n ee sky an' stucked in moi pail!'

Junty Cellarhog took it from her. 'Don't fret, marm, it missed ye!'

*

Back in the ditch, Badredd was mulling over Flinky's idea. 'How many days do we wait?'

Junty's voice interrupted further conversation. The Cellarhog was whining piteously, 'Sir, we've got somethin' here for ye.'

Badredd leaped up. 'Lend a paw 'ere, get me outta this ditch. We won't be waitin' any longer. Hah! They've seen sense at last; that'll be my magic sword!'

They boosted him up out of the ditch. He was back a moment later – dripping with leftover oatmeal, potato peelings, onion skins and old cooking oil. Laughter and hoots of derision rang out from the walltops. Badredd was speechless with rage. The crew backed off from him, holding their noses at the odour from yesterday's kitchen rubbish.

He clawed at the mess. 'I don't care how long I got to wait, they're deadbeasts, all of 'em. They can't treat Badredd like that!'

Halfchop smiled at him. 'Kachunk!'

Toran sat in the orchard, surrounded by the Dibbuns, telling the tale to them whilst Sister Setiva and Martha tended his wound. The incident, while being humorous, worried Martha.

'I wish Sarobando and Bragoon were here now.'

The ottercook patted his newly bandaged shoulder. 'Don't upset yourself, young 'un. Those vermin'll leave when they find there's nought here for 'em except the ole pail o' rubbish. Ain't that right, Sister?'

Setiva knotted off the bandage neatly. 'Aye, like as not. Ye say there's but ten o' the rogues altogether. Hmm, they shouldnae be much trouble. Aye, but 'twould be fine if we had some otters or shrews aboot the place.'

Toran stood up and flexed his paw. 'Huh, ye'll not find otters around here, save for me. They've gone off to camp on the seashores all summer. As for shrews – well, they go wherever the streams an' rivers take 'em. I know we ain't got many at Redwall of fightin' age, but we'll do at a pinch.'

Martha folded the rug across her lap. 'I hope you're right. I'd hate to see vermin get into Redwall. What would happen to these little ones?'

Muggum picked up a stick. 'Uz foight 'em, miz, we'm gurt fierce Dibbuns. B'ain't that roight, Shilly?'

The squirrelbabe, and all the other Dibbuns, set up a fearful clamour. Brandishing sticks, wooden spoons and stones, they paraded up and down, scowling, growling and shouting dire threats.

Though Martha could not help smiling inwardly, she covered her ears and looked shocked. 'Dearie me, I wouldn't like to be a vermin with all these great rough warriors around. Would you, Toran?'

Her friend nodded. 'Aye, miss, thank the seasons we can sleep safe in our beds. These liddle 'uns are reg'lar terrors!'

The smallest of the Dibbuns, the tiny shrew called Buffle, picked up a stone which was far too big for him. He fell over backwards and sat there muttering unintelligible sounds.

'Gurrumvurbilbultumcuchachukchuk!'

Toran removed the stone from Buffle's stomach. He picked the babe up with one paw and set him on Martha's lap. 'Well, I wonder what that's all about?'

Yooch, who seemed to be the only one who could understand Buffle, translated. 'Buffle sez he eat vermins all up!'

Sister Setiva cleaned a few dandelion seeds from the shrewbabe's whiskers. He tried to bite her paw. Setiva raised her eyebrows. 'Och, ye wee terror, don't ye dare tae eat me all up!'

Buffle clenched his tiny paws and came out with a long torrent of garbled baby talk.

Martha turned to Yooch. 'What's he saying now?'

Yooch giggled. 'Buffle sayin' lotsa naughty fings!'

Sister Setiva looked shocked. 'Time for your nap, young shrew!' She swept him off protesting loudly. Setiva was a no-nonsense shrewnurse and ignored Buffle's tirade. 'Och, ye can stop all that gobbledygook – ah'm no' impressed!'

22

Badredd and his crew had left the ditch and crossed back into Mossflower Wood. With all manner of fruit, berries and wild vegetables to be had there during this summer season, the vermin had no difficulty finding food. Crinktail and Juppa gossiped as they prepared food for the others. Neither was very optimistic.

Juppa plucked away at a moorhen, which Rogg had brought down with his bow. 'I tell ye, 'twill be a long time afore we see the Northlands again. Badredd's more determined than ever now.'

Crinktail chopped away at dandelion roots and wild celery with a thin-bladed dagger. 'Aye, that's true enough. Where is our fearless chief? I ain't seen him round lately.'

Slipback strolled in and threw down a sizeable bunch of watercress. 'Who, Badredd? That 'un's takin' a bath in the stream, tryin' to get the smell o' that rubbish off 'im. He ain't too pleased, I can tell ye, two baths in two seasons is hard on a beast. He only took a bath last spring.'

Flinky emerged from the undergrowth, his tunic full of pears. 'Ah sure, any vermin knows that bathin' weakens ye. How's the vittles comin' along, me ould darlin'?'

Crinktail winked fondly at her mate. 'They'll be ready soon enough, ye great starvin' stoat. Sit by the fire here an' stir the pot awhile. Ye can give us a song while yore at it.'

Flinky knew more vermin songs than all the crew put together. He sang aloud, hoping the strains might reach Badredd whilst he was taking his bath in the stream not far away. The rest of the crew drifted in to listen, sniggering and nudging a bit at the words.

'Oh hear my song, young vermin,
and take heed to wot I say,
I had a fine young son like you,
who bathed most every day.
Whenever he saw water, straight off he'd dive right in,
a-scrubbin' an' a-washin' of himself, then he'd begin:

Oooooooohhhhhhh! I smell just like a rose,
from me tail up to me nose,
why, even all the blossoms envy me.
'An' all I'll ever lack,
is a mate to scrub me back,
I'm the cleanest vermin that you'll ever
see . . . eeeeeeeeeeeeeee!

I'm clean as a weasel's whistle,
shiny as a stoat's best coat.
Just pass the scented essence,
in camomile I'll float.
All lathery suds an' lilac buds an' pine tree fragrance,
    too,
with me teeth so white an' me fur so bright an' eyes of
    baby blue.'

The last verse was sung sadly and with great feeling.

'But then one summer dawn,
I had to weep an' mourn,
I went down to the bathing pool that day.
There was not one poor young hair,

just a sweet aroma there.
Alas, he'd gone an' washed himself away.
Awayeeeeeeeeeee!'

Badredd strode to the fire, dripping wet. Jiggling a claw in one ear, he gave Flinky a frozen stare. 'Get them vittles cooked an' shut yore stupid gob. When we've eaten, we're movin' on, fast!'

Flinky returned his stare blankly. 'Ah sure, an' wot's the hurry, yore 'onour?'

The little fox buckled his cutlass on. 'I want to take a look round the back o' that Abbey, there's got to be a way in!'

Flinky passed a secret wink to Crinktail, who tried to fob Badredd off with an excuse. 'But, Chief, by the time we've finished the meal and got round there, it'll be dark.'

Badredd picked up a bowl and held it forth to be filled. 'Good, that'll be the ideal time to get the job done!'

Abbot Carrul felt much relieved as he surveyed the path and the ditch from the west walltop. 'Thank goodness there's no sign of the vermin. What do you think, Toran, have they gone for good?'

The ottercook had lashed sharp kitchen knives to the tops of two window poles. He and Junty each had one. Toran peered up the path into the gathering darkness.

'Looks like they have, Father, but I'm takin' no chances. Me an' Junty'll stay guard up here an' keep a weather eye out. If the things are still all clear tomorrow, we'll do a patrol around the outer wall just to make certain.'

Carrul patted his friend's stout back. 'As you wish; I'll have food sent up to you.'

It was a fine warm night. Cavern Hole was packed with Redwallers, all happy and relaxed since hearing the news their Abbot brought, that the vermin fear had passed. Granmum Gurvel and her molemaids served a celebratory supper of mushroom and barley soup, harvest-baked loaves and a dessert of apple and blackberry crumble made from fresh ingredients, which the Dibbuns had gathered from the orchard.

Foremole sat down next to Sister Portula, digging into his bowl of crumble and smiling happily. 'Gudd arpatoit to ee, marm, ee trubble bee's gonned naow!'

Portula raised a beaker of October Ale. 'Good appetite to you, sir. Hmm, look at young Martha, she doesn't seem to be enjoying herself. I wonder what's the matter with her.'

Foremole pondered the situation for a moment, then pronounced his judgement. 'Oi 'spec Miz Marth's missin' urr bruther.'

Sister Portula called across to the haremaid, 'Don't fret about Horty, he'll be back soon, eating us out of house and home, no doubt. You'll see!'

Martha smiled wanly. 'I'm sure he will, Sister, but I can't help feeling concerned about him.'

Abbot Carrul put aside his supper and stood up. 'What you need is a jolly song. Shall I sing you a little ditty I once learned from a sea otter?'

This surprised Martha. 'You singing, Father Abbot?'

Carrul raised his eyebrows. 'What's so odd in that, may I ask, miss? Gurvel once said I had a voice like a bird!'

Brother Gelf chuckled. 'Aye, a dying duck. Come on then, Carrul, let's hear ye.'

The Abbot took a deep breath. 'Right, here goes. But you must sing this line at the end of each verse. *Heave haul away, twice around the bay. Yaah!*'

All the Redwallers wanted to see their Abbot singing, so they agreed readily. Carrul tapped the tabletop until he had the rhythm, then launched into the song. For an old mouse, he had quite a strong, ringing baritone.

'On the good ship *Leakylea*,
the captain was a frog,
the mate was a bumblebee,

and the cook was an old hedgehog.
    Heave haul away, twice around the bay. Yaah!

I was born at an early age,
and sent straight off to sea,
with a flea in an iron cage,
on the good ship *Leakylea*.
    Heave haul away, twice around the bay. Yaah!

We sailed the seas so rough,
and never washed the dishes,
ate pans o' skilly'n'duff,
and laughed at all the fishes.
    Heave haul away, twice around the bay. Yaah!

We ate all we could chew,
my flea grew bigger'n me,
'cos he'd ate more'n all the crew,
aboard the *Leakylea*.
    Heave haul away, twice around the bay. Yaah!

Then the ship sank in a gale,
I was rescued by my flea,
we're all that's left to tell the tale,
of the poor old *Leakylea*.
    Heave haul away, twice around the bay. Yaaaah!'

Martha applauded, laughing along with the other Red-wallers.

Abbot Carrul bowed modestly and winked at Brother Gelf. 'Not bad for a dying duck, eh?'

Remembering her responsibility to the Dibbuns, Martha called to them, 'Bedtime, little 'uns, come on now!'

Strangely, the three who were most likely to protest – Muggum, Shilly and Yooch – went quietly. The other Abbeybabes made their usual loud protest, but to no avail.

Sister Setiva wagged a severe paw at them. 'Up tae your beds, this verra instant, or ye'll have me tae reckon with!'

Martha watched the last one – Buffle the shrewbabe – scamper through the doorway, where he turned and glared at everybeast. 'Kumfuggleworragarrumbubbub . . . Kurch!'

Setiva picked up a ladle and made as if to chase him. 'Ah cannae tell what you're sayin', ye wee rogue. But, like as no', 'tis somethin' verra naughty! Ye'd best get toddlin' afore I catch up wi' ye!'

Buffle stood his ground long enough to twiddle a paw to his nose at the shrewnurse, then he bolted off, giggling.

Martha tried hard not to laugh. 'Perhaps we'd better go up and tuck them in, Sister?'

Setiva waved a dismissive paw. 'Och no, we can do that later. Ah've got tae go an' take supper tae Toran an' Junty first.'

The haremaid pushed her chair away from the table. 'I'll come and help you. Poor old Toran, I'd forgotten about him. Never mind, there's plenty of crumble left.'

Badredd halted his crew at the east wickergate. There was a small door set in the centre of the Abbey's rear wall. He held up a paw for silence. Gently pressing his weight against the timbers, the small fox tried the circular iron ring handle. It was firmly locked shut.

Plumnose held up a little lantern close to the door. 'Huh, id's shudd, Chief!'

Badredd had difficulty controlling his voice. 'Is it now! Thanks for lettin' me know, bouldernose!'

Plumnose grinned. 'T'ink nodding ob it.' He turned to Halfchop. 'Duh likkel door's locked, I t'ink.'

The rat wiped a ribbon of drool from his chin. 'Kachunk!'

Badredd rounded on the pair, hissing viciously, 'Shuttup, you two, an' get back into the trees – go on! Flinky, are ye any good at openin' locks?'

The stoat scratched his grimy cheek. 'Ah, well, there's locks an' locks, if ye get my meanin', yer 'onour!'

Badredd whipped out his cutlass and thrust it under Flinky's nose. 'I never asked ye for a lecture about locks! I said, are you any good at openin' 'em – well, are ye?'

Flinky heaved a sigh and took the cutlass from his chief's paw. 'Sure an' I don't know until I try. Shall I give it an ould go?'

Badredd waved him to the door impatiently. 'Well, put a move on, we haven't got all night!'

Flinky wedged the swordblade between the door jamb and the wall. He slid the blade down until it clinked dully against something.

'Hah, there's yore problem, Chief, 'tis a bolt. D'ye want me to try an' chop through it?'

The fox exhaled irately. 'Anythin', just get on with it!'

Flinky requested the aid of Floggo and Rogg. 'Come over t'this door, buckoes. Now put yore shoulders to it. Push now. That'll widen the gap so I can get a grand swing at the bolt. Push, put those ould bows down an' push!'

The door moved slightly under the pressure, creating a thin space. Flinky took the cutlass in both paws, raising it within the gap. Then he struck, whipping the blade down with all his might.

Piiing! As it struck the iron bolt, the blade snapped in half.

Badredd stared in silent horror at the stoat, who – still holding the handle and half a blade – was hopskipping in agony, both paws numbed by the reverberation of metal upon metal.

The vermin leader's voice rose to a disbelieving squeak. 'Me sword! Me luvly cutlass! Ye've ruined it! Idiot!'

Tears squeezed from the corners of Flinky's eyes as he flung the half cutlass on the ground. 'Aarh, it broke its stupid self. Yore s'posed t'be the chief, why didn't you have a go?'

Badredd seized the broken weapon. 'Have a go? I'll have a go at you if ye ain't careful, idiot! An' you lot, a fine crew

I've got, sittin' round scratchin' yerselves among the trees. Up on yer paws, doltheads, we'll have to find someplace else where we can get in. Jump to it!'

As Badredd strode off in foul mood, Plumnose called to him, 'Chief, me an' Halfchob hab got de door oben!'

Badredd dashed back to where Plumnose and Halfchop stood in the small doorway. Finding the door still closed, he fumed at them, 'Ye blither-brained, wobble-nosed, broken-snouted loafheads! Get goin', afore I carve cobs off'n ye with what's left o' me sword!'

But then, as Plumnose pushed the wicker door gently, it swung inwards. 'Duh, hawhawhaw, oben!'

Halfchop walked through the open door and grinned. 'Kachunk!'

Flinky inspected the wall alongside the door. 'Well now, ain't I the clever beast! I must've hit the bolt so hard that it broke through the ould soft sandstone it bolts into. See, there's a chunk of it missin'. Oh, here's the rest of yer grand cutlass, Chief.'

He presented the fox with the other half of the blade. Flinging it from him, Badredd turned on the crew and hissed, 'You lot, keep yore mouths shut, not a sound out of ye. Foller me, don't go cloghoppin' all over the place. We're goin' to take a look around. Next move is t'get inside the big buildin'. Quietly now . . .'

After taking food out to the west walltop for Toran and Junty, Martha and Sister Setiva returned to the Abbey. Martha stayed in her chair below stairs whilst Setiva went up to the dormitory to check up on the Dibbuns. The shrewnurse was away only for a brief space of time when a dismayed cry reached Martha. Setiva came hurrying back downstairs carrying little Buffle, who was imprisoned in a pillowcase with only his head sticking out.

The Sister's voice shook with barely controlled anger. 'Och, jist let me get mah paws on those rascals. Ah'll give 'em somethin' tae remember me by!'

Buffle strained against the pillowcase knotted at his neck. 'Goourr, 'ascals!'

A look of fear crossed the haremaid's face. 'What's happened, Sister?'

Setiva began trying to release Buffle. 'Ooh! Those Dibbuns, Muggum, Shilly an' Yooch. They've gone missing. All the rest o' the wee ones were fast asleep, except Buffle. D'ye see what they did? Trapped 'im in this auld pillowslip so he couldnae follow 'em. Where in the name of all fur have they got to?'

Buffle pulled a paw free and pointed out the Abbey door.

Junty Cellarhog ran his paw around the inside of his bowl and licked it. 'Ah, apple'n'blackberry crumble, mate, nothin' like it!'

Toran gazed longingly back towards the Abbey. 'Aye, pity we're on wallguard all night. If the Abbot sends out a relief, there might be some left when we get off duty.' Toran's keen eye suddenly noticed three small, white-clad figures trundling across the lawn in his direction. Two were waving sticks and one swinging a ladle. He peered hard.

'Look there, mate, that ain't no relief!'

It was at that moment when things began happening fast.

Framed in a shaft of golden light from the Abbey door, Martha and Sister Setiva were pointing to the Dibbuns and calling aloud to them, 'Come back here this instant, or you're in real trouble!'

The trio split, Muggum running south and the other two hurrying off to the north.

Toran saw them and chuckled. 'Escapin' Dibbuns, eh? They won't get far . . .'

Junty interrupted him roughly. 'Look, vermin!'

Badredd and his crew were sneaking quickly out across the lawn, trying to grab Muggum, who was heading for the pond where he planned on hiding in the reeds. The little mole was completely unaware of the enemy. Sister Setiva had come out on to the Abbey steps. As soon as she saw the vermin crew, she began dashing to save Muggum.

Junty was already hurtling down the gatehouse wall-steps, calling back to Toran, 'Get the other two little 'uns inside!' He shouted at the shrewnurse, 'Stay where ye are, Sister. I'll bring that Dibbun in!'

With his paws, Toran swept up the giggling Shilly and Yooch – this was all one big game to them – then the otter-cook turned and pounded towards the Abbey door.

Slipback came within a paw's length of grabbing Muggum, when Junty fetched him a massive whack to the chest, laying the weasel out flat. Then the big Cellarhog seized the molebabe and ran as fast as his footpaws would carry him, with Badredd and the crew hard on his heels. Without stopping, Junty snatched up Sister Setiva from where she had been standing in his path, rigid with fright.

Thud! Thud!

Two arrows from the bows of the ferrets buried themselves in the Cellarhog's broad back. He staggered slightly but kept running. Muggum was screeching; the hedgehog's sharp spines were sticking in his paws as the molebabe tried to struggle free.

Toran sped into the Abbey, dropped both of the other Dibbuns into Martha's lap. 'Get ready to slam the door shut!' He panted as he turned and ran back outside to help Junty.

One arrow grazed Toran's cheek, another hit Junty in his right shoulder. Toran shot past the Cellarhog, whirled hard, and caught Crinktail across the face with a huge smack of his rudder. He turned and pushed Junty, with both his burdens, up the steps and into the Abbey, roaring, 'Bar the door!'

Redwallers, who had come pouring out of Cavern Hole to see what all the commotion was about, assisted the hare-maid in slamming and barring the door in the face of the charging vermin crew. Two more arrows made a hollow sound as they flew into the strong oak timbering. A crash and a tinkle sent Foremole and Brother Weld hurrying to the lower windows.

Toran urged others along with him. 'Get tables an' benches! Barricade the lower frames before they get in!'

Badredd waved his broken cutlass. 'Keep at it there, crew, we've got 'em on the run!'

Flinky watched a dining table blocking a broken window. He muttered out the side of his mouth to Juppa, 'Keep slingin' rocks, but let 'em barricade those windows. They'd eat our liddle gang if'n we got inside. We'd be well out-numbered, mate.'

Juppa looked puzzled. 'Well, if'n we ain't goin' in, wot's the next move?'

Flinky had served under lots of different vermin chiefs, all a lot smarter than Badredd. He winked confidently at the weasel.

'Lissen t'me. If'n we ain't goin' in, well they ain't gettin' out. Did ye see that great orchard we passed as we came through?'

Badredd came marching around, prodding Flinky with his broken blade. 'Wot's that sling doin' empty? Keep chuckin' rocks at those windows until I tell ye to stop. Both of ye!'

Flinky loaded a large pebble into his sling. 'Ah, we'll be doin' that, yer 'onour, right away. I was just tellin' ould Juppa here what a clever move ye made.'

Badredd was eager to know just what the clever move was. 'Aye, well that's alright. You explain it to 'er, she was never too bright. Go on, tell the long-tailed oaf.' The small fox stood listening to Flinky's explanation.

'Hoho, we've got the sillybeasts locked up tight now. Prisoners in their own Abbey, 'tis called a siege. There's only a limited supply o' food an' drink in there. Take us now, the chief knows we got the orchard an' the pond. They'll either starve t'death in the Abbey or surrender after awhile. Ain't that right, Chief?'

Only a moment before, Badredd thought he had lost the encounter, but the realization of what Flinky had just said made him shudder with delight. So that was what a siege was all about.

Keeping a straight face, the fox nodded wisely. 'Aye, 'tis a siege, sure enough. Now you two keep slingin'.' He swaggered off, shouting orders to the other vermin. Juppa watched him go. 'A siege, eh? What a clever idea!'

Flinky launched another stone but missed. He jumped neatly aside as it bounced back at him. 'Ah sure, the ould chief is full o' clever ideas, especially when some otherbeast thinks 'em up for 'im. Little fool, he couldn't find his bottom wid both paws!' The weasel and the stoat loaded their slings again, laughing hilariously.

Martha had pulled herself from her chair. She sat on the floor, both eyes shut tight, clutching Junty's paw to her cheek as she rocked back and forth. The Cellarhog was lying where he had fallen, face up. Muggum was wailing as Sister Portula pulled spikes from his side and paws.

Sister Setiva was similarly engaged. 'Och, ye've got some fine sharp quills on ye, mah guid Cellarhog. Ah'll be with ye soon as I've got them out o' me. Hauld him still, Martha, how is he?'

With her eyes still shut, Martha kissed his limp paw. 'He's dead, Sister. Junty is dead!'

23

A squabbling flock of starlings, disputing rights to an ants' nest, woke Jibsnout in the hour following daybreak. With a cavernous yawn, the big sea rat heaved himself upright. He cast a jaundiced eye over the three sons of Wirga who were curled up together, sleeping beneath a wych hazel.

Jibsnout cuffed the trio roughly, stirring them into wakefulness. 'Up on yer hunkers, whelps, we're on the move again!'

The three smaller rats rose reluctantly, one of them glaring balefully at the Tracker and hissing, 'We only lay down an hour afore dawn.'

Jibsnout smirked. 'Aye, 'tis a shame, ain't it? Move yerself, snotty snout, an' don't argue wid me. If'n I say ye march, then ye march, so button yer lip!'

Quivering with anger, the smaller rat picked up his little spear – each of his brothers carried one, too. Jibsnout had seen them use the deadly weapons, but not as spears. Although they were actually hollow rods, the spearpoints could be removed, transforming them into blowpipes through which poisoned darts could be shot with lethal accuracy. The big sea rat stroked his long dagger fondly and moved closer to the sons of Wirga. He fixed the angry one with a cold stare.

'Go on, mamma's liddle rat, use it, I dare ye. Think yore brave enough t'slay me, eh?'

Lashing out swiftly, Jibsnout knocked the spear from the smaller rat's paws. Whipping out his blade, he menaced the other two. 'Just try raisin' one o' those things against me, an' poison or not, I'll rip yer throats out! Well, come on, ye gutless wonders, who's ready fer a fight t'the death?'

The sons of Wirga stood silent, their eyes cast down. Jibsnout curled his lip scornfully, turning his back on them. 'Hah, I thought so! There's more backbone in an egg than in youse three put t'gether. Scringin' cowards!'

Each of the three blowpipes was already charged with a poison dart. Silently slipping the head from his spear, the rat whom Jibsnout had insulted placed the hollow rod to his mouth. His cheeks bulged as he prepared to propel the dart.

Zzzzzzip!

A long arrow struck the little rat, driving him back a full four paces. He was dead before he hit the ground.

Diving to either side, the remaining two sons of Wirga sought cover. Lonna emerged from out of the trees, fitting another shaft to his bowstring. The badger's eyes were red with the light of vengeance, the snarl on his scarred, stitched face transforming him into a terrifying apparition. Frightened though he was, Jibsnout, a seasoned fighter, acted swiftly. Wielding his dagger, he dashed forwards, hoping to get so close to his adversary that the bow and arrow would be rendered useless.

Lonna was in a dilemma: he could see one of the sea rats glancing around a treetrunk, ready to fire a blowpipe, and Jibsnout thundering towards him. With lightning speed the badger acted. Falling into a crouch, he fired his arrow, but only narrowly missed being shot himself as a poison dart whipped by overhead. Jibsnout roared in pain as the arrow transfixed his paw to the ground. As Lonna rose, taking another shaft from his quiver, the sea rat who had fired the dart fled off into the woodlands.

The remaining son of Wirga came from behind a fir tree,

certain that he could not fail to hit a target as big as the badger. As he placed the blowpipe to his mouth, Figalok the squirrel appeared directly in front of him, hanging by her tail from an overhead branch. She grabbed the opposite end of the vermin's blowpipe and blew hard. Clutching his throat, the horrified rat fell writhing to the ground, choked on his own poison dart.

Figalok dropped out of the tree, nodding to Lonna. 'Chahaah, gotta be plenny quick wirra sea ratta!'

The big badger put up his bow, striving to master the Bloodwrath that was coursing through him. 'You saved my life, friend, but I'll have to thank you some other time. One of the sea rats got away. I must hunt him down now while his trail is still fresh.'

The squirrel gestured at the wounded Jibsnout. 'Warra 'bout dissa one, ya goin' to slay 'im?'

Jibsnout crouched over, his face creased in agony. The arrow that had pierced his footpaw was buried half its length into the ground. He glanced up at Lonna, expecting no mercy from him.

'If'n yore gonna finish me off, make it quick, stripedog!'

The badger strode over and grasped the arrow. With a sharp tug he pulled the arrow out, growling at Jibsnout, 'I'm no sea rat, I don't kill defenceless beasts!' Ripping the sleeve from the rat's frayed tunic, Lonna grabbed a pawful of damp moss and dockleaves.

The puzzled rat watched his enemy binding the wound up tight. 'Ye mean yore lettin' me live?'

The badger hauled him upright, slamming him against a tree. 'My name is Lonna Bowstripe. Take this message to Raga Bol. Tell him that he and all his crew of murderers are walking deadbeasts. I will find them and slay them, one by one. Even you. Now begone from my sight and deliver my message to your captain. Tell him I am coming; nothing will stop me!'

Lonna and Figalok watched Jibsnout limping painfully off until he was obscured by the trees, then together, the two friends took a brief meal. The squirrel wielded a blow-pipe spear and poison darts taken from the slain sea rats.

'Chahaah! Me betcha dis keep Ravin away from squirrel. Lonna Bigbeast, ya goin' after dat sea ratta who runned away? Me go witcha, we find 'im afore tomorra.'

But the badger would not hear of it. 'No, my friend, you have your own home and kinbeasts to protect. This is something I must do by myself. I am sworn by my own oath to rid the earth of Raga Bol and all his vermin. But I thank you for saving my life, Figalok!'

The elderly squirrel took his paw. 'Chahaaw, so be't, Lonna, ya are d'true warrior. Ya saved us fromma Ravin, glad Figalok could save ya, too. Me no ferget ya alla me life, always think of ya!'

Averting his eyes, Lonna inspected the long dagger he had taken from Jibsnout, pleased that it was a good blade. When he looked up again, Figalok had gone, vanished into the treetops.

The sea rat's trail had gone off to the southeast. Lonna picked it up and followed the tracks. As he walked, the badger fashioned a holder for his dagger, fitting it to his upper left arm close to the shoulder. By late afternoon, the dense woodlands thinned out into pine groves and sandhills. In the distance, Lonna could make out a dark shape to his left on the horizon. The trail of Wirga's remaining son was running parallel to the mysterious mass. Just before sunset, the badger crested a rise which afforded a clear view of the country he was travelling through. On the one side, the hills bordered a vast, dusty plain, almost like a desert wasteland. On the other side, the odd dark mass reared up into a towering line of forbidding cliffs. After awhile it grew too dark for tracking. Reaching the cliff face, Lonna sighted what he knew was a cave. He climbed up and made camp there for the night.

There was no need for a fire. The night was still and

warm, with heat waves drifting in from the plain. Knowing he could pick up the sea rat's tracks at dawn, Lonna sat in the cave entrance, eating an apple and some dried fruit. He gazed up at the night sky, where a sliver of moon, resembling a slice of russet apple, was surrounded by myriads of stars twinkling in the firmament. The words of an old song rose unbidden to his mind.

'When weary day does shed its light,
I rest my head and dream,
I ride the great dark bird of night,
so tranquil and serene.
Then I can touch the moon afar,
which smiles up in the sky,
and steal a twinkle from each star,
as we go winging by.

We'll fly the night to dawning light,
and wait 'til dark has ceased,
to marvel at the wondrous sight,
of sunrise in the east.
So slumber on, my little one,
float soft as thistledown,
and wake to see when night is done,
fair morning's golden gown.'

Since Lonna had no recollection of his parents, he surmised that the lullaby had been taught to him by Grawn, the old badger who had reared him.

Lonna stayed that night in the cave on the cliffside. As day dawned he spotted a tiny puff of dust, on a hilltop off to his right. The big badger knew instantly that it was his quarry. The sea rat must have spent the night amid the hills, not far from the cave. Pausing only to grab his bow and quiver, Lonna set off in pursuit.

He had travelled no further than the base of the first foothill when he was faced by a small patrol of ten Darrat rats. Their leader eyed him insolently up and down.

'Dis be Darrat land. You give me bow'n'arrers, stripedog. We take ye to Hemper Figlugg!' He grinned at the other rats, murmuring to them, 'Much Burcha Glugg, eh?'

Had it been ten rats or twenty, Lonna did not like either their manner or their disposition, so he charged them without warning. They went down like ninepins under the giant badger's onslaught. Seizing the leader of the patrol, Lonna hurled him bodily into the other rats. Then the big badger was among them like a whirlwind – punching, kicking, butting, thrashing them with their own spears. So surprised were the Darrat that they fled in panic, kicking up sand widespread as they scuttled off amid the hills.

Lonna picked up his bow and quiver. Then, throwing back his great striped head, he gave vent to the fearsome warcry of hares and badgers, 'Eulaliiiiiaaaaaa!'

However, with much more urgent business to attend to, he let the Darrat be, and didn't give chase. Instead, Lonna set off swiftly on the trail of the sea rat.

When the Darrat saw they were not being pursued, they halted on the plain beside the foothills. The patrol leader limped up, carrying half a broken spear. He watched the big badger crossing a hilltop, some distance off.

Turning to his subordinates, who were sitting licking their wounds, he snarled, 'We was sent to catcher rabbert, mouse an' squirri', not stripedog! Huh, let High Kappin catcher that 'un – 'e be over dat way wid many Darrat!'

The sea rat saw Lonna coming after him. Deserting the hills, he dashed out on to the dusty plain. It was a mistake, the last mistake he was ever to make. The badger's arrow found him. Once Lonna had the range, nobeast could outrun a shaft from his big bow. Though Wirga did not know, she had lost all three of her sons.

Lonna sat down in a hollow amid the hills and made breakfast from the food in his pack.

Out on the flatlands the five travellers pushed forwards, keeping the distant cliffs in view. They marched shoulder to shoulder because, as Saro had pointed out, that way they would not be eating one another's dust. Since their rescue, Springald and Fenna were paying more attention to Bragoon and Saro. Seasoned campaigners both, the squirrel and the otter were ever ready to share their knowledge with the younger, less experienced trio.

Horty was feeling rather chipper now that any immediate danger was past. He struck up a jolly marching song, to which he himself had written the lyrics. As was usual with hare songs, it dealt mainly with food.

'Oh wallop me left an' stagger me right,
an' buffet me north an' south,
if I could teach a stew to walk,
it'd march right into me mouth!

To pasties an' pies of convenient size,
I'd beat a tattoo on me drum,
so jolly forceful, each tasty morsel,
tramp over me gums to me tum!

As each of 'em trips in through me lips,
all skippin' along to the beat,
why all of a sudden I'd grab a fat pudden,
an' leave it no way to retreat!

Form up in line, you vittles so fine,
watch y'dressin' that salad back there,
a quick salute to trifle'n'fruit,
then charge down the throat of the hare!

Quick march! One two! Scoff 'em all! You an' you!
Left right! Left right! Here comes supper for tonight!'

A grey, black-flecked Darrat scout came loping into the camp in the foothills of the high cliffs. He threw himself flat in front of High Kappin Birug, the Darrat leader. Pointing back to the scrubland, the rat scout shouted, 'Burcha Glugg!'

Birug dashed past him to the top of a hill. He crouched, peering at the small dust cloud with the travellers marching in front of it, not half a mile away. Smirking with satisfaction, Birug turned to the others who had followed him.

'Hemper Figlugg, trus' me, ho yar, I know dey only go one way. Run for bigrocks. We wait, they be come to us. Burcha Glugg!'

Darrat vermin shook their heads in admiration of Kappin Birug's cunning. One of them piped up, 'Hemper be 'appy to see Burcha Glugg come back.' The more excited of the Darrat leaped up and down, waving spears.

Birug growled a warning at them. 'Keepa 'eads down, idjits!'

Horty glanced up at the sky. 'Cloudin' over up there, chaps. We might have a spot of jolly old rain before nightfall, wot?'

Bragoon sniffed the light breeze. 'Bit more'n a spot, matey. Looks like we're in for a downpour afore dark. Keep movin', step the pace up. Mebbe we'll find shelter in the lee of those big cliffs.'

Fenna let out a gasp and sat down. 'Ouch, my footpaw!'

They gathered around her, crouching down to take a look. The squirrelmaid spoke through lips that hardly moved. 'Stay down, all of you, don't look towards those foothills!'

Bragoon kept his eyes on Fenna. 'Why, what's goin' on?'

She quickly responded. 'Rats ahead, they look like those flesh-eating ones!'

Springald automatically began to look up, but Sarobando pressed her head back down. 'Listen to Fenna an' keep yore eyes down, miss. How many d'ye reckon there are?'

Bragoon interrupted. 'Plenty, I'll wager. Too many for us to fight off. I told ye, those vermin don't give up easily.

They've been waitin' in the foothills for us to show up. Well, mates, wot's t'be done, eh?'

Fenna shrugged. 'I suppose we'll have to run for it.'

Bragoon shook his head. 'Bad idea! They'd outcircle us.'

Horty began shrugging off his backpack. 'Does any chap mind me makin' a suggestion, wot?'

Saro saw that the young hare looked serious. 'As long as 'tis sensible. Go on then, wot's yore idea?'

Horty shed his backpack. 'Give me some old, dead brush, an' I'll decoy the rotters. A hare can jolly well outrun 'em if anybeast can. I'll take the villains off one way, while you lot go runnin' off the bally opposite way. See that black hole up there, about halfway along the cliffs? I'll meet y'back there after dark. Well, what d'you think?'

Springald objected. 'It's far too dangerous. You'll be caught.'

Saro stared at Horty. 'I say give it a try, it might work. Otherwise, we'll just stick together and get nabbed.'

Bragoon winked at the hare. 'Right, go to it, young 'un. Good luck!'

Two Darrat spies peeped over the hilltop, to where the dust cloud had stopped. One whispered, 'Warra dey do now, jus' lay dere?'

The other one leaped up as the dust plume started again, moving swiftly north. 'Musta see'd us, dey runnin' now, fast!'

He waved his spear, calling to Birug, who had the rats standing ready, 'Kappin, dey go lef' plenty fasta!'

Horty pelted along with a bunch of dead bracken tied to his tail, raising a dust cloud that stood out light brown against the lowering clouds. Glancing sideways, he saw the Darrat rats pouring over the hill, veering in his direction. He muttered between clenched teeth, 'Ahah! That's the way, you vile vermin. Come on, you shower, follow Hortwill Braebuck, skimmer of the scrublands!'

Fenna raised her head. In the distance she could see the

dust cloud off to her left. 'Good old Horty, he's whipping along like a whirlwind!'

Still crouching low, they watched their friend's progress, comparing it to the crowd of Darrat vermin chasing him. Horty was indeed a Redwaller, brave and courageous. Springald felt elation and pride surging through her. She clenched her paws.

'Go on, mate, there's none faster than you! Flesh eaters, hah! All those scum will eat is the dust in his wake! Run them, Horty, show those rats what a hare from our Abbey can do!'

As soon as Bragoon saw the two dust plumes, he realized that the Darrat had come out of the hills and hit the scrubland. Their intended quarry was far and away out in front. The otter's eyes shone with admiration.

'I said that young 'un has the makin's of a real warrior. He'll lead 'em a merry dance alright. Oh, drat, here comes the rain!'

24

Large drops began falling, slow at first, sending up small puffs of dust as they struck the dry plain. A distant thunder rumble echoed from the high cliffs, followed by a faroff flash of lightning that illuminated the southeast horizon. Then the deluge fell in earnest. Saro stood upright, blowing water from her nosetip as she blinked at the sheeting curtains of heavy rain.

'Nobeast can see us now. Let's head straight for the cliffs!'

Joining paws, they jogtrotted towards the foothills, battered by the relentless downpour. Lightning ripped over the dark skies in blinding sheets, while thunder boomed and banged overhead. Dust turned quickly to mud, their paws squelched into it. Springald tightly gripped the paws of Fenna and Saro. The intensity of the storm was frightening, she had never been out in open country at such a time before. At Redwall, it had been relatively easy to run inside and shelter from the elements, but out here it was different.

They gained the foothills, slipping and sliding up the wet grass. Bragoon shielded his eyes as he glanced upwards.

'Keep goin', it ain't too far now. Yonder black hole that Horty spotted looks like it could be a cave of some sort. Let's make it up that far an' shelter.'

Horty's wet paws slapped down in the sludge and mud. Wiping water from his eyes, he chanced a backwards glimpse at his pursuers. Although the main body were still a respectable distance off, three fast runners had broken away and were coming doggedly onwards, closing the distance considerably. The young hare bit his lip. The trio were armed with spears; if they got within throwing range, he would be finished. It was time for a change of plan. Still with stamina in reserve, Horty shot off to the right, back among the foothills, where he stood a chance of losing the Darrat mob.

Birug panted, squinching his eyes against the rain as he saw the hare change course and dart into the dunes. The High Kappin urged his rats on. 'Catchim, or Hemper Figlugg make Burcha Glugg outta you!'

Topping a rise, Horty spotted the barely discernible hole in the cliffside, far along to his right. He tripped and went rolling downhill. Spitting grit and coated with sand, he swiftly picked himself up and pounded on to the next dune, muttering to himself, 'Ears up, old lad, keep pickin' 'em up an' puttin' 'em down, wot. Huh, if only the young skin'n'blister could see her handsome brother now – a blinkin', gallopin' sandbeast!'

A spear buried itself in the sand, not far behind him.

Birug appeared at the top of the hill that Horty had just come over. Two others trailed behind him. He seized the spear from one of them and flung it. The Darrat leader's aim was bad – he watched the spear strike the hillside flat and slide back down. Birug rested a moment on all fours, fatigued.

Horty gained the next hilltop and turned. Holding a paw to his nose, he wiggled it and called out cheekily, 'Bloomin' old flesh scoffer, go an' boil your own head an' eat it, wot wot!'

Stung by the hare's jibe, Birug hauled himself upright

and came after the hare with renewed energy. Horty scuttled off, chiding himself for his momentary foolishness.

'Have to keep the old lip buttoned, wot! Seems a jolly determined type o' cove for a rat, full of the old vermin vinegar. Curse his caddish hide!'

Afternoon passed, without the rain slackening its intensity. It was humid, without a trace of breeze. Rivulets gathered into swollen streams, racing down the cliffside in floods of umber-hued water.

Bragoon was first to reach the black hole. His prediction had been correct: it was a cave – large, dark and deep. He helped Springald and Fenna enter first, while Sarobando brought up the rear. Once inside, all four flopped down, exhausted. The otter shook himself like a dog and shrugged off the packs he had been burdened with.

'Whoo! Wretched weather, wonder when this rain's due to stop?' He sat up against the right wall, peering out. 'Come on Horty, mate, where've ye got to?'

Fenna joined him. 'I hope he's alright!'

Springald rose and began to wander off to explore the big cave, but Bragoon pulled her back.

'You stay close up here, miz. We don't know wot might be back there. Can't risk a fire, either – too dangerous. Break out some vittles, if'n they're still dry enough, and a drink, too. Funny how ye can be out in the rain all day an' still be thirsty.'

The mousemaid found dry oatcakes and some crystallized fruit, which they washed down with some home-brewed cider. Fenna stared out into the persistent downpour, then jumped slightly as thunder boomed out overhead.

Saro patted her shoulder. 'Nought t'do but sit an' wait, matey. Don't fret now, that young rogue'll make it.'

The squirrelmaid forced a smile. 'If he's not here soon, I'll light a fire and make a pot of soup. Horty can smell vittles a league away. He'll show up then, I wager.'

She sat miserably, pondering the foolishness of her statement. Horty could be lying slain out there in the rain.

Horty staggered gamely on, the three rats not more than six paces behind him. They had picked up their spears again and thrown them at him several times. With the courage of desperation, the young hare, having managed to avoid the throws, remained unscathed. Birug and his two rats had left the spears where they fell, and carried on, stubbornly pursuing the fugitive. It was only a matter of time now, and they would have him. As the High Kappin blundered forwards, Horty moved out of his reach.

With his tongue lolling, the rat gasped out, 'We . . . catcha!'

Horty stumbled, tripped and wriggled out of his reach. Gaining his footpaws, he stood panting. 'Couldn't . . . catch your old . . . grannie . . . Slobberchops!' He blundered on another pace or two, then collapsed.

Birug nodded to the other two rats. 'Gerrim . . . now!'

All three crawled forwards on their bellies, reaching out to lay paws on the fallen hare when, without warning, the hillside gave way, sliding down a tremendous avalanche of wet sand. It enveloped the three rats completely, burying them under a huge mound.

Horty lay at the edge of the mass, covered right up to his neck. He was trapped fast. A paw, almost the size of his own head, seized both of the hare's long ears and yanked him out with one mighty pull. Horty revived with the pain, his eyes flickering open. He stayed conscious just long enough to see a lightning flash illuminate the head of a giant badger with a scar running lengthwise down its striped muzzle.

The young hare blinked. 'Nice weather, wot . . . Oh, corks!' Then he passed out.

Only the Dibbuns slept upstairs in their dormitories that night, while every other Redwaller guarded the barricades.

It was the longest, saddest night Martha had ever witnessed. The still form of Junty had been wrapped tenderly in blankets and borne down to the place he loved best, his cellars. Clearing the barrels and lifting some floorstones, Foremole Dwurl and his crew dug a grave for the good Cellarhog. Junty was laid to rest. Once the grave was filled in and the flooring stones replaced, Abbot Carrul took a charcoal and wrote words upon it. At some later day the moles would chisel the words into the stones as a permanent epitaph for a beast whom all Redwallers loved dearly. Tears often smudged the charcoal letters as Carrul wrote:

'Here lies a fallen warrior, slain by vermin whilst helping his fellow creatures. Hard working, good and faithful. A credit to his kind. Always a kind word or smile to all. Junty Cellarhog, Keeper of Redwall Abbey cellars. His October Ale was the best. Rest peacefully, old friend.'

Above stairs, Martha rolled her cart around Great Hall, relieving those who were wearied. When she was not doing that, the tireless haremaid helped Granmum Gurvel to ferry food from the kitchens.

Toran watched Martha – she was never still, always finding something to do for the common good. He halted the little cart with his rudder. 'Come on, beauty, time ye took a nap or ye'll be worn out.'

Martha protested, 'I'm fine, honestly I am!'

But, deaf to her pleas, the ottercook opened the lap rug and tucked it beneath the haremaid's chin. 'No arguments now. I'll wake ye if'n yore needed, miss. You stay out the way here, in this quiet corner away from broken glass an' slingstones. I'll have t'go an' get more stuff to barricade those windows.'

He hurried off to assist Brother Weld, who was struggling with a door he had taken from its hinges. 'Here, Brother, you take one end an' I'll take the other.'

Weld sighed thankfully. 'We're getting a bit old for this sort of thing. D'you think we'll hold them off, Toran?'

Gritting his teeth, the big otter growled, 'Filthy scum, if

they get in this Abbey, 'twill be over my dead body. Don't worry, Brother, we'll keep 'em out!'

Old Phredd helped them to shore the door up against the windows. 'Huh, the way I see it, we're under siege. 'Tis those vermin who are keeping us in!'

Toran clenched his paws tightly. 'That's right. Strange ain't it, bein' kept prisoner inside yore own home.'

Old Phredd added miserably, 'Aye, what do we do if the food runs out?'

Toran's clenched paw wagged under the ancient Gate-keeper's nose. 'Quit that kind o' talk now, d'ye hear me? There's vittles aplenty for all, so don't go scarin' every-beast!'

Badredd watched the dawn wash the skies in rosy hues. The small fox was in his element. 'Flinky, Crinktail, c'mere. I got a plan o' me own at last!'

Both stoats, stuffing themselves on orchard produce, continued eating as Badredd explained his scheme.

'Load up a couple o' sacks an' take a stroll through the woods south of here. Eat what y'like as ye go.'

Flinky tossed away a half-eaten pear. 'Sounds like a good ould job, Chief, but what're we supposed t'be doin'?'

The little fox grinned craftily. 'Recruitin' more vermin. We need more beasts to take this place. Tell 'em that Redwall is bein' conquered by Badredd an' a vermin crew. Aye, an' tell 'em there'll be plenty o' vittles an' booty for anybeast who'll serve under me. Have ye got that?'

Flinky saluted elaborately. 'Leave it to us, Chief. We'll bring ye back a gang o' the best, so we will. No old or feeble ones, just grand fightin' vermin. But wot about all this ripe ould fruit?'

Badredd snorted impatiently. 'Use yore head, give it away to any vermin ye come across. Show 'em we got plenty of vittles. Say there's lots more where that comes from, if they'll come an' serve under me. Do I have to tell ye everything?'

Crinktail touched the side of her nose knowingly. 'We unnerstand, Chief, leave it to me'n Flinky.' The pair hurried off to the orchard to load up sacks of fruit.

Badredd began issuing orders to his depleted crew. 'Floggo, Rogg, watch that big door, an' the windows, too. Keep yore bows'n'arrows at the ready. Kill anybeast wot pokes his nose out!'

The little fox was glad he had the weasel brothers to serve him. They never argued and usually obeyed all orders.

'Juppa, Slipback, Plumnose, Halfchop, keep slingin' stones at those windows. Whatever ye do, don't stop!'

Juppa was pawsore and weary of slinging stones. 'But we've smashed all the windows. Wot else is there t'keep slingin' stones at?'

Badredd could feel his temper fraying. His voice gained a squeak as he shouted in the weasel's face, 'The idea of breakin' the windows is so that ye can hurl stones through an' hit anybeast inside the place. Or are ye too stupid to realize that?'

Juppa stood her ground, arguing back swiftly, 'No, I ain't stupid, but I'm hungry an' tired! Us four've been chuckin' stones at that Abbey all night. Oh, an' there's one more thing we ain't too stupid to realize. We're runnin' outta stones to throw, while yore marchin' about givin' orders out an' doin' little else!'

Badredd waved his broken cutlass about threateningly. 'Don't ye dare talk t'me like that, I'm the chief around here!'

Slipback muttered loudly, 'Wot're ye goin' t'do, run 'er through wid a broken sword?'

The little fox threw his half cutlass aside and stamped his footpaw down so hard that it hurt. 'I heard that, Slipback. Do? I'll tell ye wot I'm goin' to do. I'm goin' t'show ye three how to sling stones properly! Throw down wot stones ye got left an' give me yore slings. Plumnose, Halfchop, start slingin' alongside me. Come on, move yoreselves, take these slings an' load up!'

Halfchop picked up a sling and loaded it with an apple he had been munching on. He grinned at Badredd. 'Kachunk!'

The little fox glared speechlessly at the hapless rat. He shouted to Plumnose, 'Teach that idjit to throw stones!'

Furiously, Badredd began slinging at a mad rate. The slingstones went everywhere – a few through the window spaces, some backwards across the lawns when he released them too early. Others bounced back off the solid sandstone walls.

Slipback dodged a ricochet, grinning slyly. 'Hah, let's see 'ow long the mighty chief can keep that pace up!'

Juppa started moving out of range, ducking a pebble that had gone the wrong way. 'Let's get out of 'ere afore we get slain!'

She raised her voice, calling to Badredd, 'We're goin' to get somethin' to eat an' take a rest!'

The fox kept hurling stones like a madbeast, panting, 'Get out o' my sight, ye useless lumps! When y'come back, bring more stones, a lot more!'

Plumnose, who was slinging at a much steadier rate, called happily to Badredd, 'Huhuh, we'b godd lots ob stones, me'n my mate!'

The fox screeched back at him, 'Sharrap an' get slingin'!'

Halfchop had found a black-and-red banded pebble among his stones. He polished it on his fur and spoke to it. 'Kachunk!'

25

Abbot Carrul and Granmum Gurvel were going around Great Hall, distributing beakers of hot barley and leek soup to the defenders. Martha was wakened by a stone pinging off a nearby column. Gurvel ladled soup from a cauldron standing on a trolley. The Abbot served it to Martha. Then Carrul called Toran over and gave him some.

Toran accepted it gratefully. 'Well, Father, the windows are barricaded tight now. There's only the odd stone comin' through. Let the vermin wear themselves out. Apart from broken panes, there ain't much damage – unless they try burnin' the window barricades.'

Carrul tried to remain calm, though he could not help sounding anxious. 'Have you a plan in mind, Toran?'

Scratching his rudder, the ottercook stifled a yawn. 'I wish I had, but I'm far too tired an' upset about pore Junty.'

Martha straightened the rug across her lap. 'We'd do better if we went upstairs to the dormitories. Perhaps up there we could retaliate against the vermin.'

Abbot Carrul nodded. 'Sounds sensible to me, Martha. Carry on.'

Warming to her own idea, the haremaid explained, 'We could make slings and throw stones at them. I'll wager Foremole and his crew could provide us with rubble.'

Gurvel sighted Foremole Dwurl coming up from the cellars. She beckoned him to join them. 'Coom over yurr, zurr.'

Dwurl waved a heavy digging claw. 'Wutt can oi do furr ee?'

Martha made her request. 'Would it be possible to get a load of rubble and pebbles up to the dormitory windows, please?'

The mole nodded his velvety head. 'Surpintly, miz! Oi take ett ee bee's goin' t'give yon varmints a gudd peltin', hurr hurr!'

Immensely fond of Foremole Dwurl, Martha took his work-lined paw in hers. 'Great minds think alike, my friend. We need lots of stones, and some rubble, to tip on the vermin if they start lighting fires. Water is too precious to waste in our present position.'

Toran looked at his young friend with a new respect. 'Hear that, Carrul? Our Martha certainly has a wise head on her shoulders, eh?'

Martha turned to the ottercook, her eyes shining fiercely. 'Aye, and I don't intend to lose it to a band of murdering vermin. It was vermin who slew my family when I was a babe and too young to do anything about it. This time 'tis going to be different. No matter what happens, those evil scum are not going to take Redwall Abbey from us. We'll defeat them!'

They all clasped paws on the arm of the haremaid's chair. Her resolution ran like wildfire through them all.

Father Abbot Carrul's voice echoed around Great Hall. 'Everybeast upstairs to the front dormitories. We're going to fight them. Redwaaaaaaalll!'

A great cheer went up as Martha had united them in a common cause: taking the attack to the foebeast. The Redwallers thundered upstairs, shouting and roaring.

'We'll teach 'em a lesson they won't forget!'

'Aye, they'll regret the day they came to our Abbey!'

'No vermin's goin' to bully us!'

'Blood'n'vinegar, that's what they'll get!'

Sister Setiva was minding the Dibbuns as the dormitory door was flung open wide. Redwallers crowded in, still shouting. The Abbeybabes did not quite know what was going on, but they joined in lustily, issuing dire threats against the enemy.

'Cutta tails off wiv rusty knifes!'

'Boil ee varmints in roasted baffwater!'

'Gurr, smack ee bottoms wi' gurt sticks!'

Little Buffle stuck out his stomach and bellowed, 'Yukkumbumgur!'

Setiva was becoming able to translate Buffle's baby language. She raised her eyebrows in horror. 'Och, ye wee scallywag, I'll wash your mouth out wi' soap if ye even think o' sayin' that again!'

Martha was carried up, chair and all, by Brother Weld, Toran and several stout moles. Immediately she related her plan to all the Abbeybeasts.

'Sisters Setiva and Portula, could you set about making lots of slings? Good, strong braided ones. Brothers Gelf and Weld, I want you to check the downstairs barricades as often as you can. Make sure they're still holding firm, and report back to me each time. Foremole, sir, can you bring up as much stone and rubble as you can lay your paws on?'

Dwurl saluted. 'We'm got loads o' rubble an' rock frum our diggin's in ee basement, miz. Oi'll bring et roight aways.'

The haremaid nodded to Toran. 'Can you search about, friend, to find anything we can use as weapons? Anything!'

Muggum and the Dibbuns clung to the chairarms, pleading, 'Uz 'elp ee, Miz Marth', give us'n's summ jobs!'

Sister Setiva turned in the dormitory doorway, shaking her blackthorn stick and berating the Abbeybabes. 'Och! Ah'll give ye jobs. Get straight intae yon beds an' stay oot o' Miss Martha's way, this verra instant!'

Martha saw the sad little faces on the Dibbuns and interceded on their behalf to the strict Infirmary Keeper. 'Please,

Sister, they only want to help. Let me find a job for them. Granmum Gurvel, have you any sieves or riddles? We'll need them to sift out slingstones from Foremole's rubble when it arrives up here. Could you find some?'

Muggum brightened up. 'Oi'll tell ee a riggle, Miz Marth'.'

Gurvel took the molebabe's paw. 'Gurr, liddle pudden 'ead, that bee's ee wrong sort o' riggle. Cumm to ee kitchens, an' oi'll foind ee sum proper riggles.'

Everybeast hurried to their tasks, while Martha tried to keep some organization amid the ensuing chaos.

Molecrews trundled in and out of the dormitory, bearing stretcherloads of rubble. Sister Portula and some elders ripped old fabric into strips and began weaving slings. Redwallers on kitchen duty came scurrying up with drinks and meals. Martha wheeled her chair about, giving directions, calling encouragement and keeping the constant traffic moving back and forth.

'Don't block the doorway, please. Bring that stretcher right in and empty it there, by the window.' She seemed to be everywhere at once. 'Oh, that's a nice strong sling, put it over there with the others. Don't leave that cordial and soup by the rubble, it'll get dust all over it. Shut it inside that wardrobe for the present.'

Badredd soon grew tired of slinging stones. His paws were aching: more than once, a stone had stayed in the sling, causing it to wrap around his paw and strike it sharply. That, plus the fact that he was an abominable shot, made him toss the sling away angrily.

'Blood'n'skulls, I've got better things t'do than stand here chuckin' stones all day. Where's the rest o' this lazy lot, eh? Stuffin' vittles or layin' about sleepin', I bet. Well, I'll soon liven their ideas up, the dirty layabouts!' He stalked off in high dudgeon.

Plumnose and Halfchop dropped their slings and trailed

after him. The little fox turned on them furiously. 'Where are you two deadbrains goin'? Did I tell ye t'stop slingin'? Get back there afore I flay ye both!' The pair went back wearily and continued slinging.

Plumnose complained resentfully to his companion. 'Huh, he'd inna bad mood, iddent he?'

Halfchop nodded in agreement. 'Kachunk!'

Martha kept track of Badredd from her position at the front dormitory windows. 'I wonder where he's off to now.'

Toran stood behind her chair. 'Who knows, miss. He's up t'no good, though, an' jumpin' mad by the look o' him.'

Foremole gestured at the considerable mound of earth and stone piled up close to the windowsills. 'Hurr, ee vurmint can jump all ee looikes, we'm ready for 'im!'

Granmum Gurvel staggered in, dragging a bulging sack. 'Yurr, lookit oi finded, ee gurt sack uv 'otroot pepper. Ee 'hotters leaved it yurr afore they'm go'd off. Oi'm b'aint a keepen it in moi kitchens, no zurr, orful sneezy stuff!' Gurvel dumped it next to Martha's chair. The haremaid quickly pulled out her kerchief as dust rose from the sack. 'Kerchoo! Aah . . . Aah . . . Achoo! Beg your pardon, dearie me!'

Baby Buffle stared down at the sack from the top of the rubble mound. 'Sumakivalikkasaccasaccavurgimchoochoo!'

Martha dabbed at her nose with the 'kerchief. 'What's he chunnering on about now, Sister?'

Setiva translated the shrewbabe's language. 'Och, pay no heed tae the rascal. He says we should throw et at yon vermin. 'Tis a silly idea – we'd be sneezed tae death doin' a thing like that. The breeze'd carry et right back in 'ere.'

Gurvel spoke up. 'Nay, marm, not if us'n's makes ee likkle sacks uv pepper, boi 'okey. We'm cudd frow slingers at ee varmints.'

Martha clapped her paws delightedly. 'What a great plan! Thank you, Buffle and Gurvel. Let's try it!'

The ancient molecook took charge of the operation. Soon, she and several Dibbuns donned bandannas of wet cloth to protect their noses and mouths against the fiery hotroot pepper. Carefully, they ladled measured portions of the pepper on to flimsy squares of thin, birch-bark parchment. Each of these was fashioned into a tiny bundle, tied at the top with thread. Toran weighed one in his paw. 'Just right for throwin'. Hoho, these'll cause a few sneezes if they land on some scummy noses!'

Yooch the molebabe had scrambled up on to a windowsill. Jumping up and down, he waved his tiny paws and squealed, 'Look out, look out, d'vermints bee's cummin'!'

Badredd kept a paw on the broken cutlass in his belt, not drawing the weapon lest they see it was only a half-bladed thing. Behind him stood the rest of the available vermin crew – Halfchop, Floggo, Rogg, Slipback, Plumnose and Juppa.

The little fox shouted boldly, 'Where's yore chief? I wanna talk!'

Abbot Carrul showed himself at the dormitory window. 'Say what you have got to say, fox!'

Badredd puffed out his narrow chest. 'Lissen, we've got ye well boxed in up there. You ain't warriors, ye can't fight back or hurt us. So I'll tell ye what I'll do. Open yore doors, we won't attack. Just let me'n one o' my crew come in. When we've found yore magic sword, an' other bits o' loot that we fancy, we'll leave ye in peace an' go.'

The Abbot shook his head firmly. 'Never! You'll not set paw in Redwall Abbey, none of you!'

Badredd passed a paw signal to Rogg from behind his back. The weasel casually notched an arrow to his bow-string.

Keeping his temper in check, the fox replied, 'Never? We'll see about that. Wot ye got to unnerstand is that yore under siege – we could starve ye out or keep attackin' until one by one yore all slain. Oh, I've got lots o' bright ideas, mouse, take yore pick. Either that or just do as I command. 'Twill save ye a lot o' grief.'

Carrul stood his ground. 'No matter what you say, you will not enter this Abbey. Now, let me make a suggestion. Take your vermin, plus all the fruit you have stolen from our orchard, and leave here. If you do this, you will save yourself a lot of grief. Take my word for it!'

Badredd shrugged. 'Ain't no use of talkin' to ye, mouse.'

As the vermin leader stepped aside, Rogg hurried forwards and let fly. Inside the dormitory, some of the pepper dust had got to the Abbot, causing him to sneeze. 'Yaachooo!'

As Carrul's head went down with the force of the sneeze, the arrow tipped his headfur, ending up quivering in the dormitory ceiling.

Cursing inwardly, Badredd forced himself to stay nonchalantly calm, even to smile. 'Saved by a sneeze, eh? Yore a lucky mouse!'

Suddenly Toran appeared at the window, a pepper bomb in each paw. 'You won't be so lucky. Sneeze on this, snottynose!'

In quick succession, two bags of pepper struck Badredd's face. Then the dormitory windows were packed with Redwallers, hurling their new weapons and shouting.

'Try a sniff of this, uglychops!'

'Yurr, stuff this'n oop ee nose, zurr vurmint!'

'Och, take a whiff o' this, ye wicked rabble!'

'Sorry we ain't got no salt, so here's a little more pepper for ye!'

Literally peppered by bags of the stuff, the vermin crew fled – spitting, sneezing and rubbing at their burning eyes as the fierce hotroot pepper did its work. Between sneezes, they bumped blindly into one another, wailing and screeching.

Martha held up a paw. 'Stop now, no use wasting pepper. They've learned their lesson, a good hot one!'

A rousing cheer went forth from the Abbeybeasts. 'Red-waaaaaallll!'

Martha hugged Toran's waist from her chair. 'We did it, friend, we defeated the vermin!'

The ottercook stood watching the vermin as they hurled themselves into the Abbey pond. He stroked the haremaid's head absently. 'Aye, beauty, we did it for now. But they'll be back, an' next time they do, those vermin will try to slay us all.'

Sister Portula was in agreement with him. 'Right, Toran, so what'll we do then?'

Martha surprised herself by shaking a clenched paw. 'We'll just have to give back as good as we get. Don't forget, there's more of us than them. I'd risk my life willingly any day if it meant defeating those scum!'

Growls of agreement rang out, even from the Dibbuns. Abbot Carrul was taken aback by the warlike mood of the Redwallers, and even more so by Martha's fighting spirit. He held up his paws until order was restored.

'You are right, of course, my friends, but let us not do anything haphazard. There has to be a proper plan to rid our Abbey of these vermin!'

Flinky and Crinktail were in no special hurry to run about seeking recruits for Badredd's gang. The pair wandered deep into Mossflower, glad to be away from the bickering and squabbling of the small vermin gang. They rambled onwards, consenting with each other to desert their fellow vermin and find a new life together, far away from it all.

Unfortunately, they walked right into trouble and ambled straight into the camp of Raga Bol. A huge, fat sea rat with one milky, sightless eye grabbed the luckless pair by the scruffs of their necks. Both their stomachs churned in fear at the sight of the savage sea rat crew. For the first time in his life, Flinky was rendered speechless as he beheld a real sea rat captain.

Raga Bol was the complete picture of a barbarian chieftain – from his hooped brass earrings and tawdry silk finery, to his silver hook, gold teeth, curved scimitar and the lethal stiletto he was using to pick at a roasted pike. He spat a fishbone into the fire and picked at his teeth with the hook. Looking both stoats up and down, Raga Bol consulted the fat rat.

'Who are these two barnacles, Glimbo?'

Flinky began stammering out an answer. 'If it please, yore 'onour, we was just . . .'

Splat! Raga Bol leaned forwards and struck Flinky a slap across his mouth with the pike. 'Did I speak to ye, stoat?'

The hook shot out, catching Flinky's jerkin. He was yanked forwards, under the cold glare of the wickedest eyes he had ever looked into.

He felt the sea rat's hot breath on his face as the rasping voice growled out, 'Guard yore tongue, mudbrain, or I'll carve it out an' feed it to ye. Speak now, wot's in those sacks?'

Flinky's throat bobbed as he gasped out, 'F . . . f . . . fruit, sir!'

Raga Bol stuck his stiletto in the sack Flinky was holding. He booted the stoat backwards, causing the blade to rip through the sack. Flinky went sprawling amid the fruit which spilled out on to the ground.

The sea rat scowled. 'Fruit? Is that all ye brought? No booty, weapons, not even a brace o' birds or a decent fish. Just fruit!'

Glimbo wrenched the sack from Crinktail. He emptied it over Flinky, who lay cringing on the ground. 'Sink me! This 'un's brought fruit as well, Cap'n. They must be both stoopid in d'brain!'

Gripping hold of Crinktail, Glimbo shook her until her teeth rattled, bellowing in the hapless stoat's face, 'Yore stoopid in d'brain, wot are ye?'

Crinktail gabbled out something that sounded like 'Stooballainnabrab!'

The sea rats crowded round laughing. They tore the

jerkins from both stoats, and robbed them of their belts and knives.

Stripped to the fur, Flinky and Crinktail huddled together, eyes wide with terror as the sea rats licked their knifeblades and winked wickedly at them.

Raga stroked under his chin, with the polished curve of his pawhook. 'The woodlands round here are packed with fruit, an' ye bring me two sacks o' the stuff? Right then, me beauties, I'll tell ye what we'll do. What'd ye like, an apple or a pear?'

Crinktail spoke, her voice quivery with terror, 'Apples, sir.'

Raga smiled, showing several gold-capped fangs. 'Haharr, apples it is then. Ferron, jam an apple apiece in their gobs, 'twill stop 'em singin' out while they're roastin'!'

Ferron, a tall, gaunt-faced rat, sorted through the fruit until he came up with two large, rosy apples. He strode over to the two victims, but before he could start, Flinky yelled, 'Loot! Treasure! Booty an' magic swords!'

Raga's long blade rasped out of its scabbard. Resting the point against Flinky's nose, the captain spoke just one word – 'Where?'

The stoat answered speedily, knowing his life depended on it. 'Sure, 'tis at the Abbey o' Redwall, sir, only a good ould march from here. All the plunder yore 'eart could desire!'

The swordtip lifted as Raga looked around the ugly faces of his leering crew. 'Give 'em back their stuff. Come 'ither, mates. Sit 'ere by me, where I can carve cobs off'n ye if yore tellin' me fibs. I can't abide fibbers, can you, messmate?'

Flinky shook his head vigorously. 'Sure those fibbers are the worst ould kind of beasts ever born, ain't that right?'

Crinktail hastened to agree with him. 'Fibbers are villains!'

Raga Bol narrowed his frightening eyes and glared at his prisoners, who sat as if hypnotized. Suddenly he threw back his head and roared with laughter. 'Aharrharrharrharr!

That's wot I like to 'ear, me liddle fishes. Avast there, Blowfly, bring grog fer our messmates!'

Blowfly, a malodorous, greasy-looking rat, brought three gigantic pottery jars and a keg of grog, which he rolled along by kicking it. He filled the jars brimful, issuing one to each of them. Both stoats quailed at the sight of the fearsome-smelling brew. Bol drained half of his at one huge swig, smacked his lips and winked broadly at them. 'Good 'ole seaweed'n'fish'ead grog, ain' nothin' like it! Aharr, Raga Bol can't abide prissy liddle creatures wot don't like grog. Drink 'earty now!'

Gagging and spluttering, Flinky and Crinktail tried to sup the fiery liquor. The sea rat crew gathered round, grinning and guffawing as they watched the stoats trying to cope with the grog. Finishing his swiftly, Raga observed his victims closely. 'Cummon, buckoes, no shilly-shallyin' there, bottoms up, an' don't ye leave none for the fishes!'

Grog was dribbling down Flinky's chest fur by the time he finished. Something odd was happening to his eyes. In front of him sat three Raga Bols. His head was whirling, and his tongue felt as though it belonged to someone else. He hiccupped. 'Heeheehee, hic! Sure, that was a prime ould, hic, droppa grog, hic hic! Ain't that right, hic, eh, Crinky, hic!'

Crinktail gazed woozily at her empty jar and giggled. 'Sh'marvelloush! Makesh y'feel like a battlin' badger, hee-hee, whoops!'

She was knocked flat on her back. Raga, who had kicked her over, stood glaring down at the stoat, his sabre drawn. 'Badger, wot badger? Is there a badger 'ereabouts? Have ye sighted a great giant of a stripedog? Tell me!'

Crinktail attempted to rise, but fell flat. She looked up at the sea rat captain with owlish solemnity. 'Wot badgersh? Heehee, we ain't seen no shtripedogs around 'ere. Don' worry, Bragger Roll, we'll fight 'em all for ye, me'n Shlinky!'

She giggled again, then passed out, senseless. A fleeting

glimpse of relief crossed the sea rat's face. He turned his attention to Flinky, who was swaying from side to side, and blinking drunkenly. 'Ahoy, bucko, let's talk, me'n you. I'll ask the questions, an' ye give me all the answers. The right ones if'n ye value yore skin! This Abbey o' Redwall, tell me everythin' about it. An' worrabout yore crew, 'ow many strong are they, who's yore leader, wot's 'e like? No lies, now, c'mon!'

Raga Bol's crew listened avidly as Flinky related the entire sorry tale to their captain. The stoat was drunk, but not so drunk that he didn't know what would please the murderous Raga Bol. A good portion of his story was outright lies. He told of witless Abbeybeasts, and a fabulous treasure, laying great emphasis on the magic sword. Flinky was good at what he did, having spent most of his life lying and pleasing others. The captain and his crew believed the yarn. There followed much winking, nudging, whispering and gleeful rubbing of paws, even from Raga Bol. This was going to be a picnic, an orgy of looting and slaughter. A real sea rat's dream come true!

The sea rat crew made ready to march. Raga Bol delayed moving, since there was one thing still bothering the captain's mind – the fate of the giant stripedog. Giving orders for the crew to stand ready, he marched back along their trail alone, looking for signs of his assassin's return.

After an hour or so, Raga Bol glanced up at the sky. Dark rolling clouds, coupled with the distant rumble of thunder, presaged the arrival of a sizeable storm. He turned his gaze to the path ahead, where the foliage was swaying in the hot wind. The sea rat's keen eyes and ears missed nothing. He saw the shrubbery moving the wrong way at one point and heard the moans and laboured gasping of somebeast coming slowly up the trail towards him.

It was Jibsnout, leaning heavily on an impromptu crutch he had fashioned from a branch. Raga Bol hastened to intercept him, frowning with false concern. 'Jibsnout, matey, are ye wounded? Have ye news of the stripedog? Where are those sons of Wirga, 'ave they deserted ye?'

The stolid sea rat slumped wearily down, his tongue licking the first fat drops of rain that fell through the woodland canopy. He looked up at Raga Bol kneeling at his side.

'Cap'n, we stood no chance! That stripedog 'ad a squirrel wid 'im, they ambushed us! Two of Wirga's sons were slayed. The other one ran away, though 'e wouldn't'a got far, I wager. I was shot through the footpaw by the stripedog, then 'e took my blade. I thought 'e was gonna kill me, but 'e tended to the wound an' sent me back to ye wid a message, Cap'n. The stripedog sez to tell ye that 'is name is Lonna Bowstripe, an' that 'e's comin' after ye, Cap'n Bol. Aye, yoreself an' all the crew, me too. We're all deadbeasts, d'ye hear me, walkin' deadbeasts! That big Lonna beast is goin' to slay us one by one, every ratjack of us! Take me word fer it, Cap'n, 'e's a mighty warrior but a real madbeast! I saw it in 'is eyes, they was red as fire. The stripedog'll finish us, all of us, I believe wot 'e said!'

A jagged lightning flash lit up the gloomy woodlands; thunder rattled closer and the rain came in earnest. Raga Bol held Jibsnout close to him, murmuring softly, 'Hush now, mate, no stripedog's goin' to harm ye. This storm'll wash out all our tracks, nobeast'll find us then. Besides, we'll be snug inside of a big stone fortress, wid vittles to spare an' more loot than ye've ever clapped eyes on. Hahaarr, 'ow'll that suit ye matey, eh?'

Jibsnout blinked rain from his eyes. 'That'll suit me good, Cap'n.'

Bol held him closer, whispering in his ear, 'Ye won't breathe a word about no stripedog to the crew now, will ye, me ole mate?'

Jibsnout smiled at his captain. 'You know me, Cap'n Bol. None of 'em will 'ear a word from my mouth!'

Raga Bol smiled back at Jibsnout. 'So they won't, mate, yore right.'

He slew Jibsnout with a single thrust of his stiletto. Shoving the body into the bushes, Raga Bol sloshed back through the battering downpour, muttering to himself. 'They all talks sooner or later, but you was right, Jibsnout. Nobeast'll 'ear a word from yore mouth.'

26

The storms which had been battering the high cliffsides slackened off to a steady downpour. Fenna popped her head outside the cave, shielding her eyes. 'It's hard to see anything properly on a rainy night. No sign of Horty yet, I do hope he's alr . . .'

A monolithic shape loomed out of the darkness, silent as a moonshadow. The squirrelmaid staggered backwards as a badger of massive proportions padded in. Over his shoulder lay Horty, draped like a limp rag. The badger carried on past them, to the back of the cave, his deep growl echoing.

'I found your friend, never fear, he'll come to his senses before too long. Be still now until I get a fire going.'

Bragoon's paw stayed Springald from rising. 'Be still, Spring, do as our friend says.'

They heard steel strike flint, as the badger's soft breath coaxed flame from the sparks that fell on to the tinder. Soon a pale light flickered. It became a proper fire when the badger added dried grass and twigs to it. He banked it up with broken pine branches, waited a moment, then turned to face the travellers. Bragoon had encountered a badger or two before, but none like this one. Warrior was written all over this giant beast – from the great bow he carried, to the long quiver full of arrows, to the lethal dagger strapped below his shoulder. He wore a simple smock of rust-hued homespun, belted with a woven sash.

But it was his face that denoted his calling. A deep, jagged scar ran lengthwise across the broad-striped muzzle, with stitchmarks pocking either side. The dark eyes remained impassive, reflecting the firelight. The otter judged him to be one of those fated creatures cursed with that malady called Bloodwrath – the red tinge mixed with the creamy eye whites betrayed it. Bragoon had heard tales of such badgers that described them as terrible to behold and unstoppable in battle. The otter held out his paw, flat, with the palm upwards, a sign of peace. The badger did likewise. Then he placed his paw on top, making Bragoon's look like the tiny paw of a Dibbun. He introduced himself.

'I am Lonna Bowstripe. This is not my cave, but you are welcome to stay here until the hare recovers. I saw you escape those rats today and knew you would shelter up here. I watched from the hills what a brave thing your friend did. I killed those three rats who tried to capture him – vermin are bullies and murderers, they are no great loss to anybeast. Who are you, why are you in this country?'

The otter bowed respectfully. 'I am Bragoon. This is Saro, Fenna and Springald. The hare is named Horty. We are travellers.' He gestured upwards towards the plateau on top of the cliffs. 'We are seeking a place called Loamhedge. It lies somewhere up there.'

Lonna began stringing his bow. 'A dangerous quest, friend. There are many Darrat rats out there still. Their captain was one of the three I slew. You need to reach the clifftops without interference from them. Your journey will be hard enough without rats following you. Perhaps they are camped in the area. I will warn them off. Pass me an arrow, Fenna.'

The squirrelmaid took a shaft, nearly as long as she was, from the badger's quiver. They watched Lonna blunt the point by jamming an old pinecone over it. He held it to the fire until it was blazing and crackling. Testing the air out-side the cave, the badger seemed satisfied.

'It's not raining too heavily now, the shaft should burn for a bit before it goes out.' With a single graceful move, Lonna set the blazing arrow on his string, drawing the shaft back until the burning end almost touched the bow. *Whooooosh!* It shot off like a rocket, into the night sky above the dunes.

Throwing back his head, the big beast roared out in a thunderous voice that echoed around the cave and along the cliffsides. 'I am Lonna Bowstripe! I eat rats! I will taste the blood of any who are here by dawn! Eulaliiiiiaaaaaaaa!'

He returned to the fire as they took their paws from ring-ing ears and began tending to Horty. Lonna smiled and shook his head as Horty began to stir. 'He looks hard to kill – I've heard it said that hares are perilous beasts. This one will be a warrior one day.'

The giant badger looked so large and ferocious in the fire-light that Springald could readily understand how the rats would fear him. She enquired politely, 'Sir, you didn't really eat three rats, did you?'

The smile still lingered on Lonna's lips. 'Nay, little maid, don't believe all you hear. The language of death and vio-lence is all that vermin understand. I'd sooner devour a crushed toad that was four seasons dead than eat rat. I eat only the same food as you do.'

'Eat? I say, did some chap mention eats? I'm famished!'

Bragoon assisted the incorrigible hare to sit upright. 'Oh, this 'un's awake, sure enough. Well, how d'ye feel, young famine belly? Oh, ye'd better thank the beast who saved ye. This is Lonna Bowstripe.'

Horty did an exaggerated double take at the huge badger. He winked cheekily. 'Good grief, sah, bet you can pack the jolly old provisions away, wot wot?'

They pooled the resources of their packs and were soon toasting yellow cheese and oat scones over the fire. Saro poured dandelion and burdock cordial for the company.

Springald split some loaves of nutbread and spread them with honey.

Lonna glanced sideways at Horty, taken aback by the young hare's appetite. 'Great seasons, talk about packing provisions away! Where do you put it all? You're a bottomless pit!'

They all burst into laughter at the sight of Horty's indignant face.

Over the next few hours, they exchanged their stories. The five friends told Lonna all about Redwall and its creatures. They also explained Martha's situation and the reason for their quest. When the giant badger related his own personal history, they were greatly saddened and angry, too. There was a hushed silence when he came to the end of his narrative. Lonna ran his paw down the fearsome scar, tracing it across his still face.

'They will pay with their lives, Raga Bol and all his vermin crew. As sure as the days break and the seasons turn!'

The five travellers did not doubt a word that he uttered.

Lonna rose and replenished the fire. 'You must sleep now. Tomorrow will be a hard day's climbing. I think the plateau above the cliffs is no place for the fainthearted. Take a good rest tonight, I'll guard the cave entrance.'

Bragoon uncovered his sword. 'I'll keep ye company, Lonna. Two guards are better'n one, an' four eyes can see more than two.'

They sat together at the cave entrance. Lonna could not take his gaze from the otter's sword, drawn to it like a magnet to metal. 'That is indeed a wondrous weapon you carry, Bragoon.'

The otter let the firelight play along the blade. 'Aye, 'tis so, though it don't belong t'me. Abbot Carrul of Redwall loaned it t'me the day we left. I think he did it not just for our protection, but as a sort o' good-luck charm for the journey. This sword belongs at the Abbey. 'Twas owned in the far olden seasons by a mouse. His name was Martin the Warrior, one o' the founders of Redwall. I was told stories of Martin an' his sword when I was nought but a Dibbun. They say it was forged an' made by a great badger lord, a warrior himself, an' a very skilled swordsmith, as ye can see. He made it from a lump of ore that fell from the sky, a piece of a star, I was told. This badger, he was Lord of Salamandastron, a mountain fortress. Did ye ever hear of that place, Lonna?'

The dark eyes of the giant flashed. 'Every badger knows the name of Salamandastron. I will go there myself someday. I feel my days will end there – but only when my score with Raga Bol is settled.'

Bragoon sat up with a start, realizing that he had dropped off to sleep during the night, something he would never have done in his younger seasons. Dawnlight was filtering into the cave, and Lonna Bowstripe was gone. As Saro was rekindling the fire from its embers, the three young ones were just waking.

She gave Bragoon a beaker of hot mint tea. 'Mornin', matey. Well, our bigbeast left while it was still dark. I saw 'im go, y'know.'

Fenna poured tea for herself. 'Lonna's gone?'

Saro nodded. 'Aye, you lot were all asleep. Horty's snorin' woke me, sounded like a tribe o' stuffed-up frogs.'

The young hare huffed indignantly at her, but Saro carried on. 'I was lyin' there wide awake, watchin' Lonna in the fireglow. He'd picked up the sword o' Martin to admire it. Well, next thing that badger went stiff as a frozen pike, sittin' there starin' at the blade as if it was speakin' to 'im. I watched for a while, then Horty started snorin' agin. So I gave 'im a good kick an' settled back to catch a nap.'

Horty interrupted. 'Blinkin' cadess, kickin' a chap in mid slumber? Rank bad manners, I'd say. Hmph!'

The elderly squirrel shrugged. 'When I woke up agin, he'd gone.'

Bragoon slapped his rudder against the rock floor. 'I'll wager 'twas Martin the Warrior, speakin' to Lonna through the sword. He told the badger where t'find Raga Bol, an' Lonna took off after the villain!'

Bragoon wrapped the sword up reverently as Horty chuckled. 'I bet old Raggaballoon wotsisname wouldn't be too pleased with Martin, if he knew. Snitchin' about him to that bally great hulk. I'd hate to be in his way when he feels peevish. Frazzlin' frogs, imagine what old Lonna'll do to that vermin when he catches up with him, wot wot!'

Bragoon began packing his belongings. 'I wouldn't like to imagine, mate. That's Lonna's business, an' I'm sure he can take care of it well. But we've got our own problems to tend. Up an' on to Loamhedge, mateys!'

Morning boded bright as they left the cave and began climbing the cliff to its top. It was hard going until the two squirrels, Saro and Fenna, went ahead. Soon they were on top of the cliff. Lowering down a rope, they heaved up all the packs, then secured the rope around a rock, allowing the other three to haul themselves up.

It was a breathtaking panorama from the plateau. Horty's keen eyes spotted a small dark smudge, moving across the scrublands in the distance. He pointed. 'I say, you chaps, that could be thingummy, er, Lonna!'

Springald shaded her eyes. 'So it could! He's headed northwest, that's the direction we came from. Saro, d'you suppose he's going to Redwall?'

Sarobando felt they were wasting time sightseeing. 'I couldn't really say, missy, but one thing's shore, we ain't goin' to Redwall. 'Tis Loamhedge we want. So stop lookin' backwardss an' let's go for'ard. Quick march!'

Shimmering flatlands, devoid of vegetation or shade, rolled out before them. Small swirls of dust eddied in spirals on the hot breeze. Sarobando squinted her eyes against the distance.

'Miss Fenna, yore in charge o' the drinks; we'll have t'be stingy with liquid. It might be some time afore we run across water by the look o' things.'

Immediately after the squirrel mentioned drinks, Horty

began feeling thirsty. 'I say, Fenna old gel, pass me that canteen, there's a good little treebounder. I'm parched!'

Fenna marched right on past him. 'We'll drink at midday and not before, so forget about it and keep going.'

The young hare appealed to his comrades. 'Wot? Did you chaps hear this heartless curmudgeon?'

Bragoon grinned pitilessly at Horty. 'Aye, loud an' clear, mate. Wot's the matter, are ye thirsty already?'

The incorrigible hare clapped a paw to his throat dramatically. 'Me flippin' mouth's like a sandpit, an' the old tongue feels like a bally feather mattress. A drink, for pity's sake, marm!'

Saro levelled a paw at him. 'Ye drink when Fenna tells ye. Now get a slingstone pebble an' suck it. That'll keep the thirst off as y'march, 'tis an old trick.'

Horty pulled a pebble from his pouch, looked at it in disgust, then put it back. 'Permission to sing, sah!'

The otter waved a paw in the air. 'Sing y'self blue in the face for all I care, but forget about drinkin'.'

Horty had to dig through his store of ballads and ditties, but he soon came up with an appropriate one.

'I knew a jolly old spider, and she always used t'say,
she could dive in a bath of cider, an' swim around all
    day.
Oh I would like to be that spider,
floatin' round in sparklin' cider,
she'd drink an drink, 'til she started to sink,
there'd be so much cider inside o' that spider!

I once knew a friendly flea, to whom I used to chat,
his favourite drink was ice-cold tea, what d'ye think of
    that?
Oh I would like to be that flea,
sippin' cups of ice-cold tea,
all in fine fettle from a rusty kettle,
'til I drank as much tea as that flea!

O cider spider, tea an' flea,
'tis all good manner o' drinks for me.
I'm an absolute whizz for strawberry fizz,
I'll sup old ale 'til I turn pale,
I'd never bilk at greensap milk.
Give this ripsnorter some rosehip water,
or cordial fine made from dandelion,
give me a barrel, it's mine all mine,
just tip me the nod or give me a wink,
an' I'll drink an' drink an' drink . . .
an' dri . . . hi . . . hi . . . hiiiiiiiink!'

Saro covered her ears with both paws and roared, 'Enough! I can't stand no more o' that caterwaulin', give that hare a drink. Give everybeast a drink!'

Fenna passed the canteen around, allowing each of the group one good mouthful. Horty was on to his second swig when the otter snatched the canteen from him and stoppered it. 'Ye great guzzlin' gizzard, don't ye know when t'stop?'

Horty gave him a hurt look and belched. 'Beg pardon, sah. Miserable blinkin' bangtail, I barely wet me lips, wot!'

Bragoon grabbed the young hare by his fluffy tailscut and tugged hard. 'One more word and ye'll be wearin' this as a bobble twixt yore ears. Now belt up an' march!'

It was hard, hot and dusty out on the flatlands, but they trekked doggedly onwards. Even the breeze was like the heat from an open oven door. With neither shade nor shadow to shelter from the ruthless eye of the blazing sun, it soon became an effort to walk.

Bragoon licked his dry lips. Dropping his pack, he crouched down on his hunkers. 'Phew! I tell ye, mates, I never knew a day could get so hot. We'll rest here awhile.'

The aged squirrel set about making things comfortable. She laced their cloaks together and made a lean-to. Weighting one end of the cloaks with their supply packs, she propped up the other end with two travelling staves.

'That'll give us a bit o' shade. Get under it, an' we'll take another drink. Mebbe we'll have a nap 'til it gets cooler. Then we can travel in the evenin'.'

The otter dug a beaker out of his pack. 'Good idea, mate. Fenna, pass me the canteen. I'll measure our drinks out, so nobeast gets any less.' Here he glanced at Horty. 'Or more than the others!'

They were each allowed one half-beaker, which they sipped gratefully.

Horty quaffed his off in a single gulp. 'Bit measly, wot! Where's the food?' He was the only one who felt like eating; the others stretched out and tried to rest.

Fenna watched the hare stuff down candied fruits. 'That will make you even thirstier. The sweetness will start you wanting to drink more.'

Horty waggled his ears at her. 'Oh pish tush an' fol de rol, miss, I like eatin', doncha know!'

Bragoon opened one eye, remarking ironically, 'Ye like eatin', really? I'd never have known if'n ye hadn't told me so! Put that haversack back on the cloak ends, or the wind'll blow our shelter away.'

Springald dreamt she was back at Redwall, paddling in the Abbey pond. Cool, wet banksand slopped between her footpaws as she splashed happily about. Sister Portula and the Abbot came strolling across the dewy lawn. Although the mousemaid could hear what they were saying, their voices sounded different.

'All gone! Every flippin' thing is confounded well gone, wot?' Springald wakened to see the reddish evening light through clouds of dust. Horty was stamping about outside the lean-to entrance, sobbing hoarsely. 'Every blinkin' drop t'drink, an' every mouthful of scoff. Gone, gone, we've been robbed, flamin' well looted!'

Bragoon grabbed the hare and shook him. 'Stop that bawlin', calm down an' tell us wot 'appened.'

Springald gathered round with Fenna and Sarobando to hear Horty's woeful tale.

'Couldn't sleep, y'know, too bally hot, wot. I was jolly thirsty, too, so I got up an' went outside t'get the canteen out of the haversacks. Some blighter's filched the lot. They've left rocks in their place. Go an' see f'y'self!'

It was true: five rocks sat holding down the rear of the lean-to, where the five packs of food and drink had been stowed.

Saro held up her paws. 'Be still, there may be tracks, paw-prints or dragmarks!'

She went down on all fours, eyes close to the dusty earth, nose twitching as she sniffed. A moment later, she stood up with a look of disgust on her face. 'Nothing! Not a single trace. Must've been an experienced thief who did it.'

Bragoon commented wryly, 'A beast would have t'be clever to survive in this wasteland. Well, that's it! No good weepin' o'er stolen supplies, we'll just have t'get on with it. While 'tis dark the weather's cooler, so we'll travel by night, at the double. Right, Saro?'

The old squirrel nodded and began issuing guidelines. 'Aye, mate. March fast an' silent, no talkin'. We don't know wot's out there in the darkness. 'Tis strange territory, so stick together an' hold paws. There'll be no time for restin'.'

She wagged a stern paw at the young hare. 'Listen good, Horty, this ain't a game anymore, see. If you start yammerin' on about food'n'drink, or causin' any upset, ye'll be riskin' our lives. Just march, do as yore told an' shut that great mouth o' yours, d'ye hear?'

Horty placed a paw over his own mouth and drew the other paw across his throat in a slitting motion.

Springald nodded. 'I think he's gotten the idea. Quick march!'

Off they went into the day's last crimson-tinged twilight – without food, drink or any hope of rest. The five small figures were dwarfed by the immensity of a dust-blown, trackless desert. Hidden eyes watched their departure, and sinister shapes rose from the earth to follow the questors.

27

The storm broke over Redwall at about the same time that Raga Bol killed Jibsnout. Foremole Dwurl gazed gloomily out of the dormitory window at the windswept deluge outside. He blinked as lightning illuminated the room and thunder barraged overhead.

'B'aint no use a throwen pepper at vurmints in ee gurt rainystorm. Bo urr, nay, zurr!'

Martha wheeled her chair to the window and peered out. 'Hmm, I wonder how the vermin are coping with this downpour.'

Abbot Carrul sighed. 'Who knows? Martha, please keep an eye on them. Right, let's get on with this Council Meeting.'

Outside, fat raindrops beat a deafening tattoo on the walls of the Abbey, its lawns nearly underwater. Badredd and his gang had commandeered the gatehouse. They lay about, wrapped in sheets, blankets and window curtains, using the material to dab at their sorely inflamed nostrils. Sneezing had become pure agony, with the membranes of their nostrils and throats red-raw from the bombardment of hotroot pepper.

Plumnose was having the worst of it. Each time he

sniffed, his pendulous nose wobbled and vibrated. Throwing off the bedspread he had been wearing, the suffering ferret made for the gatehouse door.

'Duh, I'b goin' oudd inna rain tuh lay dowd an' ledda rained water clear be node. Id mide wash idd out!'

Halfchop sneezed painfully as he volunteered to accompany him. 'Kachuuub!'

The Abbey Council had decided on a desperate scheme. Twoscore of the most able-bodied Redwallers would storm the gatehouse and make an end of the vermin. They stood ready to go, each armed with some form of homemade weapon: kitchen knives tied to window poles formed spears, long-handled garden spades, forks and hoes, together with coopering mallets and stave hatchets from the cellars.

Toran, serving as commander of the group, leaned against the windowsill, going over the scheme for a second time. 'Listen, friends, 'tis no use barricadin' 'em in the gatehouse. We've got to make an end to it, invade the place, break in an' slay every last one o' them. No half-measures if we want a peaceful life for us an' the little 'uns. I'll go through the door first, the rest o' you follow me. Show no quarter once yore inside! Sister Portula, Foremole Dwurl an' yore two moles there, Burney'n'Yooler, you stay outside an' get any who tries to break out an' run off. Any questions?'

Muggum saluted with a copper ladle he had brought from the kitchen. 'No, zurr, oi'll do moi dooty, doan't you'm wurry!'

Martha lifted him on to her lap and took the ladle. 'Your duty is to stay here with the rest of us and guard the Abbey door. This storm has set in for a good while yet. Once it goes dark, Toran and his friends will have the advantage of night cover and rain. The vermin won't be expecting them to attack. Meanwhile, we'll guard the door and make sure only Redwallers get back inside. It's a very important job, Muggum. Can you do it?'

The molebabe narrowed his eyes, glaring suspiciously at Toran's attack party. 'Ho, oi can do et, Miz Marth', doan't ee fret. They'm b'aint a-getten back in yurr iffen they'm b'aint theyselves!'

Toran shook the molebabe's paw. 'Well said, matey!'

Abbot Carrul stood up on one of the truckle beds and delivered a homily to his beloved Abbey creatures. Everybeast fell silent, respectfully bowing their heads as he spoke out.

'Fortune and fates be with you all,
you who fight for the right,
some will stand, others fall,
never to return this night.

But fear ye not, my loving friends,
be strong of limb and heart,
knowing that peace depends on you,
let courage play its part.

Tranquillity and calm spread wide,
through this our dear homeland,
justice and truth go by your side,
which evil cannot withstand.'

Though Martha did not say it, she wished now more than ever that her two friends, Sarobando and Bragoon, had stayed.

Thunder exploded overhead; jagged forks of lightning tore through the fading light. Raga Bol and his sea rats pounded on Redwall Abbey's main gate. Hearing the noise, Halfchop and Plumnose padded soggily to the gate.

Plumnose placed an ear against it, calling out, 'Who'd dat?'

A sabre was at Flinky's neck as he answered, 'Sure, 'tis only me'n me mate Crinktail. We're gettin' drowned out here. Open up an' let us in, Plummy!'

The two crewbeasts lifted the wooden bar, allowing the door to swing inward. Flinky and Crinktail were flung in, landing face down in the mud as the sea rats poured through. Raga Bol seized the ferret's nose and twisted it, bringing Plumnose up on his pawtips, squealing in agony.

'Yeeee! Ledd go!'

The captain let go and kicked Plumnose flat in the mud. 'So yore the big bad warrior wot put this place to siege, eh?'

He roared with laughter as the ferret held a paw tenderly around his bruised nose and pointed to the gatehouse. 'Nodd me. Badredd's in dere, he did idd!'

The little fox was half asleep as the gatehouse door crashed off its hinges. He was dumbstruck at the sight that greeted him. Raga Bol strode forcefully in, squinting one eye as he glared ferociously around.

'Which one of ye is Badredd?'

The crew, terrified out of their wits by half a hundred sea rats leering through the doorway at them, pointed quickly at the fox. Raga's polished pawhook latched into Badredd's belt, jerking the fox face-to-face with him. The barbaric captain's murderous eyes bored into the fox's numbed gaze. 'So then, liddle laddo, yore the mighty Badredd?'

Speech deserted him; Badredd could only stammer, 'Y . . . Y . . . Yu . . . Ya . . . y-y-y–'

Raga Bol shook him like a rag doll, covering the little fox with spittle as he roared into his face, 'Don't stan' there makin' noises like an idjit! Are ye or aren't ye Badredd, ye runty buffoon?'

The fox nodded furiously, as he heard his own voice squeak out, 'Yis!'

The sea captain turned to his crew, gold fangs asparkle as he grinned at them. 'Well now, ain't that nice. Say 'ello to our new cap'n, buckoes!'

There was loud guffawing and shouts of ridicule from the sea rats.

'Pleased t'meet yer, I'm shore!'

'Mercy me, 'e do look fierce, don't 'e?'

'I'd watch 'ow ye talk to ole Badredd. Looks like an 'ard master t'me, a cold 'earted killer!'

'Hawhawhaw! Aye, lookit 'is sword. Hawhawhawhaw!'

The sea rat captain wrenched the broken cutlass from his victim's belt. He held it under Badredd's nose. 'Does your mamma know ye've been playin' wid this? Dearie me, yew could cut yerself. Naughty fox!'

Raga Bol's crew laughed until tears ran down their cheeks. When the fox's own crew began smiling and chuckling, the big sea rat turned on them savagely.

'Wot are you lot laughin' about, eh? Stupid clods, lettin' yoreselves be ordered about by a liddle oaf with a busted sword. Gerrout of 'ere, all of ye, clear out!'

The vermin scurried to obey, cringing and ducking as they had to pass Raga Bol, who was partially blocking the doorway. Still dragging Badredd along by his belt, Raga strode out into the sheeting rain, issuing orders to his sea rats.

'Glimbo, Ferron, Chakka, you stay in the liddle 'ouse wid me. Ringear, lock that big gate, nobeast gets in or out. Post a watch on it. The rest of ye, take shelter where ye can find it. Blowfly, take a rope's end an' keep an eye on this lot.'

He indicated the fox's crew with a nod. Finally, Raga turned his attention to the hapless Badredd. Thrusting the broken cutlass into the fox's shaking paws, he snarled, 'Now then, me laddo, yew'd better be a good cook, or ye'll find yoreself bein' served up as vittles. D'ye hear me?'

Badredd nodded miserably as Raga Bol continued barking out orders. 'Git yoreself down t'that pond an' take yore crew along. I wants fish fer me brekkist, a good fat 'un, an' no excuses. Just 'ow yer catches an' cooks it is yore bizness. But if'n it ain't on the table, done perfectly, when I wakes up . . . then ye'd best cut yore own throat wid that toy sword, 'cos ye won't wanna face Raga Bol. Now get to it sharpish!'

He flung Badredd face first into the mud. Then, turning on his paw, the big sea rat strode inside the gatehouse.

The little fox raised his head, weeping and spitting out wet soil, thankful he was still alive. But for how long? The barbarous rat had set him a near impossible task. How was he going to catch a big fish and cook it in the midst of a thunderstorm, with rain pounding furiously down?

Thud! A blow from a knotted rope's end made him arch his back. Blowfly landed another one, this time across Badredd's rump.

'Up on yore hunkers, foxy! Yew 'eard wot the cap'n said. Step lively now. Youse others, bring that blanket t'make a tent fer me. I ain't sittin' round in the rain watchin' ye makin' Cap'n Bol's brekkist. All down t'the pond now, at the double!'

He drove them forwards with the rope's end.

A horrified silence had fallen over the Abbey dormitory. One word from Old Phredd cut the air like a knife. 'Sea rats!'

Shilly followed this up with a question. 'Wot bee's a sea rat?'

Toran bent down to the small truckle bed and pulled up the covers to the squirrelbabe's chin. All around the dormitory, Dibbuns were sleeping peacefully. The ottercook wrinkled his nose at Shilly.

'A sea rat, me dear? Just some naughty ole beast. Nothin' for ye to get upset about, go t'sleep now.'

Abbot Carrul sat down on a hill of slingstones in the middle of the floor. 'How many of them are in the grounds of our Abbey?'

Martha replied from her seat at the window. 'Hard to count in the dark and rain, Father, but there's certainly more than twoscore of them, all rats, and armed to the fangs. Surely we can't overcome that many!'

An old mousewife called Mildun began sobbing in a panic. 'We'll all be dragged out of our beds and murdered, I know we will, us and those poor little babes. Oooooooohh-hhhhh!'

The haremaid immediately issued a harsh scolding. 'Stop that right now!'

Shocked into silence, Mildun shrank from the sharp reproof, listening intently as Martha continued in a stern voice. 'There's no call for that behaviour, marm, all you'll do is cause worry to everybeast. Don't let me hear an outburst like that from you ever again. Now if you've anything to say, then make it helpful. Don't be a beast of ill omen, and keep your voice down. We don't want the little ones taking fright. Do you hear me?'

Mildun sniffed and mumbled into her 'kerchief. 'Sorry, Martha.'

Abbot Carrul turned grateful eyes to the haremaid. 'Thank you, miss. Well, the whole situation has changed now – for the worse, I'm sad to say. An attack against such numbers of those savage rats is out of the question. So what do we do now? I'm open to helpful suggestions.'

Foremole Dwurl raised a powerful digging claw. 'Tunnels owt, zurr, me'n moi moles can make ee gurt tunnel. Uz'll all be safe frumm ee vurmints then, oi reckerns!'

As hope sprang anew in the Redwallers, they began chattering and clamouring aloud.

Toran silenced them with a sudden bark. 'A fine idea, sir, but let's not be too hasty. Yore plan calls for a bit o' discussion. Now one at a time – you first, Father Abbot.'

Carrul folded both paws into his wide sleeves. 'Thank you, Toran. First, let me say this. Our Foremole's plan is a sensible one. The Dibbuns, and anybeast who chooses to go with them, will be safe from harm. As for myself, I must remain here where my duty lies. I could never desert my beautiful Abbey.'

The ottercook seconded him. 'Nor I, Carrul. It ain't right leavin' Redwall wide open to sea rats an' vermin. I stay!'

Martha struck the arm of her chair resolutely. 'Redwall Abbey is my home, the only home I've ever known. I'm not moving from here!'

Every voice in the room was raised. 'We stay! We stay!'

Foremole Dwurl wrinkled his nose apologetically. 'Oi bee's sorry oi menshunned et naow.'

Abbot Carrul placed a paw about the faithful mole's shoulders. 'You've no need to be sorry, friend, it was a good idea. The trouble is that nobeast wants to go now. So what do we do next?'

Muggum would not be denied his say. The molebabe waved the copper ladle, which had become his chosen weapon. 'Us'n's foights, zurr, that bee's wot us do. Foight!'

Sister Setiva relieved Muggum of the ladle to stop him from giving anybeast a whack as he waved it about. 'Och, ye wee terror, hush now an' pay heed tae yore elders!'

Toran picked up the molebabe and made an announcement to the assembly. 'This liddle feller's right, we must fight. But it won't be no kill-or-be-killed sort o' last stand. Oh no, mates, we'll fight an' defend the Abbey, stave off any attacks. Even if that means we'll have t'fight all summer long, until the Skipper brings his ottercrew back 'ere from the Northshores. Then together we can deal with those savages outside.'

Sister Portula brandished the hooked window pole she had armed herself with. Normally a quiet and reserved old mouse, she surprised everybeast by calling out, 'Well spoken, Toran. That's the most sensible thing I've heard so far. We can be what we are, not warriors but defenders! We can stick it out and delay them all summer until help arrives from Skipper and his crew. But it will be no easy thing. Remember that we are under siege. Food will run short, drinks will have to be rationed, water cannot be used freely anymore . . .'

Baby Buffle interrupted the good sister by piping up, 'Nonomorragerrabaffinwirrawater!'

Martha gave Shilly a puzzled look. 'What did he say?'

The little squirrel grinned from ear to ear and did a somersault. 'Iffa water bee's short, Dibbuns can't not get baffed. Yeeheeheehee!'

Nobeast could resist laughing along with the overjoyed babes.

The storm finally subsided to a light drizzle. Scratching the back of his neck with his silver hook, Raga Bol rolled out of Old Phredd's bed and exited the gatehouse. Swigging from a flask of grog, he listened to the whimpers and wails from the pond. Blowfly was keeping Badredd and his little gang hard at it. The sea rat captain gazed up at the majestic grandeur of Redwall Abbey. What a sight! Anybeast would be mad to bother with ships when he could own a place like this. Smiling wolfishly, he shouted towards the Abbey, 'Yore goin' to meet Cap'n Raga Bol tomorrer, mousies!'

28

Marching all night was a harrowing experience for the younger creatures. Saro and Bragoon, being used to such hardships, plodded doggedly on in silence. Fenna stumbled alongside them, her eyes constantly drooping shut. The squirrelmaid sorely regretted ever leaving Redwall and all its comforts. She did not know which she yearned for most – sleep, food or water. Springald was of a like mind, trudging onwards in a straight line with her four companions, keeping quiet and trying not to inhale too much dust.

It was a cruel and forbidding outlook, the wasteland stretching all around, flat, silent and gloomy in the nighttime darkness. After what seemed like an eternity, daylight showed on the eastern horizon, a pale, misty mixture of dove-grey and orange.

Bragoon watched the faint apricot edge of morning sun slowly rising. He spoke softly. 'That's a pretty sight, ain't it, mates?'

Horty hardly gave it a second glance. 'Pretty, y'say? Pretty bloomin' awful if y'ask me, wot. I'd swap the blinkin' lot for a drop of water! Can't we stop now? You said march by night an' sleep durin' the day. Well, there's the jolly old day, an' I'm pawsore an' weary. So let's lay the old heads down, eh chaps?'

Saro pushed him onwards. 'Not just yet, we've got to keep goin' while 'tis cool. When the day gets hot, that's the time for sleep. The more ground we cover, the sooner we'll be out o' this wasteland. Keep marchin', don't stop now.'

None of the travellers wanted to, but they carried on, knowing that it was the only sensible thing to do.

By midmorning, the sun was beating down remorselessly as small dust spirals danced on the hot breeze. There was still no sight of trees or streams amid the dun-hued wastes.

Bragoon finally halted. 'We'll rest here until late afternoon!'

Saro began setting up a lean-to with cloaks and staves, weighting the cloak edges down with pieces of rock.

Horty raised a dust cloud as he slumped down. 'If I could only lay paws on the rotters who swiped our grub'n'water. By the left! I'd kick their confounded tails into the middle o' next season, wot!'

Bragoon rested on his stomach in the small patch of shade. 'Don't think about it, mate, yore only makin' things worse.'

Springald looked back at the ground they had covered. 'Funny how the land seems to wobble and shimmer out there.'

Fenna curled up and closed her eyes. 'That's just the heat on the horizon. It's a mirage, really.'

Saro shielded her eyes, peering keenly at the spectacle. She nudged the otter, directing his attention to it. 'Don't look like no mirage to me, wot d'ye think, Brag?'

Bragoon squinted his eyes and watched intently. His paw strayed to the sword which lay by his side. 'It might be just the heat waves, but it seems t'be movin' closer towards us. Then again, it could be the earth dancin'. Remember the ground shakin' like that the last time we was in this territory, Saro?'

The squirrel never let her gaze waver from the shimmering. 'Aye, it made a rumblin' sound, too.'

Horty laughed wildly. 'Hawhawhaw! Just listen to 'em,

chaps. We're in the middle of bally nowhere, bein' baked alive, not a flamin' drop t'drink or eat. Now what, the ground has to start bloomin' well dancin'! Am I goin' off me flippin' rocker, or is it those two ramblin' duffers, wot?'

Bragoon and Saro exchanged glances, then went back to their watching.

Horty, however, would not be ignored. Gesturing with his paws, he flopped his ears dramatically.

'They're tellin' me the ground's doin' a jig. An' here am I, without a pastie to shovel down me face or a bucket o' cordial to wet me parched lips! Ah, lackaday an' woe is the handsome young hare, languishin' out here an' losin' me mind! I'm goin' mad, mad I tell ye! Stark bonkers an' ravin' nuts! 'Tis the dreaded thirstation!'

Springald shook her head. 'Thirstation? Shouldn't that be thirstiness, or just thirst?'

Bragoon whispered to Saro, 'That couldn't be the earth dancin', or we'd have felt the rumbles.'

Horty continued with his tirade. 'Rumbles, rumbles? How could benighted buffoons such as you know about the rumblings of a sad tragic hare, whose life is bein' cut short by the contagious thirstation an' tummyrumbles?'

The otter's tail caught him a firm thwack across the rear. 'Shuttup, young 'un, get to sleep an' quit yore shoutin'!'

Horty subsided meekly, but still muttered to have the last word. 'Beaten by the bullyin' Bragoon into shallow slumber. Goodnight, fair comrades, or is it good day, wot?'

Within a short time, the three young ones were asleep. Sarobando was dozing, too, but Bragoon lay on his stomach, chin resting on both paws. Through slitted eyelids he scanned the wastelands to the rear of the lean-to. They drew closer. Now he could distinguish them, not as heat shimmers but as small, patchy bumps. Moving silently, betrayed only by odd puffs of dust, they edged nearer. Then they halted. One bump detached itself from the pack and advanced.

Saro came awake as Bragoon touched her ear. He nodded

towards the moving object, twitching his tail against the squirrel's footpaw. Saro prepared herself, knowing the signal well. One . . . Two . . . On the third twitch they both attacked. Springing in the air and leaping forwards, both beasts threw themselves bodily on the thing. It squeaked aloud. Immediately the ground came alive. Squeaking and whistling, hundreds of small shapes raised an enormous dust cloud as they fled. The captured one wriggled and bit madly, but it could not escape its captors. It was disguised by a cloak woven from tough, coarse grass. Bragoon and Saro swiftly wrapped it into a bundle, trapping the beast within.

Saro drew a small blade. 'Haharr, got ye, thief, be still or I'll slay ye!'

Bragoon crouched with his sword poised, defending his friend's back against attack. Saro dragged the bundle inside the lean-to, rapping out orders to the trio, who were now awake.

'Grab ahold o' that. Jump on it if it tries to escape!'

Springald and Fenna held the thing tight. Horty pulled off the covering. It was a small, goldish-brown mouselike beast with a long tail and a white-furred stomach. Temporarily stunned, it lay gazing up at them through huge, dark eyes.

The otter came bounding in; sword upraised he menaced it. 'Our food'n'water, where is it? Speak or die, robber!'

The creature gave vent to a piercing cry. 'Feeeeeeeeeeee!'

This was followed by a sound from outside, like hundreds of tiny drums.

Saro stepped out of the shelter. 'Curl me bush, come an' take a look at this, mates!'

A billowing dust cloud was rising from footpaws drumming the earth. When it settled, a hundred or more of the mouselike beasts stood facing them. They all wore grass cloaks about their shoulders.

Fenna whispered to Saro, 'Good grief, what do we do now?'

The older squirrel answered quietly out of the side of her mouth. 'Say nothin'. Leave this to me, mate.'

Bragoon emerged from the shelter, dragging his prisoner by the tail. Hoisting the creature up, he swung the sword of Martin. The otter's voice roared out, 'Give us back our food'n'water, or this 'un's a deadbeast! D'ye understand me? I'll slay 'im if'n ye don't obey!'

For an answer, they once again set up a loud drumming with their footpaws: *Brrrrrrrrrrr!* Then they stood silent, watching Bragoon as the dust settled.

The captive one glared fearlessly up at the otter. 'Chiiiiiiirk – kill me! We of the Jerbilrats give nobeast water. Chiiik, sooner give our blood than water!'

Springald was surprised. 'Rats? They're handsome little things. They've got beautiful, big dark eyes. They look far too nice to be rats!'

Saro turned fiercely on the mousemaid. 'Just shut yore mouth, miss, I don't care 'ow nice they look. They've told ye wot they are – a rat's a rat, an' that's that. Hold yore tongue, an' leave the talkin' to Brag!'

The otter yelled back at the massed Jerbilrats, 'Hah, so ye can unnerstand me. D'ye think I'm foolin'?'

He struck with the sword, snipping a whisker from the Jerbilrat. As the drumming resumed, Bragoon raised his sword. 'Next one takes this robber's head off. Give us our supplies!'

Fenna whispered urgently to Horty, 'He's not really going to chop off a defenceless creature's head, is he?'

Horty shrugged. 'Simple case o' survival out here. Either we get the rations back or we peg out an' perish, wot!'

The Jerbilrat actually smiled at Bragoon. 'I die, one less mouth to feed – that saves water. Kill me, riverdog.'

Saro sighed. 'Don't give us much choice, does 'e?'

The otter let his sword drop. 'I never slew a helpless beast.'

Saro winked. 'I know, mate, we ain't murderers. Let me try.'

Hauling the Jerbilrat up by its ears, she dealt it a slap. 'I know ye ain't givin' us our supplies back, but I'll slap ye round 'til sunset if'n y'don't tell me where water is.'

Saro made a wavy motion, describing a stream or river. 'Water, like this.' She gave the beast a heavier slap. 'Talk!'

The Jerbilrat shrugged. 'Two days southeast maybe, don't know.'

Saro struck again. 'Then find out, 'cos yore comin' with us!'

The creature snarled. 'I'm Jiboa the Jerchief. I'll kill you – I'm not afraid to kill, like that riverdog is!'

Saro took a length of rope, knotting it firmly around Jiboa's neck. She smiled grimly. 'Ole Bragoon's the merciful one, I ain't so soft 'earted. I don't take no lip from cheeky-faced rats. Now take us to the water, or I'll make ye wish my mate had killed ye!'

A swift kick to the rear set Jiboa moving. 'Your water might be gone now. Dancing earth can shift streams down great cracks in the ground.'

Saro flicked the rope against the back of his neck. 'Ah, go an' tell that t'the frogs. Ye just get us there.'

Cancelling all plans to sleep by day, the travellers broke camp and set off into the dry, hot morn. They kept glancing back as the entire Jerbilrat pack continued to follow them. When Jiboa thrummed his footpaws, the rats drummed back in answer. He smirked at Saro.

'Feeeeeee! Old toughbeast, eh? Jerbilrats can go without water longer than you and the others. You'll weaken sooner or later. Then my rats will slay you all, you'll see.'

Saro jerked the rope sharply, causing Jiboa to fall on his own tail. She winked craftily at him. 'Funny 'ow ye can't do two things at once. Seems every time ye try, then ye fall over.'

Jiboa scrambled upright. 'Stupid treejumper, I can walk'-n'talk!'

Saro tugged the rope and pulled him over again. 'Wrong! Every time you say somethin' nasty, bump, down ye go.

But if'n ye was to shout out that y'can see water, ye'd regain yore sense o' balance right away. Unnerstand?'

There was neither shade nor shadow when the sun was directly overhead. Horty began complaining once more. 'Oh shed a tear for a thirsty young hare, an' if it's wet I'll drink it, wot. I say, you chaps, wouldn't you just love to wet the old whistle at a cool runnin' stream? If the odd fish swam by, then one could eat an' drink at the same jolly old time, wot. Phew, I'm so hot'n'dry that you could make a blanket of my tongue!'

Fenna gave him a sharp nudge. 'You're showing us up in front of those Jerbilrats, moaning and whining like that. They'll think we're soft and weak. Now try to behave like a Redwaller, and stop all that nonsense!'

Horty stiffened his ears, saluted and stepped out smartly. 'Right, old gel, leave it to Hortwill Braebuck, Esquire. I'll sing t'the clod-faced old savages, wot, here goes!'

Horty, with his talent for making up songs as he went, launched into an insulting ditty about Jerbilrats. Fenna and Springald giggled as they joined in the refrain at the end of each verse.

'Oh a Jerbilrat's a creature,
without one redeemin' feature,
beware of him, pay heed to what I say.
He'll sneak up on one quite sudden,
and devour one's pie or pudden,
an' he'll rob your bloomin' water anyday . . . Anyday!

If one ever meets a jerbil,
one must be extremely careful,
an' keep one's drinks tight under lock and key,
for 'tis a widely held belief,
that the scruffy little thief,
will sup every single drop quite happily . . . Happily!

For a jerbil's just a rat,
who has never had a bath,

so be careful that you stay upwind of him.
'Cos the smell would blow one's hat off,
or put any decent rat off,
an' kill all the flies around a rubbish bin . . . Rubbish
   bin!

Jerbil manners are disgraceful,
they're so spiteful an' ungrateful,
so arrogant an' sly an' so unjust.
Every ugly son an' daughter,
is a stranger to bathwater,
jerbils wallow round all day beneath the dust . . . 'Neath
   the dust!'

Horty waved to the Jerbilrats, who were squealing and
drumming their footpaws angrily. 'What ho, chaps, sorry I
can't warble anymore for you. The old tongue's all swollen.'

Saro halted Jiboa until the others caught up with her.
'This sun is gettin' too much, let's take a rest, mates.'

Shading their heads beneath the cloaks, they squatted on
the hot earth. Dozing off was unavoidable in the intense
heat. Late afternoon shadows were lengthening as Saro was
jerked awake. Jiboa had gnawed through the rope. He sped
off in a wide arc, trying to get back to the other Jerbilrats.

The squirrel chased after him, shouting out, 'Grab 'im,
Horty, he's loose!'

Quick off the mark, the young hare gave chase. He was
reaching out to grab Jiboa, when a piercing shriek came
from above. 'Kyeeeeeeeeeee!'

Jiboa threw himself flat, but Horty was knocked ears over
scut by a massive shape. A great buzzard – chocolate-and-
white plumed – snatched Jiboa up in its fierce, hooked
talons. It bore him off squeaking, high into the blue. Three
more of the deadly predators swooped down on the Jerbilrat pack, each one seizing a victim, as the rest tried vainly to
burrow into the dust. Then they were gone. The rest of them
fled westwards, thrumming and wailing fearfully.

Then there was silence. Horty sat up, dusting himself off. 'Stifle me whiskers! Did you see the size o' those birds? That's a pretty awful thing to happen to anybeast, even a Jerbilrat. Fancy bein' scoffed by a flippin', flyin' feather mattress, wot!'

Springald gazed around at the dusty, deserted plain. 'Those poor creatures, no wonder life in this area makes them hostile to others. I hate this dreadful place!'

Fenna's voice sounded small and frightened. 'How are we going to find water now that we're completely alone?'

Bragoon shouldered his sword wearily. 'Just press on. Jiboa knew there was water over this way. We've got t'keep goin'!'

They staggered onwards, but as evening arrived Fenna collapsed. Saro rushed to her side, fanning her brow and rubbing her paws. The ageing squirrel looked up at Bragoon. 'Pore young thing, the heat an' thirst have got to 'er. We don't even have a damp cloth t'wet 'er lips. Fenna'll die if'n we don't get some water soon.'

The otter covered the little squirrel with his cloak. 'Right, mates, that's it. Horty, ye come with me! Spring, ye stay 'ere with Saro an' Fenna. Me'n Horty will find water, or die tryin'. If'n we ain't back by tomorrer noon, ye'll know we never made it. But don't fret, we'll be long back by then with water!'

Sarobando and Springald shook their friends' paws.

'Good luck, an' fortune go with ye!'

'We'll be alright here, hurry back now!'

Horty bowed gallantly. 'To hear is to jolly well obey, marm!'

The two comrades struck off into the gathering dark.

Saro and Springald settled down to their vigil. After awhile, Fenna began murmuring as she tossed and turned feebly, 'A beakerful, is that all, Father Abbot? I'm thirsty . . . so very thirsty, Father.'

The mousemaid cradled her friend. 'Hush now, Fenn, lie still.'

Softly, Springald began singing an old lullaby, from when they were Dibbuns together at the Abbey.

'Peace falls o'er vale and hill,
silence fades the light,
moon and stars watch over
little ones by night.
Dawn will send the day bright,
larks will sing for thee,
streams of slumber flow now,
round this babe and me.'

Saro smiled. 'That's a pretty song, I remember it from Redwall long ago. Ol' Sister Ormel used t' sing it in the dormitory. Happy days, Ormel was a good ol' mouse.'

Springald sniffed. 'I learned it from her, too. Sister Ormel passed on three winters back. She was well loved.'

As they nursed Fenna, in hostile country, far from their beloved Abbey and its friendly creatures, Saro and Springald sat silent with their thoughts of Redwall.

Horty staggered gamely onward, though his paws were wobbling and his body bent with fatigue. Bragoon was in slightly better shape, but every step he took was an effort. Side by side they stumbled along through the night. Then the young hare tripped and fell, bringing the otter down with him.

Through cracked and swollen lips, Horty mumbled, 'Beg your pardon, old lad, tripped over a confounded bush. Wonder what oaf left it there, wot.'

He grunted as Bragoon scrambled over him and grabbed a pawful of leaves. Thrusting his nose into them, the otter whooped. 'Wahoo! This ain't no bush, mate. 'Tis a big clump o' comfrey. There's water nearby, I'm sure of it. Water!'

Leaping up, they plunged forwards with renewed hope and energy. The otter suddenly ground to a halt, pulling

Horty back. He pointed ahead, to where a soft glow emanated from behind the bulk of a widespread willow tree. Beyond that, the trickle of running water could be clearly heard.

Drawing his sword, Bragoon thrust the young hare behind him, uttering a quiet caution. 'Stick close t'my back, an' don't do anythin' foolhardy. There's a fire burnin', t'other side o' yon tree. I 'ope there's friendly beasts sittin' round it.'

Horty snorted. 'Fat chance in this neck o' the woods, pal. All we've met is bounders'n'cads since we climbed those cliffs. Huh, friendly y'say, prob'ly so friendly they'll chop off our blinkin' heads on sight, wot?'

The otter's paw clamped over Horty's mouth. 'Stow the gab an' stay behind me, we'll soon see!'

There were six reptiles in all – two large frilled lizards, three fat toads and a grass snake – lounging around the fire. They were grilling a mess of bleak and minnow on green twigs. Having made a bit of noise as they approached, both travellers were expected. One of the lizards stood barring their way to the water, which appeared to be a small streamlet flowing away into a dense pine forest. The rest of the reptile crew crouched, ready to back the lizard up.

Bragoon nodded civilly to them, noting that all eyes were on his sword. 'Evenin' to ye, we've come for water.'

One of the lizards sniggered nastily, trying to imitate the otter's voice. 'H'evannin' to ye, we've a-come f'waterrrr!'

Horty noticed several large gourds of water nearby. 'That's the jolly old stuff, water, you know, that pleasant liquid which is rather nice t'drink. I say, those tiny fish smell rather toothsome, wot. Don't suppose you'd like to donate a few to a worthy cause, a hungry but honest hare, eh?'

The reptiles edged around, circling the pair. The largest of the lizards picked up a crude, flint-tipped spear, pointing it at Bragoon.

'Watersss not a free, iz all oursss. You wanta fisssshes an' drrrrrink, give usss bright a blade!'

Ignoring him, the otter turned to Horty. 'I don't know wot it is wid the beasts in this country, but they seem t'think we're dim-witted. Our stream, our water, our fish. While pore young Fenna's dyin' for a drop o' water. I've taken about enough of all this claptrap, mate. Ye take my sword, don't do anythin', just stay there, that's an order!'

Horty took the weapon and saluted. 'As y'say, sah! An' pray, what d'you intend doin', if one may ask, wot?'

A slow, savage grin spread across the otter's tough face. 'Nothin' much, I'm just goin' t'get us some water.'

Roaring out a warcry, Bragoon launched himself at the reptiles. 'Make way fer Bragoon o' Redwaaaaaallllll!'

Horty could not have moved if he had wanted to. He stood wide-eyed with shock, watching six reptiles take the most fearsome beating he had ever witnessed.

Bragoon broke the spear of one of the lizards over its head, then picked the reptile up and hurled it into the stream. He went at the others like a madbeast. Flinging himself through the air, he butted a toad heavily in its enormous stomach. As air shot out of the toad in a whoosh, he rudderwhipped it hard, thrice across the head, laying it senseless. He turned and grabbed the other lizard, running it forcefully, snout on, into the willow trunk. Seizing the grass snake, he used it like a flail, cracking the jaws of the other two toads with the snake's head. Bragoon leaped high. Still holding the grass snake, he landed on the two toads' stomachs, then booted all three toads into the stream. The other lizard sat facing the tree trunk, nursing its broken snout. Knotting the snake around its neck, the otter looped them both to a low branch.

Dusting off his paws and breathing heavily, Bragoon took the sword from the astounded young hare. Putting the swordpoint at the lizard, he growled, 'In the future, mind yore manners an' be polite to visitors!'

The lizard clutched on to the coils of the senseless grass snake around its neck. The snake was looped to the branch above, keeping the lizard on tippaw. Bragoon put his face close to the reptile and roared thunderously, 'Yore all dead-beasts if'n I clap eyes on ye agin! D'ye hear me, slimeguts?'

Dipping a paw into one of the gourds, the otter tasted the water and spat it out in disgust, then called to his companion. 'Git yore gob out o' that stream, young 'un. Wash these things out an' fill 'em wid fresh water. I'll get the fish.' He stowed the sword over his shoulder. 'Don't dillydally, mate. Fenna an' the others'll be waitin'. Put a move on!'

Horty hurried to do Bragoon's bidding, holding a conversation with himself as he rinsed and filled the containers. 'Seasons o' soup'n'salad, 'pon my word! That crackpot must've been a right terror in his younger days, wot? Curl me crusts! A chap'd do well to stay the right side o' that otter, he's a bloomin' one-beast army!'

Bragoon's voice cut sharply into his meanderings. 'Stop chunnerin' an' get 'em filled, ye great gabby windbag!'

Horty filled the last gourd with one paw, saluting furiously with the other. 'Chunnerin', sah, who, sah, me, sah? No, sah, not never, nohow. Last one filled, sah, all correct, wot wot!'

Bragoon had chopped branches with his sword. He and Horty carried the gourds, strung on the wood and yoked across their shoulders, two to each of them. They had drunk sufficient water and chewed on the cooked fish as they trekked back to their friends.

Sighting the lean-to in dawn's pearly light, they dashed forwards, slopping water, with Horty yelling, 'Toodle pip there, you idle lot, here come two handsome water carriers. I say, we've got fish, too! Jolly good, eh?'

There was no reply from the shelter. Bragoon hurried forwards, only to find it deserted.

BOOK THREE

'We lived one summer too long'

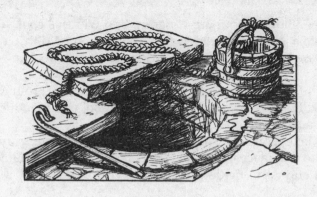

29

Morning sunlight filtered like molten gold through the gate-house. Raga Bol picked his teeth with the silver pawhook, spitting a bone back on to the remains of a well-grilled fish, which he had breakfasted on.

The sea rat captain was in a expansive mood, having slept dreamlessly without any giant stripedog nightmares. The whole incident surrounding Lonna had faded into the background since his arrival at the Abbey. He felt a sense of power, sheltered by the monumental red walls which he knew would be his new home. No more scouring the cold northeast seas. This was a place of fair weather, a fortress from where he could rule all Mossflower. Lord Raga Bol; he liked the sound of his new title.

Badredd quaked with pent-up tension as he awaited the sea rat's verdict on his cooking. Blowfly stood behind him, twirling his knotted rope's end. Relief flooded through the small fox at the sound of the captain's coarse but satisfied chuckle.

'Haharr, I've eaten worse an' lived! Wot kinda fish was that 'un, matey? Wot 'erb did ye use on it, eh?'

Badredd answered promptly. ' 'Twas a grayling, sir, grilled with button mushrooms an' dill. I did it special.'

Bol patted his stomach. 'Graylin', that's a nice-soundin'

name. Blowfly, wot are we goin' t'do wid this cook – flog 'im to a jelly wid yore rope's end or gut 'im wid this 'ook?'

Blowfly smiled, not a pretty sight. 'Gut 'im, Cap'n, go on!'

The hook lunged out, capturing Badredd around his neck. He was dragged forwards until Bol was breathing in his face.

'Make yoreself useful round 'ere, me liddle graylin'. Clean this place up, scrub it out an' make the bed. Blowfly, you stay 'ere, tickle 'im up wid yore rope's end if'n 'e slacks!'

Thrusting both scimitar and stiletto in his sash, the captain swaggered out on to the sunlit lawn. 'Glimbo, rally the crew. 'Tis time we went for a parley wid our new friends!'

All night long, Foremole and his molecrew had been carrying rubble up to the dormitory to be used as extra defence material. Martha sat close to the window with Toran and Abbot Carrul.

Granmum Gurvel laid breakfast out on the windowsill for them. 'You'm bee's h'eaten ee brekkist naow, 'tis gudd furr ee!'

The trio had already laid their plans. Toran poured honey and beechnut flakes over his oatmeal, pointing to the gatehouse. 'Stand ready, everybeast, they're comin'!'

Raga Bol sauntered up with twoscore of sea rats, as though he was out for a morning stroll. He waved up at them.

Toran grunted, 'Don't look like they're goin' to attack right now.'

'It wouldn't pay to!' Martha muttered grimly, reaching for one of Redwall's latest pepper bombs. Abbot Carrul stayed silent, polishing his glasses nervously on his habit sleeve.

A sea rat brandishing a rusty axe snarled up arrogantly at the dormitory windows, 'Get yerselves out 'ere, or we'll come in an' drag ye down!'

Drawing his scimitar, Raga Bol dealt the sea rat a swinging blow to the jaw with its bone handle. He placed a sea-booted footpaw on the sprawled-out rat and spoke reprovingly. 'Tut tut, I'm surprised at ye, mate. Is that anyways to be addressin' gennelbeasts?' Returning the blade to his sash, the sea rat captain lectured the rest of his brutish crew. 'Mind yore language when ye talks to the goodbeasts up there, that's an order!'

He winked broadly and turned away from them, performing a flourishingly elegant bow. His gold fangs glinted as he smiled up at the dormitory windows. 'My 'pologies, an' a good day to ye all, messmates. Me name's Raga Bol, fer want of a better 'un. I'm 'ere to parley wid yore cap'n. 'Twould be a kindness if'n 'e'd speak t'me.'

Abbot Carrul showed himself. 'I am Father Abbot Carrul of Redwall. What exactly do you want, sir?'

Raga Bol put his head to one side, almost managing to look coy. 'Ho, a bit o' this an' a bit o' that. Nothin' fer you to bother yore dear old grey 'ead about, Father Abbot. I'm naught but a simple beast who likes pretty trinkets.'

Toran felt that Carrul had taken enough verbal fencing. Recalling the arrow which had been shot to slay his Abbot, he came forwards, placing himself in front of Carrul. In one paw he held a long cook's knife; in the other, a pepper bomb.

'Wot would ye like, silvertongue – a bit o' this or a bit o' that?' He indicated both weapons as he spoke. 'Make yore choice, 'cos that's all ye'll get from us. Redwallers aren't born fools. We know scum, even when they try to talk fancy!'

Realizing that the otter could not be cajoled or wheedled, Raga hurled himself at the Abbey door, hacking at it with his sabre and knife and yelling to his sea rat crew, 'Attack! Break this door down!'

'Redwaaaaaalllllll!' A warcry rang out as the defenders fired slingstones and pepper bombs down upon the foebeasts. A slingstone pinged off Raga's jaw, leaving it gashed.

He retreated from the door, bellowing, 'Back! Out o' their range. Back!'

They stumbled back across the lawn to where they could see missiles coming and better dodge them.

Martha was shocked but elated. It had all happened so fast: one moment she was listening to the talk going back and forth, the next moment she was screeching like a wild-beast and madly launching off slingstones. She held her trembling paws up to her eyes, willing them to be still.

Toran winked at her. 'Well done, beauty!'

His attention was distracted by Raga Bol, shouting, 'Ahoy there! Is that the way ye treat creatures wot comes in peace? Aharr, ye wretches, I'll show ye the sea rat way o' fightin' back. I'll burn ye out!'

The sea rat captain marched off, back to the gatehouse. Some of his crew were nursing wounds, while others fled blindly, their eyes streaming as they sneezed uncontrollably and headed for the pond.

Martha could feel panic welling inside her. She clasped Toran's paw. 'Will they really try to burn us out?'

Seating himself on the windowsill, the ottercook stared down at the Abbey's main door, directly below. 'Aye, I thought they'd get around to that, sooner or later. But the sea rats' plan won't work. How much of that soil an' rubble is there, Dwurl?'

Spreading his hefty digging claws, Foremole shrugged. 'Much as ee loikes, zurr. We'm gotten gurt 'eaps o' durt'n'rubble, hooj marsess uv ee stuff!'

The Abbot looked over his glasses at Toran. 'What are you thinking of, friend?'

The ottercook turned from the window. 'Our Abbey is built o' stone, Father. Ain't many ways they can burn an entrance in. The big Abbey door is the one way. If that went afire, we'd be lost, sittin' on the other side of it, waitin' for the door to burn down. So I plan on blockin' it completely. We'll do it right now. Ain't no sense in losin' time, so we'd best work hard'n'fast. Pay attention, everybeast, this is the plan . . .'

Raga Bol's mood had turned sour. He had supposed that his show of force would have gained him an easy victory rather than a shameful retreat. But it had become apparent that the Abbeybeasts were not afraid to fight, no matter how great the odds. He retired to the Abbey pond where he sat sullenly watching those of his crew who had been struck by pepper bombs dousing their heads in the shallows. Flinky and the rest of Badredd's gang were there, ineptly trying to catch another grayling. The captain took his spleen out on them, booting Flinky headfirst into the water.

The stoat rose spluttering, as he tried to placate the irate sea rat. 'Sure we was only tryin' to catch a fat ould fish for yer 'onour's supper. Ain't that right, mate?'

Halfchop nodded enthusiastically. 'Kachunk!'

Raga Bol drew his scimitar menacingly. 'Gerrout o' me sight, ye witless idiots, make yoreselves scarce. Now!'

Avoiding the keen blade, Flinky and the rest fled the scene.

Ferron, the gaunt rat, slung a flat pebble, bouncing it over the pond surface. 'I wouldn't give 'em 'til sunset, Cap'n. I'd burn those beasts out now!'

Bol was loath to destroy any part of his new home. He looked to Wirga, his Seer. 'Wot say ye, old one?'

Wirga was drawing patterns in the banksand with a stick. She shrugged. 'If the sons of Wirga were here, they could use their darts on anybeast who showed at the windows.'

Raga Bol glared at her. 'But they ain't 'ere, are they? So do we burn 'em out, or have ye got a better way?'

The Seer sensed the danger in his tone. She made her reply diplomatically. 'Set a fire in full view of the windows. Then send a messenger to give them one last warning. The sight of flames should alter their minds.'

This was the answer the captain desired. He gave orders.

'Ferron, Glimbo, gather wood an' get lamp oil. Then set up a blaze on the lawn, where they kin see it. Wirga, take Chakka wid ye. Go an' warn those fools wot'll 'appen if'n they don't surrender t'me!'

Badredd had just finished mopping the gatehouse floor clean and was about to unbend when Blowfly slapped his rump smartly with the rope end.

'Yew missed a corner be'ind the door!' The fat sea rat caught Flinky peering in through the open window at him. 'Now then, slysnout, wot do yew want?'

The stoat smiled apologetically. 'Beggin' yore pardon, sir, but 'tis the cap'n, 'e wants ye down by the pond.'

Blowfly gave Badredd another sharp rap. 'This place better be shipshape when I comes back, or I'll flay the back offa ye. Ahoy there, stoat, lend 'im a paw. I kin find me own way t'the pond.' Blowfly waddled off, twirling his rope end skilfully.

The small fox tossed Flinky a damp rag. 'You start on the windows, I'll see t'the floor.'

The stoat pulled him upright, whispering urgently, 'We're gettin' out o' this place. Come on now, while they're all at the pond we can make a run fer it!'

Badredd gazed dumbly at Flinky, as if not understanding what he had said. The stoat grabbed the cleaning rag from him and flung it away. 'Don't stand there wid yore jaw flappin'! Are ye comin' wid us, or d'ye like bein' a slave? The rest o' the gang are hidin' by the gate, waitin'. All the sea rats are down by the pond, there's not a sentry on guard at all!'

Badredd's limbs began trembling. 'But wot if they catch us?'

Flinky could not keep the contempt out of his voice. 'Huh, some grand ould leader ye turned out t'be. Yore better off stayin' here if'n yore too scared. We're goin'!'

He ran from the gatehouse to where the others were waiting. 'Get that gate open, quick now!'

Soon Badredd came running from the gatehouse to join the escapers, shouting out, 'Wait for me, mates. I'm comin', too!'

A moment later they were off, dashing south down the path and cutting off east into Mossflower Wood, leaving the main gate swinging lazily in the summer breeze.

Raga Bol was putting an edge to his blade on a stone he had found on the pond's edge. He glanced up sourly at Blowfly's approach. 'Wot do y'want, eh?'

The fat sea rat saluted with his rope's end. 'Dat liddle stoat, the gabby one, 'e said yew wanted ter see me, Cap'n.'

Blowfly dodged a swipe from the silver hook as Bol roared, 'I never said no such thing. Get back to that gate'ouse an' see wot they're up to. Go on, move yer fat bum!'

He glanced up despairingly at the sight of Wirga and Chakka arriving back from the Abbey building. Both were caked from eartips to tails in a mixture of soil, rubble and sloppy debris, which clung to their bodies. The sea rat captain shook his head in disbelief. 'Well, make yore report. Wot 'appened to youse two?'

Wirga spat out grit. Pawing soil from her ears, she hawked and coughed to clear her mouth. 'They didn't give us a chance to speak. We went round there like thee told us, but they wouldn't listen, would they Chakka?'

She waded into the pond and began washing the mess off as Chakka continued. 'They was pourin' muck outta the winders, Cap'n. We tried to give 'em yore warnin', but a crew o' those moles lobbed a big 'eap o' rubble down on us. Not only that, but they kept tippin' stuff down until we was knocked flat. We 'ad to dig our way out afore we was buried. It looks like they're coverin' the Abbey door, so we can't put a light to it, Cap'n. Those beasts are killers, we was near suffocated!'

Raga Bol put aside sharpening his scimitar. 'Have the others lit the fire on the lawn yet?'

Wirga emerged dripping from the pond. 'Aye, the wood is burning.'

Raga Bol hurried up from the pond, past the orchard and out on to the lawn at the front of the building where he could take in the full scene. He could see the top few timbers of the Abbey's main door. The rest had disappeared under a heap of debris, which was still pouring out of the window, forming a great hill of rubble, which completely blocked the doorway.

Quivering with rage, Bol strode up to the fire, which his crew was fuelling with logs, branches and planks. He smote at the blazing wood with his scimitar, scattering it on to the lawn. 'Glimbo, git yoreself over 'ere! Stop burnin' the wood, we'll need it to pile up agin that load o' rubble!'

The one-eyed sea rat, who had been enjoying the blaze, saluted his leader quizzically. 'Ye don't want a fire then, Cap'n?' He recoiled, his face now splattered with spittle from the captain's furious rant.

'Can't ye see they've blocked the doorway, fool? Rubble won't burn, we need that wood to pile up agin that 'eap. We can climb up on it through the winders!'

Raga Bol sat down on the lawn, chopping at the grass with his blade and shouting out, 'Can't ye use yore brains? 'Ave I got to do all the thinkin' round 'ere?'

Blowfly came plodding up from the gatehouse. 'Cap'n, the vermin gang are gone. The gate's open, they must've escaped!'

Bol gritted each word out slowly, as if he was speaking to a dim-witted infant. 'Well, go an' bring 'em back! Glimbo, you go wid 'im, an' don't show yer ugly faces back 'ere widout every last one of 'em. Go!'

Martha had heard every word. She smiled at the Abbot. 'Well, that's a few less to bother us.'

Sister Setiva ducked her head aside as a stretcher load of debris hurtled out of the window space. 'Och, but did ye hear yon sea rat? They're goin' tae make a ladder tae scale the heap o' muck. Whit are we to do now?'

Just then, Foremole Dwurl clumped into the dormitory, his face wreathed in a happy smile as he announced, 'We'm no need to wurry o'er water nomores, zurr. Moi molers h'uncovered a gurt well, daown in ee cellars!'

Sister Setiva pursed her lips. 'Och grand, but ah don't see how that's goin' tae help us fight sea rats off!'

Toran shook Dwurl by his muddy digging claw. 'That's a spot o' luck, me ole mate! Keep throwin' rubble out o' the windows, an' tell yore crew to start bringin' up pails o' water, as much as they can!'

The ottercook winked roguishly at Martha. 'We'll see 'ow far the rats get, tryin' to scale a mudhill.'

The haremaid clapped her paws gleefully. 'Very good, Toran, what a splendid idea! Gurvel, keep making those pepper bombs. In a day or two those sea rats will wish they'd never heard of Redwall Abbey!'

Little Muggum flung a pawful of debris moodily out the window. 'Hurr, they'm founded watter. Oi 'speck uz Dibbuns bee's a getten barthed agin.'

Sister Setiva patted the molebabe fondly. 'Och aye, but ye can throw the soapy bathwater oot o'er the rats!'

Within the hour, Old Phredd had penned a poem about what he envisaged. Martha laughed along with the rest as the ancient Gatekeeper read it aloud to the defenders.

'They won't leave this Abbey, all filthy and scabby,
    when this war is done.
Our foes will retreat, looking clean, nice and neat,
    every sea rat's son.
Oh won't it be splendid, when this siege is ended,
    like roses they'll smell,
washed by bathwater sweet, looking fresh in defeat,
    as away they run.
Come one and come all, dirty vermin we'll call,
    should you need a scrub,

don't worry or fear, we've got bathwater here,
    you may take a tub.
Wash the mud out your ears, so you'll hear us my dears,
    for 'tis truth to tell,
you will know how it feels, with a clean pair of heels,
    from a Redwall Farewell!'

Raga Bol watched as Ferron and Rojin barred and shut the big wallgates. Wirga followed him inside the gatehouse, waiting silently on his command. The sea rat slumped down on Old Phredd's bed, speaking his thoughts as he gazed up at the ceiling.

'Tonight, once 'tis dark, we attack. You stay 'ere wid a few o' the crew. Light a fire, make lots o' noise, they'll think we're all round by this gate'ouse. I'll take the rest an' storm the Abbey by surprise. Tell Ferron to gather all the wood that ain't burned. We'll need it to get up the rubble. I'll be inside afore that ole Abbotmouse knows it. I'll teach those bumpkins to defy Raga Bol. The floors in there'll be awash wid blood by the time I'm done!'

Wirga ventured some questions. 'Do I leave the gates locked, Cap'n? What if Blowfly an' Glimbo return with the prisoners? Or my three sons, what if they return with Jibsnout?'

Raga Bol looked sideways at his Seer. 'They got paws'n'voices, ain't they? Let 'em bang on the gates or call for ye to open up.'

Wirga humbled her tone, knowing she was touching on a delicate subject. 'Jibsnout and my sons are gone overlong now, they should have returned. Thou wouldst know then if the big stripedog still lives.'

Bol snapped up off the bed. 'Wot do I care about yore whelps, or Jibsnout, eh? I gave 'em a job to do, they should be doin' it. As fer the stripedog, mention 'im agin an' I'll let daylight through yore skinny carcass. Now get out an' give my orders to Ferron an' the crew. We attack tonight!'

30

Horty looked around blankly, spreading his paws. 'Gone? Where in the name o' seasons have they gone to? They were supposed t'wait here, wot!'

Bragoon held up a paw. 'Quiet, mate, don't move, stay still!' He cast around, starting in a small circle and going wider. 'If ye go shufflin' about with those big paws o' yores, this dusty ground'll get disturbed. Ahah! Here's their tracks, aye, an' one other, too. Quick, mate, grab all the gear an' foller me!'

Horty gathered up the cloaks and staves which had formed the lean-to. Burdened by this, plus the two gourds of water on his yoke, he staggered after the otter. Bragoon, having shed his share of the water, was forging ahead swiftly.

Horty protested. 'I say, old bean, that's a bit wasteful, ain't it, leavin' behind good water that you had to carry half the blinkin' night?'

Bragoon kept his eyes on the trail as he answered. 'Can't stop now, got t'get to our mates fast – 'tis a matter o' life an' death. Keep up as best ye can!' Hurrying forwards, the otter began emitting an odd, piercing whistle.

Horty plodded on, twitching his ears in disapproval. 'Huh, matter of life'n'death, an' the bounder's whistlin' if y'please? Wouldn't mind, but it's not even a flippin' catchy tune. The bally beast's brains have gone to his rudder if y'ask me, wot!'

Eventually Bragoon spotted the three figures, out on the arid plain. Springald and Saro were shuffling along facing backwardss, supporting Fenna. Closely following the otter and his three companions, an adder was slithering, its forked tongue flickering out, sensing prey, the fatigued trio ahead of it. Hearing the sound of Bragoon's high-pitched whistle, the snake turned, bunching its coils and hissing viciously. Not as big as some serpents the otter had encountered, it was a male, just beginning to get its growth. But angry and deadly enough to deal a fatal bite with one speedy strike of its venomous fangs. Continuing to whistle, Bragoon drew his sword and moved closer, making ready to fight if necessary. The otter smiled grimly. His ploy had worked: the hunting adder had now become the hunted, its fate sealed.

Before the old warrior could strike, the young hare bawled out a warning. 'Look out, pal, here come those blinkin' buzzards again!'

Like thunderbolts out of the blue vaults of morning, two large adult birds whizzed down. With total disregard for the snake's venomous fangs, they struck their quarry with lightning speed. The murderous beaks and talons of both buzzards snuffed out the adder's life with savage skill and ferocity. The dead snake was still writhing in the dust whilst they continued their frenzied attack. Then it went still, and the hawks screeched out their victory cry.

Shielding her eyes against the sun, Saro watched the predators bearing their limp prey off into the cloudless sky as Bragoon and the hare approached her.

She shook her head ruefully. 'I wish I'd learned t'do that whistle. Never could get the hang of it, though. Burn me brush! Is that water you've got there, Horty?'

Shedding all his trappings, the young hare sank wearily

down. 'Indeed it is, marm, but I'm afraid you'll jolly well have to com'n'get it for yourselves. I'm whacked out!'

Bragoon took the yoke from him and sat it across his shoulders, then lifted the two gourds. 'Ye did well, mate, take a rest now.'

The elderly squirrel and the two Abbeybeasts sat amid the wasteland dust, gulping down the life-giving liquid. The otter soaked a cloth, allowing it to dribble into Fenna's mouth. He wiped her face with the damp material, cautioning them, 'Drink slower, or ye'll be sick. This young 'un'll be right as rain soon. So, wot 'appened, mate?'

Saro looked up from the gourd. 'Just afore dawn, I scented the adder. Huh, I can sniff those things a mile off!'

She continued drinking as Springald took up the tale. 'We knew it was somewhere close, stalking us. It was too dangerous to stay inside the lean-to, the snake would've found us. So we sneaked quietly off, but the adder saw us and came right on our track. I've never seen an adder before – horrible beast! I was scared clean out of my wits. Good job you found us in time, we couldn't have carried Fenna much further. And, Bragoon, will you teach me that whistle? It saved our lives!'

The otter lifted Fenna on to his back. 'Some other time, miss. Let's get this 'un into the pineforest shade. We found a stream over that way. I'll take ye to it.'

Saro closed her eyes dreamily. 'A pine forest an' a whole streamful o' beautiful babblin' water. Lead on, mate!'

They entered the pines when it was midday. Horty raced ahead until he found the stream. He ran towards it, turning his head to shout, 'This is the place, chaps! Hawhaw, wait'll I tell you what old Brag did to a gang of bullyin' reptiles last night. He gave 'em the towsing of their lousy lives, he . . . nunhhhhh!'

Without paying attention, Horty had run full head-on into a thick, low pine branch. He was laid flat out, unconscious.

Saro ran to him and lifted his head. 'Stone-cold senseless!

That makes two we got to nurse now. Why didn't the lop-eared gallumper look where he was goin'?'

The remainder of the afternoon was spent beside the stream. Springald looked after her two friends whilst the older pair went foraging for food. It was so pleasant in the shade of the tall pines. Besides tending the invalids, the mousemaid had time to paddle and wash in the stream. It was a cool and peaceful spot with sunlight and shadow dappling everywhere. Fenna was recovering nicely when Bragoon and Saro returned. The two old campaigners brought with them wonderful chestnut-coloured mushrooms, wild onions, dandelion buds and a variety of edible roots and berries.

Bragoon was heartened by the sight of the squirrelmaid. 'Feelin' better, eh, beauty? Well, we can't light no cookin' fires in a pine forest like this, 'tis too risky. Do ye fancy a nice salad, miss?'

Fenna watched the otter chopping everything finely with his swordblade. 'Salad would be perfect, thank you!'

The moment the aroma of freshly cut food assailed his senses, Horty revived. 'Oh goody! I say, you chaps, please pass the salad. Owchowchoooh! Me flippin' bonce is splittin'. Can y'see any of me brilliant young brains leakin' out, wot?'

Fenna could not stifle a giggle. 'Oh, poor Horty, you've got a lump like a boulder, right twixt your ears. I'm sorry for laughing, it must be very painful.'

The young hare winced when he touched the large swelling. 'Painful ain't the word, Fenn old gel, it's absobally agonisticful. Don't think I'll last the day out, actually. Don't shed too many bitter tears when I turn me paws up an' peg out. 'Twas all done bravely in the line of duty. Wot!'

Saro inspected the injury. 'Hah, it looks like a duck egg growin' out o' yore skull. Don't worry, though, you'll live. I've got just the thing for that. Sit still an' eat yore salad while I go an' make a poultice.'

She spent some time at the stream, gathering certain things and soaking them in the water. On her return, the ageing squirrel tore strips off a cloak for binding.

Horty pulled back apprehensively. 'Don't hurt a dyin' young beast in his final moments. Be merciful, marm!'

Bragoon held the hare's paws as Saro worked. She tweaked Horty's whiskers whenever he moved. 'Be still, ye great ninny! This is a compress of duckweed, dock, watercress, sainfoil an' streambed mud. 'Twill do ye a world o' good!'

When she had finished, the others had to turn away their faces to keep from bursting out into laughter. Horty sat dolefully munching salad. Atop his head sat a high turban of cloak strips, herbs and mud, secured with a tie beneath his chin. Both of Horty's ears flopped out at the sides. He glared at Bragoon, who was biting down on his lip to contain a guffaw.

'What's the flippin' matter with your face, chucklechops? D'you find somethin' funny about a wounded warrior, wot wot?'

The otter brought himself under control. 'Who, me? No, mate, but I wouldn't go near any bumblebees if'n I was ye. They might be lookin' fer a new hive! Hohohohoho!'

Seeing there was no salad left, Horty rose regally and stared down his nose at the mirth-struck quartet. 'Tut tut, I shall be carryin' on alone, without any aid from those I once called friends. Huh, bunch of whinnyin', witless woebetides. Fie upon you all, say I!' He stalked off in high dudgeon, his turban dressing awobble as he stooped to avoid branches.

Fenna grasped her sides, tears of laughter rolling down both cheeks as she gasped out, 'Heeheehee, come on, I'm, haha, well enough to travel now. Ohahahahhh! We'd better go along with him just in case he, heeheehee, backs into a sharp branch, and we, hahahahaaaa, have to tie a turban to his tail. Whoohoohoohoo!'

The pine forest was a vast area. As evening fell, it became dark, swathed in a gloomy, green light. Horty was still not talking to anybeast, but the urge to utter some noise was so great that he struck up a mournful dirge.

"'Tis a sad lonely life, I have oft heard it said,
to go wanderin' about with this wodge on one's head,
for I travel alone o'er desert an' lea.
Why, even the midges and ants avoid me,
while the ones I called pals an' the comrades I know,
all laugh 'til their rotten, cruel faces turn blue.
There's a grin on the gob of each pitiless cad,
as they scoff at the plight of a poor wretched lad,
but I'll carry on bravely, I won't weep or cry,
an' I'll have my revenge on 'em all when I die.
My ghost will sneak up while they're laid snug in bed,
an' I'll hoot spooky whoops through this thing on my
    head.
Then they'll cry out, "Oh Horty, forgive us, please do"
as my spirit howls loudly . . . "Yah boo sucks to you!"'

When night fell, Horty broke down and wept inconsolably. Springald crept through the gloom and found him sitting on a log, feeling sorry for himself. She put a paw around him.

'Horty, don't cry. What's the matter? This isn't like you.'

He shoved her paw away. 'Yaaah, gerroff me, you don't care, no flippin' one bally well bloomin' cares about me!'

Bragoon took a firmer approach. 'Come on now, mate, wot's all this blubberin' about, eh?'

Horty snapped a small twig and flung it at the otter, but it missed. 'You ain't no mate o' mine, none of you lot is! I'm starvin' t'death, I've got a molehill growin' out me head, my poor skull aches like flamin' thunder, an' now I'm goin' blind. I can hardly see a paw in front o' me!'

Fenna took over, grasping the weeping hare's shoulders.

'Don't be silly, Horty Braebuck, and listen to me. What's all this carrying on for, eh? You're hungry, right? Tell me when you *aren't* hungry! What then, your head's aching? Stands to reason, you've suffered a nasty bang on it. But as for going blind, that's nonsense! It's so dark in this forest at nighttime that none of us can see much. Here, take hold of this stick and follow me. Don't keep fiddling with that dressing on your head or it'll never get better. Saro, have you any food left?'

The squirrel produced a few mushrooms. 'I saved these.'

Fenna gave the mushrooms to Horty. 'Eat them slowly, take small bites and chew each mouthful twenty times. Come on, up you come, we've still got a lot of ground to cover yet.'

They marched all night, with Bragoon scouting ahead and Saro keeping them on course. The otter returned in dawn's first glimmer, bringing with him a heap of ripe bilberries in his cloak.

'Lookit wot I found! I think there must be a river ahead, I could hear the sound of running water in the distance. Sit down an' get yore gums round a few o' these, Horty mate, they're nice'n'ripe. We'll rest 'ere awhile.'

Horty was considerably less sorrowful when there was food in the offing. 'Mmmm, better'n those measly mushrooms. I say, you chaps, I can see better. Flippin' bandage must've fell down over me eyes last night, wot. Oh corks, now everything's gone flippin' green! Why's it all green?'

Springald explained. 'Because it isn't properly light yet, it's the day breaking over the treetops. Pines grow so thick in here that it makes the light look green.'

But Horty would not be convinced. 'Fiddlesticks, you're only sayin' that t'make a chap feel better. Ah well, I don't mind spendin' the rest o' me life in a green fug. Hawhaw, lookit old Brag, sour apple face, an' you, too, Spring, little lettuce features, an' you Fenn, young grassgob!'

Saro stared at him pointedly. 'Ye missed me out?'

Having devoured all the available berries, Horty lay back and closed his eyes. 'Hush now, let a chap get some rest, cabbage head!'

The squirrel chuckled. 'That's more like the ole Horty we all know an' dread.'

Midmorning found them back trekking once more, eager to be out of the oppressive pine forest. The further on they went, the more pronounced came the sound of flowing water.

Saro stopped to listen. 'Sounds like a fairly wide river. Have ye got that ole map from the Abbey, mate?'

Bragoon produced the map, which had been made during the journey of Matthias of Redwall in search of his son Mattimeo. He scanned it closely. 'Aye, we're on the right course, though I think we took a different route t'get to it. This is the high cliffs, here's the wastelands an' this is the pines we're in now. There should be some sort of open area ahead, then a big river. We'll soon see, mates. Press on, eh!'

They emerged on to the edge of a deep valley, the hill below them thickly dotted with smaller pines and lots of shrubbery. Below it was the narrowest strip of bank. Beyond that, a wide, fast-flowing river glimmered in the sunlight. Halfway down, the travellers halted on a shale ledge. They still had some way to go, and the descent looked fairly steep. Horty sat down, yawning in the heat. He rested his face in both paws.

Saro prodded him. 'Are ye alright, head achin' is it?'

The young hare nodded. 'A bit, but I'm more tired than anything.'

Saro indicated an overhang that was screened by bushes. 'Tuck yoreself in there young 'un an' take a snooze. I'll call ye when we're ready to move.'

The four travellers slithered and bumped down the steep hillside, grasping trees and bushes to slow their descent. They were about halfway down when Bragoon sighted the reptiles. He halted, pointing.

'Down yonder on the riverside below us. Those reptiles I dealt with last night are waitin' for us. Trouble is, they've brought a pile o' their gang with 'em!'

Saro counted the assorted lizards, newts, toads, smooth snakes and grass snakes awaiting them on the shore. There were about thirty in all, with another twoscore camped on the opposite bank of the river.

A thin reed lance zipped upward, narrowly missing Fenna's cheek. She stumbled, almost overbalancing, but Bragoon managed to grab her. 'Take cover quick, they're throwin' lances!'

To one side of the slope, a fallen pine had lodged flat between two standing trees. Crouching behind it, Saro fitted a stone to her sling and launched it off at the reptiles. Cautiously, she peered over the log, noting that a toad had hopped out of the way of her stone. 'They ain't movin', just waitin' for us down there. Let's give 'em another couple o' slingstones, mate!'

Both she and Bragoon slung more stones as Springald and Fenna threw lumps of shale. They were forced to duck fast as a half dozen of the sharp, thin lances came back at them.

The otter thumped his rudder down irritably. 'Well, this ain't goin' t'get us to Loamhedge. Those cold-blooded scum 'ave got us pinned down 'ere!'

Springald picked up one of the lances and threw it back. 'It's a stand-off, what are we going to do?'

Sarobando passed her sling to the mousemaid. 'Ye can use this, 'tis a good sling. But I'll want it back later. This is wot we'll do. While you three keep slingin' stones, I'll slide off through the trees an' take a scout round downriver. I'll find a good quiet spot where the river narrows for an easy crossin'. Then I'll slip back 'ere an' let ye know. Once 'tis dark, we can all sneak away an' escape. Right?'

Fenna nodded. 'Sounds like a good idea!'

Bragoon raised his eyebrows. 'Sounds like? Let me tell ye, missy, when my ole mate gets an idea, 'tis always a good 'un!'

Saro gave him a quick grin. 'Thankee, Brag. Now let's give 'em a good rattlin' volley to keep their 'eads down while I pop off unnoticed. One . . . Two . . . Three!'

Slingstones and lumps of shale peppered down at the foebeasts below. When Springald looked up, Saro had gone. Bragoon shoved the mousemaid's head back down as more lances came.

'Always duck fast once ye've throwed, Spring. There's more pore beasts been injured or slain in fights by lookin' up to see where their stones went. Ready agin, come on, let's give 'em a spot o' blood'n'vinegar. Yahaaar! Try some o' this, ye scum-backed, bottle-nosed crawlers!'

Horty slept on beneath the overhang, blissfully unaware of what was taking place.

31

Saro put some distance between herself and the skirmish. Ahead lay a sweeping bend in the river. Making her way down to the bank, she skirted the bend and began jogging steadily along the shore. It was peaceful and quiet, with only the crunch of pebbles beneath her footpaws mingling with the murmur of riverwater, echoing off the high, wooded slopes on either side. As she got round the bend, Saro caught the sound of deep, gruff voices singing a river shanty. She pressed on towards the singing. It was a song she knew, and she was fairly certain who the singers would be. The ageing squirrel joined in with the melodious music.

'Wally wally dampum dearie,
I'll sail back home next spring.
Kiss all the babies for me,
an' teach the lot to sing.

Toodle aye toodle oo, me daddy's a shrew,
whose face I can't recall,
but I'll stay home all season long,
until I hears him call.
Logalog Logalog Logalog Oooohhhh!

Ringa linga ling me darlin',
there's ribbons for yore hair,
I'll bring to ye a bonnet,
an' a fine red rockin' chair.

Toodle oo toodle ay, just wait'll the day,
Daddy comes paddlin' in.
I'll grow up big'n'strong then,
an' sail away with him.
Logalog Logalog Logalog Oooooooohhhhhh!'

Cupping both paws to her mouth, Saro bellowed for all she
was worth. 'Logalogalogaloga loooooooog!'

Six shrew logboats hove into view, sailing upriver. The
lead craft was by far the largest, carved from a mighty oak
trunk and fitted with a single square sail of scarlet with an
ornate letter *B* emblazoned on it. All the logboats were
packed with shrews, about a hundred of the small, fierce
beasts. Each spiky-furred shrew wore a multicoloured
headband and a kilt held up by a broad, copper-buckled
belt into which was thrust a short rapier. Their leader, a
solid old patriarch, with a thick, silver beard, stood in the
prow of the front craft. He signalled for the rowers to pull
into the shore.

No sooner had the vessel nosed in to land than the
shrew chieftain leaped ashore and seized Saro in a vicelike
bear hug. He roared cheerily, 'Sarobando, me ole squirrel-
cake, where've ye been a-hidin' yoreself? Oh, it does me
eyes a power o' good to see ye agin! Belay, where's that
rip-ruddered rascal Bragoon? Is the ole villain still alive?
Haharrharrr!'

Saro tugged the shrew's big beard and kissed both of his
cheeks. 'Log a Log Briggy, ye barrel-bellied ole riverroarer,
I knew 'twas you as soon as I 'eard yore song. Let go o' me,
mate, while me ribs are still in one piece. Lissen careful to
wot I got to tell ye!'

After loosening Saro, Log a Log Briggy listened as she told him the facts. 'There's trouble upriver. Bragoon an' some young mates of ours are pinned down on the 'illside by reptiles. There's about thirty o' the scum on this side o' the water, an' more on the other side. We need yore 'elp, Briggy!'

The shrew chieftain's brows lowered menacingly as he gritted out the words, 'Reptiles, eh? I can't abide the creepy, cold-eyed scum. They think they rule the roost up that end o' the river. Don't fret, matey, I'll put my oar in an' show 'em who the real bigbeast is in these waters. No reptile's goin' to mess wid good mates o' mine!'

He began issuing orders to the captains of the other five logboats. 'Moor those vessels on the other bank, we'll come back for 'em later. Jigger, take twenty goodbeasts an' go wid Saro. Bring extra clubs along wid ye. Raffu, Fregg, Scordo, Fludge, you an' the rest foller me along the far bank. Keep 'idden among the trees, an' don't make no noise. Bring me Aggie Frogslapper, look lively now!'

One of the shrews passed Log a Log Briggy a hefty carved sycamore war club, which he wielded lovingly. 'Ole Aggie's slapped a few frogs in 'er day. Hah, there'll be a lot o' reptiles won't be comin' back for a second kiss from ye, Aggie me old gel!'

Briggy introduced Saro to a young shrew who was the model of himself in bygone seasons. 'This is me eldest, Jigger. 'Tis only his sixth season out as a Guoraf warrior, but he's shapin' up well. Jigg, me darlin' son, go wid Saro. When ye get yore fighters set up, wait for yore dear ole dad's call afore ye charge the scurvy foe.'

Jigger shook Saro's paw. 'Let's make tracks. I hate bein' late fer a fight, marm!'

Armed with clubs, rapiers and slings, the shrews set off with Saro and Jigger at a swift trot around the riverbend. Log a Log Briggy took his logboat with the other five craft across the river to the opposite bank. He was first ashore, stroking his club, Aggie Frogslapper, and murmuring fondly, 'Aharr, 'tis a long time since ye had a good outin', me dearie!'

Night had descended over Redwall Abbey. Brother Gelf and Brother Weld sat by the dormitory window with Toran and Martha. The vermin had extinguished the fire on the Abbey lawn. Only the glow from a fire by the gatehouse could be seen. Abbot Carrul came up from the kitchens, threading his way through the Redwallers, who were resting on the dormitory floor. He pushed a trolley along to Martha and the watchers.

'I thought you might like some leek and chestnut soup. There's freshly baked cheesebread here, too.'

Toran nodded admiringly. 'Ole Granmum Gurvel's a treasure. All the strife we're goin' through, but she still finds time to cook good vittles for us. Thankee, Father!'

Abbot Carrul stared out the window. 'Pretty calm out there. I imagine the vermin are taking their supper by that fire near the gatehouse. You can hear their voices when the wind drifts this way. Do you think they'll bother us tonight?'

Brother Weld exchanged glances with his friend Brother Gelf. 'Well, you heard them say they'd attack us when it got dark. Don't let that little decoy by the gatehouse fool you, Abbot, they'll be coming shortly.'

Carrul poised his ladle over the soup cauldron. 'You'll excuse me saying, but we don't look exactly ready to stand off an attack, with everybeast sitting about on the beds and the floor. How will you know if the sea rats are stealing up on us under cover of darkness?'

Brother Gelf chuckled. 'Oh, we'll know sure enough, Father.'

From out on the lawn, shrieks and curses rent the air, together with the clatter of falling wood. Martha said calmly, 'That'll be them now. Right, friends, all to the windows and take up your positions.'

The Abbot ducked to avoid a hooked window pole that Foremole Dwurl was carrying. 'Will somebeast pray tell me what is going on out there?'

Martha patted the paws of the two brothers beside her. 'It was their idea. We knew Raga Bol and his sea rats would come once night fell. So Brother Weld and Brother Gelf had the bright idea of throwing broken glass, from the windows of Great Hall, out on to the lawn. Then, if the sea rats tried to sneak up in the dark, they'd naturally let us know. It worked rather well, Father. Just listen to them!'

Raga Bol lurched about on the darkened lawn. He grabbed one of his crewrats, cuffing him about his ears. 'Silence, ye fool, wot's all the yowlin' about?'

The sea rat limped this way and that, trying to dodge the blows. 'Somethin' sharp is stickin' right into me footpaw. I couldn't 'elp it, Cap'n, I swear!'

Bol shoved him away scornfully. 'Somethin' sharp, eh? I'll give ye somethin' sharp if'n ye don't shuttup. Any chance we 'ad of a surprise ambush is long gone now. Never mind yore footpaws, get some fire in yore bellies an' try t'be like real sea rats. Avast there crew . . . Charge!'

Keeping his voice low as he heard the captain bellowing, Toran the ottercook gave his own orders. 'Up t'the winders, mates, let go the water!'

Sturdy moles trundled forwards to the windows. They hurled out the contents of bowls, pails, pots, pans, cauldrons and buckets. Water cascaded over the rubble heap, which piled outward, protecting the Abbey door.

The first ranks of sea rats flung tree limbs, planks and long branches against the heap. Raga Bol dashed about, shouting encouragement. 'The fools won't stop us wid a drop o' water! Up ye go, buckoes. Board the place like it was a ship an' slay 'em all!'

Crewrats began scaling up the timbers. Unfortunately for them, the wood started sinking into the rubble, which had turned into a big mudheap, owing to the water drenching it. However, three of the longest planks spanned the mess, their ends resting on the sandstone lintel above the door.

When Raga Bol saw this, he waved his scimitar about wildly. 'Ferron, Hangclaw, Rinj, gerrup those long bits. Come on, all paws t'the planks. Get through those winders, look sharp!'

Clenching blades in their fangs, the sea rats clambered skilfully up the wooden lengths. The planks bellied under their combined weight but held.

Raga Bol laughed like a madbeast. 'Haharr, keep goin'. We'll make it, mates!'

But they never quite made it. Hotroot pepper bombs burst on the heads of the lead climbers. Vermin wobbled on the planktops, trying to hold on whilst fending off the searing packages that pelted them.

Toran and the Redwall defenders appeared at the window spaces bringing their long, hooked window poles into play. The ottercook and four others latched on to a centre plank and heaved it out from the wall.

'Push, friends! Put yore backs into it an' shove!'

Under the concerted effort of the Abbeybeasts, the plank was forced outward. Sea rats clung shrieking to it, as the pole moved it away. With nothing to support it, the plank teetered for a moment, then toppled over backwardss with vermin clinging to its underside.

Willing paws plied more window poles. Sister Setiva, Sister Portula and a crowd of elders pushed the left plank. Brothers Weld and Gelf, assisted by Gurvel, Foremole and three of his crew, pushed the one to the right. They strained and grunted, leaning their weight against the bending window poles.

Martha gripped the arms of her chair, lifting her body forwards. She could hear herself roaring, 'Push hard as you can. Push!'

The planks fell, one to either side of the windows. Wood scraped against stone as they plunged sideways. Wailing sea rats threw themselves clear – some going headlong into the mudheap, others thudding on the paving stones below.

The defenders fell in a heap on the dormitory floor, yelling out a great victorious cry. 'Redwaaaaallllll!'

Martha was about to drop back into her chair when an awful sight froze the breath in her throat. The sea rat Ferron was crouching before her, framed in the window. He had leaped from the first plank before it had begun its backwards journey. Latching on to the sill, Ferron had hauled himself up on to the windowledge. Now he perched there, snarling, a long dagger in one paw, ready to kill. In front of him, the Abbot had risen from the jumble on the floor and was standing with both paws raised wide, joining in the joyous shout of Redwall, with his back to the window.

Time stood still; Martha's voice had deserted her. She was holding herself up, with her paws still gripping the chair arms. In front of her, Abbot Carrul stood, smiling at the haremaid and cheering lustily. Behind him, the sea rat raised his dagger, preparing to stab at the Abbot's unprotected back. Alarm bells were clanging furiously in Martha's brain, coupled with the voice of Martin the Warrior, thundering at her, 'Save your Abbot!'

It was over in a flash! Martha stood upright. Charging past Carrul and pushing him to one side, she hit the sea rat, knocking him right out of the dormitory window.

Toran came bulling forwards. He grasped the haremaid's waist, pulling her back into the room. 'You walked, Martha! You walked! You walked! You walked!'

32

Down on the lawn, Raga Bol turned and strode away from the scene of his defeat. The sea rat Rojin limped up to him. 'Cap'n, there's no way we kin get at 'em. Those beasts ain't as simple as they look.'

Bol carried on walking without even looking back at Rojin. 'Have ye only just realized that? Call the crew off. There's got t'be a way into that Abbey, an' I'll find it. Ye can take my oath on it, 'cos I ain't movin' from Redwall. 'Tis mine, d'ye hear me? Mine!'

Somewhere southeast, deep along a woodland trail in Mossflower Wood, Flinky stopped running. Breathless and shaking, he collapsed to the ground. The little gang of escaped vermin flopped down beside him. Badredd slunk at the back of the group, with nobeast paying him the slightest attention. Gone were his days as gangleader. Now all the vermin looked to the stoat, Flinky, as their saviour. He had taken them out of the sea rats' clutches.

Panting hard, Crinktail clutched her mate's paw gratefully. 'We did it, we got away!'

Halfchop grinned fondly at Flinky, his new hero. 'Kachunk!'

Understanding what his pal meant, Plumnose nodded in agreement. 'Wodd duh we doo's now, Flink?'

The triumphant stoat was never stuck for words, despite trying to regain his breath. 'Ah well, Plum, we can't run anymore tonight. Let's just stow ourselves under those bushes an' take a good ould rest while we lay low there an' 'ide. Tomorrer we'll 'ead south, where nobeast will ever find us agin. Sure, we'll find a comfy spot where there's plenny o' vittles growin', clean water an' grand weather. That'll do fer us, a good plan, eh?'

Juppa's voice was full of admiration. 'Aye, that it is. We're with ye all the way, Chief!'

Rolling beneath the bushes, Slipback settled down amid the leaf mould. The rest joined him, with Flinky still chattering on.

'Ah, sure, we musta bin mad, lettin' greedy ould fools an' oafs lead us. Ferget all the magic swords, sieges an' great abbeys. Wot more could a body want than layin' round in the sun all day, fillin' yore stummick wid vittles an' never an argument twixt the lot of us anymore? After wot we bin through, I reckon we deserves a taste o' the good life, mates!'

Owing to the size of his nose, Plumnose was gifted with a keen sense of smell. His voice carried a note of disgust as he called out in the darkness beneath the bushes. 'Duh, sumthink smells h'awful round 'ere!'

Juppa gave vent to a horrified gurgle. 'Yurgh, wot's this?' She shot out of the bushes on to the other side of the trail. Wringing her paws, the weasel performed an anguished little dance.

'There's a deadbeast in there! Yukk, I put me paw on its face. Creepy crawlies were all over its eyes!'

A mad scramble ensued as the gang ran out from beneath the bushes, shuddering and dusting themselves down.

Flinky was the first to express an urgent desire. 'Let's get outta 'ere, run mates! We'll keep goin' 'til it's light, then I'll pick a better spot. Keep goin', don't stop fer nothin'!'

Their sounds receded south into the distant woodlands, until everything was still and silent once more. The only things that moved were the insects crawling over the lifeless carcass of Jibsnout – lying stretched beneath the bushes where Raga Bol had flung his slain body.

Around the midnight hour, two others came along that same path. The sea rats, Glimbo and Blowfly. It was the latter who searched the ground closely for signs of the fugitives.

Sceptical of ever finding them, one-eyed Glimbo complained volubly. 'Wot'n the name o' Hellgates do ye expect to find in this forest at night? We ain't even got a lantern!'

Blowfly wheezed as he heaved his bulk upright. 'I got good blinkers, don't need no lantern. I've tracked 'em this far, an' I'll keep on 'til I lays paws on dat scurvy liddle crew!'

He unwound a long whip from about his flabby waist and cracked it. 'I'll teach 'em t'run away. They'll be lucky to 'ave a hide to their backs by the time they git back to the Abbey!'

Glimbo watched him track on a piece, then come to a halt. Blowfly inspected the ground carefully, going back and forth over the same piece, muttering and cursing.

Glimbo relaxed, leaning against a tree. He scoffed sarcastically, 'Ye've lost our liddle pals, I thought ye would. Nobeast kin track anythin' at night through 'ere. Give up, mate, let's git back t'the crew. They're prob'ly inside that Abbey now, grabbin' the loot an' plunderin' the place. Yore wastin' time out in a forest when we could be back there snatchin' our share.'

Blowfly gave him a surly glare. 'Huh, 'tis alright fer you, I'm the one t'blame for lettin' them escape. 'Tis me who Cap'n Bol will take it out on. I can't go back empty-pawed!'

His companion did not agree. 'Aw c'mon, Bol won't be frettin' over a few runaway fools. The cap'n 'as other things t'think about. A kick in the tail an' a few 'ard words is the most we'll get. Huh, we've 'ad plenny o' those afore now. Belay there, shipmate, wot are ye doin'?'

Blowfly looked up from his task of striking flint to steel. 'Wot I shoulda done awhile back, makin' a torch. I'll find these runaways, just ye wait'n'see!'

Glimbo seated himself with his back against the tree trunk. 'Well, ye can find 'em on yer own, 'cos I ain't goin' anywheres. When ye come back this way widout 'em, gimme a shake. I'll be right 'ere, takin' a nap.'

Blowfly held up the burning torch he had fashioned. Silent and stubborn, he trudged off alone into the night.

Lonna Bowstripe saw the glow from between the trees where he sat resting. It appeared like a small floating island of light in the darkness. Silent as a wraith he arose, becoming one with the forest as he stood motionless against the elm trunk. Blowfly walked by within a paw's reach of the big badger. Staring at the ground, the sea rat mumbled bloodthirsty curses as to the fate of the lost fugitives. Lonna saw his face in the torchlight, and a trigger went off in his mind. He recalled brief flashes of the night he had been attacked by the sea rats. Blowfly's coarse, ugly features were instantly identifiable. Swiftly, the badger strung his bow and stole up behind the unsuspecting sea rat.

Blowfly was jerked back as the tightly strung bow trapped his neck between wood and twine. The big badger managed to catch the torch before it fell.

Craning his head around painfully, the sea rat caught a glimpse of his captor and spoke almost indignantly.

'Yore dead!'

Lonna drew him in until they were face-to-face. Only the pressure on the bow held the sea rat upright, his limbs having turned to jelly.

With torchlight flickering over his scarred features and the light glinting in his vengeful eyes, the giant badger resembled some beast straight out of a nightmare.

Blowfly's tongue suddenly ran away with him. 'It was

Bol . . . it wasn't me . . . I wasn't nowhere near ye. I swear me oath on it, I never did nothin' . . . Gurgg!'

A sharp tug on the bowstring silenced him. Lonna's voice left the sea rat in no doubt that lies would not save him. 'So you never did anything, you were nowhere near, it all had nought to do with you, you are innocent of everything?

'How many times has that same excuse been made? Think of every bully, cheat, plunderer or murderer before you who has lied with those same words. Once a villain is caught with no pack around him, then everybeast is to blame, except himself, of course. He will lie, betray and cheat to save his hide. But sometimes there is justice in the world, and fate catches up with him. So speak truly to me, or you will die slowly. You have my word on it – and I never lie.'

Blowfly sighed with relief. He told Lonna all he needed to know, and he spoke truly. The big badger kept his word: the sea rat did not die slowly. A single, mighty jerk of the bow, and Blowfly died quicker than he had ever expected to.

Awakened by flaring torchlight, Glimbo yawned and stretched his paws. 'Betcha never caught 'em, I told ye afore y . . . Ukkk!' The sea rat's paw shot to his neck. Blowfly's long whip was tied around it, holding him fast to the tree he was sitting against.

A deep, forbidding voice warned him, 'Be still, vermin!'

Automatically he raised his other paw, trying to free his neck. There was a hissing sound, like an angry wasp. An arrow of awesome length buried its point deep in the tree trunk, a hairbreadth from his neck. Glimbo froze.

Lonna revealed his face in the torchlight, laid another shaft on his bowstring and unhurriedly explained his purpose to the petrified sea rat. 'You will take me to the Abbey of Redwall. I am going to release you, but play me false, you'll wish you hadn't. Is that understood? Speak!'

Glimbo's good eye rolled about alarmingly in its socket – he was completely terrified. 'Unnerstood!'

The badger drew a long knife from his arm sheath and severed the whipcoils with a swift stroke. The sea rat shot off like a hare at top speed. Lonna drew back the bowstring, homing in on the fleeing figure.

'Never mind, I'll find my own way.'

33

Fenna lowered her head quickly. More thin, sharp reed lances whipped viciously by. 'Don't they ever run short of those things?'

Without raising himself, Bragoon hurled off a slingstone. 'There's always reeds aplenty on riverbanks. They just cut 'em an' point one end – it makes a good throwin' lance, sharp an' dangerous. I've used 'em meself in the past.'

Saro suddenly rolled in beside Springald. 'Aye, but ye weren't much good with lances, too 'eavy pawed.'

The otter scratched his rudder. 'Where did you come from, mate?'

Saro smiled, secretly enjoying the surprise she had in store. 'I found a bend in the river down that way, an' guess wot else I found?'

She signalled with her paw. Suddenly Springald found herself being jostled by a score of shrews who had crept out from behind trees and bushes to join them in the shelter of the log.

The otter uttered a delighted growl. 'Guoraf shrews . . . Great!'

Saro pointed to Jigger. 'Aye, Guoraf shrews, an' who does this 'un remind ye of, Brag?'

The otter inspected Jigger's face, noting the beard he was starting to cultivate. 'Wait, don't tell me, are ye a kinbeast to Log a Log Briggy, young 'un?'

Jigger expertly caught a reed lance as it flew by. As he cast it back downhill, he was rewarded by a reptile's scream. 'Briggy's me old daddy. You must be Bragoon, the mad otter. Daddy's tole me about you. Pleased t'meetcha!'

Fenna whispered to Saro, 'What's a Guoraf shrew?'

The squirrel explained, 'That's just the first letters of their tribename. Guerilla Union of Roving and Fighting Shrews. They're good friends an' fearsome warriors. Sometimes I think that they do all their far rangin' just lookin' for fights. Me'n Brag have battled alongside of 'em once or twice through past seasons.'

When everyone was acquainted, Jigger outlined the plan. 'We've got to 'old on, 'til me dad an' the others get set on the far bank. Then when we 'ears the signal, we charge an' cut loose at those reptiles on our side.'

Bragoon mulled it over. 'Sounds like good sense t'me, mate. This crowd down below ain't goin' anyplace. They're tryin' to outwait us, an' slay us all when we makes a move t'leave.'

Jigger peered over the log and ducked a few lances. He thudded the ground with his club, chortling eagerly, 'Reptiles'll stan' about waitin' fer ages in the sun. Well, I 'ope they enjoys their sunbath, 'cos we'll be givin' 'em a different kind o' tannin'. Hahaha!'

Saro spotted slight movements in the bushes on the far hillside. 'Looks like ole Briggy's gettin' the lads into position. Won't be long now.'

Without any prior warning, Horty came skipping blithely out from beneath the overhang. He ran by the log, speeding downhill and calling back to them, 'Shrews, eh? Where'd ye meet that flippin' lot? I feel much better now, chaps. Who's for a jolly old paddle in the shallows, wot?'

When three lances came zinging at him, the young hare

stopped, but the weapons had pierced his ridiculous head-dressing. He ground to a halt, only paces from the dumb-founded reptiles.

'Great blinkin' seasons, have a flamin' care where you're chuckin' those things. A chap could get injured by them!'

Knowing that the plan had been ruined, Bragoon, Saro and Jigger, followed by their fighting force, came bounding downhill. At the bottom they found, to their shock, that the reptiles were lying prostrate, facedown in front of the young hare. Horty stood posing majestically, the three lances trans-fixing his turban.

Saro glared at him. 'Wot were ye thinkin' of, ye great idiot? Lollopin' off right into the middle of the enemy like that!'

Horty gave her a scathing glance. 'Hold your tongue, marm. These chaps are just showin' their respect to me. Hawhaw, they must think I'm the Great Hortyplonk, descended from out the bloomin' sky, wot!'

Springald scoffed in his face. 'Then they must be bigger idiots than you! D'you realize you could've been killed?'

As she spoke, there was a whooping warcry from the far bank. '*Logalogalogaloooooooog!*' Briggy had commenced attacking the reptiles over there.

The reptiles laid out in awe of Horty lifted their faces. When they saw the score of shrews brandishing their clubs, they rose, backing off into the shallows.

Horty took a few paces towards them. 'I say there, old scaly-skinned chaps . . .'

Hissing and squeaking, the reptiles fled into the water.

The young hare turned to Jigger, who was looking rather crestfallen. 'Oops, sorry about that, old lad. Were you goin' to give those bounders a good drubbin'? I didn't realize. Oh well, never mind. Come on, we'll pursue 'em into the river an' deal 'em a few severe whackin's, wot!' He trotted into the shallows but was immediately set upon and hauled back by four shrews.

Horty protested vehemently. 'Wot the . . . ? I say, unpaw

316

me, little sirrahs, I'm not scared of a few mangy reptiles, by the left, I ain't!'

Jigger remarked caustically, 'Oh, we know ye ain't, lopears. But it's not the reptiles that's the danger on this stretch o' the river. Watch!'

He picked up a lance and went into the shallows, holding the weapon out into the water at paw's length. Suddenly it began to shake and vibrate. When Jigger pulled it out, the tip was ripped and ragged. A small fish, which seemed to consist of only big, needlelike teeth, was clinging doggedly to it. Jigger flicked the creature back into the water.

' 'Tis the fish that are the slayers 'ere!'

The reptiles were being swept downriver, shrieking unmercifully as the water about them reddened.

Horty sat down in a collapse on the bank, looking pale about the gills.

'Oh corks, I feel quite ill all of a sudden!'

On the far bank, the reptiles were taking a colossal walloping from Briggy and his command. They had tossed a big logboat sail over their foes, capturing most of them beneath the spreading canvas. Some of the Guorafs held the ends down, while others galloped about on the sailcloth, dealing great whacks with their war clubs to any bump that appeared – be it head, tail, back or limb. Gradually the canvas subsided and was still.

Log a Log Briggy waved over to them, his stentorian bass voice booming over the waters, 'Stop there, friends, I've sent a crew to git the boats. They'll pick ye up an' bring ye over!'

It was a glorious evening on the far bank. Six logboats lay prow-on to the bankside, as the travellers sat among their shrewfriends.

Horty sniffed the air appreciatively, his whiskers atwitch at the aromas of cooking. 'I say, old Briggathingee, is that supper I detect? Jolly nice of you chaps, wot!'

Briggy pulled a mock glare at Bragoon. 'So, ye had t'bring

a starvin' hare along with ye this trip. I'll wager that lollop-lugged young famine maker can shift a tidy few platefuls, eh?'

Horty smiled primly. 'Oh, I just nibble a bit here'n'there, y'know, sah. Actually I've not been feelin' too chipper of late. But if the scoff's as good as it smells, well, I might persuade myself to try it, wot.'

Jigger looked askance at him. 'Lissen, mate, if'n ye want to sail wid the Guorafs, ye've got t'be a big eater an' a great bragger, like Drinchy 'ere. Ain't that right, Drinch? Show the harebeast 'ow 'tis done.'

A fat, powerful-looking shrew stood up, smirking, then launched into Riverbraggin, an art much admired among the longboat crews. Drinchy thumped the ground with his club and commenced roaring, 'I wuz borned on a river in a thunnerstorm, an' wot did I do? I ate the bottom outta the boat an' fought six big pike who tried to eat me! Though I wuz on'y a babe, I scoffed three of 'em, an' tossed the rest on the bank an' fried 'em for me brekkist! Aye, mates, I'm Drinchy Wildgob, the roarin' son of a roarin' son who killed 'imself tryin' to feed me. I can outeat, outchew an' outswaller anybeast alive – includin' long-pawed, flop-eared, fancy bunnies!'

Finished with his mighty brag, Drinchy bowed as the shrews cheered him raucously.

Saro nodded to Horty. 'I think you're bein' challenged, young 'un. Think you can do better than Drinchy?'

Horty stood up, bowing elegantly to Saro. 'Marm, my dander has risen since the remarks that chap made about me. We of the Braebucks are not backwards in coming forwards. I shall accept this curmudgeon's braggin' challenge, forthwith!'

Without further ado, Horty bounded up, spreading his paws dramatically and yelling like a madbeast, 'I'm the son of the howlin' hare! I was born on a winter's night in a gale. My parents took one look at me, chewin' on the chimney, an' left home! There ain't a cauldron big enough to hold my dinner, not one in all the land! I've ate every jolly old thing – fried frogs, toasted toads, boiled badgers, roasted reptiles, an' shrews, too! Shrew stew, shaved an' shrivelled shrews, shrew soup an' simmered shrew! I've got a stomach of iron an' a mouth like a steel trap! I'm the Horrible Hortwill Braebuck, an' nobeast steps over my line! Even little fat wretches with bellies like balloons an' spiky fur an' names like Drinchy! D'ye know what the Horrible Horty likes for supper? Daintily diced Drinchy . . . with lots o' gravy. Yaaaaaah!'

The Guoraf shrews battered the ground with their war clubs, a mark of the highest honour they could show anybeast. Then they hoisted Horty up on their shoulders, cheering him twice around the camp.

With a look of thorough humbleness, Drinchy shook the young hare's paw fervently. 'Well, I more'n met me match there, mate. Ye must be the best bragger ever born, ye made me look like a beginner.'

The triumphant Horty was gallant, even in victory. 'No hard feelin's, Drinch old lad, but mind your language in the future, wot!'

A magnificent supper was served, as befitted shrewcooks, who were renowned across the waterways for their culinary skills. Huge portions were served up to Horty. The shrews gathered round, gazing in awe as he downed one dish after another.

'Mmmm yum! This is top-hole tucker, wot wot. Pass some more o' that skilly'n'duff, please. Oh, an' lob more honey over it, I like it that way. I say, is that actually rhubarb-'n'blackberry crumble? . . . Where's me blinkin' spoon? Drinch, old scout, would y'be kind enough to fetch more shrewbeer – not that little beaker, gimme the jug!'

Bragoon chuckled. 'Look at young Horty, he's in 'is element there. They'll get tired o' servin' before he does of eatin', mark my words, Briggy!'

The shrew chieftain watched Horty admiringly. 'That 'un should've bin a shrew, mate. I saw 'im march straight inter

319

that reptile crowd widout turnin' a hair. They'd already throwed three javelins an' spiked 'is hat. I tell ye, Bragoon, it takes a brave beast to do that!'

The otter poured himself another beaker of shrewbeer. 'Or a ravin' idiot! I'll tell ye the truth of it all someday.'

Horty was on to a wild grape and almond pudding. 'Never had this before. My word, it's rather toothsome, wot. Send the old cook out, an' I'll give her a kiss!'

A small, toothless, grizzled male shrew stumped out from behind the cauldrons hanging over the fire. He grinned. 'H'I'm the cook round 'ere. Wot was it ye wanted, sir?'

Horty choked on a mouthful of pudding. 'Wot, er, oh nothin', granddad. Excellent scoff, wot. Top marks, well done an' all that. Back to the old fire an' keep on cookin'. Eh, wot!'

Log a Log Briggy called to his shrews. 'Ye can let those reptiles free now, I reckon they've learned their lesson. If any of the slimy-skinned lot give ye any bother, give 'em another drubbin' an tell 'em you'll sling 'em in the river. That should scare 'em!'

He sat down with Bragoon and Saro, winking fondly at them. 'Now then, mateys, wot brings you two t'these parts, eh?'

They explained the mission for Martha's cure and their quest for Loamhedge.

Briggy stroked his beard. 'Hmm, Loamhedge eh? I've 'eard tell o' the place. But ye'd 'ave to cross the great gorge to git anywheres near where the stories say the lost Abbey o' Loamhedge lies. Did ye bring some kind o' chart along to 'elp ye find it, or are ye just trustin' to fortune?'

Bragoon produced the chart from Matthias's journal. 'It's been mostly luck to date, but we do 'ave this.'

Briggy rummaged a battered single eyeglass from his belt pouch and held it to his eye. 'My ole peepers ain't wot they used t'be, I got to use this monocle t'see. Right, wot've we got 'ere?'

He perused the dilapidated parchment thoroughly. 'Hah,

I know this country, 'tis sou'east o' where we are now. I've seen these two rocks an' all. They're called the Bell an' the Badger's 'ead, great big lumps o' stone they are. Wot's this, a large tree called the Lord o' Mossflower? Huh, that was long gone in the seasons afore my father's grandfathers. Blowed down, or collapsed more likely, when the earth trembled.'

Saro looked anxiously at the shrew chieftain. 'But ye do know where the two big rocks are?'

Briggy stowed his monocle away. 'Ho, I knows that place sure enough. East along this river for a day or so, then cut south when ye leave the bank. Wicked country, 'tis.'

Bragoon patted his swordhilt. 'That don't worry us, we've travelled wicked country afore. So will ye take us up-river to the Bell an' the Badger's 'ead, me ole mate?'

Briggy held out his paw. 'Course I will, 'ere's me paw an' 'ere's me heart on it. But afore ye gets to the big rocks, ye've gotta cross the great gorge. I never knew of anybeast who's done that yet.'

Saro winked at him. 'You leave that to us. We've done lots o' things nobeast 'as ever done, me'n my mate.'

Jigger joined them, taking a great interest in Bragoon's sword. 'That's a fine-lookin' blade ye carry, mate.'

The otter drew the sword, holding it out to let the firelight play along its blade in the gathering twilight. It shimmered and glinted like a live thing. 'Aye, a fine blade it is, young 'un. My friend, the Abbot o' Redwall, loaned it t'me for the journey. 'Tis the sword of Martin the Warrior!'

The shrews had evidently heard of Martin. As word ran through the camp, they crowded around Bragoon, straining to catch a glimpse of the legendary weapon.

'So that's the sword o' Martin. 'Tis a sight to be'old!'

'They say 'twas made at the badger mountain from a piece of a star wot fell out the sky!'

'Blood'n'fur, fancy ownin' a blade like that!'

Jokingly, Jigger drew his own short rapier and waved it. 'Would ye like to challenge me to a spot o' swordplay?'

There was a twinkle in Briggy's eye as he nudged the otter. 'Go on, mate, show 'im wot a real swordbeast kin do.'

Bragoon rose casually, then moved like lightning. Jigger stood aghast, rooted to the spot as the sword encircled him in a streaking pattern of light. It clipped one of his whiskers and tipped the bandanna from off his forehead. The young shrew closed his eyes tightly.

Bragoon whirled the blade as he roared, 'Yahaarrr, ssssss'death!'

The rapier flicked from Jigger's paw. It whipped through the air, then quivered pointfirst in the prow of his father's big logboat which was drawn up on the bank.

Jigger gasped. 'Scuttle me keel! How'd ye do that, mate?'

Bragoon winked roguishly at him. 'That's a secret, young 'un!'

The Guoraf shrew greatly admired the otter's prowess. 'Could I see yore sword, sir, just fer a moment?'

Bragoon held the blade about a third of the way up. Raising his paw, he did a short hop and threw it. It turned once in the air, almost lazily; then, with a solid thud, buried its point into the logboat, next to the rapier.

The otter nodded. 'Aye, 'elp yoreself. But take care, yon's a sharp blade.'

Jigger retrieved his own rapier, but he could not budge the sword since it was too deeply imbedded in the oaken boat. Bragoon went to sit down with Briggy.

The shrew chieftain stroked his beard. 'Where'd ye pick up swordtricks like that?'

The otter shrugged. 'A Long Patrol hare from Salamandastron showed me some dodges with a blade one time. That 'un was wot they called a perilous beast, a real swordfighter, no mistake!'

Horty looked up from the remnants of a huge pastie. 'A Long Patrol hare, indeed! That's what I'd like to jolly well be someday, wot!'

Saro patted Horty on the stomach, knocking the wind

from him. 'Then ye'll have to scoff less an' exercise more. Long Patrol hares are fightin' fit.'

The young hare got quite huffy. 'Fiddlesticks, marm, one's got to get the right nourishment t'grow strong first, wot?'

Briggy smiled at him. 'Yore right there, Horty, an' ye need a full night's sleep, too. Go an' pick yoreself out a good berth on my vessel. We've got a journey upriver t'make at dawn. I'll put ye to the oars, that'll toughen yore muscles up a bit. You git yore rest now, an' you, too, Jigger.'

Horty gathered up some bread, cheese and pear cordial. 'Right y'are, Cap'n Briggathingee. I'll just take along a light snack to guard the young body against night starvation. I suffer from it terribly, y'know. I was born with the illness. I say Jigger, old lad, not takin' any rations with you? Well, suit y'self, laddie buck, but don't come pesterin' me durin' the flippin' night.'

Jigger, however, was not listening. He had found a new object for his admiration. The young shrew was all smiles and attention for Springald. Carefully he helped the mouse-maid aboard the logboat that he was travelling on.

'Watch yoreself, Miz Spring, these boats are tricky craft. You take some o' my cushions an' a soft blanket. Sleep up in the prow, that's the best spot aboard!'

The pretty mousemaid played him up outrageously, fluttering her eyelashes and allowing him to make up her bed. 'Oh thank you, my friend, that's so kind of you!'

Fenna scooted in and flopped down on the cushions. 'Plenty of room for us both here, Spring. Thanks, Jigger mate!'

Sitting by the fire with Briggy and her otter friend, Saro watched the young ones with amusement. 'Nice to see 'em gettin' on well t'gether, eh?'

Stirring the flames with his rapier, Briggy laughed. 'Ha-harr, bless 'em, they're only young once. The seasons soon fly by, ain't that right, Brag, ye ole battler?'

Bragoon polished Martin's sword with a piece of damp

bark. 'Ye never spoke a truer word, ole pal. Me'n Saro have gotten quite fond o' those three young 'uns; they're made of the right stuff. Now an' agin we gotta yell at 'em, but they learn fast. By the way, on that chart o' mine it says Long Tails an' desert beyond the river. Will that mean danger for us?'

Briggy looked scathing. 'Huh, Long Tails? My ole Granpa whopped those rats seasons afore I was born. Guorafs drove 'em off into the desertlands south o' the great gorge. They shouldn't trouble ye, though the desert might. 'Tis a long dusty trek to the gorge. D'ye want us t'come with ye?'

Saro clapped the stout old shrew's shoulder. 'No, mate, you git back to yore river, that's what ye know best. We've managed one desert by ourselves, another one won't make much difference. We'll be fine!'

Briggy seemed relieved. 'I thankee fer that, Sarobando. I don't like bein' far from runnin' water anytime. But I'll tell ye wot I'll do. We'll bring the boats back to where we drop youse off, say in about six days. I'll pick ye up for the return journey. There's a secret route I know that'll take ye back to the flatlands below the plateau. It means shootin' a mighty waterfall to git down there. But don't fret, my crews kin do it if anybeasts can. 'Twill get ye back 'ome to Redwall much faster.'

Bragoon shook the old shrew's paw heartily. 'Yore a real friend, true blue'n never fail, Log a Log Briggy!'

The shrew chieftain rose from beside the fire. 'Think nothin' of it, mate. I'm off t'me bed, if'n that young Horty ain't stolen it. Us old 'uns need sleep as much as the young do. Pleasant dreams, ye pair o' rips!'

The ageing otter and his lifelong friend sat by the fire awhile. Bragoon stared into the flames. 'We're gettin' too old for this sorta thing, Saro. I think when this adventure's over I'll settle back down at Redwall. Maybe that brother o' mine'll teach me to be a cook.'

The squirrel stared levelly at him. 'If'n that's wot ye want, then fair enough, matey. I'll be by yore side wherever ye are.'

The otter chuckled drily. 'An' so ye will be, we been together since we was Dibbuns. I wouldn't know where to turn widout ye.'

That night they slept by the fire, dreaming dreams of the sunny old days at the Abbey when they were both young tearaways together.

34

Martha was up at dawn, trying out her newfound skill – walking! At first it was painful and slow, but the progress she was making, holding on to things for support, was remarkable. With the aid of Sister Setiva's blackthorn stick, which the Infirmary nurse had parted with happily, the haremaid wandered joyfully along Great Hall.

Martha laughed inwardly at what Setiva had said: 'Och, take this auld thing an' use it in good health, ma bonny lass. Ah've only kept it tae threaten Dibbuns with – not that they ever took much notice, the wee villains!'

The young haremaid manoeuvred the stairs, pausing every few moments to revel in her newfound freedom. Walking!

Abbot Carrul came up behind her, watching Martha's progress, until she turned and noticed him.

'Good morning, Father Abbot, it's a fine morning!'

Carrul beamed back at her. ' 'Tis the finest of mornings, young miss, and all the better for seeing you up and about!'

As Toran came out on to the dormitory landing, he waved down to them. 'Now then, you two gabby idlers, why ain't ye bringin' brekkist up to the pore beasts on guard, eh?'

Martha started eagerly back downstairs. 'Breakfast for how many, sir – one, two, ten? It'll be up there directly!'

Granmum Gurvel came trundling through Great Hall, heading a small convoy of moles who were pushing four trolleys. She brandished her best copper ladle at Martha.

'Ho no you'm woant, brekkist bee's ee cook's tarsk roun' yurr. Miz Marth', you'm 'asten oop to ee durmitrees an' set ee on a churr. Rest yore paws naow. Doo ee hurr?'

Brother Weld had joined Toran on the landing. 'Best do as she says, or old Gurvel'll skelp your tail with her ladle. That's one old molecook who'll stand no nonsense.'

Breakfast in the dormitory was a makeshift affair, rather inconvenient for most but huge fun for the Dibbuns. The Abbeybabes, who thought everything was a game, perched in the oddest places, singing, playing and eating together. Sister Portula was trying to coax Muggum, and several of his cohorts, down from a shelf, where they were bouncing up and down as they squabbled over hot scones and honeyed oatmeal.

In a state of despair, she turned to Martha. 'Oh dear, I do wish the sea rats weren't here and we were back to normal. Just look at those little ones, they're getting very wild. But with no Abbeyschool, and having to spend all day indoors, who can blame them?' Portula looked to Martha for comment, but the haremaid was not listening. Her joyous mood dispersed, she stood gazing forlornly out the window.

The kindly Sister showed concern. 'Martha, dear, is something the matter, what's wrong?'

Toran was close enough to hear his young friend's reply. 'I'm sorry, Sister, but I can't help feeling sad; I've just realized something. What a waste of time it all is. Bragoon and Saro, together with Horty, Springald and Fenna, have gone off questing for Loamhedge. Little do they know that I need no cure or remedy. Suddenly I can walk! My brother and good friends are far away from Redwall – who knows what deadly danger or injury may befall them? There was no real need for them to go. Oh, fate can be so cruel at times. I feel responsible and guilty about the whole thing!'

Sister Portula comforted her. 'You must not blame yourself, Martha. None of this was your doing, was it, Toran?'

The ottercook had strong feelings about Martha's supposed dilemma, and he minced no words in telling her so. 'Wot's all this nonsense, don't ye be talkin' that way, Martha! Huh, ye could go on all day, worryin' about this an' that, an' supposin'. Lissen, I'll give ye a suppose. Supposin' yore friends an' my brother an' Saro hadn't gone, eh? Things would've turned out totally diff'rent, fate would've cast other lots for everybeast. You mightn't 'ave been at that window in yore chair last night, but those sea rats may've changed their plans. Then where'd ye be now, Martha? I'll tell ye, still sittin' stuck in a chair!

'So don't ye dare say that there was no point in our good friends undertakin' a mission to find a cure for ye, Martha Braebuck! An' don't talk t'me of danger or injury. If'n Brag an' Saro 'ave anythin' t'do with it, the only ones sufferin' perils an' wounds will be anybeasts who tries to stop 'em! So quit complainin' an' supposin', miss. Be grateful that ye can go runnin', on yore own footpaws, to greet the travellers when they return to our Abbey!'

Martha had never heard Toran speak so forcefully, or truly. Wiping her eyes, the haremaid clasped her friend's paw fervently. 'Thank you, Toran, you're right. What a silly creature I am!'

The ottercook turned away, brushing a paw across his own eyes. 'No you ain't, yore our Martha. Now put a smile on that face, an' get those liddle villains down of'n that shelf afore they fall an' 'urt themselves!'

Sharpening his silver hooktip on the wall, Raga Bol lounged in the gatehouse doorway. Bright summer morn had done nothing to ease his foul mood. Dreams of the big stripedog had begun haunting him afresh, plus he was still smarting from the previous night's shameful defeat. Striving to put thoughts of the badger from his mind, he took out his mean temper on every crewrat in sight, snarling menacingly at them.

'Belay there, Wirga, ain't there any vittles left, where's me brekkist? Ahoy, you there, stop scrapin' mud off'n yoreself, an' grubbin' at yer eyes like some snotty liddle whelp. Go an' get some vittles for yore cap'n, sharpish!'

All four of the sea rats, not knowing exactly whom the glaring captain was addressing, ran off to do his bidding. 'Aye aye, Cap'n! Right away, Cap'n!' they chorused as they tugged their ears in salute.

Raga Bol turned his spleen upon the one called Rojin, who was sitting on the gatehouse wallsteps, poulticing a swollen eye. 'Quit dabbin' at yore lamp, ye've still got a good 'un left. I never got no brekkist, 'cos Blowfly let me servants escape. They're the beasts who should be doin' the cookin'. Git yoreself after Blowfly an' Glimbo. I want t'see ye all back 'ere by noon wid the runaways in tow. 'Cos if'n ye ain't, I'll let the livin' daylights into the lotta youse wid this 'ook. Go on, gerrout o' me sight, ye laggard!'

The next to come in for a tongue lashing was the one called Rinj, who happened to stray within earshot. 'Stan' by the big gate there, Rinj, ye useless mess of offal. Keep a weather eye out for Rojin an' the others comin' back. Report ter me the moment ye spot 'em!'

The sea rat captain stalked back into the gatehouse, slamming the door so hard that its hinges rattled. He slumped into Old Phredd's armchair, trying to banish thoughts of the badger and concentrate instead on his plans to conquer the Abbey.

Morning rolled on into the summer noon. The crew danced attention upon their captain, but he barely glanced at the food they brought. Instead, he ordered them to bring him volumes and scrolls from the shelves. Bol rifled through them, searching vainly for some clues – a reference or a sketch, perhaps. Anything that would help him gain access to the Abbey building. After awhile he tired of this pursuit and banished the crewrats from the gatehouse. Scattering volumes and parchments over the floor, the sea rat captain flung himself upon the bed and fell into a fitful slumber, the coverlet draped over his face.

On waking, Raga Bol saw that the sunlight shafts had shifted across the window. It was late afternoon, merging towards eventide. Rising, he took a mouthful of his favourite grog, swilling it around his mouth, then spat it out sourly. It was silent outside, with no sounds of activity. The sea rat captain went swiftly outside.

Rinj was standing upright, propped against the gatepost, obviously sleeping. Raga Bol dealt him a savage kick, knocking Rinj flat. He continued to kick the hapless sea rat, accentuating his words.

'Ye scabby-eyed, useless bilge swab! Did I tell ye to go snoozin' on duty? Wot's this door barred for, eh? Yore supposed t'be outside, watchin' for the others t'come back. If'n we was at sea now, I'd tie ye t'the anchor an' sling yore lazy carcass o'er the side!'

Dragging Rinj upright by his ears, Bol knocked the gate bars up with his hook. He hauled the gates open, still shouting. 'I'll learn ye to disobey yore cap'n's orders, I'll . . . Yaaaagh!'

The gates swung inward, revealing Rojin, pinned to the timbers by a huge single arrow, head slumped and footpaws dragging in the dust. Dead as the proverbial doornail!

Beyond the outside path and ditch, out on the flatlands, Lonna Bowstripe roared as he fitted a shaft to his bowstring, 'Raga Bol! Death is here! Hellgates await you, sea rat! Eulaliiiiaaaaaaa!'

Bol took one glance at the avenging giant and hurled himself at the Abbey gates, slamming them and dropping the heavy baulks that served as locks. The wood shivered under the thud of the badger's massive arrow. Raga Bol leaped back from the gates, as if expecting the shaft to come right through.

Sister Setiva was prying the paws of little Yooch from the dormitory windowsill. 'Och, come away from there, ye wee pestilence!' Attracted by the shouting from the gatehouse area, she peered over to see what was amiss there. Raga Bol's hoarse yells left her in no doubt.

'All paws to the walltops! Bring spears, slings an' bows. Jump to it, the stripedog's 'ere!'

Setiva caught Abbot Carrul's sleeve. 'There somebeast oot there, yon sea rat's howlin' like a madbeast!'

Toran was out the dormitory door, with Martha close on his heels. Carrul and Setiva followed as Toran called to them, 'Up t'the floor above, mates, ye can see better from there!'

Redwallers crowded to the second-storey windows, which gave them a clear view of all that was taking place. Out on the flatlands, Lonna was raising his bow again. Brother Weld transmitted an excited commentary of what was taking place, for the benefit of those few who could not see. 'Great seasons of slaughter, it's a giant Badger Lord! The sea rats are throwing spears, firing slingstones and arrows at him. Haha, their range is too short, their weapons can't touch him. Oh my, oh golly! Did you see that?'

Old Phredd croaked impatiently, 'See what? I can't see a thing!'

Brother Weld described what he had seen. 'The big badger fired off an arrow, huh, more like a spear. It struck a sea rat, up on the ramparts. Got the vermin dead centre and drove him clear off the wall on to the lawn!'

Sister Setiva shook her head in disbelief. 'Och, what a shot, ah've never seen aught like it!'

The Abbeybeasts set up a great cheer. Lonna caught sight of them and waved. Leaning out from the upper windows, the Redwallers waved back furiously, shouting encouragement.

'Give 'em blood'n'vinegar, well done, friend!'

'That's the stuff big feller, keep those shafts coming!'

'Hurr, zurr hoojbeast, you'm give ee vurmints ole billyoh!'

With her eyes shining fiercely, Martha yelled at Toran, 'Isn't he magnificent! Can't we do anything to help him?'

The ottercook bit his lip anxiously. 'We got nothin' to throw that'd span the range twixt this Abbey an' the wall-tops, 'tis too far off for slingstones. There ain't a single bow'n'arrer in the buildin'. I'd love to 'elp the big badger, but wot kin we do, miss, wot?'

Brother Gelf, normally a quiet, unobtrusive mouse, spoke out. 'Er, I may be able to help, but I'll need to be down in Great Hall. I think I'll need a long windowpole, some twine, a couple of those pepper bombs and a few stones. Er, make them slightly larger than slingstones, but not much.'

His curiosity immediately piqued, the Abbot bowed to Gelf. 'You shall have them, Brother. Let's go down to Great Hall. No pushing there, please, let Gelf go first.'

Up on the walltops the sea rats were lying low, stunned by the accuracy of the bowbeast. Raga Bol was trying to instil some confidence in his crew. 'We're safe be'ind this wall, buckoes. That stripedog's got to stay out of our range. Soon as 'e moves forwards we'll get 'im. Ain't been a beast born yet that spears an' arrers can't slay. All's we gotta do is stay inside these walls!'

Wirga shuffled closer to Bol. 'Aye, but while we're on the inside, the stripedog has us pinned down from the outside. No sea rat owns a weapon with the range an' power of that big bow, Cap'n.'

Bol did not want to hear this. He stared cold-eyed at the Seer. 'What would ye 'ave me do then, run out an' charge 'im?'

The loss of her three sons rankled Wirga, who now did not lose the opportunity to needle Bol. 'We outnumber the bigbeast by about twoscore. I never saw a sea rat cap'n back off with those odds on his side!'

Before Bol could strike out, or argue against Wirga, a sea

rat further along the parapet gave out a shout. 'Aaargh, wot the . . . Oooch!'

He fell sideways, slain by one of the big arrows. Raga Bol crawled swiftly along and inspected the dead crewrat. 'Wot in the name o' blood'n'thunder 'appened to 'im?'

Cowering fearfully against the battlements, the rat who had been crouching beside the victim babbled out, 'I saw it, Cap'n! Gornat was 'it by summat from be'ind. There 'tis, see, one o' those liddle bags o' pepper, tied on a string, wid a stone at the other end!'

Bol unwound the object from around Gornat's waist. 'From be'ind, this thing got 'im – ye mean from the Abbey?'

The sea rat nodded vigorously. 'Aye, it came from over that way, I swear it, Cap'n. Pore Gornat got a terrible smack from it, the thing 'it 'im an' wrapped right round 'is waist. It musta cracked a rib, 'cos Gornat shouted an' jumped up. That's when the arrer took 'im, straight through the neck!'

Turning to face the Abbey building, Raga Bol saw another of the missiles come whirling through the air. It spun round and round on its twine, weighted on one end by the pepper bomb and on the other by the stone. This time it missed and struck the wallside. The pepper bomb burst, sending its load over two rats crouched directly beneath. One had the sense to stay down and do his sneezing. The other leaped up and sneezed once, then an arrow silenced him for good.

Down in Great Hall, the Redwallers had unblocked the shutters from one of the tall windows.

Toran took the windowpole from Brother Gelf. 'Can I try yore new slingpole out, Brother?'

Gelf smiled quietly. 'Be my guest, sir.'

Laying the twine across the hooked metal end of the pole, the ottercook raised it straight up, facing out of the window. Holding the end of the pole in both paws, he let it lean back across his shoulder until it lay flat. Then he whipped it upright with swift force. The missile flew off through the high open window. There was a short interval of silence, followed by an agonized screech.

Toran grinned. 'It works!'

There was no shortage of the homemade weapons. More windowpoles were brought, and more volunteers came forwards, eager to try out the new weapons. Competition became so fierce that, owing to several of the defenders hurling the missiles at the same time, some of them missed the open window space. These projectiles struck the walls and lintels, bouncing back into Great Hall and bursting. Undeterred, the Abbeybeasts kept going, muffling their faces with towels. Soon, however, the atmosphere proved too much for the onlookers; many fled the scene, sneezing uproariously.

The Dibbuns thought the whole thing was huge fun. They chortled and giggled, dashing about and bumping into one another, shouting, 'Hachoo! Blesha! Harrachoo! O blesha blesha!'

Martha helped Abbot Carrul and some of the elders to shepherd the little ones downstairs into Cavern Hole. The haremaid actually carried two Dibbuns down the steps on her back, chuckling and joking with them.

The Abbot cautioned her. 'Careful, Martha, should you really be doing that? You don't want to put too much strain on those limbs!'

Martha deposited the Abbeybabes in a corner seat. 'Oh fiddledeedee, Father, I feel stronger than I've ever felt. It's as if I had brand-new footpaws and legs, they're as supple as greased springs!'

Granmum Gurvel sent down some kitchen helpers to carry baskets of fresh-baked tarts and pastries and jugs of sweet elderflower cordial.

Martha lent a paw to serve the Dibbuns, then went to sit on the stairs with the Abbot. She felt very happy and carefree as they shared the food. 'Oh Father, isn't it wonderful, having that giant badger on our side! I wager things will be different now.'

The Abbot seemed somewhat thoughtful, though he agreed with her. 'Yes, indeed, those sea rats obviously fear the big badger a lot. Wouldn't it be marvellous if he were inside the Abbey with us? Things would be so much easier.'

Martha sipped her cordial. 'In what way?'

The Abbot warmed to the subject, propounding a theory which had been growing in his mind ever since he had first sighted Lonna standing out on the flatlands.

'Our badger fires that bow like a mighty warrior, that's for certain. If he were inside the Abbey with us, I guarantee he'd send those sea rats packing in short order.'

Martha thought for a moment about what the Abbot had said. 'Aye, he could stand at the dormitory windows and pick the sea rats off at his leisure. They're hemmed in by the outer walls, so it would make it hard for them to avoid him. The badger could use the upstairs windows on all sides.'

Abbot Carrul put aside his food. 'But the problem is that the badger's outside the walls at the moment. Those sea rats aren't stupid, they're not likely to leave Redwall and take their chances outside. Not with that giant and his bow waiting for them.'

Martha saw the wisdom in her Abbot's logic. 'Hmm, that could make Raga Bol doubly dangerous to us because he'll probably try twice as hard to get inside the Abbey now. It would give him an advantage over the badger, who would have to fight his way into the grounds and take the sea rats on from inside the grounds. That would place him in range of their weapons. Oh dear, I wonder what the answer is to all of this!'

Carrul had already anticipated the problem. Unfortunately, he could not hold out a great deal of hope. 'We need to contact our badger friend and get him inside here, but that's not possible. The sea rats are standing between him and us. We'll just have to wait our chance, though there isn't much likelihood of that at present.'

Martha tried to hide the frustration in her voice. 'But there won't be a much better opportunity than right now.

Most of the sea rats' attention is on the badger. If only we had somebeast who could slip out unnoticed! Whoever it was could leave by the small east wallgate. They'd be shielded from any attention by the Abbey building. It wouldn't be hard to steal through the woodlands to the corner of the northwest wall. When it got dark, it would be simple to creep out on to the flatlands and make contact with the badger. Then they could both return the same way.'

The Abbot folded both paws within his wide habit sleeves. 'No, 'tis far too risky at the moment, Martha. We'll wait – tomorrow, perhaps. Oh dear, all this worry and strife. I'm longing for the day when those villains are long gone from Redwall and we can all get back to a normal, peaceful life.'

Martha stood up. 'Don't fret, Father, it'll happen when you least expect it. Do you know, I feel restless. Think I'll exercise my new walking skills. I'll go up to the dormitory windows and see how things are going. Best steer clear of Great Hall, and all those pepper bombs bursting inside.'

The Abbot smiled wearily at his young friend. 'Take things easy, Martha, don't go tiring yourself out.'

She paused on the stairway. 'Oh, I'll go as slowly as Old Phredd. By the way, Father, could you do me a favour? Will you sit guard on these stairs and make sure those Dibbuns don't go rushing back to Great Hall?'

Abbot Carrul stretched himself lengthways across the step. 'Certainly. I might doze off a little, but they won't get past me. You go on now, and remember what I said about taking things easy!'

However, taking things easy was the last thing on the young haremaid's mind. Martha had a mission: she would be the one to contact the badger. She went up to the back rooms on the east side, choosing one that was mainly used as a linen store. It was filled with blankets, sheets and table-cloths.

Knotting bedsheets together, she fashioned a makeshift rope, reasoning aloud to herself, 'Finally I can do something useful to help Redwall. Now I can walk, and run, too. After all those seasons stuck in a chair, it would be a crime to waste my new gift!'

Climbing down the rope was easier than the haremaid had imagined. She had forgotten how strong her grip had become from wheeling a chair about for most of her life.

35

Dawn light seeped over the river, casting a haze of pale green-gold mist. Saro lounged in the stern of the main logboat with Bragoon, savouring the new day, and a few scones still warm from early breakfast.

'Ah, this is the life, mate, save the wear'n'tear on me ole footpaws. There's nothin' like a nice lazy rivertrip, eh?'

The otter grinned as Horty approached them, pushing on a hefty oarpole, part of two double lines of shrews. The young hare turned and started to make his way back to the prow, where he would repeat the process of poling the craft upriver.

He glared at the otter's cheery face and stuck his tongue out insultingly at Saro. 'Blinkin' idle bounders, sittin' on your bloomin' tails, wallopin' down scones, while I slave m'self into an early grave. Huh, should be blinkin' well ashamed of y'selves!'

Briggy left the prow and strode down the centre of the logboat, between both lines of polers. Exchanging a sly wink with Bragoon and Saro, he clipped Horty lightly across the ears, roaring at him in true rivercraft language, 'Avast there, ye long-legged layabout, quit prattlin' an' git polin'. We gotta build those muscles up t'make a warrior of ye! Ain't it a wunnerful life, nothin' t'do but pole about all

day on the river, ye lucky swab! Dwingo, give us a drumbeat there. Come on, shrews, put yore backs into it. Sing
out a polin' shanty to speed us on our way. Push, ye
shrinkin' daisies. Push!'

The drumbeat rolled out, echoing around the forested
banks, with deep, gruff shrew voices singing in chorus. The
shanty was a totally untrue pack of insults about Log a Log
Briggy, but he sang along with them lustily.

'Barrum, babba, whum! Pole to the beat o' the drum!
Our Cap'n is a bad ole shrew,
I wish I'd never signed to roam.
He feeds us worms an' mudpies, too,
oh ma, let me come sailin' home.
Barrum, babba, whum! Pole to the beat o' the drum!

Ole Briggy is a lazy hog,
wid a belly like a tub o' lard,
if we don't call 'im Log a Log,
he beats us bad an' treats us hard.
Barrum, babba, whum! Pole to the beat o' the drum!

One day our logboat sprang a leak,
an' I gave out an 'earty wail,
the Cap'n gave me nose a tweak,
an' plugged that leak up wid me tail.
Barrum, babba, whum! Pole to the beat o' the drum!

We ran head-on into a gale,
our Cap'n made me cry sad tears,
'cos the wind 'ad ripped right through the sail,
so he patched the canvas wid me ears.
Barrum, babba, whum! Pole to the beat o' the drum!

Ye've heard me story, messmates all,
an' if I spoke a lie to you,
may me nose swell into a fat red ball,
an' me bottom turn bright green'n'blue.
Barrum, babba, whum! Pole to the beat o' the drum!'

Horty was astonished; he turned to the shrew behind him. 'By the left! I say, old chap, are you allowed to bandy insults like that about Briggathingee, wot?'

The shrew kept poling as he gave Horty a broad wink. 'It ain't serious, mate, 'tis all done in good fun!'

Briggy saw Horty gossiping and descended upon him. 'Stop jawin' an' keep pawin', rabbitchops, or I'll 'ave yore whiskers for desksweepers!'

The young hare gave Briggy a cheeky grin and launched into a barrage of insults. 'Oh shut your blatherin' cakescoffer, y'great bearded windbag! You sound like a duck with beakache, hasn't anybeast ever told you? Hah, tush'n'pish for all your ilk, sah, you wobble-pawed, twinky-tailed excuse for a barrel-bummed toad. Who d'you think you're jolly well talkin' to, you wiggle-whiskered, bawlin' braggart!'

Horty turned back to the shrew he had spoken to previously. 'Pretty good, wot! That told old Log-a-pudden a thing or two!'

The ashen-faced shrew hissed back at him, 'We only ever does it in songs, all t'gether like. If'n you speak like that, face t'face wid a Log a Log o' Guorafs, that's mutiny, mate!'

Horty turned round to find Briggy looming over him with a face like thunder.

The force of the shrew chieftain's roars made Horty's long ears flap. 'Mutiny, eh? I won't 'ave mutineers aboard my logboat! Grab 'old o' this mutinous beast, put 'im to task! No more rations for 'im while he's on this vessel!'

Four shrews frogmarched the hapless hare off to the stern where he was given a large sack of wild onions to clean and peel.

Bragoon made his way to the prow, where he had a quiet word with the shrew chieftain. 'Ye were a bit 'ard on Horty there, mate. The young 'un wasn't wise to yore rules an' reg'lations, he thought 'twas all a bit of a joke. Horty didn't mean ye no real insult.'

Briggy's eyes twinkled. 'I know he didn't, friend, but I

said I'd toughen 'im up. If'n that young 'un ever expects t'join the Long Patrol, he's gotta learn manners an' curb his tongue. Could ye imagine one o' those hare officers from the Long Patrol lettin' a recruit speak to 'im like that? Joke or not, some stiff-eared sergeant would clap 'im on a charge an' use 'is guts fer garters!'

Bragoon agreed. 'Yore right, Briggy, a bit o' discipline wouldn't 'urt 'im. All three o' them young 'uns've been livin' the soft life at Redwall fer too long. The two maids are much better be'aved than Horty, they'll lissen t'reason. But Horty's too wild an' 'eadstrong. One day he'll make a fine warrior – after he's learned a few stern lessons.'

Briggy stroked his beard. 'Don't fret, mate, I'll knock all the rough edges off'n Horty. My Jigger was the same 'til I showed 'im the ropes. Lookit Jigger now, commandin' his own logboat. There's a young shrew anybeast'd be proud t'call son!'

The otter went back astern and sat with Saro. Behind them Horty was weeping buckets as he peeled and chopped the pungent wild onions. He went at it with vim and vigour, though scowling and muttering about the injustices of life aboard a logboat.

'Bit flippin' thick this lot, wot? A few measly words to old Brigalog an' he treats a chap like a bloomin' vermin marauder! I mean, what did I say? The bearded old buffer should count himself jolly well lucky, wot! Oh, yes indeed, when Hortwill Braebuck Esquire starts really chuckin' insults, he could roast the flamin' ears off a milky-whiskered shrew. I could've called the chap a lot worse! Twiggle-jawed trout! Giddy-nosed toad! Pickled old pollywog! Witless water beetle! Puddle-pawed duck's bottom! Or even Skinnyforlinkee Wobblechops! Huh, I think I let him off lightly, really. Good job one can hold one's temper, wot wot!'

Log a Log Briggy came striding down between the polers. 'Ahoy there, mates, is that mutineer be'avin' hisself? I might let 'im get a bite o' supper tonight, if'n I 'ears an apology.'

Bragoon nudged Horty. 'Did ye hear that, matey?'

The young hare turned a face, still running onion tears, to the Guoraf chieftain and declared dramatically, 'Y'mean you'd restore my scoffin' privileges, sah? Merciful Logawotsyaname, I'll peel every last one of these foul fruits, I swear I will. Good Captain, I'll be the saltiest young riverbeast you ever clapped eyes on. Listen to this. Shiver me sails an' rot me timbers, fry me barnacles, scrape me keel, an' all that nautical jimjam. You, matey sah, are lookin' at a completely reformed beast!'

Briggy glanced at Saro. 'Wot d'ye think, marm, is that a rogue worth feedin'?'

The ageing squirrel saw the haunted look in Horty's eyes and took pity. 'Aye, Cap'n, only a moment ago Horty was sayin' wot a good ole Log a Log ye are. Ain't that right, Brag?'

With difficulty, the otter kept a straight face. 'Right enough, I'd give 'im another chance if 'twas up t'me.'

Briggy stroked his beard a moment, before answering. 'Aye, so be it then. Leave those onions now, young 'un, go amidship an' lend the cook a paw in the galley.'

Horty galloped off, overjoyed at the prospect of working amid food. 'Help the cook, I say, what a spiffin' job! A thousand thanks to you, Captain Briggaboat, an' you, my two chums. You have a handsome young hare's undying thanks!'

Bragoon chuckled. 'Same modest Horty, eh?'

Aboard Jigger's logboat, Fenna and Springald were being treated like royalty. Fenna had also gained an admirer, a stout young shrew named Wuddle. Both he and Jigger could not do enough for the pretty Redwall maids. The shrews brought extra cushions, erected an awning to shade them from the sun and served more delicious snacks than both of them could possibly eat. Then the two creatures vanished momentarily, to reappear grinning awkwardly, carrying with them two accordion-like instruments, which they said were called shrewlodeons. Jigger and Waddle twiddled a few keys, then launched into a song. Springald and Fenna were convulsed with laughter at the faces that both shrews pulled while singing. On verses they would be scowling savagely, whilst on the choruses they adopted expressions of peaceful concern. Both had wonderful bass voices and sang in harmony.

'When I meets a beast wot ain't polite to laydeez,
I grabs 'im round the throat 'til he turns blue,
I holds him tight in check as I squeezes on his neck,
then I boots his tail three times around the deck!

'Cos be they sisters, mothers, aunts or daughters,
all laydeez must be treated tenderly,
they're dainty an' they're neat, an' they don't have
   much to eat,
an' they rouses gentle feelin's within me.

When I'm around an' you insults a laydee,
I'll jump on yore stummick very forcibly,
then I'll punch you in the snout an' I'll prob'ly knock
   you out,
an' black both of yore eyes so you can't see!

'Cos be they sisters, mothers, aunts or daughters,
all laydeez must be treated tenderly,
they're dainty an' they're neat, an' they don't have
   much to eat,
an' they rouses gentle feelin's within me.

So mind yore manners an' be very careful,
when in the company of laydeez sweet,
or I'll shove you in a sack, after fracturin' yore back,
an' I'll stamp upon yore paws if you gets free!'

After the final chorus, they escorted both maids on a pleasant promenade of the deck, snarling fiercely at any of the poling shrews who dared to look sideways at Fenna or Springald.

Supper on a mossy bank, overhung by weeping willows, was a total success. It was all due to Horty's onion soup. The Guorafs congratulated him on his cooking skills. He lapped up any compliments with a complete lack of modesty.

'Tut tut, nothin' to it, dear chaps – a pinch o' this, a smidgeon o' that an' a sprinklin' of the other. Plus, of course, blinkin' loads of those confounded onions. I tell you, I shed many salt tears into the recipe, wot! Wild onions? Hah, I wasn't too blinkin' pleased, havin' to tame 'em down for you lot. I'd sooner be skinned me bloomin' self than have to skin another wild onion!'

Log a Log Briggy watched the young ones cavorting, singing and playing, then lay back and stretched. 'Beats me where they find the energy! Ah well, let 'em be merry while they can, 'specially those three young 'uns o' yores. I reckon we'll make our voyage end by midmorn tomorrer. That's when all the fun'n'games will finish for Horty an' the maids. I'm glad I don't have t'make the slog over desert an' gorge to Loamhedge with ye. That's country I was never fond of.'

Bragoon flicked a twig into the fire. 'They'll do alright, with me'n my mate to look after 'em.'

Saro smiled. 'Aye, but by the creakin' o' my ole bones, 'tis them who'll be lookin' after us by the time this liddle jaunt is finished!'

Next morning, they arrived on time at the spot, just as Briggy had predicted. It was indeed hard, arid country. They had been sailing upriver since the crack of dawn. Nobeast could fail to notice the difference in the terrain. Trees, bushes and grass thinned out along the banks, whilst a hot breeze wafted in dust from the wastelands.

Briggy smiled at the young creatures' downcast faces. 'Cheer up, mates, it ain't goodbye just yet. We'll be moored alongside this bank when ye come back wid a cure for Horty's sister. Get goin' now, an' good fortune go with ye!'

'Thanks for everythin', ole friend!'

'Aye, we'd a-been in a right pickle widout you an' yore crews, matey.'

'See ye in six days, eh!'

Loaded with shrew hardtack biscuits and two canteens of water apiece, the travellers set off into the unknown.

Briggy called out as the logboats pulled away, 'Keep the sun on yore right cheek, ye'll see the Bell an' Badger Rocks afore dark. But y'won't be able to reach 'em until ye figure out 'ow to cross the great gorge!'

Silence reigned over the searing, dusty flatness at high noon. Bragoon led the party, with Saro bringing up the rear.

It was not long before Horty began complaining. 'Phew, my ears are roasted, my tongue's parched an' my bally feet are fryin'. My word, it's even too hot to sweat! Walkin' walkin', always flamin' well walkin'. It's the story of m'life, chaps. First I was walkin' up'n'down on a blinkin' logboat, pushin' an oarpole. Now I'm walkin' again through this food'n'drink-forsaken place!'

Saro tugged the hare's tail. 'We're all walkin', ole gabby gob. We're walkin' t'bring back somethin' that'll make yore sister Martha walk. So stop moanin' an' keep walkin'.'

The otter glanced over his shoulder, turning his attention on Springald and Fenna. 'Ahoy there, you two. Keep yore faces like that an' it'll rain afore long, ye mis'rable pair o' mopes!'

Springald dragged her paws in the dust, replying sulkily, 'There's nothing at all wrong with our faces, thank you. Anyhow, you wouldn't understand.'

Saro piped up from behind, 'Why wouldn't we unnerstand?'

Fenna pouted. ' 'Cos you just wouldn't, that's all!'

Horty could not resist smirking. 'They're jolly miserable because they've been parted from old Jigger an' his pal, wotsisname, Cuddles! Oh lack a day an' woe are they! I expect your little hearts are breakin', wot?'

Kicking dust at the mocking hare, Fenna shouted, 'His name isn't Cuddles, it's Wuddle, and he's far nicer than you, Horty Braebuck. So there!'

Skipping ahead of the two maids, Horty made an elegant leg and bowed with a flourish. 'Fie upon you, marm, there's nobeast nicer than the charming I. Not in all the lands, or the river. Not like those two spike-headed water whompers who caterwaul songs like stricken ducks!'

This time it was Springald who kicked dust at Horty. 'You vain, pompous, floppy-eared boaster!'

Horty was about to kick dust back, when Bragoon grabbed his ear and tweaked it soundly. 'If'n ye value yore ear, then stop embarrassin' those maids, right now! All three of ye are startin' to try my patience. Come on, Spring, cheer up. You, too, Fenn. It won't be long afore ye see those young shrews agin. Quit bein' so mean to each other, an' no more teasin'!'

Horty rubbed at the ear that had been tweaked. 'Who, me? I barely uttered a blinkin' word, it was those two who jolly well started it!'

It was Saro's shout that put an end to the bickering. 'Look, mates, there's the Bell'n'Badger Rocks!'

36

Floating above the heat-shimmered distance, the tops of both stone monoliths were just about visible on the horizon.

Fenna's keen eyes confirmed Saro's discovery. 'Hooray! You're right, there they are, I can see them!'

Shading her eyes, Springald stood on tippaws. 'They look like one of those mirages that Old Phredd told us about. I wonder how far off they are?'

Bragoon squinted over the wasteland haze. 'A fair bit yet, but if'n we press on 'til they're in plain sight, I'll call it a day an' we'll make camp. I want to look at those parchments from the Abbey. How does that sound to ye, mates?'

Bragoon and Saro watched the three young ones dashing off ahead, their quarrels all forgotten as they shouted to one another.

Saro scratched her bushy tail. 'Ha, lissen to 'em, they're the best o' pals agin!'

Fenna was shouting, 'I'm going to set up camp with the cloaks an' staffs. Where are you off to, Horty?'

The young hare had put on a spurt, racing ahead eagerly. 'Gangway, m'dears, I'm your cook this evenin'. Had lots of valuable experience, y'know. Oh yes, a chap learns a thing or three from those shrew coves, wot!'

Springald kept pace with Fenna. 'I want to help Brag and Saro to study those parchments.'

Bragoon and Saro followed the young ones at a steady lope. 'Looks like we've lost command o' the quest, mate. Can ye see those rocks clearly yet?'

The squirrel looked up. 'Not quite, but it won't be long now.'

It turned out that the three front-runners were forced to halt quicker than expected. Horty ground to a stop in a cloud of dust. 'By the left, right, an' knock me blinkin' sideways! How in the name of onion soup do we get across that bloomin' thing? Looks like the end o' the flamin' earth, wot!'

Fenna and Springald joined him, gasping in disbelief at the awesome spectacle that confronted them.

'Whew! No wonder it's called the great gorge!'

'Good grief, it must be miles down to the bottom!'

Bragoon and Saro arrived on the scene. The otter ventured a glance down into the black chasm. 'If'n ye fell down there, that'd be the last anybeast'd see of ye, eh mate?'

Saro, however, was more concerned with the width of the gorge. 'Hmm, that's a wide ole canyon! Don't matter 'ow deep 'tis, we've got to think 'ow we're goin' to cross it. Any ideas?'

Food was the only idea Horty gave priority to. 'Let's get a fire goin' an' we can figure it all out over a jolly good scoff. How's that for a scheme, wot?'

The otter shook his head. 'This is strange country, mate. I don't feel too easy wid the thought of a fire. Pitch the camp an' see wot ye can make from the packs, Horty. I'll go off t'the right along the rim. Spring, you come wid me. Saro, you take the left edge. Fenna'll go wid ye.'

They set off, with Horty issuing dire warnings. 'You chaps get back here before dusk, or I'll whomp up somethin' absolutely delicious an' eat it myself!'

Saro glanced across the gorge as she and Fenna explored

along the edge of the precipice. 'Those two big rocks are plain t'see now, they mustn't be more than a couple o' sling-shot distances from the other side. We're so near, yet so far, eh Fenn?'

The squirrelmaid had noticed something down in the chasm. Suddenly her voice became shrill with excitement. 'There, that's how we'll get across, come and see!'

Saro lay flat on the edge, staring down at the solution to their problem. 'Well spotted, young 'un. I almost walked right by an' missed that. Let's go an' tell the others!'

Horty had created a fruit salad from the rations, with elderflower and dandelion cordial to go with it.

They sat eating as Saro reported, 'There's a tree trunk spannin' the gorge down that way; Fenna spotted it. About the height o' Redwall Abbey's battlement, down it lies. I don't know where it came from or whatbeast put it there, but it bridges the gap alright. 'Tis the longest trunk I've ever seen, lodged twixt a crack on one side an' a narrow ledge on the other. I think we should be able to get down to it on the rope that Cosbro, the old rabbit, gave us.'

Bragoon gathered up the parchments he was about to study. 'Let's go an' take a look at it.'

The spot where the tree trunk lay was directly in line with the two rocks across the gorge. Bragoon was thinking hard as he gazed down at the long, old span of timber that bridged the chasm.

Springald watched him as he studied the whole thing – the twin rocks, and the tree trunk wedged inside the gorge. 'You know something about this, don't you?'

The otter spread the map he had brought from Redwall. 'See here, this is the Bell an' the Badger Rocks. Now this spot is where the Lord o' Mossflower once stood. Ole Briggy said that it was a large tree, which had fallen down long ago. I reckon that tree trunk down there is the one that's marked on the map. After it fell down, some crea-tures must've rolled it into the gorge to make a bridge. I

349

wager it took a lot o' beasts t'do the job, but they didn't know they was doin' us a favour when they took on the task. Is that rope long enough, matey?'

Saro, who had fetched Cosbro's rope along with her, dangled its length over the side. 'Aye, it falls a bit short o' the trunk, but it'll do.'

Satisfied, the otter issued orders. 'You three young 'uns, go back an' break camp. Fetch everythin' back 'ere with ye. Make as little noise as possible. There's somethin' about this area I don't like. It might be only a feelin', but I'm takin' no chances. Saro, me'n you'll rig this rope up. Remember now, be quiet!'

Horty and the two maids did not take long to pack the gear and break camp. Returning to the spot, they found that Bragoon had broken his staff in two pieces and driven them into a crack near the rim. Saro tested the rope she had tied around the wood. Without further ado, she went silently and skilfully down, using her footpaws on the rock walls for balance. She dropped lightly on to the trunk and twirled her tail several times as a signal that everything was alright. One by one they descended into the dark quiet chasm, Bragoon being last to go.

The five travellers perched precariously on the tree trunk. Saro gave the rope a swift upward flick, bringing it down with them.

Horty peered across the gorge nervously. 'I say, Brag old scout, we could do with a torch to light us over this thing, it looks jolly dangerous t'me, wot?'

The otter glared at him. 'Ssshhh, don't talk, yore voice echoes off the side down 'ere!'

Saro knotted herself and the others into a line, with herself at the front and Bragoon at the rear. Getting down on all fours, the five creatures inched out on to the long trunk. It seemed like an eternity, crawling over the wide expanse with nothing beneath them but empty space and total blackness. Sometimes the big log quivered, as one of them

350

stumbled. At moments like this, they crouched there still, until Saro moved forwards again.

Bragoon emitted a hushed sigh of relief when they finally made it on to the ledge at the far side. Fenna peered into the gloom, looking fearfully at Saro. The squirrel saw three black holes, which looked like entrances, in the rock face. She nodded and placed a paw to her lips in a gesture of silence. Untying her four friends from the rope, she coiled it about her waist and began climbing up the other side of the gorge. They watched her ascending the rock face with all the grace of a born squirrel climber. Bragoon kept casting anxious glances towards the three dark, forbidding entrances, but no signs of life showed there.

Saro made it to the top in good time. Finding a convenient boulder, she tied a knot about it and lowered the rope to her companions. As they began the upward climb, the otter was still keeping a weather eye upon the dark holes.

Once all five travellers were safely together on the top of the far side, Horty laughed out loud. 'Hawhawhaw! Well, chaps, that's that! I suppose it's alright for one t'make sounds now. It's almost as bad as bein' hungry, for a brilliant speaker like me not being able to flippin' well talk. Absolute torture, wot!'

Bragoon could not help smiling at the young hare. 'Go on, mate, talk away, even sing if'n ye like.'

Ever willing to oblige, the garrulous hare burst into song.

'Oh it ain't much fun, when you must keep mum,
an' they tell you not to speak,
standin' about with a tight-shut mouth,
an' your tongue stuck in your cheek,
'cos being silent, makes me violent,
I want to roar an' shout,
Wheehooh! Yahboo! I'm tellin' you,
I've lots to talk about!
Hello good day, how are you, say,

the sky went dark last night,
but it got bright this morning,
so things turned out alright.
Well there might be rain, but then again,
we'll face the storm together,
in wind or snow, oh don't y'know,
let's talk about the weather!
Wheehooh! Yahboo! I'm tellin' you,
I'll whisper, yell or shout,
I'll natter'n'blab, or chatter'n'gab,
I've lots to talk about!'

Saro cast her eyes to the darkening evening sky and sighed.
'We'd better stop for supper soon. That's the only time
Horty goes quiet, when he's eatin'.'

Bragoon watched fondly as the young hare did some
fancy high kicks and ear twiddling. 'Aye, that rascal's like
a weed on a wall, he grows on ye. I'll say this, though –
Horty's becomin' a first-rate cook, I like 'is vittles. We'll go
as far as the Bell an' the Badger Rocks afore night comes. I
think we could even risk a liddle cookin' fire. Let ole Horty
create us one of his masterpieces. Come on, mate, it ain't
more'n a mile or two now.'

As the laughter and banter of the questers receded into
the gathering eventide, a stillness fell over the wasteland.

Three faint screams echoed into the unfathomed depths of
the great gorge. On the ledge where the tree trunk bridged
the space, several cloaked figures turned and padded
silently into the three dark holes. These were passages,
which led into a single hall-like cavern. The creatures from
outside joined masses of others, similar to themselves. A
myriad of glittering eyes were riveted on a ledge, where
burned a sulphurous, yellow-green column of flame. A
huge hunched beast, enveloped in a flowing cloak, stood
with its back to them, facing the flame. It turned slowly.

Not daring to look upon it, everybeast lay down prostrate, faces to the floor. A concerted moan arose from the masses.

'Mighty Kharanjul, Master of the Abyss! Great Slayer, in whose veins runs the blood of Wearets! Lord of Life and Death! We live only to serve thee!'

The cloak swept back to reveal Kharanjul. He was a gargantuan creature, a primitive and hideous mutation – something between a ferret and a weasel. With neither ears nor any semblance of a neck, his brutal head perched straight on to his hulking shoulders. When he spoke, his voice was a gurgling hiss, forced from between curving, discoloured fangs.

'Where are the three guards who were sleeping at their posts when strangers entered my gorge?'

One of the creatures, who had recently entered the cavern, raised his face and cried out in a reedy voice, 'Lord, they are still falling into the chasm. They felt themselves too unworthy to face thy wrath, O Great Slayer!'

Kharanjul picked up a big iron trident. He ran his long misshapen claws across the weapon's three barbed points. 'Nobeast has ever trespassed in my domain and lived to see the sunset that day. Ye will not fail me again, ye spawn of darkness. If those intruders set paw within a league of my gorge, to return whence they came, ye will let me know of it without fail. Double the guards both night and day. If the interlopers are caught, their suffering will be great. They will plead to be cast into the abyss of eternity. I have spoken!'

Still facedown, the masses chanted their reply. 'We hear and obey, O Mighty Kharanjul, Great Wearet Lord!'

37

Martha closed the east wallgate behind her but left it unbolted. Her heart pounded wildly as she stole shakily through the night-shadowed woodlands, hugging the wall. The haremaid knew it had been an ill-advised plan, but she realized that the Abbot, or any sane Redwaller, would have forbidden her to venture on this mission alone. Her footpaws were trembling as she turned the corner to the north wall. Willing them to be still, she strove to gain control of her body. Every once in awhile, she heard weapons clanking on the parapet above. The sea rats were patrolling the ramparts. The moment it went quiet, she would inch forwards again.

Lonna had lit a fire out on the flatlands facing the west Abbey wall. He piled up brush and twigs into a heap, placing it so that from a distance it could be mistaken for himself, seated by the fire in the darkness. Moving off to his left he settled down, accustoming his eyes to the night. Setting a shaft to his bowstring, he watched the battlements. Soon a vermin head poked up cautiously, seeing the decoy by the fire and mistaking it for the badger. The sea rat on the wall stood upright. Leaning outwards, he peered towards the fire, trying to make sure that it was Lonna who was sitting crouched there. The big bow twanged, and the arrow took the sea rat through his skull, sending him slamming backwards on to the walkway. Hearing the resultant commotion from the walltop, the badger shifted his position, moving closer to the wall.

Raga Bol's voice was immediately recognizable as he roared directions to his confused crew. 'The stripedog's somewhere out 'ere, on the far west end. Keep yore 'eads down, ye fools, or ye'll end like that 'un. Chakka, get over this way, the stripedog's over 'ere, not on the north side!'

Lonna edged closer, until he could hear Chakka's reply. 'But, Cap'n, there's somebeast down here, sneakin' alongside the wall. It ain't as big as the stripedog, though. Wonder who it could be?'

Crouching, Raga Bol made his way across to the north wall. He risked a swift peek over the space between the battlements. 'Gimme yore spear! 'Tis an Abbeybeast tryin' to reach the big 'un, I'll wager. Blast yore eyes, gimme the spear afore it gets away!'

Martha made a break and ran for it, out across the path. She stumbled and tripped, going headlong into the ditch, which skirted the outside path. *Thunk!* The spear quivered in the ditchside.

Raga Bol saw another sea rat getting up from a crouch to pass him a second weapon. 'Ye missed, Cap'n, but only just! Take my spear, 'tis me lucky one . . . Unngh!'

Bol hurled himself flat as the spear clattered to the parapet beside the slain crewrat. 'Down, all of ye, down!'

Lonna was running towards the ditch, firing off arrows with amazing speed, one after another. They pinged off the stonework and shattered against the northwest wall corner, keeping the vermin down.

Martha narrowly avoided the huge bulk that crashed into the ditch beside her. She gasped, 'Sir, I came from the Abbey, my name's Mar . . .'

A massive paw cut off further explanation, as she was grabbed up and tucked beneath the giant badger's quiver.

It bumped against her cheek as he rushed headlong through the ditch going northward, away from the Abbey.

A deep voice sounded close to her ear. 'Time for introductions later, let's get out of range first!'

Martha felt like a Dibbun's plaything. Everything about the badger was immense – his paw, his long arrows poking from the quiver, the great bow he carried, his colossal frame. Everything! Moonlit spaces flickered past as she and the badger left the ditch and sought the shelter of Mossflower woodlands. Martha saw the badger's face. It was deeply scarred and roughly stitched, giving him a savage and fearful appearance. But his eyes were soft and gentle, friendly, the eyes of a friend.

Lonna placed her down gently. 'Now, you were saying?'

The haremaid tried not to be intimidated by his size. 'Thank you, sir, I was saying . . . We have need of you inside Redwall Abbey. I stole out to get you . . . Oh, my name is Martha Braebuck . . .'

The bigbeast crouched, coming level with her face. 'Braebuck? I met your brother and his friends on the side of the high cliffs. Shouldn't you be in some kind of chair with wheels, miss?'

Martha found herself babbling. 'You met Horty, oh, is he alright? Bragoon, Saro, all of them, are they safe? Please tell me about them. Have they been ill or injured in any way? Oh, I've been worried out of my mind . . .'

The badger's paw covered her face as he placed it over her mouth. 'Hush, little Martha, your friends are fine. I'd like to stand here all night talking with you, but you say they have need of me inside your Abbey. Can you show me the way back in there? By the way, my name's Lonna Bowstripe.'

Martha bobbed a small curtsy. Then she was swung up and placed upon the badger's shoulder as he moved off swiftly.

'Point me in the right direction, Martha Braebuck!' Holding on to his ear with one paw and the bowstring with the other, Martha showed him the way. 'Straight ahead, Sir Lonna, you can see the belltower showing above the trees.'

He chuckled. 'Just call me plain old Lonna.'

She whispered into his ear, 'Lonna it is, you can call me Martha. I only get the full title when I'm being told off.'

Raga Bol sought out Wirga. 'Those poison darts, have ye got any of 'em?'

The old sea rat drew a rod from her cloak. 'Aye, Cap'n, there's one inside this. 'Tis the tube that I shoot 'em through.'

She unplugged the ends of the rod, letting a dart show from it. 'See, my little messenger of death!'

Bol murmured to her, 'I'm thinkin' that the stripedog'll try t'get inside the Abbey buildin'. He's got t'be stopped. Do this for me an I'll give ye anythin' y'want!'

Wirga shuffled to the wallsteps. 'My price will be high, I warn thee. I have already lost three sons.'

The sea rat captain spread his paws wide. 'Anythin'!'

Wirga looked up from the lawn. ' 'Tis as good as done!'

Abbot Carrul stood at the open window with Toran and Sister Setiva. He covered his eyes at the sight of the knotted linen rope hanging over the sill.

'I knew it, though it only occurred to me awhile after she'd been speaking with me. Oh Martha, why did you have to go and do it?'

But Toran did not stop to argue the point. He was already over the sill, clutching the linen rope and lowering himself down.

Sister Setiva leaned out of the window. 'Och, ye'll get caught by yon vermin if ye go out there!'

The ottercook dropped to the ground and drew his sling. 'Martha must've gone out by the east wallgate to find the badger. I'm goin' to look for her, you stay by here an' keep watch for us. Pull yoreself t'gether, Carrul!'

The Abbot stood by the window with Sister Setiva. 'I should have known, I should have stopped her!'

Placing a comforting paw about him, the Infirmary Keeper shook her head. 'Ah'll have a wee word wi' Martha when she returns. Ah thought it was only her brother who acted silly. Don't blame yersel', Father, yer no' a mindreader! How were ye tae know the maid wid do sich a thing?'

Toran was stealing across the back lawn, when he saw Wirga ahead of him. He crouched low and watched her as she neared the east wallgate, then halted, obviously having heard something. Then Wirga scurried to a rhododendron bush, which grew close to the wall, hiding herself behind it.

The small door creaked on its hinges as it opened. Martha entered the Abbey grounds. Her paw lost in Lonna's grip, the haremaid turned and smiled at him. 'Home at last, welcome to Redwall, Lonna!'

The badger had to stoop as he came through the gate. Toran saw Wirga slowly stand upright, placing the blowpipe to her mouth. There was no time to stop and think. He acted speedily. Bounding forwards, the ottercook threw himself sideways, slamming into the sea rat. Wirga's head hit the sandstone wall with a resounding crack, immediately reuniting her with her three sons.

Martha pulled on Lonna's paw as he whipped the long knife from his arm sheath. 'Don't hurt him, that's my friend Toran!'

Lonna took hold of the ottercook's apron and stood him upright. Toran blinked past him at the haremaid. 'Martha, is that you, matey?'

She ran forwards and hugged him. 'Oh Toran, that was a brave thing to do. Quick, let's get inside, there might be more sea rats prowling about!'

Other Redwallers had found their way to the linen room. There were many willing paws to assist Toran and Martha back inside the Abbey. Lonna, however, was a different matter. Extra cloths and sheets had to be knotted into the makeshift rope. The badger's weight was such that no amount of helpers could even raise him from the ground. Tossing his bow and quiver up to Toran, the big badger made his own way, paw over paw, up the Abbey wall to the room. At first, Martha thought Lonna would burst the window frame, but he managed to squeeze through with a certain amount of grunting and wriggling.

The haremaid beamed proudly at the Abbot as she presented her new friend to him. 'Father, this is Lonna Bowstripe. He has volunteered to help us. Lonna, this is the Father Abbot Carrul of Redwall!'

There was a deal of comment from the awestruck onlookers.

'Good grief, will you look at the size of him!'

'Hurr, oi never see'd nobeast as gurt as that 'un!'

'Look, his head almost touches the ceiling!'

Without registering the least surprise, Abbot Carrul shook the badger's massive paw. 'Welcome to Redwall, Lonna, and my thanks to you for returning our Martha unscathed. It was a brave deed.'

Lonna immediately took a liking to the dignified old mouse. 'Thank you, Father, it's a pleasure to be here. I will do all I can to rid your home of Raga Bol and his sea rats.'

Carrul bowed gravely, then turned his attention to the onlookers. They were still commenting on the new arrival's size, speculating as to how his face came to be so dreadfully wounded. The Abbot stared them into silence.

'It has always been our manner to welcome visitors and offer them refreshment. Have you nothing better to do than embarrass our guest with your remarks?'

Muttering apologies, the Redwallers hurried off downstairs to comply with their Abbot's wishes.

Carrul beckoned to Lonna. 'Come, friend, you must be hungry and tired. Let Martha and me offer you our hospitality. You must forgive our Abbeybeasts, they meant no offence.'

Lonna followed Martha and the Abbot from the linen room. 'No offence taken, Father. I would be surprised if they had not mentioned the way I look. Anybeast I've ever met does.'

Martha gave him a reproving look. 'I never mentioned your appearance. Neither did Abbot Carrul or Toran, for that matter.'

Lonna gave the haremaid one of his rare smiles. 'Then I have made three good and sensible friends tonight. I think I'm going to enjoy Redwall Abbey.'

Everybeast stayed up late that night, crowding into Cavern Hole to see the giant badger. Granmum Gurvel and her helpers trundled to and fro from the kitchens, bringing lots of delicious food for the guest, and for all present. Lonna sat staring at the array of fine things. Then Foremole Dwurl presented him with an outsized portion of his own personal favourite.

'Yurr zurr, this bee's deeper'n'ever turnip'n'tater'n' beet-root pie. If'n ee doant wish t'be h'offendin' ee cook, you'm best eat 'earty. Thurr bee's aplenty more whurr that cummed frumm, an' ee cook's a gurt fearsome ole villyun!'

The badger took an amused glance at the dumpy figure of Granmum Gurvel, then set to with a will. Redwallers gazed in wonder as the hungry giant satisfied his appetite.

Sister Setiva even ventured a wry wink at Lonna. 'Och, there's nothin' worse than a beast with a wee flimsy appetite, pickin' away at his vittles, ah always say!'

Lonna accepted a full deep-dish apple-and-blackberry crumble from the Infirmary Keeper. He dug into it with gusto. 'Aye, marm, but you must forgive me. They tell me I was a very fussy babe. It's a wonder how I survived!'

His observation broke the ice; the Redwallers burst out laughing in appreciation of their visitor's ready wit.

After the meal, they sat entranced, as Lonna related his story, which included his meeting with the travellers. The Dibbuns had infiltrated the gathering, slowly encroaching until they were sitting on Lonna's footpaws. Craning their necks, they stared in goggle-eyed admiration at the one who had confessed to being a fussy babe. Lonna gained them extra time, interceding with the elders not to send the Abbeybabes up to bed. Infants were always a source of amazement to him, he marvelled at their minute size and lack of shyness with strangers.

Having finished his narrative, Lonna asked Martha to tell him of how she came to be walking. The haremaid obliged willingly.

Muggum had managed to scale the badger's footpaws and now sat upon his lap. Tugging the badger's paw, the molebabe succeeded in gaining his attention. 'You'm surpinkly a gurt creetur! Zurr Lonn', 'ow big bee's yore bed?'

Lonna looked thoughtful and adopted a serious tone. 'Hmm, it's quite large, and wide, too, though I've given up carrying it around with me. Why do you ask, sir?'

Muggum waved a tiny paw generously. 'You'm best take moi bed, Lonn. Oop in ee dormittees et bee's!'

The talk went back and forth, encouraged by beakers of mulled October Ale for the elders and raspberry cup for the young ones. After awhile, the old ones fell into a doze; the Dibbuns, too, no longer able to keep their eyes open, curled up and slept where they chose.

Abbot Carrul took advantage of the lull in the conversation, murmuring to Lonna, 'Come up to the kitchens, there's an empty storeroom there. We'll set up a sleeping place for you. But before that, I must talk to you, friend. We'll formulate a plan to defeat the enemy and free this Abbey. Martha, Toran, Sister Portula, Brother Weld, would you come, too? I'd like you to take part in the discussion.'

That night, in the quiet of the storeroom, they formulated their plans. Lonna's status as a seasoned warrior, and his expertise in the ways of his enemy sea rats, earned him the main say in the discussion. His ideas made sense to his friends, although his first words were in the form of a request.

'I need more arrows, good stout shafts, and well pointed. Have you any in the building?'

Toran answered. 'I'm sorry, Lonna, we haven't, but I can look for some wood and make your arrows.'

Brother Weld interrupted the ottercook. 'Last winter, Brother Gelf and I found an ash tree, which had collapsed outside the east wall. Skipper and his otters helped us to chop the trunk into firelogs. Gelf and I took about six sheaves of long branches from it and bundled them up. We planned on cutting them into smaller sizes to use in the orchard, for fencing and propping up berry vines. But we never got round to it. They're still piled up under the bell-tower stairs. Those ash branches will be well seasoned now, perfect for making arrows!'

Toran patted Weld's back. 'Good work, Brother, bring them to the wine cellar. Pore Junty Cellarhog had a little forge and anvil down there. I can make arrowheads from barrel-stave iron; Junty kept a whole stock o' the stuff.'

Lonna looked from one to the other enquiringly. 'Flights?'

Sister Portula had an immediate answer. 'There's a whole cupboardful of grey goose feathers in my room. I'll be glad to see the last of them. Two autumns back, Sister Setiva fixed the wing of a gosling, whose father was the leader of a goose skein. The geese were so grateful that they donated a load of loose feathers to me. I was supposed to cut the ends and use them as writing quills. Dearie me, they gave us enough for ten recorders to use for seven lifetimes. Please, Lonna, would you take them? If you'll relieve me of the burden, I'll recruit a team of elders to shape and bind them to your arrow shafts.'

The badger agreed readily. 'Thank you, Sister, there's no better flight for a shaft than a goose feather. I've been using gull feathers from the northeast shores, but they don't have the strength and firmness of good goose plumage.'

Martha spoke. 'You'll have a full supply of arrows, Lonna.'

Stretched out on a heap of clean sacks, the big badger gazed up at the ceiling, sure now of what he was going to do. 'Nobeast can live without food and water. Martha, I want you and a few others to patrol the windows all around the Abbey, where the sea rats would find things to eat or drink.'

The haremaid replied, 'You mean the orchard and the Abbey pond? There's also a vegetable garden adjoining the orchard. Since the sea rats arrived, they've taken water and fished from the pond, and as for the orchard, they're hardly ever out of there and the vegetable garden. Isn't that right, Father?'

Carrul clenched his jaw. 'Correct, Martha. Those scum! I dread to think of the state our crops will be in. After all the hard work Redwallers did. Well, Lonna, you'll have a fair view of it. Orchard, vegetable patch and pond – they are all clearly visible from our south-facing windows.'

Lonna reached for his bow and began running a small piece of beeswax up and down the string. 'Perfect. How many arrows have I left in my quiver, Toran?'

The ottercook took a look and returned grinning. 'Twenty-three . . . and a molebabe. Muggum's sleeping in there!' The little mole grumbled dozily as Sister Portula extricated him. 'Oi got to stop urr. Lonn' bee's sleepin' in moi bed!'

Abbot Carrul took charge of the molebabe. 'Then you can sleep in my big armchair, you rascal. In fact, I think it's time we all got a rest, there's lots to do once the day breaks. Right, Lonna?'

Bloodred tinges suffused the badger's eyes, his bowstring twanging aloud as he tested it. He gritted one word from between his clenched teeth. 'Right!'

The Abbot hurriedly ushered his charges from the store-room. 'We'll leave you to your sleep now, friend. Good-night.'

There was no reply. Closing the door behind them, Toran the ottercook exchanged meaningful glances with the Abbot. 'Did ye see that, Father? Lonna's possessed of the Bloodwrath!'

Martha looked from one to the other, perplexed. 'What's the Bloodwrath, some sort of sickness?'

Toran grasped her paw so hard that she winced. 'Lissen to me, young 'un. You stay out o' that beast's way until his eyes clear up again. Badgers ain't responsible for wot they do when Bloodwrath comes upon 'em, d'ye hear?'

The haremaid managed a frightened little nod. 'Lonna wouldn't hurt us, would he?'

The Abbot signalled Toran and the others to their beds. He walked through Great Hall with Martha, who was carrying the sleeping molebabe.

Carrul talked quietly with her. 'Do as Toran has told you, pretty one. Only be close to Lonna when you have to. Creatures such as us know little of Bloodwrath, but grown badgers of his size can be very dangerous to anybeast when it strikes them. Take your friends tomorrow, patrol the south windows on the first and second floor. The moment you sight sea rats in the grounds, report straight to Lonna. Then get out of the way. Redwallers have no business hanging around a badger who is taken by Bloodwrath. Believe me, Martha, I tell you that Lonna needs to avenge himself and his dead friend upon Raga Bol and his crew. He is here for no other reason. Go to your bed now and remember what I have said.'

Carrul took the sleeping Muggum from Martha and went into his room. The haremaid looked up at the figure of Martin the Warrior on his tapestry. There was no need of visitations or dream speeches from the gallant protector of Redwall. His eyes seemed to say it all. She bowed respectfully to Martin, then went to her bed, still puzzled but obedient to her Abbot and the guiding spirit of her Abbey.

Death came to Redwall at dawn. A sea rat came bursting into the gatehouse and raised Raga Bol from the bed where he had lain sprawled and twitching in broken dreams. 'Cap'n, the stripedog's just kilt Cullo an' Baleclaw. They was fishin' in the pond an' 'e slayed 'em both wid one arrer!'

Bol came upright, his silver hook thrusting through the rat's baggy shirt as he dragged him forwards. 'Killed 'em wid one arrer! Have ye been at the grog agin, Griml?'

The rat wailed, 'I saw it meself, Cap'n. They was stannin' in the water, one afront o' the other, when a big arrer pins 'em both through their neckscruffs, like fishes on a reed!'

Bol thrust Griml roughly out the gatehouse. 'Rally the crew, an' fetch Wirga t'me. Move yourself!'

Griml's mate, Deadtooth, was crouching beside the wall-steps. He, too, had witnessed the slaying of two sea rats with one arrow. Deadtooth caught up with Griml. 'Wot did Bol say?'

Griml shrugged unhappily. 'Not much, just booted me out an' tole me t'bring the crew an' fetch Wirga.'

Deadtooth persisted. 'Don't the Cap'n know Wirga's dead? They found 'er just as it went light. Somebeast 'ad knocked the daylights outer 'er agin the wall. But ye knew that, didn't ye? Yew shoulda told Bol.'

Griml nervously looked this way and that. 'Hah, yew go an' tell 'im, if'n ye dare. I don't want no silver 'ook guttin' me. I wish we was afloat at sea, like last springtime. I tell ye, mate, we've 'ad nought but bad luck since we dropped anchor in this rotten place!'

Griml caught sight of several sea rats emerging from behind a small ornamental hedge where they had been sleeping. 'Ahoy, youse lot, Cap'n wants ter see ye, right now at the gate'ouse, ye best jump to it . . .'

There was a piercing scream from the orchard as a crewrat staggered out, transfixed by an arrow. Still holding a half-ripe pear in his claws, he took one more pace and crumpled in a still heap. Griml gestured at him wildly. 'See, wot did I tell ye? There's Rotpaw gone now, a good ole messmate like 'im, off to 'ellgates afore a bite o' brekkist passed 'is pore lips. I said this place is bad luck, didn't I?'

38

Having camped by the rocks and spent the night there, the travellers got their first clear view of them at sunrise next morn. Fenna found Horty, who had already risen, blowing on the embers of the previous night's fire and adding twigs to rekindle the flames. In high spirits, the young hare waved his ears at her.

'Mornin', fair Fenn'. Lots of twigs blown up against the rocks by the blinkin' wind, wot. Jolly useful to a first-class rivercook. What ho, you lazy lot, rise'n'shine, eh! So, here we are at the old Badger an' Bell. Thoughtful cove, whoever named 'em – they look just like an enormous bloomin' bell an' a blinkin' huge badger's bonce!'

Springald blinked sleep from her eyes and gave Horty a sidelong glance. 'Really, have you just noticed that?'

Saro got between them. 'Don't start again, you two. Horty, ole scout, ole lad, ole boy, wot's for breakfast?'

The garrulous hare giggled. 'Heeheehee, would you believe fried fruit salad, marm?'

Springald came wide awake then. 'Horty, you're joking?'

Bragoon had sidled up. With the tip of his sword he speared a slice of plum from the flat rock that served as a frying pan. The otter chewed it pensively. 'Our cook ain't jokin', marm. Hmm, it don't taste too bad!'

As Saro tried a morsel, winks were exchanged all round, behind Horty's back. The ageing squirrel merely nodded. 'I suppose y'can't be too picky out in this country. I've ate worse an' survived.'

Fenna prodded at the food with a twig. 'Do we have to eat it?'

Closing her eyes, Springald gulped a piece down. 'It's either that or starve. Fried fruit salad? Only a hare could think up a breakfast like that!' Horty's ears rose like flagstaffs and his cheeks bulged out. The outraged hare was about to give them a piece of his mind, when something out on the wasteland distracted his attention.

'Cads! Bounders! You rotten, ungrateful . . . I say, chaps, is that somebeast crouchin' down out there?'

Bragoon leaped up, wiping his swordblade. 'Come on, let's find out!'

They spread out and made for the distant shape. Slowly and cautiously they approached the object. Then Fenna, who had the best eyesight, ran forwards, calling to them, 'That's no crouching beast, it's nothing but a big battered old tree stump!'

The fragmented piece of conifer stood almost as tall as Bragoon's shoulder. He tapped it with his sword.

'Y'know wot this is? All that's left o' that big tree on the map – Lord o' Mossflower. We crossed over the great gorge by walkin' across its trunk!'

Saro circled the broad base. 'A shame, really. 'Twas a mighty tree in its seasons. Right, mate, 'tis time we took a look at the stuff you brought from the Abbey.'

Bragoon drew out the tattered scraps of parchment he had carried since the day they left Redwall. 'Let's take a look then. Loamhedge can't be too far now. Maybe we'll find some clues that'll help.'

Horty was never a beast who took kindly to studying. He watched them unfolding a scrap of parchment. 'Borin' old stuff, I'll go back an' break camp, wot!'

Bragoon passed the piece of paper to Springald. 'Yore a

bright young 'un, read this out to us. I don't see too good for readin' lately. Think I might need those eyeglasses like Carrul an' Old Phredd wears when they reads things.'

Springald studied the neat script. 'Martha copied this out. It says here that it's Sister Amyl's rhyme. Listen.

> "Where once I dwelt in Loamhedge,
> my secret lies hid from view,
> the tale of how I learned to walk,
> when once I was as you.
> Though you cannot go there,
> look out for two who may,
> travellers from out of the past,
> returning home someday."'

Bragoon winked at Saro. 'That was us, we're the travellers from out the past. I wonder how young Martha is.'

Saro folded the parchment up, returning it to the otter. 'I wish she could've been fit t'make this trip with us. Now there was a young maid who had an 'ead on her shoulders. Huh, no clues there, though. Wot does that other bit say?'

Beside the map sketch, Bragoon had only one other piece of parchment. He offered it to Saro. 'You read it, mate.'

After unfolding it, the ageing squirrel gave it to Fenna, without a second glance. 'My readin' is terrible, I never payed attention at Abbeyschool. Just like you, Brag, but I ain't makin' excuses about needin' eyeglasses. You read it, Fenna. I bet you was a good learner.'

The squirrelmaid straightened the creased document. 'Martha tells us here that this is something which was copied by somebeast named Recorder Scrittum. The words are Sister Amyl's, but Scrittum recorded them for her.

> "Beneath the flower that never grows,
> Sylvaticus lies in repose.
> My secret is entombed with her,

look and think what you see there.
A prison with four legs which moved,
yet it could walk nowhere,
whose arms lacked paws, but yet they held,
a wretched captive there."'

Springald shrugged. 'Well, there are clues in that rhyme.
But look around, what do you see? A broken tree stump,
two big rocks shaped like a badger's head and a bell!
Besides that, all we have is a map, made so far back that
nobeast can remember. Is this all the information you
brought with you from the Abbey? Bit thin, isn't it?'

Bragoon drew patterns in the dust with his paw. Then he
and Saro cast rueful looks at each other.

Fenna spoke to them. 'Wasn't there something else, a big
volume about how a party of Redwallers found Loamhedge
in bygone seasons?'

The otter explained limply. 'Aye, missy, there was, but
we never took the time or the trouble to try readin' it. We
ain't no scholars, that much is plain, ain't it, mate?'

Saro nodded dolefully. 'Right, we thought that, 'cos we'd
been atop o' the high cliffs an' on to the plateau one time,
we knew this country. Our mistake, I s'pose. We should've
let one of you young 'uns read the book out to us. You ain't
like us. Livin' in the Abbey all yore lives, you managed t'get
some learnin'. Me'n ole Brag, we ran away when we was
young, didn't get much schoolin'.'

Fenna wanted to take them to task for going off on such
a quest without proper information, but they looked so
crestfallen. She also felt it would be unfair to berate two
creatures of such skill and craft, all of which they had
gained in the hard school of travel and experience. Scholars
they might not be, but adventurers they certainly were.

A shout interrupted her thoughts. 'What ho there, you
curmudgeons! Handsome young hare approachin' with
visitors! Put aside your weapons. They're friendly, an' they
enjoyed my blinkin' breakfast, too!'

Bragoon thumped his rudder down in astonishment. 'Horty, what'n the name o' silly seasons . . . ?'

The young hare marched up to the stump with his two new friends – a large fat dormouse, pulling a cartload of twigs and wasteland debris; and, at his side, a tiny sand lizard held by a braided lead.

Horty grinned from ear to ear. 'Meet my new pal Toobledum, survivor an' hermit of the wastelands, wot! Oh, an' this other ferocious creature is Bubbub, his faithful sand-sniffer. I say, these coves really appreciate my cookin', they scoffed the bloomin' lot!'

Springald cried indignantly, 'Well thanks for nothing. I scarcely took a bite of that food!'

Horty pawed his nose at her. 'Serves you jolly well right, after the way you lot carried on about my fine cookin'!'

Toobledum, a cheery dormouse, wore an outrageously floppy woven grass hat, which he tipped to them. 'Pleased t'meetcher, one an' all, friends o' the cook, are ye! Well, Horty's led ye this far pretty good, I'd say.'

Saro glared at the young hare, paws on hips. 'Led us this far, eh? I wager you've been tellin' Mister Toobledum a right ole pack o' fibs!'

Horty waffled for a moment, then changed the subject completely. 'I say, chaps, here's a wheeze. Guess where Toobledum lives? Go on, tell 'em, Toob!'

The dormouse sat down and lightly scratched Bubbub's emerald-green sides. The little sand lizard arched its back with pleasure. Toobledum looked up at them from beneath the wide brim of his hat.

'Lives? Me'n likkle Bubbub lives at Loam'edge, that's where we lives. Sand lizards ain't like most reptiles, y'know. Get 'em young enough an' they're good likkle tykes.'

Bragoon stared open-mouthed at the dormouse. 'Y'mean to tell us you actually lives at Loamhedge?'

The floppy hat wobbled wildly as Toobledum nodded. 'All me life. Youngest o' sixteen I was, left 'ome an' came out here t'fend fer meself. Loam'edge h'aint no Redwall, like the big place Horty told me that 'e rules. But 'tis 'ome, an' we like it, don't we likkle Bubbub?' The tiny sand lizard nodded and romped over to Fenna to be stroked and tickled.

Springald treated the dormouse to one of her prettiest smiles. 'Could you show us the way to Loamhedge, sir?'

He flushed under his hat brim. 'Ain't no sir, missy, only an ole Toobledum, but I'll show ye the way willin'ly!'

Fenna left off petting Bubbub, who nudged at her for more. 'You will show us the way. Now?'

Dusting himself off, the dormouse rose with a grunt. 'Now's as good a time as any, me pretty one. Long as ye let my pal Horty cook me another good mess o' vittles.'

Bragoon clapped the young hare's back so heartily that he almost knocked him flat. 'Well o' course, the champion quest leader an' expert cook an' ruler o' Redwall would be only too glad to cook for ye, matey!'

Toobledum passed the towing rope of his cart to Saro. 'I'd be obliged if'n ye pull the ole cart fer me, marm. Me paws gets weary from luggin' it far'n'wide. Come on, likkle Bubbub, let's go 'ome.'

He trundled off into the wasteland, chattering animatedly. 'Nice to find somebeast t'jaw with, it gits lonely out 'ere. Likkle Bubbub don't speak, y'see. I collects useful stuff, goes far'n'wide t'find it. Firewood, nice stones, bits o' this'-n'that. Don't never waste nothin' out 'ere, I always sez. If'n ye got gear to cast off, then throw it me way!'

They journeyed on, mainly south by Bragoon's reckoning, with Toobledum talking ceaselessly, and Bubbub frisking along on his lead, moving from one to another in his efforts to find more stroking.

A camp was made out on the wastelands that evening. The dormouse donated some wood from his cart to make a fire. He was all agog in anticipation of his next meal.

'Well, Cooky, wot's fer supper? Me'n likkle Bubbub's feelin' peckish. Somethin' nice, I 'ope!'

Springald grinned pointedly at Horty. 'Oh, don't worry, Cooky will turn out something delicious, I'm sure.'

The young hare was beginning to tire of his role as cook. He rummaged through the dwindling supply in the ration packs. 'Hmm, I expect I'll create some superb dish, but we're runnin' a bit low on the old tucker, wot. Oh, fiddlesticks! Why's it left t'me to do all the blinkin' cookin' an' slavin' round here, while you flamin' lot sit on your tails an' loll around? Huh, bit bloomin' thick, I'd say!'

Fenna joined in the teasing. 'Cheer up, Mighty Ruler of Redwall, I expect you have an army of skivvies to serve you back at the Abbey. Excuse me, you're not frying another fruit salad, are you?'

Borrowing an iron pot that had been clanking along on a hook beneath Toobledum's cart, Horty answered airily, 'As a matter o' fact, marm, I'm inventin' some scone soup, with a few wild onions, some sage, carrots, a leek or two an' some crumbled oatscones. Followed by fresh strawberry surprise, with dandelion tea to drink.'

It was a surprisingly tasty meal. They downed it with relish. Fenna had one comment to make about the dessert. 'What's in this strawberry surprise, Cooky?'

Horty grimaced. 'Wish you'd stop callin' me Cooky. Oh, the strawberry surprise? I made it with some dried apple, preserved plums an' a piece o' fruitcake I found at the bottom of a ration pack. There ain't a flamin' strawberry in the whole thing – that's the surprise. Good, eh?'

Toobledum and Bubbub licked their bowls. The dormouse belched. 'Parn me one an' all. We liked it. Any second 'elphins?'

Toobledum listened to the rhyme which had been dictated to Recorder Scrittum by Sister Amyl. Fenna read it out to him, but the dormouse was at a loss to cast any light on it. 'Flowers wot never grows, an' four-legged prisons wid no arms? Means nought to us, does it, likkle Bubbub?'

The tiny lizard shook its head and nestled under Saro's paw. The dormouse bedded down by the fire, letting the hat brim cover his face. 'I ain't clever like you beasts, I'm just an old Toobledum. No matter, ye can search for yore own clues around Loam'edge in the mornin'. We'll git there afore midday. I'll bid ye 'appy dreams one an' all, g'night!'

Bragoon settled down with the sword close to paw. 'I'll stay awake for first watch, mates.'

Toobledum's voice came from under the hat. 'You git some sleep, I've taken Bubbub off 'is lead. That likkle feller's better'n any sentry, 'e'll stand guard all night for ye.'

Horty grinned with relief at Fenna. 'Saves us a job, wot!'

The squirrelmaid curled up in her cloak beneath the cart. 'Indeed it does. Goodnight, Cooky.'

The young hare's ears shot up stiffly. 'Cooky yourself, miss! Go an' boil your blinkin' heads, the bloomin' lot of you!' He closed his eyes, trying to ignore the replies.

'Nighty-night, Cooky!'

'Not staying up to plan breakfast then, Cooky?'

'I expect he has a special menu writer to do it for him back home at Redwall, don't you, Cooky?'

'A leader with stout paws, a wise ruler of an Abbey an' a cooky with a heart o' gold. Ain't we the lucky ones!'

Next day dawned on the wasteland, a warm flood of glorious colours, muted by dusty haze. The travellers ate a cold breakfast, eager to be on their way. Toobledum lingered, gossiping and trying to spin the meal out. It was only after gentle prodding that Bragoon urged the dormouse to get under way. Saro took Bubbub's lead, and Springald volunteered to pull the cart. They took up the rear, while Toobledum walked in front with Horty and Fenna. Ambling slowly along, the dormouse chatted with them.

They had been marching awhile, when Bragoon began having suspicions about the route. He called to Toobledum, who was still talking at length with Horty and Fenna, 'Now then, matey, when d'ye reckon we'll be at Loamhedge?'

Without turning around, the dormouse shouted his answer. 'Oh, it won't be 'til after lunch, I'm thinking. But don't ye fret, we're makin' fair progress, one an' all.'

Nodding knowingly, the otter whispered to Saro, 'Aye, I thought so, this ole buffer's got us on a vinegar trip.'

She glanced quizzically at the otter. 'Wot are ye talkin' about, mate?'

Keeping his voice low, Bragoon explained. 'See those hills off to the right? We've been followin' them east instead o' south. Can ye see 'ow slow Toobledum's walkin'? Did ye notice how he lingered over brekkist?'

Saro was becoming impatient. 'Spit it out, mate. Wot's goin' on?'

The otter conveyed his thoughts to her. 'Well, we ain't exactly goin' the wrong way, the dormouse'll get us there, sooner or later. But he's stringin' the trip out so we'll feed 'im agin at lunchtime. Trouble is, the old feller loves vittles too much, an' he mightn't have much food at 'ome. So he wants to scoff our rations an' have Horty doin' all the cookin' for 'im!'

Saro looked down at Bubbub. 'Is that right?'

The little sand lizard grinned and nodded as the squirrel patted him. 'Well, the crafty ole grubswiper!'

Bragoon winked at her. 'I'll fix that fat swindler, mate!'

He called aloud to Toobledum. 'We ain't stopping fer lunch. Best press on to Loamhedge. When we arrives we'll have a big lunch an' a good rest.'

The dormouse immediately altered course and speeded up, heading for the hills as he answered. 'Aye, good idea. Foller me, I've just remembered a good shortcut. We'll be there afore ye know it!'

Saro whispered to Bragoon, 'Lookit liddle Bubbub there, I'll swear he just sniggered.'

39

In less than an hour the travellers had reached the hilltops. Below them the land took on a complete change. Gone was the arid dusty wasteland, replaced with an expansive green valley – not lush green like Mossflower woodlands but pleasant enough to appear refreshingly welcome to desert travellers. The whole area in the dip of the vale was dotted with brush, heather, grass and some stunted trees.

Toobledum whipped off his hat and made a sweeping gesture. 'There 'tis, one an' all. Loam'edge!'

Halfway down the slope, Fenna stooped to pick a few daisies. She crumbled some earth in her paws and sniffed it. 'This was probably rich fertile country in some bygone time.'

The dormouse watched her braid the flowers into her tailbush. 'Most likely it was, young missy. Mebbe those mice who lived around 'ere long ago tended the land an' farmed it t'keep it that way.'

Horty stared about. 'Don't see any streams or runnin' water.'

Toobledum plucked a daisy stem and chewed on it. 'There's underground water at the middle o' the valley. I gets it cold'n'sweet from a well down there. Once we crosses the Abbey boundary I'll take ye to it.'

They carried on downhill. When the dormouse was almost on level ground he kicked aside some long grass and shrubbery. 'See 'ere, that's the top o' the ole boundary wall. It must've collapsed an' been buried in the long ago, when the ground used to dance an' shake.'

He exposed a line of coping stones, each one decorated with a skilful carving of a mouse. Toobledum straightened up, arching his back as he gestured around the valley bottom. 'If'n ye takes the trouble, an' yore fond o' diggin', y'can follow it all around in a big square. I've never bothered meself, 'cept when I needs stones for me 'ouse. Right then, come on one an' all, don't shilly-shally, 'tis lunchtime.'

They followed the old dormouse into a grove of stunted, knobbly trees, stopping as they reached a rickety hut, a rambling structure knocked together from odds and ends of stone, timber and debris.

Toobledum announced proudly, 'Well, this is it, one an' all, me likkle 'ome. Me'n Bubbub wouldn't trade it fer a palace!' He set about lighting a fire beneath a rock slab oven, which stood outside the front door. Bubbub frisked happily about as the old dormouse sang.

'All round an' round the land ye well may roam,
lots o' places I 'ave rambled, far'n'near,
but there ain't no nicer nest than me ol' 'ome,
'tis so comfy an' we loves it, oh so dear.
The moment that we gets 'ere, me an' me likkle mate,
we lights a fire an' puts the kettle on,
though we ain't got much to eat, we gets along just
   great,
'cos two kin live 'ere just as well as one.'

Bragoon had a quiet word with Horty. 'Give 'em all we can spare from the rations. Make it a lunch to remember for the ole beast an' Bubbub.'

The young hare saluted smartly. 'To hear is to obey,

O Wise Otter, sah. I'll make it a spread that none of us'll forget!'

Fenna blew a sigh. 'As long as you don't serve us fried fruit salad again!'

Horty began rummaging through their meagre supplies. 'Pish tush, miss! I shall treat that remark with the blinkin' contempt it bally well deserves, wot!'

He did, however, cook a very passable meal. Drawing water from the dormouse's well, Horty produced a tasty vegetable soup and some scones and honey, with penny-cress and comfrey cordial to wash it down.

Saro ate it with relish but could not resist a wry remark. 'Mmm, tastes good, but I ain't even goin' to ask wot's in it.'

Horty licked honey from his paws and reached for another scone. 'Just as well really, marm. Wild frogs wouldn't drag the recipe from me. We cooks have our secrets, y'know!'

Toobledum and Bubbub did the lunch full justice. Springald was astounded at the amount the little lizard ate.

The dormouse just laughed at Bubbub's appetite. 'Proper likkle famine face, ain't he?'

Bragoon began questioning Toobledum, warming to the aim of their quest. 'This spot we're searchin' for, it's a grave I think. Lissen to these few lines, mate, an' see if'n ye can throw any light on 'em.

"Beneath the flower that never grows,
Sylvaticus lies in repose.
My secret is entombed with her,
look and think what you see there."

'I want ye to pay attention, Toobledum. Do ye know any-place 'ereabouts that sounds like wot I've just said?'

The dormouse pulled down his hat brim, muttering darkly, 'That'll be the dead place. We never goes over there, do we, mate?'

Bubbub snuggled tight against the dormouse and shook his head.

Springald pursued the enquiry. 'Whyever not? The dead never hurt anybeast, and I wager those buried there have been dead long before you were born.'

Toobledum shook his head. 'Say wot ye likes, miss, but there's nights when the wind blows an' I've 'eard 'em moanin'.'

Horty took a light view of this sinister statement. 'Maybe they get jolly hungry down there. Come on, old scout, up on your hunkers an' show us where the old graveyard is, wot!'

The dormouse refused flatly. 'I ain't goin' nowheres near that place, ye can go an' see it for yoreselves. Walk south across the valley until ye see flat stones. They're all laid this way an' that, ye can't miss 'em. That's the buryin' garden. I think it was once inside the ole Abbey. I've only been there once, an' I ain't goin' there agin, nohow!'

Leaving the dormouse and his lizard, the five travellers set out, following his directions.

The ancient burying place was quiet and peaceful in the noontide sun. A few bees hummed, and grasshoppers chirruped on the still, warm air.

Saro sat down on one of the flat stones and looked about. 'Nice ole spot, ain't it. Sort of a garden o' memories.'

Fenna brushed the dust from a lopsided oblong of limestone. 'See what this says: Sister Ethnilla, victim of the great sickness, gone to the sunny slopes and silent streams.'

Bragoon traced a paw across the graven words. 'Pore creature, there must be a lot of her kind buried 'ere. Sunny slopes an' quiet streams, eh? I like that.'

Springald and Horty were inspecting the stones further afield.

The young hare's voice interrupted the otter's reverie. 'I say, you chaps, what was the name we were lookin' for, Sivvylaticus or somesuch? I think I've found it. Yoooohaaaw!'

Bragoon sprang upright as Horty's yell disturbed the peace. 'Wot's that lop-eared noisebag up to now?'

Springald was shouting, 'Over here, quick, Horty's fallen down a grave!'

They dashed over to where the mousemaid was hopping about agitatedly as she pointed to a yawning dark hole. 'Down there, he's fallen right through. One moment he was standing, pointing to this big stone, then something broke and he vanished!'

The otter pulled her aside. 'Stand clear, miss, or ye might be the next one to disappear.' He called down into the pitch-black space, 'Horty, are ye alright, mate?'

There was no reply, just a faint echo of his own voice.

40

Raga Bol was at his wit's end; the sea rat crew had begun to desert. He kicked out at Firzin, a rat he had posted on the main gate, screaming, 'Wot'n the name o' thunder d'ye mean, nobeast has got by ye all day? Did ye unlock this gate fer anythin'?'

Firzin cringed against the gate, which he had guarded faithfully on his captain's orders. 'On me oath, Cap'n, I've kept the gate tight locked!'

Bol glared this way and that, slashing at the air with his scimitar. 'The walltops are too high for 'em to jump, so how've they got out? Rinj, wot d'you think?'

Rinj, who had been close to Bol all day, shrugged. 'Wot about those liddle gates, Cap'n? There's one in the middle of each of the three outer walls. Bet they went through them, eh?'

The sea rat captain's gold fangs flashed as he snarled, 'I told Argubb to post guards on those wallgates this mornin'. Go an' see if'n they're still there!'

Rinj sidled out of the scimitar's range. 'They 'ad to stand in plain sight o' the winders, Cap'n. That big stripedog took the three of 'em out wid his arrers.'

Raga Bol peered around the wall buttress, which was sheltering him and his two crewrats from the Abbey windows. 'Get in the gate'ouse, both of ye, quick!'

The three rats crouched, swerving in a dead run around the buttress. They made it into the gatehouse and slammed the door. The timbers shook as an arrow hit the door, its barbed point showing through the wood.

Firzin wailed, 'We're all deadbeasts if'n we stay in this place. There ain't nowhere to 'ide from the stripedog!'

One icy glare from his captain was sufficient to frighten the sea rat into silence. Bol looked from one to the other, his face deadly calm, his voice low. 'Wot's the number o' crew left d'ye reckon, Rinj?'

The rat thought for a moment. 'Just over a score, Cap'n. That's countin' us three.'

Since early that day, Raga Bol had been scheming furiously. His back was against the wall, but he was determined that eventually he would triumph. Then it came to his mind in a flash – he knew that he had the answer. All he had to do was convince his crew.

Slumping down in an armchair, he shook his head sadly, acting more like one of the sea rat messmates than their captain. 'No more'n a score left out o' fifty, eh? I tell ye, mates, 'tis a sorry day. I suppose every one of ye wants t'see the back o' this place now. Speak up, I won't harm ye.'

Firzin summoned up his courage. 'Aye, Cap'n, they're all sayin' we're deadbeasts if'n we stays at this Abbey. Ain't that right, Rinj?'

The other rat nodded. 'Aye, mate, gettin' away from 'ere's the sensible thing to do, shore enough.'

Raga Bol gave a rueful little smile, as if in agreement. 'Mebbe yore right. But just think, mates, if we'd 'ave killed the stripedog an' won, eh? Redwall woulda been ours! The good life, me buckoes! Everybeast of us'd be livin' like kings now, wid slaves, loot, vittles an' a place t'call 'ome fer the winter. Strange 'ow things turn out, ain't it? Now we got to cut'n'run, all because o' one stripedog who should've been dead now by rights.

'Aye, we've got no ship, we're a season's march from

saltwater an' I've lost near a score an' a half of the best sea rats a cap'n ever 'ad. Now we got nothin', we'll 'ave to tramp the land like beggars.'

Rinj and Firzin had never seen their captain like this before. They shuffled their footpaws and tails awkwardly.

Then Bol dropped a single word: 'Unless!'

Both crewrats were immediately curious.

'Unless wot, Cap'n?'

'Have ye got a plan, Cap'n?'

Raga Bol leaned forwards, his eyes gleaming craftily. 'Hoho, mates, I got a plan alright. Now 'earken t'me an' lissen!'

Abbot Carrul and Toran were sitting in the kitchens. They looked up as Martha entered. The ottercook indicated a heap of arrows, lying ready on the table.

'Does 'e want more shafts?'

The haremaid shook her head. 'Not at the moment. Granmum Gurvel and I have piled arrows at every windowsill.'

The Abbot poured her a beaker of cold mint tea. 'What's going on out there, Martha? You and old Gurvel are the only ones who can get close to Lonna. What's he up to?'

Martha took a sip of the tea. 'It's all quiet at the moment. He's roaming the upper corridors, watching from the windows. It's dreadful out there – dead sea rats by the pond, on the walls and by the orchard. I think a few of them have deserted, gone through the east wallgate into the woods. Lonna is still prowling about watching the grounds, though he seems to have calmed down a little. It was frightening just to set eyes on him this morning!'

Toran brought out a stool for Martha to sit upon. 'Mayhaps the sea rats are gettin' ready to leave, or it might only be the calm afore the storm. Who knows wot Raga Bol's got in that evil brain – another scheme, per'aps. We'll just have t'sit an' wait. Wot d'ye think Martha?'

The haremaid rested her weary footpaws. It had not been

an easy day so far, running up and down stairs, keeping the badger supplied with arrows. 'I think it's gone too quiet, Toran. But who knows how things will turn out? Like you say, we'll have to wait and see.'

Sister Setiva had been listening from the kitchen doorway. 'Och, all this waitin'! Everybeasts's keepin' busy, ye ken. They're all doon in Cavern Hole makin' arrows, even the Dibbuns. Ah've come tae make some food for them. Most of us have no taken a bite since breakfast!'

Toran busied himself, glad for something to do. 'Leave it t'me, Sister. I'd forgotten about vittles today. Gurvel's helpin' Martha. I should've realized we 'ad no cook.'

Abbot Carrul climbed down from his stool. 'Here, let me help you, Toran. It's not right that my Redwallers should go hungry, even in times like these!'

Late afternoon slid into evening. Over beyond the west wall the sun set in solitary splendour. A wash of gold and purple suffused the sky, with blood red at its centre.

Lonna stood alone at the front dormitory windows. He rested against a sill, keeping watch on the gatehouse and its buttressed corner by the main gate. Now that there had been a few hours' lull from any action, the Bloodwrath had receded from him. His massive frame had relaxed. Lonna felt drained and weary, not having slept in almost two days and nights. Gradually night edged in, bringing with it a soft breeze to cool away the day's heat. Lonna began blinking a lot, nearly causing the bow to slip from his grasp. Rubbing his eyes and shaking himself, the big badger peered into the darkness, trying to keep his vision fixed on the gatehouse area. Then the voice sounded out.

Lonna came instantly alert as he identified Raga Bol's rasping tones, calling from somewhere over by the buttress where his arrows could not reach.

'Ahoy, stripedog, I see ye! Still hidin' in there be'ind the Abbot's skirts, are ye? Does yore wound still pain ye?

Haharr, I should've gone for the neck an' chopped yore 'ead off! Don't worry, stripedog, Raga Bol ain't goin' nowhere. I slayed the old stripedog an' I kin finish ye, too!'

Brother Weld, who had been checking the window barricades in Great Hall, came hurrying into Cavern Hole. 'There's something happening outside. I can hear the sea rat captain shouting to the big badger!'

Toran bounded to the stairs. 'Sister Setiva, Sister Portula, keep the little 'uns down 'ere! Anybeast who's able enough, bring a weapon an' foller me! Does anyone know where Lonna is?'

Martha seized a ladle. 'He was going towards the dormitories at the front when I left him.'

The ottercook wielded the big bung mallet, which had once belonged to Junty Cellarhog. 'Let's see if'n he's there!'

Martha and Toran burst into the dormitory, at the head of a band of Abbeydwellers. The haremaid could see Lonna's powerful back, silhouetted in the open window frame. He was shaking with rage but silent. Raga Bol was still taunting him from somewhere outside.

'I don't slay my enemies from a distance with arrers, that ain't the way a real warrior fights! But keep yore distance if'n yore scared o' Raga Bol. Come out 'ere, ye coward, an' I'll slice the other side of yer face off afore I leaves the birds to pick over yore carcass!'

Lonna leaped up on to the windowsill, roaring, 'I'll fight you any way you like, you murdering scum!'

Toran leaped forwards and grabbed Lonna's footpaw. 'Don't go, mate, 'tis a trap. There's still plenty o' sea rats out there. Ye'll be surrounded!'

The badger dealt Toran a kick, knocking him backwards. Raga Bol was visible now, standing slightly to the right on the lawn.

Paws on hips, the big sea rat laughed mockingly. 'Haharrharr! 'Ere I am, scarmuzzle! Come an' meet me paw't'claw widout yore bow'n'arrers fer once. Bring the magic sword an' cross blades wid Raga Bol if ye dare!'

'Eulaliiiiiaaaaaa!' Nothing could stop the giant badger now. Bellowing his warcry, Lonna jumped from the dormitory window. Luckily, the huge hill of rubble blocking the Abbey door had dried out in the sun. He landed upon it and managed to stay upright. Scrambling and rolling, he thundered down towards the ground. Without a moment's hesitation, Toran went over the sill after him, with Martha and the rest in his wake.

Raga Bol held the glittering scimitar ready to strike, the silver hook on his other pawstump whirling in readiness. He stood awaiting the badger's charge, about a spear's throw from the north wall.

Martha caught up with Toran. She pointed to the north walltop. 'Quick, up there, that's where the sea rats are!'

The ottercook veered, heading for the steps as he called to Martha. 'Split up, take half our beasts down to the east steps. I'll go up the north stairs. Weld, Gelf, Foremole, you come with me!'

Oblivious of everything except Raga Bol waiting in his path, Lonna rushed straight at his enemy, armed only with his teeth and claws.

Bol, judging the moment when the badger was within three paces of him, dropped down, yelling out, 'Spears, now!'

Lonna did not even bother to dodge the flying spears; three missed him, but one struck his left shoulder. He whipped it out and flung it aside, ignoring the wound. The Bloodwrath was upon him, his eyes red as the sunset he had watched a few hours earlier. His teeth shone from his scarred features in a savage snarl as his huge, blunt claws sought the kneeling sea rat captain. Bol was halfway up when the badger grabbed his neck and swung him off the ground.

Raga Bol emitted one strangled gurgle. Then four spears,

thrown by the captain's own sea rats and intended for the badger, buried their blades in Raga Bol's back instead. He died, hanging there like a rag doll in the grip of his mighty foe. The last thing he saw was Lonna Bowstripe roaring into his face.

'Go through Hellgates and burn, rat! Eulaliiiiaaaaaa!'

Holding the limp body in front of him, Lonna charged the wall, bulling up the stairs behind Toran like a juggernaut.

The ottercook shouted to his helpers, 'Look out, get to the west wall, let the badger pass! Martha, back off! Git those beasts down t'the lawn!'

The haremaid, who saw what was happening, turned swiftly to the Redwallers behind her. 'Get out of the way. Downstairs, now!'

Abbot Carrul confronted her, his blood roused. He waved a sweeping broom, yelling fiercely, 'Let me at those rats. I'll drive them from Redwall, the filthy invaders. How dare they attack my Abbey!' He was grabbed by two stout moles and hustled down the wallsteps.

The ramparts became a scene of chaos. Using Raga Bol as a flail, Lonna swept sea rats left and right. Some were knocked over the battlements, their broken bodies thudding to the woodland floor outside the walls. Any who were unfortunate enough to fall on to the lawn inside the Abbey grounds were dealt with by a horde of Redwallers, each eager to be mentioned thereafter as a beast who had taken part in the battle to win back their Abbey.

Lonna stood on the empty walkway, his chest heaving like a bellows, blood oozing from a dozen different wounds. The carcass of Raga Bol resembled a grotesque, oversized pincushion, pierced by an array of spears from sea rats who had tried to fend off the badger's advance.

Cautiously, Toran and his helpers approached from the west walltop. They froze as Lonna whirled around to face them, still holding Raga Bol's slain body, the spears hanging from it rattling against the battlements. With a powerful heave, the big badger tossed his onetime enemy over the wall, listening to his body clattering through the tree limbs. Smiling like a Dibbun who had just learned a new trick, Lonna Bowstripe sat down, letting his footpaws dangle over the lawn.

'When Martha brought me to Redwall, I hoped I could be of some help to you.'

The ottercook sat down beside him. 'Aye, an' that ye were, mate, that ye were!'

Woodpigeons were startled from their roosts in Mossflower woodlands. They wheeled about in the night air, wondering why the bells of Redwall Abbey were pealing and booming out at such a late hour.

41

Bragoon crouched, staring down into the pit of the open grave where Horty had disappeared. Saro was fashioning a torch from twigs, grass and moss. Fenna lay flat on the edge of the hole, calling down.

'Horty, if you can hear me, then shout out!'

Springald centred the light of her chunk of rock crystal on the torchtop. Magnified sunrays produced a wisp of smoke, which grew into a small flame. Saro wafted it into a fire.

'I'm the climber, let me go first. Spring an' Fenna, ye stay up 'ere in case we need anythin'. Fetch the rope, Brag.' Lowering herself over the edge, the ageing squirrel dropped a bit, then landed on something solid.

'Stone steps, look!'

A dusty flight of narrow steps ran curving downwards into the darkness. Bragoon coiled the rope about his shoulders and followed her carefully. 'Slow down, mate – we don't want t'lose you, too!'

Springald and Fenna watched until the light vanished around the curve, down into the gloom.

The mousemaid shuddered as she sat down by the broken covering stone. 'I don't like this place anymore. It looked so peaceful and sunny at first, but now there's something about it that gives me the shivers. No wonder Tooble-dum wouldn't come here. I hope Horty's alright.'

Fenna was studying the big dark headstone, perched sideways at a crazy angle. 'Horty's indestructible, you'll see.'

Bragoon's head appeared at ground level. 'Yore right there, miss. Lend a paw, you two!'

Saro was on the step behind him. Between them they carried the slumped form of Horty. Heaving and pulling, the four friends managed to lift the young hare on to solid ground, where he curled up as if asleep.

Saro patted his back. 'He took a fall an' landed on the left side of his head. Pore Horty's got a fat ear, but there's no real harm done.'

Fenna soaked some moss and dabbed at the swollen ear. 'He's taken his share of knocks on this trip. That's a real thick ear he's got there.'

The damp poultice must have worked: Horty groaned and tried to sit up but fell back, complaining miserably, 'Yowch, I am awake! I say, d'you mind awfully not scrub-bin' a chap's wounded ear with that filthy wet stuff. It stings like jolly blue blazes!'

Springald took out a flask of cordial which she had brought along. 'Could you manage a sip of this?'

Horty grabbed it and downed the lot in three big gulps. 'Not that it'll do the noble young ear much good, but I've managed to wet my parched lips with it. Ooh, my achin' lug!'

Fenna supported his head. 'Poor Horty, it must hurt terribly.'

The young hare put on a pitiful face. 'I must be close t'death. I say Fenn, old scout, you don't happen to have a bite of scoff about you, wot?'

Bragoon stifled a laugh. 'Nothin' much wrong wid that 'un! Keep an eye on 'im, you two. We're goin' back down to take a look round there. Pass me some more wood an' grass, Fenn. We got to keep the torch alight.'

Fenna bundled her cloak under Horty's head. As the squirrelmaid began gathering more fuel for the torch, she shared her latest discovery with her companions.

'Now I know why Toobledum could hear moaning on windy nights from the buryin' place. See that big dark stone, it's the one that marked this grave. There's words carved on it. Listen. "Sylvaticus. First Mother Abbot of Loamhedge Abbey. Loved by all creatures. Long in seasons and wisdom. Gone to her final rest. Forever in our thoughts." This is the very grave we've been seeking.'

Fenna indicated the beautifully carved motif at the top of the headstone. It was a lily in full bloom with a graceful stem sprouting curved and fluted leaves. The entire design was pierced right through the stonework. The squirrelmaid traced it with her paw.

'This is the flower that never dies. I'll wager that the wind sings an eerie song through this carving on windy nights. You can't blame Toobledum for steering clear of here.'

Bragoon regarded her with admiration. 'Yore a bright young 'un, Fenn, that was well thought out. Take care of Horty now, we'll be back afore ye know it.'

For the second time, the two old friends descended the stairs.

Not one to let an injury slip by unnoticed, Horty made the most of his thick ear as the two Abbeymaids ministered to him. 'Salad! Now that's the very stuff for a swollen ear, wot! Any hare'll tell you, salad's just the thing, an' lots of it. Hold hard there, Spring old gel, what's that sloppy mess? Tut tut, marm, you ain't physickin' me with that rubbish!'

Springald cradled the mixture in a dockleaf. 'Don't be such a Dibbun, Horty Braebuck. It's a mud-and-moss poultice that will do your ear a power of good. Hold him, Fenn!'

Horty struggled in the squirrelmaid's firm grip. 'Gerroff me, you flamin' torturesses. I'll bet you took lessons from Sister Setiva on how to persecute wounded beasts. Yugh! That dreadful gloop's gone right down me bloomin' ear.

You've done it now, I'll be deaf on one side for the rest of me short young life. Rotters!'

Springald tugged the hare's good ear sharply. 'Do hold still! What can you expect if you hop about like that? Now, I'll just dress it with some dockleaves.'

Horty looked blankly at her. 'What rock thieves? Speak up!'

When the dressing was completed, he lay down in a sulk, while Springald cast a glance at the grave. 'They've been gone an awfully long time. What d'you think, shall we go down there and check on them?'

Fenna nodded eagerly. 'Yes, let's do that. You stay here, Horty. Take a nap or something.'

They dropped over the edge on to the stairs, with their former patient calling after them.

'I say, what's a cap an' a dumpling? What's up, have you both gone mad?'

Holding paws, Springald and Fenna managed the steps and, placing their backs against the rough stone wall, crept forwards cautiously. The ground took a curve, dipping steeply. Slowly stumbling on, in total darkness, they were relieved to see the faint glow of a torch ahead. The muted voices of their friends could be heard.

Fenna called out to them, 'Saro, Brag, is that you? We've come down for a little peek.'

The otter's voice, which sounded rather grumpy, echoed back at them. 'I told ye t'stay on top, you should be mindin' Horty. Who knows wot that buffoon'll be up to be'ind our backs!'

Saro's voice interrupted him. 'Oh, there's no harm done, mate. Let 'em come an' take a look.'

It was quite a sight. The passage opened up into an underground chamber, lined with stone walls. At its centre stood a plinth, littered with old bones and a white cloth habit that had faded to the texture of a cobweb. In front of the plinth lay what had once been a chair with wheels but now was little more than a small heap of dry, insect-bored sticks. There were two more torches in wall sconces on one wall behind the plinth.

After Saro had lit them, she gestured about with her own guttering torch. 'Well, this is it, mates. We've travelled long'n'far, just to find this sad ole lot. Those bones are wot's left o' pore Abbess Sylvaticus. But can ye guess wot those rotted sticks are?'

Springald picked up a piece of the timber in her paw. It crumbled to dust. 'Don't tell me, this was the chair once used by Sister Amyl. Those little round black stones with holes in them must have been its wheels. Huh, they're the only things recognizable after all this time.'

Crouching down, Bragoon sifted through the debris with his swordpoint. 'Must've been 'ere thousands of seasons. How did the rhyme go . . .

"Beneath the flower that never grows,
Sylvaticus lies in repose.
My secret is entombed with her,
look and think what you see there.
A prison with four legs which moved,
yet it could walk nowhere,
whose arms lacked paws, but yet they held,
a wretched captive there."'

Bragoon rose up and put away his blade. 'Aye, that's Sister Amyl's chair, sure enough, but where's the Sister's secret?'

Saro gnawed at her lip. 'Imagine pore young Martha when we get back an' tell 'er there was nought but a pile o' dust an' four black stones!'

Springald hung her head miserably. 'It doesn't bear thinking about. Now I wish we'd never found it.'

Fenna retrieved the four little black stone wheels. She stowed two in her belt pouch and gave the other two to Springald. 'At least these'll prove we've been here. Come on, Spring, let's go back and see how Horty's doing.'

Bragoon gave them one of the torches to guide them out.

'Aye, you young 'uns go an' do that. Me'n my ole mate are goin' to stay down here awhile an' search.'

Fenna shrugged glumly. 'Waste of time, there's nothing left to search for. Oh well, please yourselves.'

The otter cautioned them. 'Don't mention anythin' to Horty, wot with Miss Martha bein' 'is sister an' all that. Tell 'im we're still searchin'. Better still, take Horty back to ole Toobledum's 'ouse an' wait fer us there. We shouldn't be too long. Will ye do that for me?'

They nodded and trudged back to Horty.

Toobledum had taken the liberty of making a meal for them from the remnants of the ration packs. His little sand lizard capered about on its back paws, delighted to see the young ones returning.

The old dormouse proudly raised his floppy hat. 'Sit down, one an' all, see wot I cooked up for ye. Me'n likkle Bubbub did ye a stew. 'Tis made of all things good, wid an apple crumble fer afters an' a drop o' me own special whortleberry cup brew to drink. Ho dear, wot 'appened to pore master Horty?'

Horty blinked oddly at the dormouse. 'What the dickens is the old chap wafflin' about? Who's he goin' to plaster for being naughty, wot?'

Fenna roared down his good ear, 'He said, what's happened to poor master Horty!'

The young hare waggled a paw in his good ear. 'No need to bellow, miss!'

Then he turned to Toobledum. 'Ah, well may you ask, little fat sir. I suffered a dreadful injury to the old ear, but I'm keepin' jolly brave about it. Mmmm, nothin' wrong with a chap's nose, though! That stew smells like just the ticket. Whack me out a large portion, sir dormouse, looks like a splendid cure for thickearitis!'

Toobledum humoured Horty by giving him a large bowlful. The young hare was halfway through it when he held the bowl out. 'Don't stint on the stew, I always say. Never mind Brag'n'Saro, they're far too old to appreciate good scoff. I say, those two relics should be back by now. Huh, loiterin' around graveyards, bloomin' bad form, they'll go all morbid.'

It was over an hour before the two searchers made an appearance. The dormouse and Bubbub welcomed them back. Springald gave them two bowls she had washed out. 'Toobledum made some delicious stew, but you'd better get some fast before Horty hogs it all down.'

The young hare looked up from a beaker of whortleberry cup. 'I heard that, marm. Why should frogs fall down? Complete gibberish if y'ask me, wot!'

Springald waited until the two had finished eating before she enquired, 'Well, did you find anything?'

Saro smiled at Bragoon, who winked back at her as he sipped his drink. 'Hmm, whortleberry juice! 'Tis a while since I've tasted that. Used t'be me favourite drink at one time.'

Fenna twirled her bushy tail impatiently. 'You haven't answered the question. Did you find anything?'

Saro tasted her drink, still smiling secretively. 'Aye, 'tis nice, a sweet taste. Mind ye, I was allus partial to a drop o' nettle beer, like those otterpals o' yores drinks, up on the north coast.'

Horty looked from one to the other. 'Who's seen a ghost?'

Fenna fumed, 'Oh, put a cork in it, Horty! Now, Mister Bragoon, Madam Sarobando, will you answer the question. Please!'

Old Toobledum chuckled. 'Heeheehee, I knows ye found somethin', yore both sittin' there lookin' like a pair o' toads eatin' trifle. Put the young 'uns out their misery an' tell 'em, mates.'

The otter produced a small cylinder of parchment. He tossed it from paw to paw. 'We found it – this is Sister Amyl's secret.'

Springald was about to reach for it, when Saro caught the

cylinder and stowed it in her belt pouch. 'No ye don't, Spring, this is for none but Martha t'read!'

Fenna pouted indignantly. 'How do you know that?'

Bragoon raised his eyebrows. 'Because, miss clever clogs, it sez so on the parchment. Read it to 'em, mate.'

Saro took out the little scroll that had been tied with a few threads to keep it closed. On the outside was some tiny, squiggly writing. She peered at it closely, reading slow. 'Only the one who needs this shall know my secret!'

Bragoon levelled a paw at them. 'None of you young 'uns needs to know, only Martha, 'cos she's the one who needs it. We haven't looked at it ourselves, out o' respect to Martha. So nobeast is goin' to find out Sister Amyl's secret except that young hare back at the Abbey o' Redwall. We're bound back there at tomorrer's dawn, with all 'aste!'

Fenna, however, still had a question that needed answering. 'But we saw the place, there was absolutely nothing down there but bones, powdery wood and dust. How did you come to find it?'

Bragoon paused briefly before launching into his explanation. 'It was at the bottom o' that stone thing where Abbess Sylvaticus lay . . .'

Springald interrupted. 'The plinth, you mean?'

Saro nodded. 'Aye, the plinth, that was it. We was about to leave the place, when I took one o' those torches off'n the wall, 'cos our torch 'ad gone out. Well, I stubbed me footpaw on the bottom o' the plinth, an' one o' the stones came loose. Brag pulled it out an' there 'twas, lyin' as safe an' neat as ye like, be'ind a stone all that time.'

Fenna pursued her enquiry. 'But why hadn't it turned to dust like everything else down there?'

Bragoon picked something that resembled a tiny pellet from under his pawnail. 'See . . . beeswax. It was wrapped tight in dockleaves covered with beeswax. I tell ye, it was difficult, separatin' that liddle roll o' paper from the beeswax, but we did it!'

Toobledum poured them more drink. 'Well done, mates,

you found wot you was questin' for. I'm 'appy for ye, one an' all!'

Horty humphed. 'Three scones on a wall, ridiculous, wot?'

Saro pulled Horty upright. 'I've had enough o' this nonsense. Toobledum, bring me some 'ot water, not too 'ot, mind. Brag, lay Horty on one side, wid that muddy ear upwards, an' sit on 'im. I couldn't put up with 'im talkin' rubbish all the way 'ome!'

Horty guffawed. 'Hawhawhaw! Walkin' cabbage an' a bone? Poor old Saro's finally gone off her rocker, wot!'

Sudden panic struck as Bragoon pushed Horty down and sat on him. 'What the . . . ? Gerroff me, you great plank-tailed bounder! Good grief, what's that nutty old squirrel doin' with a jug o' steamin' water? Help, somebeast, help! They're tryin' to kill me! Murderers, assassins! Boilin' me blinkin' brain, an' just 'cos I scoffed three flamin' bowls of stew? Spring, Fenna, strike the cads with rocks'n'clubs, save me!'

But no help was forthcoming. The otter held him tight whilst Saro washed out his ear with warm water. A moment later it was all over. Toobledum gently treated the young hare's cleaned-up ear.

'There there, Sir Horty, ye'll live t'cook agin. This is an ole dormouse remedy, my special ointment. I makes it wid sanicle, feverfew an' a few secret herbs. So, 'ow does that feel, young master?'

Horty relaxed, closing his eyes blissfully. 'Bloomin' marvellous, old top, me ear is at peace an' very comfortable. Amazin' thing, too, I can hear again!'

Saro wiped mud and moss from her paws. 'See, we never killed ye after all.'

Springald muttered under her breath, 'Pity.'

Bragoon whispered back to her, 'Shame we missed our chance.'

Fenna's eyes twinkled as she chuckled along with them.

'Just think of the food we'd have saved without a hare to feed.'

Horty opened one eye and fixed them with a baleful stare. 'I heard all that, you rotters!'

They burst into laughter; even little Bubbub did a squeaky giggle.

Dawn of the following day saw the travellers bidding farewell to the dormouse and his lizard.

Fenna hugged the pair fondly. 'Why don't you come with us to Redwall? You'd both be very welcome there.'

Toobledum's hat wobbled as he shook his head. 'Nay, pretty miss, me'n likkle Bubbub wouldn't ever leave Loam'edge. We ain't got much, but 'tis 'ome to us.'

Saro stroked the little sand lizard one last time.

Bragoon clasped the old dormouse's paw warmly. 'As ye wish, matey, take care of each other, an' live happy. Goodbye an' good fortune to ye!'

Standing on the hilltop above the valley, the five travellers looked back. Bubbub was shaking his tail as Toobledum waved his hat and shouted, 'Fare ye well, one an' all, an' take our good wishes with ye!'

Fenna wiped her eyes as they marched off into the waste-lands. 'Those poor creatures, it must be terrible for them. Living that lonely life, and with so little to eat.'

Bragoon ruffled her ears affectionately. 'Aye, they're both goodbeasts, Fenn. But don't ye go believin' all that ole dormouse told ye, miss. Yore too young an' soft'earted.'

Horty took a pull from his canteen, filled with fresh water from Toobledum's well. 'Steady on, I liked Toob an' Bub. Bit unkind to talk about the old chap like that, wot?'

Springald agreed with him. 'I think so, too. They've only got each other for company, and they shared what little they have. Why shouldn't we believe what Toobledum said?'

The otter cast a wry glance at his old friend. 'That dormouse is a hermit, he likes bein' alone. As fer not havin' much in the way o' vittles . . . tell 'em, Saro.'

The ageing squirrel explained. 'When I was swillin' Horty's ear out, I watched Toobledum goin' to fetch that special ointment. Hah, the ole fogy didn't think I could see 'im. He went into a corner an' lifted a floorstone. Do ye know wot was underneath it? A cellar, packed from wall t'wall wid vittles. Drinks, dried fruits, veggibles, nuts, enough t'feed an army fer ten seasons. That's 'ow short o' food Mister Toobledum was, mates. Brag saw it, too!'

Horty stopped in his tracks. 'Well, the flamin' old fraud, wolfin' down all our grub an' tellin' whoppin' fibs about havin' none himself. What a blinkin' cheek!'

Fenna could hardly believe what she had heard. 'That's a shameful thing to do, the old liar!'

Springald was about to add to their condemnation of Toobledum, when the otter cut in. 'Don't be too 'ard on the ole feller. Vittles an' drink is precious in this region. If ye've got none, yore a deadbeast. Toobledum was only thinkin' of hisself an' liddle Bubbub. We were just passin' visitors. Now that we've gone, he's got to provide for 'imself an' his mate. 'Tis called survival. Ye don't go dashin' to the first beast ye see an' offerin' them a cellarful o' grub; ye takes care of yore own first.'

Fenna held up her paws. 'Alright, we understand, Toobledum's only doing what's best for himself and Bubbub. Please don't rub it in by telling us we're only young and we'll learn.'

Saro winked knowingly at her. 'Wouldn't dream of it . . . young 'un!'

A raven flew out of the great gorge. Soaring high, it hovered on the evening thermals, a dark sinister shape framed against the setting sun for a brief moment. Then it swept off southwards. Down below, standing at one of the three cave entrances, a cloaked figure watched the bird's departure, then turned and went into the tunnel. Pushing through the mass of dark creatures, the cloaked one made its way to where the sulphurous flame burned constantly, a tall column of fire, giving off its acrid stench.

Kharanjul, the Great Wearet Slayer, stood waiting for the news his guard captain brought. The cloaked creature lay flat on the rocky floor and lifted its face.

'It is as ye said, Mighty Lord, the travellers are even now returning, to sully thy abyss with their presence!'

Kharanjul's hideous face stared impassively down at the captain. 'Did Korvusa say when they would arrive in my domain?'

The speaker lowered his eyes from the Wearet's piercing gaze. 'The bird said that they would reach the gorge rim in the second hour of darkness, Great Slayer.'

Kharanjul's trident pointed at the messenger. 'Take a score of my creatures across, to the other side of the long tree. Hide there and await my signal.'

Accompanied by twenty spearbearers, the captain marched out, prepared to cross the tree trunk that spanned the forbidding drop.

The Wearet's harsh voice grated out, echoing around the cavern. 'None of the trespassers must be slain, they are to be taken alive . . . to die at my pleasure!'

The dark masses rose, spearblades glinting as they chanted, 'Blood of the Wearet runs in thy veins, O Mighty Kharanjul. Ruler of the Abyss! Lord of Life and Death!'

42

Abbot Carrul sat soaking up the warm morning sun at the orchard entrance. Folding his paws across his stomach, he smiled at Old Phredd, sitting across from him at the breakfast buffet table. The ancient hedgehog Gatekeeper was chatting away to a bumblebee, which had landed on the rim of his beaker.

'Dearie me, have you seen the mess those vermin made of my gatehouse? There's scrolls, books and parchments scattered about on the floor. One would think a herd of wild beasts had been living there. Hmm, they have really, haven't they?'

The bee buzzed, vibrating its tiny wings. Phredd pointed a bony paw at it. 'Oh, that's easy for you to say, my friend. But the curtains have been ripped, the cupboards flung open and the bed linen will have to be scrubbed twice before I use it again. Thrice, even!'

Carrul reassured his old friend. 'Don't worry so! Stretch your paws and enjoy being outdoors in our own Abbey again. We've time aplenty to put everything right, Phredd – the remainder of summer and all the autumn.'

Foremole Dwurl and a crew of his worthies trundled up to the table. The mole tugged his snout in respectful salute. 'Me'n moi moles've cleared opp all ee gurt 'eap o' rubble wot was blocken ee h'Abbey door h'entrence, zurr. Et bee's ready furr use naow, arfter they'm scrubbed ee wuddwurk daown!'

Carrul beamed gratefully at the Foremole. 'Well done, Dwurl, come and have some more breakfast. There's lots of it left here, do help yourselves.'

Dwurl and his molecrew, needing no second invitation, fell to with a will.

'Thankee, zurr. Much h'obliged oi'm shurr!'

Toran and Martha came running across the lawn. The ottercook called out, 'Gangway, make room there, mates, two more 'ungry workers comin' in for second brekkist!'

Carrul indicated two spaces either side of himself. 'Well, what have you two been up to? I haven't seen you since first serving at dawn.'

Martha cut herself a slice of fruitcake. 'Unblocking the windows in Great Hall, Father. Brother Gelf says he's got extra panes in the attic storeroom. The Dibbuns have gone up there to sort them out with him.'

Foremole Dwurl looked up from his mushroom pastie. 'Hurr, better'n sennin' they'm likkle villyuns into ee h'orchard to 'elp wid ee fruit'n'berries. Hurr hurr, they'm loike to h'eat umselfs sick afore sundaown!'

Sister Setiva was next to put in an appearance. 'Och, ye should see the state o' yon dormitory, it's no fit for worms tae crawl in. Ah'm goin' tae need some bonny helpers tae make et habitable again. Martha lassie, have ye seen that braw badger taeday?'

The haremaid shook her head. 'No, Sister, last beast to see him was Granmum Gurvel. He took a few scones from the kitchen and hurried off. Wonder where he's gone?'

Toran supplied the answer. 'Lonna said he'd sworn to wipe out all the sea rats. A few of 'em escaped yesterday by the wallgates. I saw 'im fillin' up his quiver, an' waxin' that big bow, after we left the walltop last night. I thought better of askin' 'im where he was bound.'

Martha poured pennycress cordial for the ottercook. 'I

401

don't blame you, mate. Lonna can flare up like lightning. If and when he returns, I won't be pressing him about where he's been. I pity those sea rats, though. If it were me, I'd have let them go. They've learned their lesson, and a hard and bloody one it was, too!'

Old Phredd spoke to a bowl of oatmeal he was finishing. 'Ah, but Martha isn't him, is she? Big badger warriors like that are different from anybeast. If he swore to wipe out all those sea rats, well that's just what he'll do. Every one of them, down to the last rat!'

The last rat was, in fact, running for his life, out on the western flatlands. His tongue lolled from one side of his mouth as he looked over his shoulder at the distant figure of the avenging giant. Lonna was standing still, a long distance away. The sea rat stopped as well, collapsing in a heap, his limbs wobbling and trembling uncontrollably. Then he bared his stained fangs at the sky and laughed breathlessly.

'Haharrharr . . . Done it! Can't get me now, stripedog . . . Outta yore range now . . . I escaped ye . . . stripedog!'

The big badger grunted with exertion as he leaned down on the bow, bending it so that he tightened the string by taking another loop around the end of the thick yew wood. He shed his quiver. Going through the arrows, Lonna selected one. Then, holding it to his eye, he peered down the shaft to check that it was straight and true. Spreading both footpaws, Lonna gripped the ground firmly, wetted his upper lip and raised his head to feel which way the breeze was blowing. Satisfied, he looked towards the sea rat, gauging the distance. Then he placed the shaft on his bowstring and drew back. The string was resting against one scarred ear, the bow strained in a mighty arc to its full capacity. After glancing once more at the distant sea rat, Lonna elevated the bow slightly skywards and let fly.

The sea rat rose upright, waving his sword at the tiny figure out on the flatlands. 'Outran ye, stripedog! I beat ye, didn't I?'

A distant, blood-curdling cry answered him. 'Eulalilll-laaaaaa!'

The arrow came like a thunderbolt out of the blue.

Lonna strode out to view his last work of vengeance. Spreadeagled on the coarse grass, the sea rat lay face up. His eyes were wide open, staring at a sun that he would never see again, the long arrow standing out from the centre of his forehead.

The badger gazed down at the last rat of Raga Bol's once mighty crew. 'Nobeast can outrun Lonna Bowstripe's arrow. Nobeast!'

Unstringing the bow, Lonna placed it lengthways across his broad shoulders, resting his paws on the weapon. Turning his back on the sea rat, he strode east through the high summer midday to Redwall Abbey.

Night had fallen as the travellers neared the great gorge. They were weary after marching since early morning that day.

Bragoon called a halt within a short distance of the rim. 'We'll take a breather, but without any fires. Eat'n'drink wot ye need, 'cos we'll be leavin' the rest behind.'

Horty slumped down gratefully. 'I say, what's the point of leavin' bloomin' good scoff here? Silly if you ask me, wot!'

The otter spoke in a low voice to the three young ones. 'Keep yore voices down 'til we're on the other side o' that gorge, mates. I didn't like the place last time we crossed it, an' I likes it even less now. We've got to travel fast'n'light when we crosses that big tree trunk, so keep yore wits sharp!'

Saro had the rope. She tied a short, thick piece of wood crosswise to one end of it. 'Those broken staves we stuck atop o' the other side should still be in place. If'n I throws it right, this chunk o' wood will lodge atween 'em, an' we can climb up sharpish.'

Springald cast a worried glance at the pair. 'You two don't

like that gorge one little bit, do you? Don't fret, we'll cross it as quick and quiet as you like.'

Saro tested the knot she had tied around the wood. 'Aye, you do that, Spring. I'll be in front of ye, an' Brag'll bring up the rear. Just do as yore told, an' everythin' will be alright. I don't like that gorge any more'n Brag does. That place has a bad feel to it!'

Fenna's voice was small and shaky as she tried to make a joke. 'Don't worry about us. We're young and we've got a lot to learn, but we're willing to listen to experienced old fogies.'

Grasping her paw, Bragoon smiled in the darkness. 'That's the spirit, missy. Right! Up on yore hunkers, mates. Let's get ye safe back to Redwall.'

Drawing the sword of Martin from behind his shoulder, the otter led them off towards the rim.

Horty took one rueful glance at the small heap of provisions on the ground, then uttered a small sigh. 'What a flamin' waste. Ah well, this is it, chaps, off we jolly well go!'

The edge of the chasm loomed up, sooner than they had expected. Saro found the same boulder she had used on the previous trip. Making a wide loop in the rope's free end, she placed it about the big stone, lowering the end with the wood attached into the gorge below. Bragoon went first. Climbing carefully, he reached the ledge in front of the three cave entrances. He held the wood, so that it would not clack against the rock wall. Springald came next, followed by Horty, then Fenna. Saro was last to descend. She flipped the rope deftly, catching the end as it unlooped from the boulder and dropped down.

Before Bragoon stepped on to the tree trunk, he pressed something into Fenna's paw and whispered, 'Shove this in yore belt pouch, no questions.' Without a word, the squirrelmaid stuffed the object into her pouch, then followed the otter out on to the tree trunk bridge.

Total silence and engulfing dark reigned in the yawning chasm. Holding one another's paws, the five travellers edged slowly forwards, step by step. They were almost across to the far side when a harsh, evil laugh sounded out from behind them.

Suddenly the lights of many smoking torches lit up the gorge. Saro turned, gasping at the incredible sight.

Kharanjul stood on the trunk, backed by an army of vermin, each holding a torch in one paw and a spear in the other. They were mainly ferrets and weasels, with a scattering of large rats among them. Everybeast's fur was thickly daubed with a sickly yellow-and-green substance, giving them a sinister, spectral appearance. But it was the horrific form of their leader that stood out.

The Wearet swung back his cloak, revealing a misshapen but powerfully bulky torso. As he gestured at them with a big, three-pronged trident, his monstrous face split into an ugly grin. 'Stop where ye stand, trespassers! You belong to Kharanjul, Lord of the Abyss! I will punish you for intruding on my domain!'

Saro pushed Horty forwards. 'Keep goin', we're almost across!'

Bragoon was about to jump from the log on to the opposite ledge, when a score of vermin rose up in front of him.

The captain, a tall weasel, snarled in his face, 'Stand still! Obey the Great Lord of Life and Death!'

The otter laughed, then slew him with a single sword-thrust. Catching the captain's spear as it fell, Bragoon tossed it back to Saro. 'Keep 'em busy, mate. Redwaaaaaalllll!'

Hurling himself from the tree trunk, Bragoon roared like a madbeast as he dealt out death and destruction with the sword of Martin the Warrior. 'Heeeeeyaaaaaah! Grab some spears, young 'uns! No pack o' fancy-talkin' vermin are goin' to stop us Redwallers!'

Horty seized a long spear and was suddenly in the thick

of the battle, whooping and bellowing, 'Forwards the buffs, give 'em blood'n'vinegar. Chaaaaarge!'

Belting a weasel flying into the abyss, the young hare stood shoulder to shoulder with the otter – cutting, thrusting and slashing. Springald and Fenna armed themselves with fallen spears. They turned to help Saro, but the ageing squirrel would have none of it. Single-pawed, she held the centre of the log bridge, letting none pass. Using her spearblade, she slashed at a ferret, flaying his footpaw. He hopped off into midair and vanished screaming.

Saro yelled at the two Abbeymaids, 'Take this rope an' see if ye can fix it t'the top. Then go an' help Brag an' Horty. I'm fine right 'ere, they can only come at me one at a time!'

They obeyed her immediately. As they jumped off the tree trunk, a big rat charged Springald, but he vanished over the rim with a yowl of dismay when Fenna pushed him with her spearbutt.

The squirrelmaid was momentarily stunned. 'I've just slain somebeast!'

Springald shouted, 'Good! Mind your back, Fenn!'

The mousemaid deflected a spear with her own. She thrust and saw the look of surprised horror on the vermin's painted face as he fell dead.

Steeling herself, Springald stood back to back with her friend. 'Keep fighting or we're deadbeasts!'

Bragoon and Horty fought their way through to the side of the two maids. The otter despatched a charging weasel, then shouted, 'Gimme that rope, Spring. You three, cover my back!' Grabbing the rope, he whirled it and flung it up, but it fell back. Bragoon whirled it once more, gritting his teeth against the swordblade held between them. This time his throw was good; the chunk of wood lodged between the two broken staves which they had fixed into the plateau. The otter swung his weight on to the rope, testing it. The rope held firm. He turned to the three young ones.

'Come on, mates, up y'go! Horty, take this sword, 'tis too

short for fightin' spears with. Pass me yore spear an' get climbin'!'

Horty gave him the spear and took the sword, but the hare refused to climb up. There were six vermin left to face on their side. Slaying one with a slash to the throat, Horty shook his head. 'Let Spring an' Fenn go, I'm stayin' here with you, sah. True blue an' never fail, that's us Braebucks, wot!'

The otter whacked a vermin over the skull with his spear, then kicked him swiftly into the abyss. Blood was flowing from a wound on his forehead as he turned on Horty furiously. 'I said, git up that rope, hare. Do it now!'

Between them they faced off a vermin, who was very fancy with his spearwork.

Horty muttered rebelliously, 'I ain't goin', otter! I can't leave you an' Saro here to face that flamin' lot on your own!'

Bragoon's eyes were blazing as he faced Horty. 'Wot did I tell ye, I'm in charge 'ere. Obey me . . . Argh!'

The vermin's spearpoint took the otter through the foot-paw. He pulled the spear from his foe's grasp, ran him through with it and booted him into oblivion. Livid with wrath, he rounded on the young hare. 'Don't argue wid me, mate! Yore young, like them two maids, you got all your lives ahead o' ye. Get that sword back to Redwall! Me'n Saro knows wot we're doin'. We can't look after three young 'uns who are still wet be'ind the ears, we've lived one summer too long fer all that! Now git up that rope, Horty, or I swear I'll run ye through wid this spear! Look after the two maids, live yore life for us. Now go!'

Leaving Horty one vermin to deal with, the otter turned and limped out on to the long tree trunk to help Sarobando.

Horty downed the vermin in a perilous rage, needlessly striking at the foebeast's carcass. Springald and Fenna looked down from the top of the plateau, howling hoarsely at their young friend.

'Horty, come on, get up the rope!'

'You must obey Bragoon, do as you're told!'

Clamping the sword in his teeth, Horty ran to the rope. He took one backwards look at Bragoon and Saro. Though wounded in a dozen places, they were still fighting savagely.

Reeling from a blow, Saro caught his eye and bellowed, 'Get to the top an' pull the rope up, or they'll come after ye an' slay those two maids. Go! Go!'

Blinded by tears of rage and helplessness, Horty went.

Kharanjul stood on the far ledge, urging his creatures forwards. Seeing so many killed by the two old battlers who were holding off the advance, the Wearet took up his trident and went out to fight.

The vermin were still coming. Bragoon and Saro were bowed with fatigue, but covered in blood and severely injured, they were still taking on all comers. They fought side by side on the narrow causeway of timber, keeping their eyes on the advancing enemy, talking to each other as they thrust and parried.

Saro panted, 'The young 'uns are gone. Pity we couldn't 'ave gone with 'em.'

Bragoon dislodged a foebeast with his spear. 'Wot, y'mean back to Redwall? Don't think I could've stood it, mate, sittin' in the gate'ouse wid Old Phredd countin' me teeth as they fell out an' dozin' all day!'

Saro wiped blood from her eye and chuckled. 'Dibbuns climbin' all over us, ole Setiva physickin' away at us, wrappin' rugs round our laps in winter!'

Bragoon caught a ferret in the throat with his spear. 'Might be even worse – they could've sent us back to Abbeyschool. We'd 'ave Sister Portula teachin' us to read-n'write'n'figger. No, that ain't fer us, pal!'

The ageing squirrel caught sight of Kharanjul advancing. 'Oh, look out, Brag, 'ere comes the big ugly mug. We'd better start backin' off. Blood'n'fur, lookit the size o' that monster, he must've ate some dinners with that fork!'

The vermin advanced on them as they retreated. Sorely

wounded and drained of strength, the two old friends continued to hack and slash. Vastly outnumbered by their adversaries, and knowing that they would be beaten and captured by Kharanjul, they crawled down from the long bridge, with one last desperate plan in mind.

The Wearet pressed forwards, holding his lethal trident ready as he taunted his victims, 'The Lord of Life and Death will keep you alive. I will make your dying long and slow. Your companions escaped the Wearet, but you shall pay for them!'

Bragoon and Sarobando were not listening. Between them they had jammed a half-dozen spearbutts under the end of the tree trunk. With a last mighty effort, both beasts put their shoulders to the spears, using them as levers.

Saro gritted her teeth and growled, 'One, two, three. Push!'

The long trunk moved askew, with a grating of wood on rock. Panic ensued out on the tree trunk, as vermin tried to run back to the other side. Some threw themselves flat and clung on.

Bragoon yelled above the din of wails and screams, 'She's movin', mate! Again, one, two, three! Push!'

Kharanjul dropped his trident. Crouching low, he gripped the tree trunk, trying to move forwards and reach his enemy. At last the mighty trunk of the tree, once called Lord of Mossflower, groaned like a living thing as it made a half-turn to one side and slid over the brink of the ledge.

With the effort of their final push, the two old warriors had fallen flat. They watched as the log seemed to hang for a split second in space, with Kharanjul's face looming in front of them. Then the whole trunk fell into the bottomless abyss. Screeches and shrieks rent the night air, swiftly fading to echoes. Down, down, into the dark gorge it all plunged – the Wearet, his vermin army and the only solid bridge that had ever spanned the awesome space.

Bragoon and Saro lay there, staring down into the void,

their paws clasped. The ageing squirrel closed her eyes. 'Nice'n'peaceful 'ere now, mate, ain't it?'

The otter gave her paw a faint squeeze. 'Aye, restful ye might say. Summer's a good time to lay down an' rest.'

No longer able to keep them open, Bragoon slowly closed his eyes. 'Saro, ye recall wot it said on that gravestone at Loamhedge? Young Fenna read it out to us. I said I liked the sound of it.'

Saro nodded weakly. 'I remember, mate. It said, "Gone to the sunny slopes an' quiet streams." I liked it, too.'

The otter's voice grew fainter as he repeated the phrase. 'The sunny slopes an' quiet streams . . . I'll wait for ye there, Sarobando . . . Wouldn't go anyplace without ye.' His paw went limp in the squirrel's failing grasp.

She smiled. 'Wait for me, Brag ole mate, I'll be there.'

Two old warriors, who had left Redwall Abbey when they were Dibbuns, paw in paw, lay on the rockledge together. They never saw the sunrise that dawn, but they went on to the land of sunny slopes and quiet streams – still holding paws.

43

Summer's days were growing short, passing gently into autumn. Redwall Abbey was restored to its former calm and grandeur. Abbot Carrul and Martha met for their early morning stroll, now a regular thing with the two friends before they took breakfast. A light mist – like golden gossamer – lay over the Abbey pond. They saw a grayling leap to catch an unsuspecting fly.

Carrul watched the ripples spread across the water. 'I had a dream last night. It was a vision of Martin.'

The haremaid was startled by her Abbot's revelation. 'A dream of Martin the Warrior? Did he say anything, Father?'

The Abbot paused before answering. 'He did, indeed, Martha. These were his very words.

"When autumn brings the harvest time,
good food you shall not lack,
when fruit lies heavy on the bough,
and travellers come back.
Look for the one who holds my sword,
these words of mine recall,
someday you will esteem that one,
as ruler of Redwall!"'

Martha sat down on a log, puzzled by the rhyme. 'Good grief, Father, there's a lot of information in Martin's words. Aside from the fact that there will be a fine harvest, our friends – Horty, Bragoon and the others – must be returning. Isn't that great news! But I never guessed you were thinking of retiring from being Abbot of Redwall.'

Carrul sat down beside her. 'The thought never crossed my mind, Martha. But Martin said someday, and someday in the future I would have to give serious thought to appointing my successor. Martin has saved me a lot of pondering, I'm grateful to him for that. However, his words are causing me a little concern. Think. Who did I give the sword to?'

The haremaid replied promptly, 'You gave it to Bragoon.'

Carrul nodded his agreement. 'Which is why I'm worried, Martha. Bragoon is a good friend, we were Dibbuns together. But he's a rover, an adventurer. Ask Toran, Bragoon's his elder brother, he'll tell you. Bragoon's too old and too wild to be Abbot.'

Martha held up a paw. 'Not so fast, Father. The rhyme said ruler of Redwall, not Abbot. It may be an Abbess!'

Carrul clapped a paw to his cheek. 'Fates forbid that it might be Sarobando! It would be woe to my poor Abbey.'

Martha could not help laughing. 'Hahaha, oh Father, think for a moment. It could be Springald, or Fenna or . . .' Now it was Martha's turn to look apprehensive. 'Or Horty?'

Carrul placed a comforting paw on the haremaid's shoulder. 'Oh, come on now, miss! Martin the Warrior was renowned for his wisdom. What are we thinking about? He wouldn't inflict any of those three rascals on our Abbey!'

Martha gave an audible sigh of relief. 'You're right, Father. But it might be nobeast we've thought of. What if they bring somebody back with them?'

Carrul pursued this idea enthusiastically. 'Of course, there may have been other creatures living at Loamhedge.

Say a sturdy young mouse, steeped in wisdom? Or a sagacious squirrel, the very model of common sense?'

Martha giggled. 'Or a studious frog with the brain of an ant!'

Abbot Carrul smacked her paw playfully. 'Now stop this nonsense, you young rip. Look, here comes breakfast!'

Toran had resumed his role as cook. He and Gurvel headed a procession carrying tables and benches, trolleys, dishes and food. He waved his ladle.

'Set 'em all up at the edge of the pond there, next to those two pore beasts who've been waitin' out here all night!'

Carrul chuckled. 'So ends our moment of peace for the day, Martha. Besieged by breakfasters!'

The haremaid went to help the servers. 'Let's join them, I'm starving!'

Setting up the tables, Brother Weld pulled a ferocious face at the Dibbuns, who were buzzing around like playful bees. 'I'll toss the lot of you into the pond if you don't sit still and wait to be served. So behave yourselves!'

Muggum the molebabe clambered up on a bench, next to Buffle. 'Hurr hurr, ee'm a gurt bold crittur t'be assultin' uz loike that! Wot do ee say, Buff?'

The tiny mousebabe scowled darkly. 'Gurrumff um burble fink!'

Old Phredd looked over his glasses at the infant mouse. 'What did he just say?'

Sister Setiva tied a bib about Buffle's neck. 'Och, ah be a-feared tae repeat it. But if the wee scamp says it again, ah'll wash his mouth out with soap!'

The Dibbun squirrelbabe Shilly tugged at Martha's paw. 'When izza harviss gonna be, Marth'?'

The haremaid gave the reply she had been repeating to the Abbeybabes for the past few days. 'On the first morning after the night of harvest moon. Be patient, it shouldn't be too long now.'

Granmum Gurvel looked up from a pan of corn and fruit slices she was doling out. 'Payshunt? You'm doan't tell ee

Redwallers t'be payshunt when they'm a waitin' to get ee
'arvest in, Miz Marth'!'

The Dibbuns cheered Gurvel loudly, glad to have an ally
on their side. Most of the babes had never been to a harvest
before, so they were eager to take part in one, knowing
there would be a Harvest End Feast. The little ones began
clamouring for Martha to sing the Harvest Song. Knowing
they would not be quiet until she did, Martha obliged by
singing the lively air, which included much tapping and
paw stamping.

'Open the cupboard, the bins and the stores,
go fetch out the trolleys and carts,
then out to the orchard, the gardens and fields,
for a harvest to gladden our hearts.

Rappety tap, the Abbot'll call,
watch out for those Dibbuns 'cos they'll eat it all!

There's blackberries, blueberries, raspberries too,
strawberries and redcurrants bright,
wild cherries, blueberries and blaeberries ripe,
to be all gathered in by tonight.

Rappety tap, wait for the feast,
just look at that Dibbun, the greedy wee beast!

Bring basket and barrel and bucket and pail,
pick rosehips, red apples and pears,
greengages, damsons and plums big and fine,
roll your sleeves up and banish your cares.

Rappety tap, that babe's the worst,
if he eats another I swear that he'll burst!

There's almond and hazel and chestnut in bloom,
and a crop of good acorns there'll be,
if you hold the ladder I'll climb to the top,
and I'll knock them all down from the tree.

Rappety tap, flat on the ground,
he's rubbing his tummy and rolling around!

Let's gather our harvest and bring it indoors,
then the Abbot'll cry out, "Well done!"
We've filled up the cupboards, the bins and the stores,
in good time for the winter to come.

Rappety tap, quick close the door,
he's up on his paws and looking for more!'

As usual, Martha had to sing the whole thing again so the Dibbuns could show off their fancy paw tapping. Whilst this was going on, the Abbot took Toran aside. He related what Martin the Warrior had told him in his dream. The ottercook was overjoyed at the news.

'As soon as the 'arvest moon shows, we'll mount a watch on the walltops to welcome them back 'ome!'

Breakfast was about finished when Foremole Dwurl, who had been gatekeeper in Phredd's absence, came trundling up with Lonna in tow. He hailed Toran. 'Gudday, zurr. Lookit who'm just cummed a knocken on ee gate!'

The ottercook quickly cleared a place for them both. 'Sit ye down, mates, an' break yore fast. Lonna, where've ye been since yesterday? Everybeast was wonderin' where ye'd got to.'

The big badger seated himself, allowing Gurvel to heap food in front of him. His fur was coated in dew, and the blood had matted on his wounds, but he looked happy. 'The sea rats are all accounted for – down to the last vermin. I was tired, but glad that I had ended my mission, so I lay down on the flatlands, about half a league from your Abbey. I must have slept deeply, because it was the sound of larks rising at dawn that awakened me. I was hoping there'd be a bite of breakfast left for a hungry badger. Thank you, marm!'

Granmum Gurvel piled corn and fruit slices on a platter.

'You'm eat 'earty, zurr. Oi'll cook more furr ee if'n ye be still 'ungered!'

Abbot Carrul beckoned Brother Gelf. 'Draw off a pitcher of our best October Ale for Lonna. Nothing's too good for the beast who saved Redwall from the sea rats. Lonna, after you've eaten, Sister Portula will find you clean robes, and Sister Setiva will care for your wounds. You must rest now, friend!'

Seating themselves around the badger, the Dibbuns watched in awe as he satisfied his appetite.

Muggum nudged Buffle. 'Yurr, ee'm gurtbeast surpintly can shuv ee vikkles away!'

Stifling a smile, Martha chided the molebabe. 'Really, Muggum, mind your manners!'

Lonna sat Muggum on his paw and lifted him to face-height. 'Listen to me, young sir, never mess with your food. Eat it all up like I do, then someday you'll be a great warrior!'

Muggum nodded sagely. 'Them bee's woise wurds, zurr!'

It was five nights hence when the harvest moon waxed fully. Most Abbeybeasts were in their beds. Toran stood watch from the ramparts on the southwest corner, where he could view both the path and woodlands. Martha and Abbot Carrul, neither of whom felt like sleeping, joined the ottercook on his vigil. The three stood there, unaware that Lonna had come up behind them. For a beast of his size and weight, the badger could move silent as a shadow. They started slightly as he spoke.

'That nice old molewife in the kitchens asked me to bring some hot vegetable soup up for you.' Lonna poured the soup from a jug into four basins.

Toran sniffed it, exclaiming gratefully, 'Good ole Gurvel!'

They sipped at their basins in silence, contemplating the serenity of a late summer's night.

*

Nocturnal birdsong drifted from the shadowed trees of Mossflower. The path stood out like a tranquil stream, curling southwards. Galaxies of twinkling stars pinpointed the cloudless vaults of sky above. A single comet streaked through space in brief silent glory. The harvest moon ruled over all, surrounded by a soft nimbus, resplendent in its own golden solitude.

None of the others noticed Lonna fitting a shaft to his bowstring. He peered towards the foliage which fringed the pathside. Drawing back his bow, Lonna called down, 'Are you friend or foe?'

Three figures stepped out on to the path. One shouted, 'Ahoy the walls, we come as friends!'

Martha's good eyesight allowed her to quickly identify the caller. 'It's a shrew. There's two more with him.'

Lonna relaxed his bowstring. 'What do you want, friends?'

The lead shrew's rapier blade flashed in the moonlight as he made a salute and offered it hilt first. 'I am Jigger, son of Log a Log Briggy, Chieftain of the Guorafs crews! I carry news of your friends. My father sent me ahead to tell you of their approach!'

Toran and Lonna were already down and unbarring the gates as Martha assisted the Abbot to negotiate the wall-steps.

Old Phredd lit extra lanterns as they crowded into the gatehouse. When the introductions were completed, the young shrew made his report. It was not a happy tale that he had to relate. Martha was stunned beyond tears at the news of Bragoon's and Saro's death. Abbot Carrul hung his head and wept openly. Lonna stood by in respectful silence. Toran was the only one to speak.

'The young 'uns, are they all safe'n'well?'

Jigger nodded. 'Aye, sir. Apart from a few scratches an' sore footpaws, they're fine. Miss Fenna told me that Bragoon was yore brother. 'Twas a brave thing him'n Saro did.'

The ottercook drew himself up straight and spoke proudly. 'Aye, Bragoon an' Sarobando was true-born Redwallers! No two like 'em, they was both wild warriors. But they did their duty an' saved their friends. I wager they took a few o' those vermin with 'em, eh?'

Jigger's eyes were shining with admiration as he replied, 'From wot our scouts said, they took 'em all, every last vermin, an' their chief, the Wearet. That must've been a powerful battle, I'll tell ye!'

Toran opened the gatehouse door. He took a deep breath of the fresh night air and smiled. 'Funny, ain't it, some'ow I couldn't imagin' Saro an' Brag growin' old like peaceful Abbeybeasts. Not those two. They went like they wanted to, the bravest o' the brave!'

Lonna offered his paw to Toran. 'True warriors have no fear of death. I only met your brother and his friend once. They were rare beasts!'

Abbot Carrul wiped at his eyes with damp habit sleeves. 'Look at me, I must have forgotten my manners. Come to the Abbey, Jigger. Bring your two friends. You must be hungry after travelling so far. Lonna, will you wait by the gates and show the rest of them to the kitchens when they arrive?'

Jigger hitched up his rapier belt eagerly. 'Lead on, Father. If'n the vittles at Redwall are as good as Horty tells me, I can't wait t'get at 'em!'

It was some time thereafter when Lonna herded the Guoraf shrews into the Abbey kitchens. Martha and Toran forged their way through the crowd to Horty, Fenna and Springald. They fell upon one another, hugging and shaking paws as the Abbot joined them.

'Welcome home, you weary travellers! Springald, what's up, miss, are you ill?'

The mousemaid was staring at Martha in disbelief. 'Look, she's walking! Martha's walking!'

Horty held his sister at paw's length. 'But how the . . .

what the blinkin' flip . . . I mean, the bloomin' skin'n'blister trottin' about like . . . like? Explain y'bally self, miss. How did y'do it, wot wot?'

The haremaid stared down at her brother's bandaged right footpaw, having noticed he was sporting a gallant limp. 'You'll get to know all about it later. But what happened to you, Horty, are you hurt?'

Trying to look brave and nonchalant at the same time, Horty waffled, 'Oh this, line o' duty an' all that, y'know!'

Springald raised her eyebrows scathingly. 'Line of duty, my tail! You great fibber, tell the truth. He was messing about with Martin's sword, showing off to the shrews, when he dropped it, tripped up and cut his footpaw on the blade!'

The Abbot exchanged a glance with Martha before he asked, 'Well, who has the sword now?'

From beneath her cloak Fenna produced the sword, neatly wrapped and tied in a piece of sailcloth. 'I took it off Horty and bound it up for safekeeping. Don't worry, it's in perfect condition and quite undamaged.'

She looked from the Abbot to Martha. 'Why, what's the matter, did I do anything wrong, should I have left the sword for Horty to fool about with?'

Both Martha and the Abbot hugged the squirrelmaid.

'No no, you did the right thing!'

'Yes, you did, Fenna, thank goodness! Please accept the gratitude of an old Abbot!'

The squirrelmaid passed the sword over to the Abbot. 'Why, Father, what's this all about?'

Abbot Carrul looked over his glasses at her. 'Nothing for you to worry your head about, miss. I'll tell you everything in a few seasons' time – that's, of course, providing you don't plan on leaving us to go somewhere else.'

Fenna replied promptly, 'Why would I go anywhere else? Redwall Abbey's my home, I'd never leave it for anything!'

Martha clasped her friend's paw. 'Neither would I, Fenna. There's noplace dearer than our Abbey!'

Whilst the shrews were sampling the delights of the kitchens, the three young ones went down to Cavern Hole with Toran, Martha and the Abbot. There, away from the hubbub, they sat by the embers of a glowing fire, recounting their journey to and from Loamhedge. It was an engrossing story, vividly illustrated by the young creatures' first real experience of the outside world – enemies they had encountered, friends they had met, hardships they had undergone. Horty, Springald and Fenna each related the parts they had taken in the epic quest. Throughout the narrative it was clear that the entire thing would not have been possible without the heroism, guidance and assistance of Bragoon and Sarobando.

By the time the dawn bells were tolling, the trio had reached the end of their tale. Fenna reached into her belt pouch and drew forth the slim package of parchment which Bragoon had entrusted to her. 'This is Sister Amyl's secret. Take it, Martha, it's meant for you alone. I know you don't have any need for it now, but I feel you should have it.'

They watched in silence as the haremaid undid the wrapping and began scanning it.

Horty leaned forwards eagerly. 'Well, are you goin' to jolly well read it out to us, or are you goin' to sit there bloomin' well gazin' at the blinkin' thing until next flippin' summer, wot?'

Martha hesitated. 'I'm not supposed to, really. It says on the other side of this parchment that only the one who needs this shall know my secret. But I don't think it will do any harm now. Here's what it says:

"The body is ruled by the mind,
I tell you this be true,
by willpower you may find,
nought is denied to you."'

Abbot Carrul took the parchment from her paws. He stared at it, turned it over, studied it a moment longer, then chuckled as he passed it to Toran. 'So, that's Sister Amyl's secret, eh? Take a look at that, Toran, my friend!'

After a brief glance the ottercook burst into laughter. 'Hohoho, Sister Amyl my granma's rudder! Hohoho, those rascals!'

Martha was astonished at the attitude of her friends. 'Excuse me, I fail to see what's so funny. Those are the words of a young Sister who suffered the same as I did. I can see that it's written in an old-fashioned style, and the writing isn't too neat. But what's that to laugh about?'

Abbot Carrul explained. 'This was never written by Sister Amyl. She was a young Sister who was well educated, her spelling was faultless and she had a neat writing paw. Remember the history of Loamhedge you were reading, the one you borrowed from Sister Portula? Amyl had written part of that, but she certainly never wrote this!'

The light of recognition dawned across Fenna's face. 'I'll wager I know who did write it. I've just remembered where I've seen that parchment before. It's a piece torn from the edge of the Loamhedge map we took with us. See, there's a line on it that was the rim of the high cliffs. Bragoon or Sarobando must have written it. Everything they found in Abbess Sylvaticus's tomb had mouldered away to dust. So they invented Sister Amyl's secret themselves rather than return to Redwall empty-pawed. That's it! Either Saro or Bragoon did the writing.'

Abbot Carrul patted the squirrelmaid's shoulder. 'Well done, miss! Actually, Bragoon or Saro didn't write this singly, they both did! I recognize the writing on the outside, Sarobando did that. She was better at spelling but worse at writing than Bragoon. He had the neater paw but oh, dear me, that otter's spelling was dreadful, look at it!'

They examined the short rhyme closely.

'The body is rooled by the mynd,
I tell you this be troo,

by willpower you may fynd,
nort is denyed to you.'

Toran wiped tears of laughter from his eyes. 'Aye, that was
my brother, alright. Old Brag never won any prizes for his
spellin'. But he did it so ye wouldn't be let down, Martha.
So I think ye could forgive 'em both for it.'

Martha stared into the fire embers. 'Forgive? There's
nothing to forgive. They did it for me, undertook that whole
long quest, protected my brother and his friends, then
sacrificed their lives for them.'

Toran did not know whether he was smiling or weeping.
He scrubbed a paw across his eyes again. 'So they did,
Martha, so they did!'

Epilogue

Ten seasons have passed since that night of the harvest moon. Fate and fortune have allowed our Abbey to prosper in peace. We had some visitors to Redwall the other day, a column of fighting hares from Salamandastron, sent by Lord Lonna Bowstripe. They were led by Captain Hortwill Longblade Braebuck, who was visiting his sister. What a change the Long Patrol has made to Horty! He went off all that time ago, with Lonna, to enlist at Salamandastron, carrying the scimitar that the badger had taken from Raga Bol. Horty is now twice as big, and twice as hungry, as he once was, a fine figure of a Long Patrol captain with a bristling military moustache. The young hares under his command admire him greatly. Abbess Fenna was delighted to see him, and so was I. We sat up until late last night, chatting about the old days, with Carrul our Gatekeeper and Cellarmole Muggum. Yes, Abbot Carrul became Gatekeeper, by his own choosing, four seasons back. He shared the task with Old Phredd until the ancient hedgehog went to his long rest last winter. Ah well, such is life, and such is its passing; not even Phredd could live forever. Horty and his hares are staying until after the Harvest Feast. (Trust hares never to miss a chance of several days' good feeding.) Those are Ottercook Toran's words, not mine, though I share his sentiments.

On the night of the harvest moon, all our Abbeybeasts will gather on the lawn near the front wallgates. We will watch Martha climb the steps to the threshold. First she will sing the beautiful ballad, 'The Rose of Redwall'. Then she will carry out the promise she made to Bragoon and Sarobando. They say that, on the day they left to search for Loamhedge, she vowed that when they returned she would dance for both of them, on the walltop, right over the threshold of our Abbey. Martha has kept her promise every season since then. After singing her song, she dances – swaying, bending, curtsying and leaping – graceful as a breeze-blown flower in the golden moonlight, for the memory of her two friends. I remember then that long ago summer when we stole out of the Abbey, rebellious young creatures embarking on a great adventure. We returned at the end of that season – wiser, more obedient and more reasonable. It was the summer of growing up.

If you, too, are travelling, questing or journeying any-where, remember this. You will always find a welcome here at Redwall Abbey, young or old. As friends come by, they often call in to enjoy Redwall hospitality. Who knows, maybe we will see you here someday. You can sit with us, rest and be refreshed and learn. Young ones have much to learn and old ones, too. Carrul said to me only the other day, we are never too old to learn. He was a wise Abbot; he is an even wiser old Gatekeeper. I hope someday I may grow as wise as him.

Springald. Recorder of Redwall Abbey in Mossflower country